SAINT OF SIN

DELILAH MOHAN

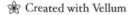

TRIGGER WARNING

Saints of Sin is a dark romance with dark themes that may be uncomfortable to some readers. Please keep in mind that the list provided may not contain all possible triggers and to read with caution if you have sensitivities.

- **Sexual Assault**
- **Sexually explicit scenes (that could contain BDSM content)**
- **Violence (including gun, knife, torture and blood)**
- **Drugs**
- **Kidnapping**
- **Murder & Death**
- **Gore**
- **Dub-con**

For the good girls with scars on their heart and blood on their hands.

CHAPTER ONE

WICK

The sun was just rising over the horizon, but the man under my knee would never see it crest. I leaned into him, knowing damn well what it meant to take his life and not give a fuck. "How does it feel to be number ten?"

The number meant nothing to him, but fucking everything to guys like us. Three years. Three fucking years without the feel of skin against my own and with my tenth kill under my belt – the last of my group to earn theirs – it meant we could move forward. It meant taking on the fourth and final member of our team and finally stepping toward what we worked so damn hard to become.

I toyed with him, savoring the moment, sliding the cool blade of my knife slowly over his jugular as sweat poured down his temple and his chest rose and fell. He barely put up a fight. Fucking politicians. All of them were weak and crooked, standing by the government as they spouted false promises, assuming they would be protected. Little did they know, the government is who they needed protection from.

"Hurry the fuck up. I've got chemistry at eight," Austin ordered.

I looked over to my friend, my partner, my team-mate of three years, furious that he was taking this moment from me. "Shut the fuck up and let me savor it."

"My chem partner will bust my fucking balls if I'm late again." His voice was nearly a whine, so at odds with our reality.

"You're a fucking SAINT. A fucking lashing of words from a five-foot female will not kill you."

"No?" He walked closer, using the tip of his steel-toed boot to dig between the ribs of Senator Marc Lawson as he screamed for a mercy he never received and begged a god that didn't exist. "Want to fill in for me today, then? I hate that fucking class."

The only reason he even bothered with it was because I suspected he had a crush on that ball buster of a female he was too afraid of silencing. "Are you asking me to take your woman? Because after I make this kill..." I gave the senator a wink as I ran the blade over his chest, using it to slice off his necktie. "I can finally have a good fuck."

God, I craved it. My cock was hard just thinking

about sliding into a body after the longest dry spell of my life.

Austin's voice turned hard, his anger directed at me even as he took it out on the man pinned under me. "You're not fucking touching her. She's too sweet to be anywhere near any of us. We aren't the men to steal her innocence."

"It's a shame. I've always liked the sinless type," I mused, knowing damn well I wasn't touching the girl.

Asa's phone beeped from twenty feet away, where he lounged casually against the senator's kitchen counter. "I am getting hungry, man. We've got five minutes according to intel, then his dog walker shows."

Now that he mentioned it, I was too. My stomach growled at the mere mention of food. "I could use a snack."

The other two mumbled their agreements as I threaded my fingers into the senator's hair and pulled his head back. Thirty minutes ago, his hair was immaculately combed, not a strand out of place. Now? It lay haphazardly in all directions, reflecting the distress his body was under. I leaned in as I pulled him up close to my face, allowing him to hear every word I spoke.

"When you die — and you are about to — I want your last thoughts to be of those little girls who begged you for their innocence as you stole it."

I planted the last thought in his mind as my blade sliced deep into his jugular, spraying blood into an arc across his wall and covering me. The thought of being covered in the blood of this scum was repulsive. The scandals that surrounded him, those horrific things that came to light and shamed the leaders of this country, were only one reason we got the order to make the kill, but I would have done it without the order. He deserved nothing less than death, and it thrilled me to deliver it.

When I was sure he was dead, I dropped his head, savoring the sound of his skull bouncing off the tile before coming to rest in a growing puddle of blood. Bracing my hands on my knees, I forced myself to a stand, kicking the body one last time before stepping away from the corpse. Careful not to touch more blood than I needed to, I walked toward my friends, a smile plastered on each of our faces.

After a long pause, Asa burst out, "We get a fucking housekeeper."

Three long years of waiting for a housekeeper, and now she's fucking ours.

"Let the fucking hiring begin."

It was noon by the time we could sit down with the organization. It always made me nervous, wondering if there was something we could have done differently, something that might have gone wrong, something that would end with our names next on the death roster. But this time, I was confident. More than confident because every blow this guy received was well-deserved and his death was quicker than a man like him should have gotten.

"The dog walker found the body around six thirty this morning." The agent in front of us steepled his fingers. We called him Jones, but fuck if I knew if that was his real name or not. All I knew was he issued orders. We all followed. Simple as that. It's what we signed up for. "They are calling it a break-in gone wrong."

If that's what they wanted to call it, then it meant we did our job correctly.

"As we planned," Asa informed him.

"Where's the information?"

Asa pulled out a clear plastic zipped bag, handing it over. "It's all in there, along with a list of names and objects to support the break-in theory."

"Excellent." Jones reached over the table, taking the bag from us. Fuck, Asa always thought of all the minor details. I never would have remembered to grab supporting evidence to assist in our staging. I placed the bag in front of him before he leaned back in his chair, assessing us. "This kill makes thirty. Ten each, correct?"

"Yes sir," I answered for the group.

"By our rules, you qualify to add a member. But judging by the grins that are toying on your lips, I suspect you know that."

"Yes, sir." This time, we spoke in unison. We were all too fucking giddy, craving the flesh and excitement they had forced us to live without for so long.

"You know the rules; you know how to get her. The stakes are high, boys. If she dies..."

"We won't let that happen," Asa assured Jones.

"They never intend to let it happen, but initiation is rough." He leaned forward, looking us dead in the eyes. "It's deadly. If your recruit is weak, your team will forever be three."

Sure, now we could fuck around. We met the requirements. But having these two fucks with me day in and day out, especially in a lengthy job with no outlet, was not my idea of a good time. I wouldn't always have the opportunity to fuck around when needed, especially on jobs that require hours of watching and waiting. We needed that fourth. I had to have a fucking fourth.

"We're the strongest team in the training organization. You think we'd pick someone weak?"

"I think that one chip in a single link can break an unbreakable chain of strength." Jones shrugged. "I'd hate to see you all go down. It's your job to train her. Strengthen her. You never know when your brothers will come after her during the sweep, or what they plan to do. You never know what challenges are coming, and until we've inked her body with our emblem, she's not officially protected."

It was like a giant game of steal the bacon. Only the bacon was our housekeeper, our girl, our fourth. And the players, all members of the Saints, all teams under the same organization throughout the state, try to take her. Harm her. Do as they wish to what's ours. Our number has been called, our conditions met, and now it was our turn to grab the bacon and hold on tight. It's the biggest challenge, the toughest job, the hardest assignment we've had to face since joining the Saints our freshman year of college at Sablewood University.

"We aren't afraid of blood," Austin chimed in.

"But are you willing to watch her die?" Jones questioned.

We squirmed uncomfortably because we weren't monsters, despite our profession. We didn't kill innocents. But to protect this girl, the girl we hand-picked and deemed worthy, we'd have to be willing to do everything that went against our morals.

"If she is dying... bleeding out... suffering..." I spoke. "Then it means each of us is already dead and it's in fate's hands."

I understand the importance of having a housekeeper. We all weighed the pros and cons. She is optional, but taking on the responsibility of one, keeping her safe, protecting her and cherishing her, that's on us. She enters her contract as innocent, and it's our job to prepare her for what's to come. It's one of the most important jobs we could have because she is ours, a part of us, one of our group.

Jones's fingers tapped against the table. "Sounds like your minds are made up."

"Yes, sir," I agreed with him.

"And you know of the application process and

what you need to do prior to us deciding to start the testing."

"Yes, sir." I nodded my head.

"Three other teams have decided to take on a housekeeper in this region thus far." Three? That number wasn't as high as I hoped. The more who take on housekeepers, the fewer teams involved in trying to take her. "You will need to keep connected with these teams if you proceed. For the women's sake."

"We understand." We fucking know already. We've done our research, we've talked to others, we learned about the initiation, the training, the application. We fucking know what we are doing, and if we don't, that's on us.

"I'd like you to really understand what you're getting into, boys. You're in this life until we let you free. Is that what you want to drag a woman into?"

"It hasn't been so bad," Austin responded, and I wished he didn't open his fucking mouth because it could get worse, so fucking worse.

"We'll see." Jones smirked, and it was fucking terrifying. "Start the process. Let me know when you've found her and have moved forward with training. You have a month before the next gathering. It will be finalized then."

A month before the next gathering, another month before the hits may come after it's announced publicly. Two fucking months. We had two fucking months to find the girl and train her before assassins come for her and our world implodes into utter chaos. And this was what we wanted. This was what we chose.

"Understood." We spoke at the same time because speaking what we really wanted to say wouldn't be welcome in this room.

"If I were you boys, I'd already be on the interview process. A month isn't a lot of time. Use it wisely." He stood, nodded to all of us before grabbing the bag of evidence from the senator's place and strolling casually out the door.

Asa waited until the door slammed shut before he said a word. "I didn't even know that was a fucking option."

"Me either," Austin chimed in.

"It doesn't matter." I cracked my neck. "He means get to it and get to it now. I want the application posted online by tonight. Flyers out before the first class tomorrow. The application is a three-step process, and most won't even get an option to move forward onto step two if they don't have acceptable answers in the first section."

"When are we planning the cut off?" Austin stood, stretching his limbs.

"A week and a half. That should give us enough time to find the right fit." I hoped. "Well, at least on paper. We can't afford more than that. We'll go through the applicants and whoever we narrow down to will begin the tests before they even realize they're being tested. I want the final applicant to be signed on, knowing what she's getting into, before we present her as ours."

Asa blew out a breath that whistled between his teeth. "We're fucked, aren't we?"

"In the worst and the best way," I confirmed. "Get to class, we'll go live with it tonight."

We left the building and divided up, going our separate ways to various spots on campus, knowing I wouldn't be able to focus. My mind was on the name-less, faceless girl who would be ours and the bullshit of blood, guts, and death we just signed up for.

CHAPTER TWO

MAC

Help wanted: Housekeeper

The Saints of SU seek female with qualifying credentials to operate as a live-in housekeeper. Must have immediate opening with a clean background and health.

My heart pounded as I read the rest of the ad. I saw the words, but I couldn't compute. Everyone knew about the Saints. The surrounding mystery, the unknowability of its members, the questions that are always asked and never answered. Until now. This position had the potential to expose it all, and all I needed to do was get the job.

Which, honestly, was nearly impossible.

I heard about their jobs before, vaguely. Hundreds apply, but no one ever seems to get through to an interview. If the Saints weren't huge supporters of charity and local events, I would almost think that fraternity was a farce. But they are everywhere and nowhere, and the aspiring journalist in me was dying to understand what made this group of men so special.

I had arrived early to chemistry, setting up my laptop as I waited for others to file into the lab. It was now or never, while I still had the guts to even attempt to infiltrate the Saints and find out who they really were.

Glancing at the sliver of paper I tore from the flyer, I typed in the web address, pulling up the application and skimming through it. I didn't think I had enough time to complete it before class started, but if I worked on it a little throughout the day, I could have it finished before work tonight.

The questionnaire was extremely personal, and though I didn't think it would make a difference, since no one ever really gets through to get a position with the Saints, I still felt the need to lie.

How many have I slept with? According to this application, five because if I had to admit to being twenty-one and only having two mediocre experiences, I'd die. Anything more than my fib of five seemed slutty, and I didn't want to come across too willing. I wasn't a prude, but I'd be damned if I put some crazy number and somehow that surfaces in the rumor mill.

Major? English. Did they need to know that I was an aspiring undercover journalist and that my main reason to even apply was to write the article of the century, at least by school standards? Nope.

Biggest fantasy? I snorted when I read that one. It was clear by the time I reached this page, section two apparently, that they weren't looking for a house-keeper, they were looking for a bedmate. I was fine with that. I could use more sex in my life, even if it was from some mediocre frat boys.

I had just typed kidnapping when a voice behind me startled me half to death, causing me to slam my laptop shut. "What?"

"I asked what you were working on." Austin's brows were furrowed, and I wondered if he had seen more of my screen than I would have liked.

"English," I answered lamely.

"Didn't look like English," he muttered to himself before tossing his bag on the ground and taking the seat next to me. "Aren't you even going to scold me for being late?"

I looked at my watch. "You're late again."

"It's compulsory." He shrugged before reaching over and picking up the crumbled tab of paper I accidentally left next to me. I should have been more careful, but I was being sloppy, clearly. "What the fuck is this?"

The look in his eyes told me he knew what

exactly that paper was, and he wasn't thrilled about it. "It's just something I got off a flyer. You know me, always job hunting."

I actually rarely job hunt. In fact, my job at the student store was cushy enough for me at the moment, but Austin and I rarely talked outside of chemistry assignments and lab work, so I didn't think the lie that slipped from my lips to be decisive.

"Mac, you and I both know that anything to do with the Saints isn't a real job." He glowers before he crumbles up the paper and shoves it in his pocket. "This isn't for you."

How the hell would he know what's for me? We hardly knew each other. "It said housekeeper," I pointed out, even as I knew they weren't looking for an actual housekeeper. If they had been, then applicants' STD track record (which, by the way, was a hundred and ten percent clean, and I planned to keep it that way) wouldn't have been needed. Unless they were all pervs, which, now that I thought about it, was a big possibility.

Austin flicked one of my pigtail buns. "I've seen inside your backpack. You have no right to apply for any jobs that could require cleaning."

"Hey." I acted offended, but honestly, he was right.

"Seriously." Our professor cleared his throat, trying to get our attention. "Promise me you won't apply for this. It's not worth your time, and you're above whatever bullshit they have planned."

I didn't promise. Our attention got caught by the elderly man at the front of the room, droning on and on about the alkali metals like we hadn't heard about them before a day in our lives. This was college, not high school. We knew our periodic tables and if we didn't, we deserved to fail.

I looked over at Austin, suddenly wondering if he knew anything about alkali. "Do you need my notes on alkali?"

He scoffed. "Am I in middle school? I've got it."

Cocky much? "Fine. I was just checking."

"I appreciate it." His eyes never left the front of the room.

By the time our lab work rolled around, his thoughts were clearly somewhere else, because dragging any sort of words out of him seemed near impossible. Turns out, receiving only grunts from your lab partner is quite infuriating, and by the time class was over, I was eager to get out of there.

My shift at the student store didn't start for another forty-five minutes, which gave me enough time to settle in the library and open the application again. I answered the questions. Only half of them came from a place of honesty. The rest of them were complete bullshit.

WWMW? I asked myself on repeat as I typed in the most untruths I've ever put on paper. What would men want? Food and sex, from as far as I knew, but judging by this questionnaire, I was completely off on that assessment.

How fast could I run a mile? If my chance of hiring was based on my mile time, I was fucked. I'd be better off surrendering my life to bears chasing me than outrunning any of them. Were you even supposed to outrun bears?

Five minutes before my shift, I hit the final submit button and hoped for the best. If I wrote my final paper on this, on them, I was sure to hit the ground running on my journalism career the minute I graduated.

After putting my laptop back in my bag, I walked through the library and into the next building. There was a back room for our belongings, so I shoved my bag into a cubie, grabbed an apron, and hit the time clock.

The student store wasn't the worst place to work. Students got allowances, and those allowances were spendable at our mini convenient store which sold a wide variety of chips, energy drinks, and microwavable delicacies. A college student's dream marketplace, I suppose.

It was two hours into my shift when the bell on the door rang. It rang a lot, but rarely was Asa Domingues the one causing the annoying little ding. My spine straightened as I watched him, caught between lusting after him and wondering how someone could walk around looking that good without having a single flaw. He had to have one, didn't he? No one was that perfect. Except everything I heard about this man claimed differently.

He grabbed an energy drink, an apple, and a bag of potato straws. I nearly fell over the counter as I watched him, my body stretching over the Formica counter, not willing to lose sight of his ass, which looked absolutely delectable clad in a pair of denim jeans.

When I could stretch no further, I pulled back and sighed. He was out of my league. That was a truth I couldn't dispute. But damn, a girl could dream, couldn't she?

And I dreamed. I dreamed about all the perfectly formed parts of that man I'd never get to touch, right up until the man of my dreams plopped his purchase onto the counter in front of me, tearing me from my daydream and causing me to nearly trip on the rubber rug under my feet. I rushed to take a step back after realizing my body was still slumped over the counter, with my chin in my palm, dreaming.

I looked at him, the corner of his lips tilted as he watched me try to compose myself. His tongue came out, licking his bottom lip and damn, I thought I'd die on the spot.

"Makenna, right?"

"I-um-I-" I couldn't get words out. "I'm Makenna."

Oh, my god. I felt my cheeks heat, embarrassment flooding me as I stumbled through my stupidity.

"I thought so. You're Austin's lab partner, right?"

His voice was like pure sin. I could listen to him read my shampoo bottle and I wouldn't be mad at it.

"Yeah. We're partners. When he shows up. How did you know?"

He bit his bottom lip, clearly amused by me, and I wasn't sure why. "Sorry. Some of that's my fault. The downside to carpooling to early morning classes. I'll try to be more punctual for you."

"I- it's not- I mean..." Shit. This man had my mind in all sorts of frenzies. "You don't come in here often."

Good save, girl. Change the subject.

He chuckled. "Did you mean to say that out loud?"

Shit. "I-"

He cut me off before I answered. "I don't come in here often. But I heard I should check it out. Good prices on the energy drinks." He held it up as if to prove it was his main point for coming in. "Among other things."

"Oh yeah. We are known for our prices." I smiled, which probably looked creepy because we absolutely were not known for our prices. In fact, our prices were shit. Absolutely fucking shit. But people bought them because they were paid for by the school credit system.

The machine beeped as I finally scanned the pile he had placed in front of me. "Put your student ID number into the pen pad, please."

He typed in the number, and immediately his

photo popped up. Jesus, was that a modeling snap-shot? I froze in my movements for a moment as I looked at the perfect photo of a golden skinned god with black hair that had to be as soft as it looked. My fingers itched to run through the shoulder-length locks, dying to find out.

"Are you going to ring up the rest?" he asked, tearing me out of my ogling.

I swallowed hard, trying to ignore the picture on my screen. "Yep."

We were silent as I scanned each item in, tossing the stuff into a plastic bag before printing out a receipt. "It seems you've got about a million bucks to spend. It's clear you don't come in here enough."

He reached over the counter, taking the bag from my grip. "Well, Makenna. I'll have to change that. Have a good night."

He gifted me with the godly sight of his dark eye winking at me, then he turned, activating the bell on the door as he disappeared onto campus, leaving me to wipe the drool from my chin as my eyes tried to track him.

CHAPTER THREE

ASA

"Absolutely fucking not," Austin insisted as we went through the applicants that made it to round three.

"She's on the list. We only have five who made it to the final round of the application out of seventy who applied. That's saying something," Wick pointed out.

"Not Mac. Anyone but Mac. She's not made for this," Austin tried again.

To be honest, he was probably right. I visited her while she worked hours after the application came through to us. She was cute, even if she wasn't my normal type. Though it's been so long since I could fuck, I wasn't even sure what my type was anymore. Still, her innocence shone through, and I wasn't sure if I could bring myself to corrupt it.

"Is it because you have a crush on the girl?" Wick pushed. "Because you would think that would be reason enough for you to want her in."

"Not Mac," he gritted out.

"She's going through the pretests like the rest of them. You think she didn't know what was coming when she answered these questions?" Wick flipped through the printout. "5'1? She's a little short for this, though, isn't she?"

"She can fit into small places," I pointed out.

"Her weight is a little-" He paused, and I corrected.

"Perfect. Trust me. It's all hourglass and curves."

Austin's head whipped in my direction. "When did you see Mac?"

"Calm the fuck down." He really was hung up on this girl. "I met her at the student store."

"You never go to the student store," he reminded me.

I shrugged. "I had credits."

"I fucking told her not to apply." He was practically pulling at his hair. The worry was genuine.

"We would take care of her, you know that," Wick clarified in case there was any question in our mate's mind.

"She could die."

"So could we," I added in case he needed the reminder.

"Pick someone else," Austin demanded.

"She's in the running. It's final." Wick turned to

the next candidate; his nose scrunched as if he wasn't nearly impressed with her application as he was with Mac's. Absentmindedly, he asked, "Do women really have these types of kinks? Some of these are just... wow."

"You're gonna give it to them." I smirked, knowing damn well we don't have limits.

"Fucking right I will." He scratched at a spot under his eye. "Scouting begins tomorrow. Stay in the shadows, don't give shit away. Pay whoever you have to in order to slip a secret to them, see how long it takes to get out. Track their answers. Can they really run..." He flips the pages, "You've got to be kidding me."

"What?"

"Mac's mile time is atrocious. That alone should be enough to disqualify her."

"I told you she wasn't made for this shit," Austin spouts.

"It's doubtful that Cyndi really runs a four-minute mile, though." He raised a brow. "Weed them out. Mac's might not be great, but at least she's not a liar."

He had a point. I can't even run a four-minute mile and I run every damn day.

"I'll take Mac," I volunteered, giving Austin a mischievous smile, knowing damn well he didn't agree with having her here on our team. "Give me another one, too. I'll double time it."

One glance at Austin proved that the man was fuming. He could kill us, murder us all right now, and all that would happen was the government would aid in the clean-up. It was how our job worked. But he wouldn't. "We'll switch off on Mac. As much as I hate to trust Austin on this one, he has better access than either of us do."

"I'm telling you; Mac is not the right fit for us. She's not even your type," he pointed out, though I'm not sure which of us he was talking to.

"My type is one who puts up a fight." Wick's eyes burned at the possibility. "Other than that, I'm not too picky. We can't have all our types in one girl. That's impossible and you fucking know it, Austin. At the end of a day, it's a girl to fuck and keep our secrets. Nothing more, nothing less."

"It's just..."

He let his argument drop, though I could feel the tension radiating off him. But Wick was right. We can't all be pleased by everything about one girl, but she would be ours. That is all that matters. And why did I picture my hands wound tight in golden brown hair when I thought of our future housekeeper? Golden brown hair that looked suspiciously like those messy little pigtail buns I saw on the awkward girl at the student store.

I knocked that thought right out of my mind because I couldn't be biased when deciding. We had criteria, and we needed to stick to it. It was for our own good. I picked up my bag, looking at the clock, noting we would be late by a few minutes to our first class. I winced, thinking of the curvy little spitfire that was sure to drag Austin through the mud for his tardiness. Guess I've already failed on the promise to keep him on time.

"We're late," I announced. "Text the information and we'll reconnect tonight on our findings."

I didn't wait for an answer. I knew that we'd do what we had to do. Our time frame was limited. We'd already wasted over a week while we waited for the girls' applications to file in. Now we had three weeks to figure our shit out, and I hoped we figured it out before then because it was going to take some hard-core preparation for our lady to learn what she'd gotten herself into.

The sun was down by the time we could meet again. Austin had grabbed some take out, and we were lounged in the living room of our home, a craftsman gem that was on loan to us until we moved on to a permanent placement for the Specialized Agents in Intelligence and National Tactics force. More secret than the CIA, it was our job to follow through in obtaining information and assassinations that the government didn't want public. We were recruited in the program our freshman year of college, and so far, our team's record was spotless.

It took hours of training. Hours of blood, sweat, and I won't even lie, some tears to get to the level that we are at now. With the addition of a house-keeper, the only allowed female to our team, we would be unstoppable. When we signed on, we were initiated in a bloody oath. They clarified that the men next to me would be my team for life. We didn't know each other the first week, but now I knew how many times their hearts beat a second. I knew everything about them, every fucking detail.

I plopped down with a carton of lo mein in my hands. "Cyndi is out. Her mile is damn near twenty minutes, and I only got her to run it by paying someone to issue a dare for cash. Her body is banging, but her trap won't keep shut. I hung around for less than thirty minutes and I already gathered all the gossip about people I didn't even know existed."

Austin and Wick both winced in unison. Yeah, that's terrible, I know. It was insufferable for me too, just gathering the information. Wick's nose crinkled as he added. "Lisa is out too. Her health checks don't pan out. According to the school's health clinic records, she's had three STIs in the last two years."

I swore Austin's face turned a little green as he leaned forward, placing his carton of food on the table before grabbing his soda instead. "Melanie seems solid so far. Health checks out. I caught her on the track. She ran a twelve-minute mile, not the worst. I paid to have a secret drop; we'll see if that happens in the next few days."

"Brenda and Mac?" I questioned.

The mention of the girl had Austin's mood seriously souring further. Wick didn't seem to notice the change in our teammate. "I've not gotten Mac to run yet. I was hoping Austin could. Brenda's on track, so she clearly has a good time. I just pulled up her records. Eight-minute mile. Could be improved on, but not the worst. I'll have someone hand her a secret tomorrow. Austin, can you test Mac's ability to keep her mouth shut?"

He grumbled something that neither of us heard. "What?"

He repeated the grumble, and Wick, clearly annoyed, shouted, "Grow a pair and speak the fuck up."

"She can keep a secret," Austin finally admitted reluctantly.

I rose a brow. "Oh yeah. Care to share how you know?"

"She's my lab partner," Austin stated, as if that was fact enough to support him.

"There is more to it than that," Wick pushed. "What secret did she hold?"

"If I told you two fuckers, it wouldn't be much of a secret, would it?" He spat the words out, rising from the couch, clearly agitated.

I laughed. "I will find out before I die. It's my only goal in life. Tell me, is it personal?"

"Of course it is." He gave us a deadpan stare. "And none of your fucking business."

"Oh, this has to be good," I taunted. "Does this have something to do with why you don't want the girl to join our team?"

"Partially. But also, she's too good to take a life.

She deserves better." Austin's statement was clear: better than us.

"We aren't trash. She won't be treated better by anyone, not better than we could provide," I pointed out. Which was partially true. We'd treat her well, we'd spoil the fuck out of her, as long as she behaved.

"You and I both know that my definition of treated well and yours are vastly different." Austin walked through the doorway to the kitchen and tossed his food in the trash, clearly losing his appetite.

"Well, we'll treat her like a whore and let you pick up the teary, cum-filled pieces that are left then." Wick shoved a massive bite in his mouth and chewed around his words. "Bet she isn't as sweet as you think in the dark."

"Never are." I confirmed.

Austin walked back into the room, the fury clear on his face, but he wouldn't act on his anger. He knew we were right. "I've got a lab tomorrow. I'll see if I can feel around on her capabilities."

"And report back, honestly?" I prompted.

"I won't fucking lie. You know that." I did. But the way he'd been so worked up over this girl, you just never know.

"We are already running out of time," I pointed out, more of a reminder than something he didn't know. We had to act swiftly on this. If we didn't have a housekeeper in a month, we'd have no other chance in our lifetimes to get one.

"I won't fuck it up. I promise you that."

"Good." Because I knew both Wick and I would watch, ensuring that his need to protect the little girl didn't fuck up our chance at becoming a team of four. I wasn't fucking around about it, and I knew Wick wasn't either. A lifetime of meaningless sex, or a lifetime of a connection when you had not a single other one. The choice wasn't that fucking hard, and I'd not let Austin's wariness fuck it up for us.

"Good." Austin nodded once before taking the stairs two at a time, heading up to his room and away from us, sulking like a fucking child.

CHAPTER FOUR

AUSTIN

For once this semester, Asa made sure we arrived on campus on time. He made no secret that if I didn't do my job, he'd be forced to go back to her work and probe around. I didn't want that. I didn't want them anywhere near Mac, if I was honest. Not because I didn't trust them with her, because I knew they played dirty and they would never truly hurt her. But because Mac was mine. My secret infatuation. The girl next door. My dream I never could have since the moment I signed over my life to the Saints.

I strolled into class, not missing her face lighting up when she saw me. I walked the length of the room until I found our table, placing my bag on the floor. She turned toward me. "On time? What is this anomaly?"

I spread my hands wide. "Sometimes I like to shock you."

My heart raced at the secretive smile she offered me, then immediately ached when I thought about the deception I'd have to do for the stupid application process. I didn't want to hurt her, but somehow, I suspected she wouldn't leave this process without her share of bruises and scars. I just hoped it wasn't the scars that settled so deep they never healed.

"I got the good Bunsen burner today. You can thank me later." She flipped open her notebook, already dating the page.

"I owe you one," I stated, meaning it. Getting the shit Bunsen burners ruined the lab work and sometimes forced us to stay after class, which I just didn't have the time to afford. "Hey, do you have plans after class?"

"Lunch," she stated. "Well, breakfast, actually."

I sighed, not liking the way she didn't eat breakfast. I licked my lips, feeling how dry they were and knowing that I was buying time because I was nervous. "Can you do me a favor?"

"Isn't me being your partner a favor enough?" She joked, but she didn't realize just how true it was. I looked at the rest of the class, and I would hate to be stuck with any of the other classmates. They were not favored in the personality department.

"An additional favor," I amended.

"Let's hear it." Her arms crossed in front of her,

bringing a little cleavage to display. I lost my thought for a moment as I stared.

When I finally could focus, I cleared my throat. "My running partner bailed on me."

"Okay?" She waited for me to continue.

"Will you go for a run with me? I hate not having someone to talk to, and I don't have many friends." This was true. That was for a reason. The reason being I kill people for a living.

"I-" She started, then stopped. "Look, Austin. I would love to help, but I don't run."

"Please. Just for today," I begged. "You won't have to do it again."

"Austin. Have you ever seen a penguin run for a fish?"

"What?" I was confused.

"That's me trying to run." She clarified, "It's slow, it's a waddle situation, and I guarantee my thighs will create a fire that might burn down the whole campus."

I braved a glance at the thighs in question, encased in jeans. "You'll be fine."

"I really don't think—"

"Please, Makenna." I pulled out the big guns, her full name. "I have a heart condition. I don't want to run solo in case I collapse."

Her eyes softened at my lie. "Has that happened before?"

"Always a first time," I pointed out.

"Mr. Bruin, Miss Wright, is there something you'd

like to share with us all since you are dead set on delaying us today?"

My head snapped up. I hadn't even heard the class start. "No sir. Sorry."

The professor nodded. "Don't let it happen again."

When he continued on, I looked over at Mac and whispered, "Pretty please."

I saw her resolve crack moments before she grumbled, "Fine. But I hope you like walking because I might be the one to collapse otherwise."

I smirked, knowing I planned to fucking push her. "Perfect."

Three hours later, I was waiting outside the ladies' dorm for Mac to reappear. She'd been gone for a while, and I wondered if she ditched me. I was ready to beg the next person who entered to let me through, but then she appeared, wearing an old school t-shirt and a pair of tight-fitting black leggings. The sight made me speechless, which was ridiculous because she was fully dressed.

"Are we going or not?" she grumbled as she tightened one of those pigtail buns she favored. The water she carried was wedged between her legs as she adjusted her hair, and I wanted to reach over and grab it, feel the warmth her thighs created against the plastic. Was that weird? That was totally weird, and I was completely fucking aware.

"I appreciate you going with me," I offered, noting that she wasn't too thrilled to be joining me today.

"Talk to me after we're finished, if I make it out alive." She stretched her muscles.

"An aggressive exerciser. Noted." I followed her lead, stretching my muscles. "I'm not planning to kill you, though."

"You clearly underestimate what my body can take." She raised her arms above her head in a stretch that pushed her boobs out.

"I think I have a pretty good idea of what a girl's body can take." Wick appeared behind me, and I swear to God, if that voice registered a second slower in my mind, I would have sucker punched him out of reflex.

I spun around. "What are you doing here?"

"Just taking a shortcut through campus on my way to math. Glad I did." His eyes sparkled as he looked toward Mac. "Are you going to introduce us?"

If I could glare any harder at my friend, he'd have physical repercussions. Before I could offer an introduction, Mac stepped forward, her hand out to shake Wick's. "I'm Mac. I'm um, Austin's chem partner."

"Oh yes." Wick smirked. "Aussie has told me about you."

"He has?" Her brow rose in question while my face heated.

"Mainly along the lines of, 'Hurry Wick, Mac will

rip me a new one if I'm late again,' but that counts, right?"

Her eyes narrowed. "He's always late."

"My fault." Wick rose his hands in an innocent gesture meant to look like a surrender, but I knew it was all an act. "I'll try to get him to class on time."

"That's what the last guy said." Her eyes grew hard. "He was late for the next class again."

"We're men. Without a female to keep us on track, we get easily distracted. Like puppies, really." He gave her his best charming grin, one that usually would have women's panties falling to the floor, but for Mac, she was anything but impressed.

She crossed her arms in front of her, seeming to guard herself against the onslaught of pheromones Wick was pushing at her in waves. "I'm more of a cat person myself."

Her glare was epic, and Wick, who had probably never heard no in his whole life and always had females begging him, seemed to take a step back. "I've nothing against cats. Claws can be good sometimes."

After a stare off that lasted way too long, with intent that we all knew had nothing to do with animals and everything to do with her disinterest in Wick, she finally broke. "Well, it was nice to meet you."

She turned and walked away, heading for the trail and leaving me standing there with my friend. When she was out of earshot, I growled, "What the fuck was that about?"

"How was I supposed to know she was easily annoyed?"

"I have told you that the thousands of times I mentioned not wanting to be late to chem." I rubbed my forehead, feeling the tension grow.

"I like her." He pointed toward her. "Let's keep that one."

"She hated you," I scoffed.

"I know." He pulled out his phone. "I'm texting Asa now."

I pushed his phone down. "Absolutely not. I'm doing this to test her because I fucking said I would. But she will not be the final one. We both know it."

Wick walked backward. "Get back to your world of delusions, Aussie. Our partner is waiting for you."

I told myself I wouldn't look after he referred to Mac as our partner, yet my head still twisted as I looked over my shoulder to see Mac standing fifty feet away, her hand on the curve of her hip as she waited impatiently. I turned back around to face Wick. "I will not leave her waiting. But don't expect a miracle to come of this. She needs to run so we can move on with the process. She won't pass. Don't fucking forget that fact."

"I don't think our girl will let us down. She loves me. She can't fucking wait to join us." He leaned over, giving her a little wave that I know caused her to fume. "See you at the finish line, mate."

When I turned back, Mac looked less than pleased. I closed the distance between us, hoping she wouldn't drop me for something a little more interesting. When I got to her, she stared, not trying to make it easy for me and fill in the awkward.

"I didn't know I'd run into him," I admitted.

"Should have invited him to run."

We started walking side by side, getting closer to the trail. "He was on his way to class. He couldn't go."

"Convenient."

I blew out a breath. The shade on this girl always got me. When she was in a good mood, it was hot. But something about her with claws out made my dick impossibly hard. Not ideal when I'm about to go for a run. "Have I told you how much I appreciate you doing this for me?"

"Have I told you how much I hate running? If the threat of having to find a new lab partner midway through the semester wasn't looming over my head, I'd have said no in a heartbeat."

I placed my palm over my chest. "And here I thought you just cared about me or something."

"Or something," she replied. "Are we doing this or chatting?"

"We're doing this," I stated as I started jogging.

She followed me, shockingly, keeping pace next to me. I increased speed slowly, and through it she stayed at my side. I wasn't running my fastest pace, but I wasn't doing it slowly either. We reached the mile marker, and I cursed internally when I looked up, seeing Wick leaning against a tree. He held up his palm, smirking as he flashed eight fingers.

Eight minutes.

I cursed under my breath at the realization that she made the fucking cut on this part of the physical assessment. Her head turned to me. " Are you okay? Do you need to stop? Is it your heart?"

Fuck. "No." I was breathing slightly heavy. "I just ..."

"Just what?" Her hand touched my forearm, and I nearly froze.

"I just remembered I forgot to take meat out of the freezer." I didn't know what kind of lie I was telling, but I was stuck with it.

"You cook?" She hardly seemed winded.

"Don't you?" I cooked. The entire team did, so that part wasn't a lie.

Her eyes narrowed. "I live in a dorm room."

"Oh yeah." I forgot they don't have all the fancy things like a basic kitchen in there. "I'll have to cook for you sometime."

What the fuck was I saying? I'd never get an opportunity to cook for her. I wouldn't want the opportunity, because that means she would be our housekeeper and I wanted so much more than risking her life for her future.

I slowed my steps and turned to run back to the front of the trail. "I thought you didn't run."

"It's atrocious," she stated.

"You're not slow at it," I pointed out.

"I'm trying to get it over with, so I'll never have to do it again."

Looking at her now, I can see the wear this jog is doing to her. It made her cheeks red, her eyes brighten, and with a slight sheen of sweat, she looked fucking beautiful. I slowed when I realized she was struggling a bit. "I appreciate the support."

She grumbled something under her breath but said nothing the rest of the way back to the start of the trail. When we reached the end, we both stopped. She leaned over, her hands on her knees as she tried to regulate her breathing. I wasn't winded. I could have gone for another few miles before I even felt a bit of a twinge in my lungs that begged me to stop.

"Want to do this again?" I teased, knowing full well she would reject me so fast.

"I'd rather die," she deadpanned.

I didn't want to tell her that hanging out with me might ensure that dying was a possibility. "You did great. Honestly, you're a natural."

"I'm going back to my dorm and napping," she declared.

"It wasn't that bad," I cooed.

"I'm dead inside." She groaned as she stretched. "This experience won't be receiving a five star from me."

"Having me as company had to add some positivity."

She tilted her head toward me as she crossed an

arm in front of her, pulling it to stretch. "It's the only reason this experience got any stars."

"I don't know if I should feel honored or insulted."

"Sorry, I'm not here to stroke your masculinity. If that was what you were looking for, maybe ask a girl from an elective class to run instead. If they can commit to one extracurricular activity, surely they will be all over you for the opportunity for more." She walked away from me, not bothering to look at me as she said, "See you in chem. Don't be late."

Then she left me standing there at the end of the trail while my phone buzzed with a text from Wick. *Looks like she's still in the running for housekeeper. Wonder if she is a good fuck? With a mouth like that, I'd love to find out.*

CHAPTER FIVE

MAC

My whole body hurt. Throbbed. Screamed. And it was all because I took pity on Austin and went for a jog with him. I might die. In fact, dying was at the forefront of my mind when my phone buzzed with a text message.

Austin: *How was the nap?*

Me: *Why are you texting me?*

It may have been rude, I'd admit it. But damn it, I was pretty sure it hurt to blink, and I couldn't even figure that one out because I used no muscles in my eyelids to jog.

The text from him came through swiftly, not making me wait. *Don't be like that, Mac. I appreciate you going. Can I make it up to you? Do you play darts? I'll buy you dinner and we can do a game or two in the student hall.*

The offer sounded strangely like a date until he sent a second message with, *Just a friendly thank you. That's all.*

That was a relief because I didn't think I could ever date Austin. Not because he wasn't handsome, because he was a fucking stunner, but I had friend zoned him since week two of us being chemistry partners, and I wasn't willing to make the rest of class awkward.

I don't know how to play darts. I sent off the text, hoping the fact that I was shit at anything that required socializing would deter him from wanting to hang out.

No such luck, though. A minute later, my phone pinged. *We'll teach you.*

We'll? My stomach balled, suddenly nervous that there would be more people than just me there with him. I didn't do well with people. I didn't socialize. The most I can manage is ringing up people at the student store, and even then, I make a fool of myself often doing that simple task.

Another ping. *Asa and his friend are coming.*

Oh, because that made it so much better. Asa was a full-on snack. Accompanied by the hotness that is Austin, and the two were going to earn me all the glares. I couldn't go. In fact, I absolutely refused. I had just typed just that when a message came through once more.

We'll be there in five minutes.

I rapidly fired off the text, begging him not to

come. When those went unanswered, I urged him to reconsider. When no response happened, I panicked and fumbled around my dorm room, grabbing clothing while also trying to brush my teeth. My mouth was full of toothpaste foam when my intercom rang.

I hurried and spit it into my sink before answering. "Hello?"

"It's Austin. Want me to come up or are you coming down?"

I looked at my dorm room. It was a simple room with an attached bathroom. Private, which was lucky because some colleges don't even offer that. But it also was a small space that was a complete mess. I needed to clean it this weekend. In fact, I'd clean it the first chance I got.

I pressed the button. "I'm coming down. Give me a few minutes."

I released the button, then stumbled as I tried to wiggle into my jeans at the same time as removing my dirty shirt. The act wasn't successful, and I fell onto my bed before finally getting the pants pulled up fully. After tossing my shirt to the side, I pulled on a cute tank top, thankful I had at least one thing clean. I really needed to do laundry. It took me another three minutes to toss up my hair into a few little buns and make sure I didn't have food on my face. A little deodorant, a splash of my favorite body spray, and I was closing my door behind me, feeling oddly nervous.

Two flights of stairs later, an impossible task since my legs were already burning, I made it to the exit and pushed it open. Like Austin promised, he was sitting on the thick rim of a cement planter outside, waiting for me. Next to him were Asa and a girl I vaguely recognized from around campus and the dorm.

Austin stood, pulling me into a hug as if he truly was happy to see me. Odd, we'd never hugged before. His friends stood as Austin smiled down at me. Why were they all so damn tall? "Thanks for coming Mac. This jerk right here threatened to kick my ass at darts, and you know I couldn't have that. But I didn't have a partner either, and I needed one because he brought Brenda."

Brenda. That was her name.

"Nice to see you again." Asa lifted his chin at me in greeting and damn it, why did that simple gesture cause my insides to warm? Did this man know what he does to a woman? It had to be the hair. Men with wild hair are wild in—

"Are you going to say something?" Austin leaned in and whispered.

Shit. Had I only been staring? I cleared my throat, trying to buy myself time and clear my mind before offering a simple, "Yeah. You too."

"I believe I offered Mac food," Austin told Asa. "So I hope you two are hungry, too."

"Starved." Asa gripped his stomach like he hadn't eaten in ages, while his girl's face scrunched up a little. Asa looked at her with concern. "You're not hungry?"

"Oh no. I had a big breakfast."

All of us were silent as we blinked a few times, trying to absorb what she said. Finally, it was Asa who brought words to thought. "It's eight at night. Breakfast was hours ago."

"Yeah, but I like to—"

"I don't care what you like to do. It's not healthy to starve. We're getting dinner." Asa's brow furrowed as he took Brenda's hand, already pulling her toward the row of restaurants just outside of campus.

She tried to argue. "I'm on track. I can't just be filling up. It will weigh me down."

"Have a salad then." He shrugged off her words. "You aren't doing yourself any favors by not giving your body fuel to replenish the energy spent."

When Asa and Brenda were far enough in front of us that they couldn't hear our conversation, Austin asked, "You like to eat, don't you?"

"I do prefer not to perish away." I tried to hide my smirk, but I wasn't that successful at it.

His lips twitched in amusement. "Good girl."

My body instantly turned to fire at his praise and embarrassment followed because this was Austin, and I knew he would want nothing sexual with me, but he was attractive and honestly, the words falling from his lips in that husky tone should have been illegal. They counteracted the boy next door vibes he threw off and my mind couldn't compute, or maybe it didn't want to, that Austin couldn't be anything but an innocent, wholesome human. Especially since I once learned that he was a—

"Why are your cheeks so red?"

"My cheeks aren't red!" Though I said the words a little too forcefully.

I hadn't realized we had caught up to Asa and Brenda, but clearly Asa had heard Austin because he looked over his shoulder and winked at me while saying to his friend, "Maybe Mac likes to be a good girl."

I wanted to die. I begged the earth to open into a giant sinkhole and swallow me down, offering me the most swift and dramatic death a girl could ask for. "Absolutely not."

He ignored Brenda's chattering as he looked over his shoulder again. "It's cool Mac, no need to hide from us. We see you."

"I want to die," I whispered, which only caused both men to laugh, their rich amusement bursting into the dark.

"Come on now Mac, we're only teasing you." Austin bumped my shoulder. "Dinner's on me, in case there was any question. I owe you for making sure I didn't die on my run."

Asa gave his friend a confused look, but said nothing as he approached a diner, pulling open the door and holding it for us as we walked in. "Take the booth in the corner, girls, we'll be there in a moment."

Brenda and I walked to the booth and took our seats, one on each side, as the boys hung back, discussing something just out of our earshot. Brenda said nothing to me, only looked pouty and annoyed that she was forced to go to a place that served food, which she had no intention of eating. Her loss. I was hungry enough to eat it for the both of us.

"So. Hi," I offered. Awkward. Yes. But it let her know I was up to being friends, or at minimum, allies.

She didn't answer, so I asked, "Have you known Asa long?"

Her eyes watched the man from where he stood, talking privately with Austin. "We just met, but I've known who Asa is for a long time. Now that he is finally showing me attention, I'm not letting anyone else get to him. He's mine."

The creepy ownership statement, combined with the glare she was giving me, made me wonder if she thought I was a threat. I held my hands up in surrender. "You can have him."

I'll just look from afar. But I wasn't willing to make that statement out loud in case she had some sort of secret arsenal of weapons hidden under that too short skirt. Saved from further conversation, the boys appeared, and I scooted over, allowing room for Austin to slide into the booth.

"What are we eating?" Austin asked me as he picked up a menu.

"Do you eat burgers, Mac?" Asa asked from across

the table. "They have a killer Ortega burger. Peppers roasted in house."

"I've been coming here at least twice a month since freshman year, and I've never seen that on the menu," I stated, as I looked through the trifold, laminated list.

"Got to know the right people." He winked. Again. And I damn near swooned.

Austin's thigh bumped against mine even though he hadn't looked up from his menu. "It really is killer."

Brenda, feeling left out of the conversation, chimed in. "Do they have it in a vegetarian version?"

All eyes fell to her, but it was Austin who spoke. "You can't ruin perfection with a plant-based soy protein patty. Trust me, eat it as beef or don't do it a disservice."

"Well." She tilted her head and rolled her eyes at Austin. A move that made me feel strangely overprotective of him. "I only eat vegetarian."

I reached over the table and patted her menu. "Salads are there."

Beside me, Austin snorted, a sound so soft that only I would hear. Brenda looked annoyed as she leaned forward. "They sell veggie burgers. I think I'll have one of those."

"Suit yourself." Austin smiled. "I hope you don't mind that we all eat meat."

"It's a little offensive, if I'm honest." Brenda crossed her arm over her chest.

"Good. I'm glad it's only a little. I'd hate to be fully offensive." Austin smile widened as he raised his hand, flagging down the waitress.

She came, taking our orders of three Ortega burgers with fries and one Ortega burger, soy patty, salad as a side. A round of iced teas closed off our order, and the waitress left, promising to return in a few minutes with our drinks. Which she did, and it was a nice break from the tension at our table.

When the waitress left again, I turned to Austin. "You're going to teach me darts? Because if this is a team effort, I'm bringing you down."

"I don't know how to play darts. No one said anything to me about darts," Brenda cut in.

I gave her a quick glare before bringing my attention back to Austin. He didn't bother to give her attention, which was strangely satisfying because we were here together as friends. And the conversation was between us. No one invited her into our bubble. He looked down at me, licked his lips for a moment, not answering, like he was stuck in a trance. When he finally spoke, it was a low, husky sentence that scratched against his throat as it left him.

"I'll teach you anything, Mac."

I smiled up at him. Had my chem partner always had those gold flecks in his eyes? "I am not a fast learner."

"We've got time," he stated before daring to look at his friend. "All night, in fact."

"Asa," Brenda whined. "Are you going to teach me?"

I could tell that Asa was regretting today's decisions when he volunteered to take Brenda out for the night. He took a slow sip of his drink, drawing out the time before he answered, "Of course."

"I'm quick at learning things," she pointedly said, as if we were in competition. She clearly wasn't quick at learning the room because everyone at this table thought she was annoying.

"Good." Asa looked at her, giving her a smile that didn't reach his eyes. "I expect us to win, then. I hate losing to Aussie. It doesn't happen often, but when it does, complete and utter disappointment."

"Is that true, Aussie?" I whispered.

His thigh bumped hard into mine at the use of his nickname that clearly all his friends use. "Absolutely not, Makenna."

"Point made. Might be worth suffering through my full name if it means calling you that, though."

We were whispering, our heads close together like we were having a private conversation that the rest of the table wasn't privy to. He leaned closer, putting his lips close to my ear. "So is Mac the ball busting lab partner and Makenna the girl that's here for a fun time?"

"Guess we'll find out." Was I flirting? With Austin Bruin?

"I, for one, am looking forward to it." Both our heads turned together to look at Asa, who was clearly not entertaining his date but was up in our business. When we said nothing, he lifted his shoulders. "What? I like to have a good time."

An hour later, we were in the student hall. Our stomachs were full, except for Brenda, who decided she hated the Ortega burger because it didn't taste good with soy. Did Austin not warn her? Most of the flavor came from a mix of beef juices and cheese mixing perfectly to add an artery clogging layer of perfection. But Brenda even opted to not have the cheese as she's lactose intolerant.

Turns out, darts were easy, and after one full round of playing with the boys, I practically aced it, while Brenda still couldn't even hit the board. By the end of the evening, I even got a few right in the center, causing a round of cheers from both the guys, while Brenda sulked and told us we weren't playing fair because she wasn't getting enough practice in.

It was close to one when we left the hall, and the guys walked us both back to the dorm. Brenda made it a point to stomp into the dorm, clearly annoyed that she lost the game. It didn't bother Asa at all. Instead, he waited back with Austin, both men giving me a hug before waiting for me to get into the building. I watched from my window as they walked away, and it left me wondering if I had a crush on my lab partner. And his friend?

CHAPTER SIX

WICK

I was infatuated with the girl, and I'd only been in her presence for a few minutes. Long enough to know she didn't favor me much, and I didn't really care. It made for a bigger fight and a hotter fuck. Anger equaled passion and all that jazz. "So Mac then..."

"I don't really think—" Why was Austin dead set on denying us this girl? She could die, but then so could we.

"She did way better than Brenda with precision. She was a fast learner and, let's be honest, Brenda was insufferable." Asa turned to me. "And a vegetarian."

A hiss whistled through my teeth. "That was not answered on her questionnaire."

"Clearly also a liar," Asa clarified.

If she had admitted that on her questionnaire, she

would have been skipped. We had no room for picky eaters. Sometimes we are on jobs and those jobs cause us to eat what's available, good or bad. Accommodations can't be made. "And Mac? She eats meat?"

"Faster than we do." Asa looked proud. "The girl was starved, for sure."

"You'd feel starved too if most of your meals came from the campus cafeteria," Austin defended her.

"You clearly misread the conversation, Aussie. I'm pretty sure that's an attractive quality, not a turnoff." I leaned back in my chair, the plastic squeaking and threatening to tip. "We're doing this then. We're getting us a fucking housekeeper."

"Tomorrow night." Asa leaned forward, bracing his elbows on his knees as he looked between us. "Aussie will take her out for a drink and slip in something extra. And before you argue, it needs to be done. Get her out of there, and we'll get her back to our home."

"We can't hurt her." Austin was already on the edge of his seat, ready to fight for this girl before we laid a single finger on her. Didn't he realize that action alone, that feeling she ignited, the need to protect, was reason enough to keep her as ours? If we didn't have a desire to protect and cherish, she wouldn't be worth joining our team.

"We won't hurt her. Much." Though I did plan to play. It was required. We needed to see how much she could handle. "I won't take more than I know she can give. You know the rules. She has to consent to be ours."

"Couldn't we do it without drugging?"

"That's not how it works, and you know it." Asa rubbed his eye, clearly tired from the long night they had. "If she sees our faces before we've got her tied up, we're screwed. The entire organization is screwed."

"Plus," I gave them a wicked grin I couldn't hide, "she did claim to have a kidnapping fantasy. Look at the bright side. You're helping her live her dreams."

"Fuck," Austin growled. "Why are girls so damn weird? Why can't they have normal fantasies, like schoolgirl outfits, mixed with some teacher vibes? Kidnapping? That's fucking insane."

"If you like the schoolgirl, I bet we can get her to comply," I offered, knowing damn well that his crush on this girl had grown exponentially. It was the only reason he was trying to warn us away so badly, even when she was clearly the best choice for us all. And the way Asa was texting me last night, not talking about his date, but Austin's, he clearly agreed.

"I don't have a thing for schoolgirls," Austin clarified.

"Lies. All men do." I laughed, knowing it would annoy him further. I stood up and checked the time. Seven. "I've got to go."

"Where are you going?" Asa asked automatically, even though I knew he didn't care. We weren't clingy.

We could do what we wanted, even if we were an inseparable team.

"I've got some energy drinks to buy." The grin I was sporting couldn't be hidden. I knew Austin would object, but fuck him. This girl, she was ours now. May not be official, but it was official enough. She passed all the tests, and I knew in the very pit of my stomach she would succeed in the rest of them. I saw the fire in her eyes. Fire never let me down.

"You don't need energy drinks." Austin crossed his arms over his chest.

"Sure I do, Aussie. We've got a long night of planning. I've got to stay awake for it." I confirmed, "You're welcome to come. The more the merrier."

"I'll fucking pass," he fumed.

"Suit yourself." I grabbed my keys. "It's happening tomorrow night, Aussie. Get your thoughts and shit together because if you fuck this up for me, for us, I'll slit your throat myself. If I have to pick, I'm picking pussy over dick."

In less than ten minutes, I was entering the student store, announced by the tiny little bell on the door. The place was dead inside, but somehow, I was very much alive as I stepped through the door. My heart raced, my pulse sped, and when my eyes met Mac's, the tiny scowl that furrowed her brows only made my cock hard.

I strolled through the aisles, grabbing a few

energy drinks, cheese puffs, and restocking the fruit in our house. It was all about balance, and sure, we ate like shit, but we also worked out so damn much that it all burned out in fuel. With an arm full of goods, I made my way to the counter and plopped my stuff down on it.

Without a word to the girl, I stepped away again, gathering some nuts, protein bars, and a few cans of vegetable juice. I swear each item I threw down, tossing it without a care, caused the girl to glare harder, intensely wishing me harm without words.

A jar of peanut butter rolled in front of her, and she stopped it with her palm. I tried not to smirk. "You'd think they would offer hand baskets in this joint. Am I right?" She didn't respond. "Okay then..."

I continued gathering things, more intending to annoy her versus actual need. Every time I added to the counter in front of her, I swore her eye twitched and nose flared. I wondered if she'd have the same look on her face right before I forced her to her knees to suck my cock.

"Would you like me to ring you up, or do you plan to purchase the entire store?"

I twisted my neck, looking over my shoulder at the fiery girl. "Could I do that? Just have you bag it all up and toss it in my truck?"

"Hilarious," she stated. Then, without taking her eyes off me, she picked up an item and scanned it into the system. "When you're ready, I'll need your ID so I can put this on your tab."

"You're a true joy, aren't you Mac?" I taunted her as I walked up to the counter, placing the last items on it.

"I'm here to serve." Another beep and an emotionless glare as she scanned an item.

If only she realized just how she was about to be here to serve me. "I'll take the survey. Let them know what a joy it is being your customer."

Beep. Beep. "Please do. Type in your number, please. I'd like to not hold up the line."

I looked around. The place was still completely empty. Not a single person in line, or in the store. "I'd hate to do that." I leaned against the counter. "Say, you don't seem to like me much, do you, Mac?"

"I talked to you for less than five minutes and I learned all I need to know." In a mocking voice, she added, "We're men. Without a female to keep us on track..." Her voice trailed off before she continued. "We are not put on this earth to babysit your gender. That's a dated point of view, and I'd rather never see a man again than let one think it's my job to babysit them. Please type your number in."

I typed my student number into the pen pad. "I think maybe you misinterpreted how I live my life."

"I think you misinterpreted my lack of care." She smiled brightly as she looked at the screen. "Will that be all, Chad?"

"It's Wick." Nothing I hated more than to be called Chad. Chadwick was an unfortunate name, I was aware. But nothing is more unfortunate than the shit people associate with Chads.

"I think I prefer Chad." She pulled out a receipt. "Here's your total, and here's your remaining balance. Enjoy your night, Chad."

I would fuck that name out of her vocabulary or I'd die trying. She was practically asking for it, begging for it, really. She'd learn, and I couldn't wait for the day she did. I leaned in, my voice a whisper. "When I fuck you, Chad won't be the name you're screaming."

"I'd die of desperation before I let your dick inside my body," she declared.

"We'll see about that, Makenna." I let my eyes roam over her, zooming in on the pigtails that I was dying to pull and use as handles as I rode her from behind. "And when it happens, and make no mistake about it, it will... I want you to remember this moment. Then I want you on your knees apologizing, before you suck my cock."

"Pretty sure this is sexual harassment." She stood tall, not even afraid of me, though I loomed a good foot taller than she stood.

"Want to report me?" I let my eyes linger on her chest for a moment.

"I want you to leave."

I picked up my bags. "I was planning on it."

"Don't come back," she demanded.

"I make no promises," I admitted. "See you tomorrow, Makenna."

"I hope not."

I smiled so hard my cheeks hurt as I carried my bag out, knowing damn well that tomorrow I'd have her strung up bare for me. I wonder what she'd taste like. I couldn't fucking wait to find out. I didn't plan on fucking her. At least not yet. But I wanted to hear her moan my name, pant for me, beg me to give her what she really wanted. Us. All of us.

CHAPTER SEVEN

MAC

"I don't even drink," I told Austin on the phone when he called. He wanted me to go to the bar with him, promising I was only going to be his wingman... errr wing woman.

"They think I like guys, Mac. That's how little they've seen me flirt. I need someone to dispute it."

"You haven't flirted," I pointed out. "At least I think you haven't, and I'll be honest, if you have, and I didn't notice, it's a little concerning."

"I haven't flirted," he confirmed.

Even though he couldn't see me, I placed a hand on my hip. "Why haven't you? Should I be offended? Do you like guys?"

"What? No!" I heard a rustling on his side of the

phone. "You're perfect, Mac. You don't need me flirting to confirm that."

"No," I answered tartly, "but it would help."

"Are you coming or not?" he huffed.

"Is 'not' an option, really?" I looked up at the ceiling as I held the phone to my ear. When had this even happened? When had I become accustomed to hanging out with Austin when I normally had absolutely no friends? It's been a wild week, for sure.

"I'll be there in five," he announced.

"What! That's not enough time to really get ready," I pointed out.

"It would have been ten if you didn't give me so much bullshit and wasted the time." I heard keys jingle. "I've got Asa's truck."

"Fancy. It's still going to take me over five minutes to get ready." I used my shoulder to hold the phone while I shifted through the closet. It was only a beer, or so he said. But somehow, I felt like it was so much more than that. I rarely drank, and yet I felt the need to make sure I looked impeccable while I was there.

Maybe it was the company? Did I want to impress Austin?

"Buzz me up when I get there. I'll wait for you." The phone clicked without even a proper goodbye, and I hadn't even agreed to go, not completely. Was I preparing myself? Yes. But I hadn't said the words to him, and yet once again, I was faced with a tight time frame and panic as I rushed to prepare myself to face Austin at a time that wasn't during class hours.

In the back of my closet, I pulled out a black dress. After undressing from my baggy shirt, I squeezed into the dress, cringing a little as it barely hit mid-thigh. Then I stumbled to my bathroom and plugged in my curling iron. While that heated, I leaned over my tub, trying to shave away the stubble on my legs. I could do my makeup with Austin here, but shave my legs? I'd die first.

I had just finished shaving when my intercom buzzed. I didn't even bother to answer. I just hit the button, unlocking the door that allowed him to enter. Why was I even doing this? This was Austin. My annoying lab partner, who would come to class late, let me act annoyed, then offer me witty banter to ease my annoyance. We weren't friends. Though if you wanted the truth, he was probably the closest thing to a friend that I had. But we definitely didn't have the friendship where we went out on Friday nights or where I frantically rushed to shave my legs, just in case.

Was I hoping for a just in case?

Hell, I didn't even know what I was hoping for at this point. It was just nice to get out.

I opened the door when a soft knock rattled the cheap particle board on its hinges, but I didn't bother to look at him. I turned, taking the five steps it took me to enter my bathroom, but leaving my door open in case he felt like talking. He entered, shutting the door behind him as he took in my space.

With a soft chuckle, he joked, "Wow, and you wanted to apply for a housekeeper's position."

I shot a glare over my shoulder before I picked up my curling iron and began winding my hair around the strands. "If it pays..."

He was right though; I was shit at cleaning. But that didn't matter because it had been nearly two weeks since I submitted that application, and though I had thought about it a few times, I hadn't heard a thing back from them. Plus, it wasn't like there was contact information. They had no phone number, no address, no fucking email. Just a web-based application and a thank you for applying page.

"How's the job at the student store?"

"Provides me with an adequate supply of ramen with the occasional splurge of coffee from the shop in the student square." I had a full scholarship to Sablewood University, complete with paid housing, so I couldn't complain. But school wouldn't be around forever to house me, and eventually, I'd graduate. I didn't want to be on the streets begging for change when that happened.

Glancing at him through the mirror, I saw him cringe at my admission before he leaned against the door frame, his eyes traveling the length of my body. "Drinks are on me tonight. I've never seen you in a dress before."

"I own three." Our eyes connected through the mirror. "That means we've got two more occasions before these suckers hit a repeat cycle."

"I'd change that," he muttered.

"Excuse me?"

"Nothing." His teeth gleamed as his lips spread wide, gifting me with the angelic look that I knew would have all the girls going wild for him if he tried. He didn't. Actually, now that I thought about it, none of them did. It was known that Wick, Austin, and Asa were inseparable. Women swooned when they walked, but they always seemed to reject any advances.

Curious.

"Question," I stated.

"Answer," he replied. "I've never seen your hair down."

"I rarely like to have it down. It gets hot, and it never behaves."

"You should do it more." His fingers flexed at his side as he watched me with fascination.

I wound another strand of hair. "So, question: Wick and Asa are inseparable from you." I led with a statement, not sure how to ask.

"Yes? We've been friends since freshman year. We've gone through a lot together."

"You guys don't date?"

"No." He didn't offer me more than that, even though I was begging with my eyes to tell me more without me asking.

When he didn't say more, I finally blurted out, "Are you guys some sort of throuple?"

He choked on his own spit as he sucked in a

breath, causing him to lean over the door frame and cough uncontrollably. When he finally stopped coughing, his watery eyes met mine. "Are you serious?"

"Well, it's not that far off. Everything I've ever heard about you three is about how you turn down any passes anyone makes at you, which makes you that much more desirable. Everyone wants to conquer you three, but if it's because you guys just don't like females, it would all make sense. And the world is so progressive these days. A throuple isn't that odd. I've seen it before. And—"

"Mac, stop."

"There is no need to be ashamed," I added.

"Mac. We aren't a throuple. Or a couple. Or anything. They are my best friends, that's all."

"Then why don't you date?"

"It's complicated. We'll talk about it sometime, just not now."

I sighed, hating answers that put off the information I really wanted to know. "I don't understand why we can't talk about it now." I released the strands of hair and picked up another one.

Austin stalked forward, his chest suddenly hitting my back. He reached for my curling iron, releasing the hair and setting it onto the counter before leaning into me, bracing his hands on the sink and caging me in. Our eyes were locked in the mirror. The flecks of gold in his blue seemed to dance and shift, doing something to my insides, turning them into lava the longer we stared down.

"I promise you, they are not the one I want," he finally whispered. His breath fanned against my hair, causing gooseflesh to raise on my skin and my nipples to pebble.

I swear my breathing was uneven as I tried to gather myself enough to talk. "Oh?"

"Yeah." He leaned into my hair and inhaled. "I thought we established on the phone that they thought I liked guys, and that's why we were going out."

"I just... people hide."

His eyes looked down at my cleavage before roaming back up. "More than you know. Hurry! I could use a few drinks tonight." His fingers left the sink to squeeze my hip before he pushed away, strolling into my room and out of view. Seconds later, I heard the springs on my bed creak under the weight of him. As if he didn't just set my body on fire and make me blaze with a single touch and a slight whisper, he added, "I thought the campus provided funds to replace these awful beds."

"I wish." My voice was hoarse, cracking as I spoke the words.

"You'll be out of here soon," he reminded me. "You won't suffer much longer."

Except if I didn't come up with better savings, I might do just that. I wonder if I slept in a tent in the park after graduation, if any of my classmates would take pity on me and offer me a couch to crash on. I could couch surf, except I didn't really have many friends. Actually, practically none.

The bed squeaked again as he got comfortable, then it was silent. That was okay enough for me. It gave me time to finish curling my waist length hair and to apply a light coat of makeup. I didn't do makeup, not normally. I didn't see the reason when I had absolutely no one to impress. But here I was, trying to impress, and I wasn't even sure who. My lab partner? His friends? Did I want some random stranger to see me across the bar while I was drinking with Austin and make a move? Would he be jealous? Did I even want him to be jealous?

I promise you; they are not the one I want. His words were like fire to my nerves and left me with so many questions. Was he talking about me? And if so, why not say it? How long had he hidden his feelings? Was I that oblivious? Shit, why was I so bad at this peopling thing? Deep down, I knew the reason. I was so emotionally damaged and closed off that I was afraid to even try to let a person in.

I finished lining my eyes, painting black on them so that the color popped out, and brushed on a little more mascara. I leaned back, looking at myself, pulling down my dress before pushing my barely there breasts together, trying to give them a little lift. With a sigh, I exited the bathroom, knowing this was as good as I was getting.

He was asleep, his eyes closed, his face soft, and

he looked so damn peaceful that I almost didn't want to wake him. I crept forward, taking in everything about him while his guard was down. His large frame barely fit on my school issued bed; his crossed ankles hung at an angle, making his shoes hang off the bed. His palms were hidden behind his head, where his arms were up, bracing himself on my pillow. It wasn't until I was standing over him that I noticed slight scars peppering his skin, tiny iridescent lines that broke into his flawless flesh. How had I missed them before?

I reached forward, my fingers ready to trace the line of one, but as I was just about ready to run my fingers over his skin, his hand shot forward, gripping my wrist tightly as his eyes opened, his gaze slightly cloudy before he blinked a few times, clearing it.

His chest heaved before he wordlessly released my wrist. Both hands came up to scrub his face before he pushed forward, forcing himself to sit up. Another heavy breath of air left him before he turned his head toward me. "Sorry."

I shook out my wrist, still feeling the tight band of his fingers against my skin. "It's fine."

It was my fault. I shouldn't have crept up on him. Shouldn't have tried to touch him. But it was like I couldn't resist. My fingers, my body, were drawn to the flaw that hid so well against his flesh. If he had this many scars on the outside, how many did he have hidden on the inside for only himself to acknowledge?

"It's not fine," he clarified. "I didn't know it was you."

"Who the hell did you think it was?" I huffed.

He shook his head as if he didn't have an answer. "Nothing. No one. Are you ready?" His eyes roamed over me. "Mac. You look..."

When he didn't seem to come up with a word to finish that sentence, I offered, "Like I didn't just roll out of bed five minutes before I needed to be somewhere?"

"No." His eyes found mine for a second before he looked away. "You look beautiful even then. But right now, you look..."

I laughed, suddenly feeling self-conscious about his compliment. "I look what?"

"Spectacular," he breathed out, the word barely audible.

I flushed, my skin heating under his gaze. "Thank you."

The springs creaked under his weight as he got up, standing an inch away from me, his height suddenly hovering over my own. I could kiss him from this distance, and it wouldn't take much. Just a slight lean, maybe a pull of his shirt to drag his lips down to my own. I suddenly wanted to do just that, lab partner be damned. He smelled divine, and the burn in his eyes was a temptation I wanted nothing more than to explore.

Did he sense it? Maybe, because his hands came up, his fingers running gently along my shoulders before he gripped them and turned me around. "Grab shoes."

Oh yeah. I had forgotten I needed those. I reached into my closet and found a pair of black stilettos. With one hand on the door frame, I used the other to strap on my heels, aware that Austin's eyes burned into me, watching every move like he was memorizing them to replay later. When both shoes were on securely and I could balance without face planting, I let go of the door frame and grabbed a sweater.

"I think I'm ready," I announced.

Austin pulled open my door. "You're perfect."

He placed his hand on my back, guiding me out the door, giving me the sense that somehow, I was about to embark on something new, and the knot in my stomach told me it had everything to do with the man at my back and nothing to do with the alcohol I was about to consume.

CHAPTER EIGHT

ASA

They were late. Not that it mattered. Austin had texted us, letting us know as much. But each second they didn't come made my nerves do funny things and let tiny waves of guilt creep in. I wasn't proud about what we were about to do, but we both knew that it had to be done. She knew our faces. Hell, she might even know us by our voices at this point. But the funny thing about being under the influence of foreign substances, sometimes it twists things up in such a way that even though your mind is telling you something is familiar, you just aren't quite able to grasp it.

"I'm so fucking strung tight." Wick cracked his knuckles from where he sat in the booth across from me. "We're about to have a fucking housekeeper."

"In theory," I pointed out.

"What the fuck is that supposed to mean?"

"It means she still has to stand strong while we've got her tied, and she has to agree to this." Consent... that's going to be the hardest part.

"She'll agree."

"How can you be so confident about that?" I leaned back, causing the booth to make a squeak.

"She owes me an apology. I intend to get it." I swear for a moment Wick's eyes glazed over with a thought.

"Owing an apology doesn't mean she will agree," I pointed out the obvious.

"She'll fucking agree. She's a loner. Just like we were. She has no attachments that I know of. At least not here. People like us, we crave whatever acceptance we can get."

I hated that he was right. When I got nudged toward the Saints, the thought of being a part of something, of being less lonely, pulled me toward it, not away. I could have died, I still could, and I have only my team to care about me. I'm not sure what type of life that is, what this will hold for my future, but even the promise of a few friends at my side until the day my last breath leaves my body is better than knowing I could die on a curb right now without a single person caring to identify or claim the body.

My mouth opened, no words leaving it because just then the door opened, and in walked Mac and Austin. At least, I think it was Mac. It was damn near impossible to tell with her hair down her back in a mix of waves and curls, and heels on her feet that made her at least three inches taller. And her thighs... I nearly forgot to breathe as my eyes traced every curve of them, the thickness and curve of her hips nearly making me drool.

"Holy shit." Wick must have realized the same thing, must have locked onto the vision in front of us. He swallowed hard. "She fucking cleans up nice."

I licked my lower lip, damn near falling over as I watched her walk to the bar. "I didn't fucking know her thighs were that gorgeous."

"Not an inch between them. I could slide my cock in them and fuck them without even touching her pussy." Wick leaned forward, his palms on the table as he strained to not lose sight of her. "In fact, after she fucking apologizes, I might just do that."

"I'd rather use them as earmuffs, squeezing against my skull until I can't breathe without consuming her."

"To each their own." Wick picked up his beer, taking a gulp. "Cunnilingus is an act earned. I'll gladly eat her for lunch, when I know she'll be a good girl at dinner."

His words had my body on fire, and I suddenly wanted nothing more than to watch him fulfill that statement. I wanted to see her thrusting wildly against his lips until she came apart against him. And the thought of him taking her, punishing her for whatever her sins were that day, made my body strain with lust.

"She's got a drink," I observed.

"He won't slip it into her drink until the second one," Wick reminded me. "*If* he does it. I haven't decided if he has the balls enough to go through with it. There's something about this girl that he doesn't want to fuck with."

"He's practically in love with her," I pointed out. "He has been since freshman year and that was before they even talked. Hadn't you noticed?"

"I..." His brows scrunched up. "I had not."

"It should have been obvious the way he insists we all can't have her, and I started thinking about why. It took a day or so to click, but it did. She was the girl he always sat facing when we ate at our table in the lunchroom freshman year. Remember? He'd flip out if either of us took his spot."

"Hm." The brows pulled deeper. "I just thought he was eccentric."

"Yeah." I leaned back, sipping on my beer. "Well, he's that too."

"Knowing that is going to make fucking with her so much more satisfying. I love when he loses his shit. He's so fucking easy to rile up sometimes."

We watched, the minutes dragging on torturously slow as I sipped my beer like a pansy. Never in my life had I drank so slowly, but never in my life had I wanted to be completely sober more than I did at this moment. I couldn't have a fuzzy mind, not when it came to Mac, not when it came to offering ourselves up as a unit, as the Saints, and asking her to join us, to be part of our team.

It was a lot, I knew. Not everyone was cut out for the life we lived. Not everyone could trustingly take a life, be coated in the blood of another, and accept that it was the right course of action. But Mac was strong enough to stand against Wick, and soft enough to make our heads turn when she thought we weren't looking. She was perfect for the job of housekeeper. She wouldn't just be a group accessory; she'd be an asset. A part of the team that strengthened us, didn't weaken our fortitude, only our hearts.

Maybe that should be warning enough. A weak heart could bring us all down. But the need to protect the heart of the team could be enough to strengthen our bond like never before. We could be unstoppable. Unbreakable. Undefeatable.

It was an hour before Austin spilled Mac's drink. It looked like an accident, but training and planning told us it absolutely wasn't. When he leaned over, helping sop up the mess, I barely glimpsed when the powder dropped from his sleeve and into his drink. He leaned back, grabbing his drink, using that as an opportunity to swish the straw a little before he used his free hand to gather the soaked napkins in a pile. I couldn't hear what he was saying, though I assumed it was some sort of apology.

"I'm glad he had the foresight to knock it away

from that dress," Wick muttered as Austin handed Mac his drink instead. "I can't wait to cut it off her."

"It would be a shame to destroy that master-piece." Mac took her first sip.

"I'll buy her a new one, all the new ones. I just want that one in a puddle on the floor. Or maybe bunched around her waist. Shit, I don't know if I can wait for an apology to fuck her. Initiations don't count, right?"

"Depends on your morals."

"I'm giving myself a free pass." He pushed his beer away, watching in fascination as Mac trusted Austin completely, a move which could cost her so much, or gain her so much more. "It's almost time."

I stood, adjusting the collar on my shirt before reaching into my pocket, pulling out my wallet, and tossing a handful of bills onto the table. "I'll meet you out back."

I slipped out the back door, and not a single eye noticed my departure. It's how we were trained. It's how we liked it. The fewer eyes we drew our way, the fucking better. Especially when we were taking a drugged up female home with us. I slipped into the driver's seat of our black car, the most nondescript vehicle we own. Masking up, I waited another fifteen minutes before Austin helped a stumbling Mac around the side of the building. As soon as he entered the dark alley, Wick appeared, his arm suddenly around Mac's waist, preventing her from stumbling.

I popped the locks, tapping my fingers on the

steering wheel, waiting until the door opened behind me, forcing my gaze to look toward the backseat. Mac was still conscious; how, I wasn't sure... but it didn't matter. The only true face she saw was Austin's. Wick and I had already placed our masks on, making us unrecognizable and no doubt fucking with her blurry mind.

"Austin?" Her voice was faint, the drug taking her out slowly, her words slurred.

"You're okay, Mac. You had a little too much to drink." For a moment I wondered if his conscience would hate him for giving her such a lie, for causing this state and fucking with her trust, but instead his eyes looked into the mirror, the orbs as hard as diamonds as he demanded, "Drive."

CHAPTER NINE

MAC

My head throbbed. I tried to open my eyes, but the heaviness weighed down each lid, making the act a struggle. I shook my head, trying to clear the fuzz that lingered in my mind, trying to grasp a full thought, but each time I was close to grasping it, the thought would flicker away in a blur, tearing from me, leaving me in confusion.

"She's waking up," a muffled voice announced. Why did it seem so familiar?

"Makenna," a voice cooed, and it was so rich, the sound so alluring I almost fought to get near it, except I was weak. I couldn't move. My arms were heavy and—

I shook them; the chains rattled with the movement as panic settled heavily in my chest. On reflex, I forced my eyes open as I attempted to scream, but the tape that covered my lips stifled the noise, allowing only a muffled sound to escape.

Beside me, the faintest touch ghosted against my cheek, and I tried to turn my head, but it was held down, strapped to the hard service under me, preventing me from turning. "Shhh. You're okay, Makenna. We will not kill you, if that's what you're worried about."

I was worried about that, actually. I was terrified. I'd never been tied up, strapped down so immobile that I couldn't even turn my head.

A masked face appeared, leaning over me as the back of his fingers brushed my face. "It's perfect, isn't it? You had a kidnapping fantasy and we, well, we needed to kidnap you."

Kidnap fantasy? What the fuck? My mind was still swimming, my thoughts not fully cleared yet, and I wasn't sure what he meant. Never had I asked to be kidnapped. Fantasy? I didn't have any real fantasies.

"Have you ever fucked two men at once, little vixen?"

I couldn't speak. The only things that fell from my lips were muffled cries to answer. Tears finally fell from my eyes, trailing down to nestle by my ear as I shook my head, denying that I had.

"Then you lied?" What? I never lied. I never spoke of being with more than one man. "What else did you lie about, I wonder? How many men have you fucked, Makenna? I want to know. We need to know."

I didn't know what kind of sick game this was, but I wanted out. I pulled against the chains again, the metal tightening painfully as I struggled. "Shhh," another voice soothed. "Tell us what we need to know."

Something cold brushed against my skin, skimming down my neck before it sliced through the material of my dress. "I carved this knife myself out of the femur of my first kill."

My back arched as I screamed, hysterical pleas leaving me, even though I knew the pleas would go unanswered, unheard. They were nothing but sounds, grunts, mumbles with inaudible meanings. The blade toyed against my skin, the cold bone pressing deep enough to cause an indent, but the pressure wasn't hard enough to draw blood.

"Now answer my question, vixen. Eight?"

I shook my head no.

"Seven?"

Another shake, more tears fell.

"It better be lower because if you've fucked over eight men, I might have to kill them all."

He kept listing numbers, and I denied them all until he finally asked, "Two?"

I had a moment of hesitation before I nodded. He leaned forward, bringing the knife to my neck and teasing me, "What a good girl. Only two cocks. I bet you've got a lot to learn. I'll teach you." There was a pause. "After you apologize."

That phrase sounded familiar, like I had heard something recently about me apologizing, but all my thoughts were just out of grasp, still too clouded by the fear for my life. The blade traveled down, pressing flat against the tips of my nipples. "You went braless for us? You wanted us to see these perfect pert nipples and take what was ours, didn't you?"

I fiercely shook my head. Not like that would make much of a difference. They would do what they wanted. They had all the power. Chained, I wasn't capable of any defense. Hell, even without the chains on my body, I was outnumbered and outsized.

"I bet you did." He leaned down, his face traveled the space between my breasts as he inhaled. "Perfect. Anything more than a handful is a waste. If I remove the tape, will you be a good girl?"

I didn't respond because I could make no promises. My silence did not deter him. His fingers came up, smoothing down my hair before letting one hand travel to the tape on my mouth. With one painful pull, he tore it from my face, and before I could even scream, his hand covered my lips. "Shhhh. We have a deal, remember, little vixen."

His hand fell away, and the words fell out of me before I could think better of it. "Fuck you."

I clearly had no self-preservation. The knife was back, this time the ivory bone weapon taunting my vision with what he was capable of. "I plan on it. Just this once, it's my pass. I'll make you cum. After that, I'll wait patiently for my apology. Or maybe not so patiently, depending on what this mouth can do. Judging by the words you spout, I have high expectations."

"Apologize for what?" My voice was hoarse, a scratch of confused words leaving me.

He tsked, "I'm hurt you don't remember, but I'll remind you. Later. How was your drink?"

Drink? What? I held my eyes closed tight, trying to remember what drink he was talking about. "I don't know."

"You'll have to think harder than that, vixen. I know the thought is in there. It hurts, doesn't it? Our first time getting drugged left me with a headache for days. I puked all over my interrogator. You're doing better than I did."

At the mention of my pounding head, a masked guy off to the corner stepped forward. With a nod of approval from the one with the knife, he shoved something in my mouth. "Swallow."

Someone suddenly poured water, splashing over my face, down my cheeks, covering my neck as I gasped and gulped, swallowing down the pills that were offered. The other one, the one who wasn't threatening me with a knife or drowning me with water, tried to offer comfort, but comfort can't be had when you're tied up by three masked men. "It will help with the headache."

The knife traveled down, curving over my hips,

and dancing over the material that pooled there while another hand grazed up my legs, teasing as the fingers traced against my inner thigh. "Do you know how easy it was to snag you?"

"Clearly incredibly easy. I'm fucking in chains," I spat.

"Feisty. It's how we like them." He sighed as fingers got closer to my lace underwear. "You should never drink out of an open glass, little vixen. Let that be lesson number one."

Drink out of an open glass? I racked my mind, trying to think of what the night had held before everything went black. It was foggy in my brain, but I pushed through the fog, picturing images of me getting ready, of curling my hair, of finding Austin on my bed. I gasped. "Austin! Where is he?"

"You worried about him?" There was a laugh as the knife's blade taunted my skin, drawing a sharp bit of pain and the faintest line of beaded blood.

"If you fucking hurt him, I swear I will—"

"You'll what?" he barked.

I hadn't thought that through. I wasn't sure what I'd do, but clearly it didn't matter. I'd not get free unless they released me. No matter how much I had tried to pull and twist my wrists, they clearly knew what they were doing when they put the restraints on me. "Don't fucking hurt him."

He ignored my order. "Do you know who we are?"

"No."

"You don't?" his voice rumbled as the knife cut off

my underwear. The thin flap of fabric fell forward, leaving me exposed to the chill in the air and eyes of the men. I tilted my head, looking away from them as mortification filled me. I let the tears fall even as anger built inside of me.

"Isn't she pretty?" he asked.

Another answered, "So fucking beautiful."

"Do you want to play our game, Makenna?"

"No." My voice was weak, nearly defeated from the drugs that ran through my body. The drugs made my skin buzz, and the mortification of being exposed to these strangers' eyes added to the burn of my body. I was spread wide, offering them an intimate view.

"Here's how it works. We'll ask you questions, you answer them. If we're satisfied, you get to cum."

I couldn't look at him. I didn't want to see his grotesque mask. "Fuck you. You're a fucking monster."

He continued on. "And if we aren't satisfied, you bleed."

"I thought you weren't going to kill me." I tilted my head, glaring at him.

"We're not. Since when does blood have to do with death, little vixen?"

"Blood is literally the source of life, dumb shit."

He laughed. "Or the source of pleasure."

"Don't fucking touch me, you prick!" I screamed when his finger stroked at the crease of my thigh.

He didn't listen as he continued, "Do you have a family, Makenna?"

"Not really." Just admitting that sent a sharp pain in my chest, and it had nothing to do with the pain they were threatening to inflict and everything to do with the soul-crushing betrayal I felt over my family and the situation of my upbringing.

A blade skimmed against my thigh, causing a sharp sting. "That wasn't an actual answer, Makenna." He brought his blade up, showing me the tinge of red that coated the edge. "Now that you're aware of answers that won't work, you can do better."

One man leaned forward. His eyes through the mask looked vaguely familiar, but I couldn't place them. His voice, a deep timbre that I swore I'd heard before. "Do you have family, princess?"

The way he spoke to me — kinder, gentler than the first man — made me wish it was him who led the interrogation instead of the monster with the knife. "A brother. I haven't heard from him since I was twelve. My parents are dead, and no family wanted me."

I admitted this to complete strangers, even though I struggled for years admitting it to myself. I made excuses for them. They had poor health. They didn't have the funds. They were too busy to add an eleven- and seventeen-year-old to their life. But it was all excuses for them not caring enough to disrupt their comfort to accommodate two orphaned children.

"Good girl. That's the type of answer we want. The trust." The one with the blade praised as the other man's hand slipped between my legs, cupping me.

"Don't," I begged.

"Shhh. It will be okay," the one with the knife promised. "Why haven't you heard from your brother?"

"He went to college and disappeared. Never contacted me again," I whimpered out an answer as a thumb grazed my clit, causing my hips to jolt.

"I heard you're good at secrets. Why?" The knife was cold as it traveled up my stomach.

"Who the fuck am I going to tell?" I spat out.

"Filthy mouth for such a pretty girl. Makes me want to shove my cock in it." His blade traveled between my breasts and left a stinging trail behind it. "Not the right answer. You never answer a question with a question, Vixen. Try again."

My chest heaved. "I don't see the point of telling other people's lives. Why? To cause them damage? It's not fair as a human being. I wouldn't want my secrets to be told."

The thumb drew a gentle circle on my clit and I gasped, the contrast against the knife was more enjoyable than I'd ever admit. "Do you have secrets, Makenna?"

"No." None that mattered. Only to one day aspire to be like my mother, to travel the world writing stories about the lives of others and share the views that are so often hidden. The only difference is I didn't want to die.

The circles on my clit were drawing a fire inside of me, one I didn't want to ignite. "You lied to us about how many men you've been with. Why?"

"I never lied to you. I don't even fucking know who you are, you asshole." I pulled against the restraints, the chain rattling.

"You haven't figured it out yet, have you?" His voice taunted, knowing I was clearly confused. Instead of responding, I spit at him, landing a wad of saliva on his mask. The spit slid down his mask slowly, and he didn't speak until it fell from the chin. Then his hand shot out, his fingers wrapping around my throat in a tight grip as he leaned in. "I wouldn't do that again, Vixen."

I tried to swallow, but his grip stalled the movement. Still, I grated out, "Fuck you."

"You sure like that word, don't you?" He ran his free hand between my breast, bringing it back up to my vision coated in the red of my blood. "I plan to fuck you later. For now, I plan to jack off, coating my cock in your blood as I do it."

"You're fucking sick," I got out after his fingers loosened slightly. "All of you are some sick fucks who get off on a helpless girl."

"I doubt you're helpless, Makenna." A bloody finger came up, sliding over my cheek. "You applied, Makenna, don't you remember? You asked us to take you. To kidnap you, to make your fantasy come true."

My eyes opened wide with the realization of who stood in front of me. I asked for this. I wanted this. I wanted to be a part of them. And yet, now with these men in front of me, I was suddenly terrified. I asked for something I did not know about, clearly. I wanted in, thinking I could expose them, use the knowledge to become the influential journalist my mother once was, but I got myself a hand wrapped around my throat and a knife of bone pointed at my chest.

"You remember now," the one who touched my body way too intimately for a stranger mused. "Do you still want this? To be ours."

"I..." My chest moved rapidly with my breath as his finger slipped from my clit to dance along the entrance of my core. "I don't know."

"Tell us you want us," his voice was husky. The tip of his fingers dipped in slightly, teasing me with a promise.

My neck was released, the fingers that curled around it now rubbing gently against the skin. "Why did you lie?"

His fingers lightly stroked against my neck as he looked down at me, the movement giving a calming effect, drawing the confession from me. "I'm not that experienced. It's embarrassing. No one would want me willingly, knowing I don't know what I'm doing."

A finger plunged into my body as my hips jolted, a hiss leaving my lips. "Good girl." His finger pulled out before plunging in again. "That's our good girl."

"Do you want us to teach you, little Vixen? Show you all there is to know?" The figure eights he drew on my skin with his blade tickled, the sensation somehow not unpleasant.

"I - I don't know." Did I want them to teach me? I wasn't sure. I apparently did not know what the hell I was signing up for. I should have listened, should have not applied like Austin begged me not to do, but I had to do what I wanted. I had to chase a dream that I knew would be ridiculous to fulfill. But if this was how they did things, chaining their girl up and torturing truths out of her, I probably didn't belong in this life.

But then why did the slow torture of the finger drawing in and out of my body feel so fucking good?

The finger drew out as the knife dragged down, past my stomach, below my belly button. "That's not an answer. We've already talked about that. Are my punishments not enough to deter you?"

"I-It's not a lie." I sobbed the words out, afraid of what he would do next. "I don't know what I want. I don't even know you."

"But you do, Makenna, haven't you realized that yet?" The knife trailed lower, before he flipped it. I hadn't had a moment to think or worry about what he was about to do before he pushed the handle into my body, the force and size causing a scream to tear from my throat. "Shhh. It's okay, I promise, we'll make it good for you, if you'll let us show you. Will you let us?"

"I..." My chest was rising rapidly, falling just as quick, and with the finger gone, now rubbing my clit in circles while the handle stretched me wide, filling me up, I couldn't fucking think about what I wanted. I squirmed against the restraint, trying to force the knife to move, the feeling too torturous to handle. "What will you do to me?"

"Do to you?" He leaned down. "Isn't it obvious? We'll worship you."

"And?" I groaned when he finally reached down, twisting the knife.

"And what? Isn't worshipping you enough?"

"What do you want from me?" I whimpered.

"What do you mean?" The knife got pulled out slowly, every ridge of the handle rubbing against me, and I hated to admit it, but it felt so damn good. "You applied. You asked to work for us. To be one of us. Do you want to take that back now?"

"I..." I didn't know what the hell I wanted anymore. I could blame the drugs, but my body was screaming, and it wasn't in protest. The more they touched me, the more my body liked it, even when my body knew it was wrong. I applied for this with the suspicion that they were more than they claimed to be. I submitted the application, asking for their acceptance, and I'd gone this far, further than anyone had before, and I couldn't take it back. "I don't. But there has to be something you want in return. I applied to be a housekeeper."

"And you will, if you accept." He pulled the knife out and brought the handle up, the bone glistening. "You're so fucking wet for this. It's glorious." His tongue darted out, licking the handle, traveling up to the hilt. "Fucking delicious."

He handed his knife to the third man, the quiet one who stood off to the side, not taking part in the delicious torture they were partaking in on my body. Then he bent down, his fingers grabbing my hair to tilt my head back before he crashed our lips together brutally, forcing his tongue into my mouth. When he pulled away, he didn't drop my hair; instead, he gripped tighter. "Did you taste it? Did you taste yourself on my tongue?"

I nodded my head, afraid to say anything, not trusting my voice when my body was so clearly already betraying me. He turned to his friend. "Do you want to taste?"

There was a moment of hesitation before his friend agreed. "It's all I've thought about."

"Good. Go ahead then. Have your fill while I talk with Makenna a little more about the position." He dismissed his friend, his focus on me as he talked. "Housekeeper is the most important part of our group, Mac."

The way he said my name, the name only people I'm familiar with called me, had my ears perking up. I knew him. I had to. "How?"

"The housekeeper is our glue. Our one person we all vow to die for. Do you want us to die for you, Makenna?" I opened my mouth to answer, my words replaced by a moan as a tongue licked over my clit, before fingers parted me wider. The tongue lapped relentlessly, the sensation so intense I arched. I shouldn't be so turned on, but I was. The heat in my core was telling me that if this kept up, I'd crumble. "If you don't answer, he'll stop."

"God no," I cried out. "I don't want anyone to die."

"We'd die for you. I wouldn't question it, just do it. You wanted to be a housekeeper, a fourth member of our group. Would you kill for us, Mac?"

"I don't even know you." My voice sounded distant, I was barely holding myself together as my hands stretched against the chains, pulling them as I struggled to move my body, nearly begging him to put his lips and tongue in the exact spot I needed him the most.

"Yes or no, Vixen. All that matters is you're with us or against us. Tell us now, and we'll share all our secrets." He leaned over, his lips wrapped around my breast, and the sensation, combined with the tongue lapping against my clit, was too much, and the ball that had been slowly building crested into an explosion, sending shock waves of pleasure through my body.

Another pull of his lips had my hands begging to reach for him, stretching and straining as my thighs clamped around the other's head, holding him to my core so tight that I was sure he'd never be able to escape. The waves of ecstasy came fast, rolling through me with such ferocity that all I could do was scream as tears stained my cheeks. I didn't know what I was agreeing to. At this moment I didn't care, as long as their lips never left my body and I could feel this every second of every day. I didn't fucking care. If they killed me, so what? I doubt they would let me leave here alive. Right before I blacked out, when my vision grew hazy and my mind blanked to absolutely nothing, seconds before my body finally gave out from the stress and strain of the drugs and the assault, I said a single word.

"Yes."

And I only hoped that when I woke, I'd not regret it.

CHAPTER TEN

AUSTIN

I watched as Mac crumbled, fought, and surrendered to Wick, and I hated that I had to stand back and not help either of them. I kept quiet, knowing damn well that a single word from me would give away who I was. We didn't want her to know, not yet, not until she agreed to join us.

"She said yes." Wick was practically beaming as he released her wrists.

"Under duress," I pointed out.

"Doesn't matter." He looked toward me, and if I wasn't so familiar with him, I wouldn't know it was him hidden under the mask that matched my own. "She knows what we can do to her now. Who would say no to that?"

"Mac, that's who. She's stubborn." I leaned over, helping to release an ankle.

"She tastes fucking amazing," Asa muttered.

"That's the deprivation talking. It's been ages since you've been able to have a female in any capacity," I pointed out.

"You didn't taste her, man. You can't imagine." Wick leaned over her, gently brushing long strands of hair back. "She's going to be ticked off when she realizes it's us." He looked at me. "And you're going to be the one to tell her."

"Fuck that. She'll hate me."

"She already hates me. It won't hurt that bad. She trusts you," Wick reassured me.

"Trusted me. Now she'll probably think about my murder in her sleep." I looked down at her body, so peaceful in sleep. I knew it was the drugs I slipped her. I'd forever feel guilty about that fact. But it had to be done. There was no other way.

"Sometimes I think about your murder in my sleep, too," Asa added as he freed her other leg, his hand running up her calf tenderly for a moment before he looked at me. "She might be mad for a while, but it will be okay. She signed up for this, remember? She said yes."

I only wondered if that yes would hold once she was clear-minded. "Go run a bath. I'll put her in it."

Asa nodded before leaving the room, heading upstairs to get the bath water going for her. She earned a good bath, especially because she had those fucking cuts that Wick inflicted. I knew it could have been worse. In fact, it should have been, but they still infuriated me to look at. Her beautiful skin marred by a man who was destined to love and care for her. It didn't seem right.

After every restraint was off her, I leaned over, taking Wick's knife. My stomach tightened as I cut the rest of the material off her body. "She's going to be ticked about the dress."

"I'll buy her a new one." Wick shrugged it off. "Fuck, her body is art. I want to paint it. Only her skin would be a decorated canvas, painted by my bloody brush strokes."

"I'm sure you'll get your opportunity." The jealousy in me hated that fact. I didn't want to share her. She had been mine since freshman year, and these guys are my family, but I didn't want to share this part of me with them. "She's ours for life now."

"For life." The corner of his lip quirked up. "I can't fucking believe this is happening."

"What exactly did you expect when you signed up to get a housekeeper?" I asked, my eyes rolling at his shock.

"I - I don't know. It's been three years. It was more a dream than anything. Something intangible that I never thought would come true. She fucking said yes, Aussie!"

"I was there." And I wasn't happy about watching.

I let my arms snake under her and lift. She was so fucking light, it was like carrying air. I shimmied her body toward me, shifting her until her sleeping head rested against my shoulder. "We have little time before she's fully awake. How are we telling her?"

"You mean, how are you telling her?" Wick dared to reach over and touch her hair. If I had a hand free, I'd stab him. "Take the mask off. It will scare her to wake to that."

"Well, no shit." He'd pointed out the obvious. I hadn't planned to keep it on.

"If she sees you, she has to know the others are us, right? She's a smart girl."

"Too smart," I sighed. "Too fucking smart for her own good."

I turned, giving Wick my back as I climbed the steps of our basement and up to the main floor. I continued, taking the second set of stairs up to the bathroom that was already billowing with steam and the smell of lavender. Asa met me at the door, bouncing on the balls of his feet, eager to do anything to help with our female. There was nothing to do, not now, at least. She was going to wake, and she wouldn't be thrilled, but that was a problem we'd have to work through when the time came.

Kneeling beside the tub, I slowly lowered Mac into the water, noting that she was already stirring. Asa handed me a rolled towel, and I used it behind her head as I shimmied my arm out from behind her neck. Mac sighed in her sleep, the heat clearly easing whatever ache she was feeling.

I took off my mask, tossing it to the floor before I

reached into the water, taking her wrists in my hand
and massaging the marks that cut into her skin from
the chains. They would heal, but the guilt of causing
them would probably always sit heavy on my chest.

"Mac, wake up." I lifted a washcloth, aware that
Asa stood by the door, looming over us, shifting from
foot to foot. The water from the washcloth dribbled
over her skin, and I ran it between her breasts,
soaking up the dried blood that was marring her skin.
"Wake up, baby."

I knew she heard me because her brows pinched
together, and a little sound escaped her lips. But I
also knew that she had stayed awake longer than we
had expected earlier and that the drugs weren't fully
out of her system yet. Probably wouldn't be for
another day or so.

"Makenna, wake up, baby. We need to talk." I
rubbed my thumb against her jaw, trying to bring her
out of the sleep that had taken her. Her head shook
slightly as she fought the haze. I hoped at least now
she wouldn't have the awful headache that came with
consuming the drug. "You can do it, baby."

"Austin?" Her voice was soft, her eyes closed, but
her calling my name fucking gutted me.

"Yeah, baby. It's me. Can you hear me?"

One of her hands came up and rubbed at her eye.
Her voice was still foggy as she asked, "Are you
okay?"

"I'm perfect, baby." I felt nauseous at her
concern, knowing I was never in danger and that I

was the one who slipped her the drug. Probably the shittiest friend there was. "Can you open your eyes for me?"

Her face scrunched up for a moment as if she was trying to figure out how to do that task. Then they fluttered before they popped open, gifting me with the sight of green eyes. "What happened to you?"

Her concern made me close my eyes for a moment, trying to gather myself. "There you are." I smiled. "How are you feeling?"

"Sort of shitty, if I'm honest." She lolled her head toward me. "Everything feels so buzzy and gritty."

"It will go away when it wears off," I informed her as I lifted the washcloth up, running it over her neck, then her forehead.

Her eyes shifted away from me, taking in that she was naked and in a bathtub. Panic set in. "Oh god. I'm fucking naked." Her voice rose. "I'm naked."

"It's okay." I tried to calm her. "What do you remember?"

"I - nothing. Just..." She closed her eyes. "They had me, Austin. They had me and they had you."

"It's okay." I rubbed my hand down her hair. "It's fine."

"It's not fine. I - they - I let them touch me." She seemed ashamed and fuck, there wasn't anything shameful about it.

"Worship," I corrected.

"What?"

"You let them worship you."

She shook her head. "I didn't know they were real. I mean, I guess I did, but not really. You warned me not to put in the application, and I didn't listen."

I let my chin fall to my chest and my eyes closed. "You didn't."

"They want me," she stated.

"They have you," I corrected.

"What?"

"You said yes, Mac."

"I don't understand." She was growing agitated, and I hated this. I hated having to be the one to break this news to her, to ruin every thought she ever had of me.

"They asked you if you were in or out. Yes or no."

Her gaze trailed off as she stared at the wall. "And I said yes."

"You did."

She shifted her gaze to look down at the water. Her chest rising and falling rapidly, her panic clear even if she wasn't voicing it. "What happens now?"

"You're a housekeeper."

Even in her state, she managed a laugh that was borderline hysterical. "Something tells me it's more than that."

"A housekeeper, Mac. The one who makes a house of Saints a home, the one who keeps the peace between men, the satisfier, the lover, the center of everything that drives us."

Her head whipped toward me so fast I swore she

would get whiplash. "Us? You. You are a Saint? The whole time?"

Shit, I could tell she was fuming. I let my eye fall to Asa, a glance that was so quick that normal people would miss it. But Mac wasn't like normal gals. Her eyes locked into my gaze and they followed it to where Asa stood, leaning against the door frame. A whimper left her before she cursed, suddenly using her arms to cover her body that we'd all laid eyes on.

"I should have known. There had to be some reason that you had been inseparable over the years and everyone else was just blind to it." She paused. Her eyes went wide with fear. "Oh god, where is he? Please tell me I'm wrong. Tell me, Austin."

I knew what she realized. I knew all about their interaction and I could only assume her feelings about him. "You're not wrong, Mac."

She refused to look at me as a tear fell. "I'm going to die, aren't I? He'll kill me."

"Is that what you think?" She didn't have to say anything else for me to know that she really thought that. She didn't like him. It was clear. "He'll protect you with his life. We all will. And we're going to have to. It's part of the job."

"The job?"

Wick strolled in, causing her body to grow more tense than it already was. "Yes, job. Did you think we were just a club, Makenna? Some frat for shits and giggles?"

"I... I don't know what to think." She refused to look at him, but it did not faze Wick.

Instead, he leaned over, placing the femur knife on the edge of the tub. "You're about to learn a world of secrets, and we need to trust that you won't spill the beans. Can we trust you?"

Her eyes didn't leave the knife, clearly getting the threat. He wouldn't kill her unless she gave him reason to do so. "Y-yes."

"Good." He leaned down, forcing her eyes to meet his. "You're ours. You know what that means, don't you?"

She didn't answer, her eyes hard as they had a stare off of secrets that spoke of hatred and, if I wasn't mistaken, lust. When neither of them broke, I tried to speak up. "Wick, she's had a long night. I'm sure she's sore and the drug hasn't fully worn off."

His hand reached out, gripping her chin. "Do you know what that means?"

"That I belong to you," she spoke, her voice a whisper.

"No." Wick's eyes dropped, and I knew they had zeroed in on the spot between her thighs before he dared to look back at her. "It means we belong to you just as much as you belong to us. We're a team, so whatever shit you have against us, against me, set it aside because from this moment, this is life or death. You want out, it's in a casket. Do you understand?"

For a long moment, she didn't answer. Then her jaw tightened against his firm grip and her eyes turned to shards of rough-cut jade as she answered, "I prefer cremation."

"Is that a declaration that we can't trust you, Mac?" Wick growled.

"No." Her eyes fell to his lips for a moment before they met his eyes. "I just thought if I'm in it for life, you might as well get to know me a little."

It was a long second, probably the longest of my life, as I waited to see what Wick would do. Seconds passed before he smiled. The look so sinister it gave me the creeps, but Mac didn't even flinch. She held his gaze, her chin high in challenge as they fought for whatever dominance that could be exchanged. Finally, he muttered, "Ready to apologize?"

"I'd rather be ash."

"Unfortunate." He released his grip on her before he turned to me. "Finish bathing her and take her to bed. Training starts early tomorrow. We've not much time."

"Training?" Her head cocked to the side in confusion.

"Oh, my little vixen. Did you think it was all going to be fun and games? Fucking? There will be plenty of that too, but if you can't fight, you're dead by the next full moon." He picked up his knife and walked away. "Tomorrow. Six AM. Don't let her be late, Aussie, or it's you who will fucking pay."

CHAPTER ELEVEN

MAC

I woke with the feeling of being weighed down. An iron band pressed down on my back, making it impossible to move, and I panicked. For a moment I assumed I was back on campus, in my dorm, sleeping away a night of drinking, but then the room came into focus, a room I'd never once seen.

I tried to lift again, and this time the band on my back moved with a groan. My head whipped to the side, spotting Austin as he fought through sleep, attempting to wake up. I rolled to the side, scurrying up and away, trying to put some distance between the man on the bed and me. Hysterical fear bubbled inside of me, but I couldn't let it take hold.

This was what I wanted, wasn't it? I'd asked for this, for them, and now I needed to own up to my decisions. Except, part of my decision was made of desperation. The other part was pure duress. I couldn't be held accountable, right? Surely, they didn't want me to go through with this. It was a game. They were only messing with me, taunting and teasing me to see how bendable I could be.

"I brought you breakfast."

I jumped, crashing into the dresser that was near my back, sending whatever bottles that were on the top crashing to the floor.

I turned, seeing Asa standing there, a hand in his pocket as he held up a bag to me. I stared at him a moment as Austin seemed to wake a few feet away before I finally blurted out what I was thinking. "This is a joke, right?"

He looked around, clearly confused by my confusion. "Why would we joke with you?"

"I don't know," I admitted. "Maybe it's a dare? A bet? What do you get by convincing the nerdy loner she belongs to you?"

"Nerdy loner?" He raised a brow. "Oh, wait... is that supposed to be you? Because there is nothing nerdy about you, Mac. And as far as being a loner, you can't be a loner when you've got the three of us."

"But—"

"But nothing. You're ours now. Do you want out? Say it now. Because the moment you leave this room, you'll no longer have an option." Asa stepped forward, placing the bag on the dresser that I had just backed into. His hand came up, tangling in my mess of hair. "I should make it clear to you, though. I don't want you to be out. In fact, there is no one I would rather own more than you."

His words made my spine tingle, but his eyes told me he spoke nothing but the truth. "What are you getting me into? Is it dangerous?"

"Extremely." His eyes fell to my lips.

"Should I be scared?" I bit my lip.

"You'd be dumb not to be." His fingers flexed.

"Then why would I volunteer for this?"

He smirked. "Now Mac, I think you know the reason for that. Why did you volunteer? Why did you say yes?"

My face flushed. I signed up because I wanted to expose who they were, and now I knew. But I didn't know the secrets they held, not yet at least. But I said yes because I would have done and said anything as long as they didn't stop touching me, as long as that orgasm lasted.

When I didn't answer him, his smirk grew into a full grin, because he knew why I said yes. "Are you going to eat your bagel and meet me downstairs? We've got some work today, and Wick doesn't want you to be late."

"Fuck him," I growled, hating him the most.

"You will, princess. You will." He leaned forward, kissing my forehead. "See you downstairs."

And damn it, I was inclined to follow him, because even now, knowing he was leading me into danger, my body leaned toward him as he tried to pull away. He was magnetic, and I got stuck in his pull.

Thirty minutes later, I was in the living room surrounded by three men that I barely knew. One had been my lab partner, and besides daily banter, I knew nothing about him. Another was the tall, dark, and mysterious guy on campus that had all the girls' heads turning and a trail of swoons left in his wake. But then, there was the other male in the room. The infuriating, cocky, tall asshole that I now somehow tied myself to. I wondered if I could get by with just interacting with two out of the three. After all, having three guys trail me would make people suspicious, right?

"I see someone brought some of my things." I pulled at the thigh of my leggings before releasing, snapping them in place.

"All of your things," Austin corrected, and I swear my brows shot to my hairline.

"Excuse me?"

"While you were sleeping, we moved you into our place. Everything is here."

Jesus. That was productive of them. We hadn't even fully agreed to this thing, and they already moved me in. "How long was I out for?"

"Total?" Asa crossed his arm over his chest, drawing my gaze to his bulging biceps.

"Yes," I answered, even when my mind fizzled out watching him.

"About a day and a half." He shrugged. "Wasn't as bad as we thought it would be."

"Oh, well, I'm happy to make it easy for you. About my things, I would actually like them put back, please."

"No." Wick's voice made my teeth instantly grind.

"What do you mean, no?" I growled out the words, already annoyed with the man standing in the way of my familiar comfort.

"I mean no. No fucking way. No. The house-keeper was clearly a live-in position, and you applied for it, or have you forgotten? Our lady stays with us. No negotiating."

"It's just that..." What excuses could I even give that would be believable? The truth would sound ridiculous, and I knew that, no matter what, I wouldn't change Wick's mind. So I needed to appeal to the others instead. I turned toward Asa and Austin. "Please. I don't sleep well in unfamiliar environments."

"Seemed to sleep just fine with Austin last night," Wick pointed out.

"First, I was still groggy from drugs that you assholes gave me. Second, I don't even remember going to bed with him."

"Look, Mac." Asa stepped forward, moving closer. "It's actually out of our hands. You staying here is an organization rule. If we break it, you could be rejected."

"Oh, I'd hate that," I responded sarcastically.

"You'd hate it when rejection means death." Wick's voice was hard. Not bothering to sugarcoat the truth, like I'm sure Asa and Austin would have. "Stretch. We've got five miles to run before it gets hot."

I choked on whatever spit I had still in my mouth. "Five miles? Are you insane?"

"We do it daily," Austin offered, as if letting me know they truly hate themselves by running five miles daily wasn't concerning. "It's our warmup, mostly."

"Warm up?" My voice came out high. "That's not a warmup. I've never run five miles in my life, and I don't plan on doing it today."

"You will," Wick assured me.

"It's cute that you have so much confidence in me. However, I promise that confidence is ill-placed."

"No." Wick closed the distance. "I've actually got little confidence in you." Ouch. Jerk. "But if you can't run five miles and learn how to do it soon, it means in a month and a half, when they come for you, you'll be dead."

"When they what?"

"Survive the test, Mac. That's all you've got to do." Austin stepped up to me, placing a gentle hand on my shoulder.

"No one ever mentioned that the tests were

someone trying to kill me." I was close to hysterics now.

"If we had, would you have signed up?" Wick's glare penetrated in me, and I knew he knew the answer. I wouldn't have signed up. I would have stayed as far away from this position as possible. Hell, if I knew it required running, I'd probably never have applied either. Then again, they asked my mile time on the application. That should have given it away.

"I think we both know the answer to that." I glared back at him, hoping he blinked first.

"Too late now." He looked down, his nose scrunching up, and I hated it was a look of disgust and yet it still looked attractive on him. "You need new shoes. Those make for shit running support. We'll get you some this afternoon."

"I can buy my own shoes, and these are just fine." He was right, I knew it. These weren't running shoes. These were barely walking shoes if I'm honest. These were fashionable fake chucks I got marked down at the local shoe outlet because one of them had a questionable scuff on the side. It was what I could afford.

"I said, we'll get you new shoes." Wick turned and walked toward the door. "I'll meet you outside."

When he was gone, I growled to myself, "I hate him."

"He grows on you," Asa laughed.

I spun toward them, temporarily forgetting that they were in the same room as I was. "I'd rather him not grow on me. He's insufferable."

"But he's quick," Austin offered. "The best really. Place a knife in his hand and he'll carve up an army to protect you. You may not like him much, yet, but you will. And he's the one you want on your side. There is a reason we're the top team, and a portion of that reason has to do with Wick. He's a jackass for sure, but he's fiercely loyal, and if you haven't realized, he picked you to be loyal to. We all did."

"I still don't understand what's going on," I admitted, feeling an odd warmth in my stomach over the fact that these men picked me to give their loyalty to for some unknown reason.

"You will, in time." Austin pushed me toward the door that Asa was already exiting. "For now, know you're beginning to train for a lifetime, and you won't regret a second of it."

Two hours later, I regretted every second. I hated them. Hated them all. How could they run five miles in under an hour while I was practically dying after two? Austin at least had the decency to jog my pace and whisper words of encouragement as I huffed along. Asa and Wick, the fuckers, passed me up within the first minute and a half and sat at the finish line eating parfaits when I finally dragged my way to it.

"Your time was atrocious," Wick stated, shoving a mix of strawberries and yogurt in his mouth. "Embarrassing really."

"I'm half your height! My legs are smaller than yours! I can't cover as much distance as you as quickly."

"You being half my height and as puny as a kitten means you're not carrying around as much weight as I am. You should have scurried your way through the five miles in record time." He mixed his food around. "You put us behind schedule."

"Fuck your schedule," I growled.

He raised a brow. "My schedule won't be what you're fucking. Take a water break. We've got weights in five."

"Water break? But you're eating a full-on meal!" I pointed out.

"Improve your time and you'll have time to eat meals, too." He shrugged before spooning another mouthful into his mouth.

"That's not fair." I knew I sounded like a whiny child, but five miles took a lot out of me. I was surprised I was even standing. If he wanted me to move more than five feet from this spot, I was surely going to need some fuel. "You're used to running this much, I'm not."

"You will be." He stood, tossing a nearly full parfait into the trash. I nearly rushed to the can and pulled it out for myself, but barely refrained. "You don't seem interested in your water break. Guess it's time for weights."

"I didn't say that."

"Actions speak louder than words." He walked

away, expecting me to follow him like Asa and Austin did.

"Wait."

"I expect to see your ass in the school's weight room in five minutes, Makenna," he shouted over his shoulder.

"And if you don't?"

"I'll whip your bare ass until you can't sit down, then make you run again."

I didn't think he was joking about spanking me, so I went to the weight room, though it took longer than he demanded for me to get there. Once I stopped running, my muscles decided they no longer wanted to work, and I was nearly hobbling when I got there. I pushed the door open, the eyes of the trio narrowing in on me, but naturally it was Wick who had to open his fat mouth first.

"You'll be punished for your tardiness later." I flipped him off. "And for that too."

"I'd like to see you try." I spat the words out like he wasn't double my size and could have me pushed over any of these machines, crying my eyes out in seconds.

"How much weight can you lift?" Asa intervened.

I puffed my chest up proudly. "I'm positive I could lift twenty pounds."

"Each arm?" Austin questioned.

"No, total. Wait? You can lift twenty pounds per arm?"

Austin rubbed at his temple. "Mac, please."

"Fine," I growled. "I can't lift shit. I never lift more than like a case of soda at work."

"That's a start," Wick mumbled as he went to a rack and pulled out various weights in various sizes and sat them all in front of me, like I was supposed to do something with them. I'd never lifted weights before. I'd not had an interest. In fact, my health was pretty low on my priority scale. When I didn't reach to lift anything, Wick crossed his arms in front of me.

"What?"

"Well?" he asked.

"Well, what?" I challenged him, standing in the same stance, even though I didn't look nearly as powerful as he did.

"Pick them up," he demanded.

"Why are you so fucking bossy?" I placed my hands on my hips as I stared at him.

He stepped forward, his feet bringing him so close that I could feel him breathe. He was invading my space, and when fingers touched my throat, before yanking me into his chest, I had no room to fight him off. The grip tightened, and my air stuck, unable to leave me.

His voice was dripping with anger when he brought his face to mine, not even flinching as I clawed at his arm, trying to force his fingers free. "I'm so fucking bossy because I lead this team. I'm so fucking bossy because I know if I wasn't, all of us would die. I'm so fucking bossy because if you don't learn how to do shit right the first time, we've wasted our time and our only opportunity for you. I'm so fucking bossy because if I'm not, you die. Do you understand?"

It had to be a rhetorical question because the only thing I could do was give a slight nod as my eyes watered and tears involuntarily poured down my cheeks. He muttered a low, "Good." Then, with one more flex of his fingers, a single extra show of power, he released me, leaving me to hunch over, hands on my knees as I gasped for air.

Asa leaned in. "We're all not nice people, Mac. You've got to learn that now. It may be him that's an asshole today, but tomorrow it can be any of us pushing your buttons, and you need to learn how to navigate it and do what you're asked, perform how you're told, because he's right. It could mean your death. Or ours."

I fucking hated all of them. I wanted nothing to do with any of them at this point. I pushed Asa, forcing him away and out of my face as Wick barked another order. "Pick up a weight. Let's assess what you can handle."

I picked up a weight as they demanded, knowing I couldn't handle much. But I kept my mouth closed, refusing to give in to the temptation of arguing further when it got me nowhere. *This was for your breakthrough story, Mac. Remember that.* That reminder was what drove me to struggle through each exercise they forced on me until my body was literally shaking and I couldn't go any further.

"Eyes on me," Wick demanded, and when my head turned, my eyes automatically finding him, he muttered, "Eyes on me, baby. Your thoughts are elsewhere, your focus is split. We can't afford a split focus. Keep your eyes on me and focus."

I did one more squat with the kettlebell tucked tight against my body, and that was all I had left in me. "I can't do anymore."

"Three more," he demanded.

"I won't be able to walk back home."

"Three more, and I'll carry you home." His eyes never left mine as he pushed me. Asa and Austin had long since abandoned me for their own workout.

I didn't believe him. I couldn't let myself believe a single word from this man's insufferable mouth. "I'll do three, and then another three until you see fit, and you'll still make me walk."

"I'm a man of my word," he pointed out.

"You're barely a man," I ground out as I did one more.

"Two more," he counted down. "Insults don't hurt me. I've got childhood trauma."

I did one more. "Don't we fucking all."

"One more, come on, baby. Don't take your eyes off me."

"I fucking hate you," I growled out, my molars grinding together as I did one more squat and tried not to die.

"That's okay, little vixen. You can hate me all you

want as long as none of us die. Go stretch, walk off the burn a little. I'll get the boys."

He turned, giving me a view of his stupidly perfect ass, and I wished he would just trip already, fall flat on his perfectly handsome face so I could know for sure that he wasn't as flawless as his jerky self presented. But he didn't. He disappeared through a door and came back five minutes later, with Asa and Austin in tow. Without a single word, he stalked toward me, bent slightly, and tossed me over his shoulder, carrying me in the most undignified way.

"I can walk," I finally ground out when the door to the gym nearly smacked me in the head.

"A promise is a promise." I felt his words rumble through his body, and I knew if I were to look at him, he'd be smiling smugly, proud of himself for ticking me off again. "Besides, we've got to get you home. You've got chemistry in less than an hour, and I know how much you'd hate to miss that class."

"You guys go to class after all that work?" My voice was a pained whine. The thought of going back to bed, any bed, had already taken root. How the hell did they go to class after doing more exercise than any human should ever do in a single week?

A low rumble vibrated through him. "Oh, little vixen. We go to class, then we'll do it again tonight."

New fear, unlocked.

CHAPTER TWELVE

WICK

That smart mouth of hers. It was like she was begging for punishment. I'd give it to her, and fuck me, it might even be my punishment, too. I would deserve it. After all, I pushed to take her on as our housekeeper, and with each squat she did, I half regretted it. Not because she was bad at it, because for as much as she bitched, she wasn't the worst I'd seen. But I hoped she would collapse at my feet, and I could bribe her to take my cock between those perfect little lips before I helped her.

I was fucked. I was aware. I couldn't help the perverse thoughts that danced in my head, begging me to take whatever I wanted, when I wanted, because she was ours and we owned her. A primal need in me screamed to just pee on her leg and mark my territory, get it done with already so I didn't bash the head in of any man who watched her. And there were a lot of men. Half of the damn gym had their eyes falling out of their head, watching her ass in those pants. It was infuriating. I'd have to get her something else to wear.

I hefted her higher on my shoulder, giving her ass a satisfying smack as I carried her the few blocks to our place. She hardly fought, resigned to the fact I wouldn't put her down. Or maybe just too exhausted to care that it was me whose fingers danced along her inner thigh under the guise of securing her on my shoulder.

"I think you worked her too hard." Austin spoke low, trying to keep the words between us. "I don't even think she's conscious."

"I didn't work her hard enough." I lifted my chin to Asa. "I made him do double when he joined us halfway through our first year."

"I'm built for this shit," Asa confirmed. And he was. His physique was magnificent, a true athlete waiting to be unleashed as he crept stealthily along the floor, hunting his kill.

"She's not," Austin continued.

"I can hear you." Mac sat up a little, using her elbow to prop her head up as she leaned against my shoulder.

I continued, like she wasn't listening. "You're right, she's not. It's like working out with a newborn giraffe. All stumbling limbs and awkward stances."

"Excuse me," she fumed.

I ignored her. "But she'll get there."

"How quick though?" Austin questioned. "She has less than two weeks until the party. Then a month after that."

"What party?" She was getting too damn squirmy, too fucking nosey, too. We didn't want to tell her shit yet, not until we knew she was solid.

"You think I'll let her get killed?"

"Wait a damn minute!" She demanded as she stretched her body in my arms, trying to see my face. "You were serious about the whole death thing."

"Did I give you any indication that I was joking?" I pinched her, trying not to smirk as she yelped in pain.

"No, but I was just thinking you were all being intense. Not serious."

"I don't joke about death, Makenna. You shouldn't either."

"You can put me down now," she instructed, her body suddenly more tense than it was before.

"Not a fucking chance. We're almost home, anyway."

"Someone might see us," she pointed out.

"Let them see."

"But they might think..."

"Think what, Mac? That I'm carrying you back to our place for a good fuck before class? They wouldn't be wrong most times." I walked up the steps of our home while Asa unlocked the door. "Imagine all the ways we're going to do it." I paused. "After you apologize, of course."

"Never." Her voice was like stone as she denied the apology she owed me. I couldn't even remember what it was for, but I knew I wanted the words to fall from her pillowy lips before my cock slid between them. I stepped into the house. "You can put me down now. We're inside."

Asa jogged upstairs, and I heard the water of a bathroom turn on. "No."

I walked up the stairs slower, letting her feel each time her abdomen jostled into my shoulder and my hand drifted up her thigh. Her hair fell around her face, but I knew if I pushed it aside and craned my neck to see, she'd be furious under the layers blocking my view.

When I entered our bathroom, I didn't bother removing her clothes as I pitched her forward, landing her right in the middle of our shower. She squealed and cursed, calling me a bastard, then quickly went silent as she watched each of us remove our shirts. "What are you doing?"

"Showering," Asa answered.

"But I- I'm clearly in here." She looked around.

"Baby, it's a multi-person shower. You never get to shower alone." Asa untied his sweats, while her eyes looked ready to fall out of her skull.

"You can't be serious." She wrapped her hands around her fully clothed body, as if that would protect her from our gazes.

Austin, who was still a little standoffish, added, "As a team, we do damn near everything together. You'll get used to it."

The way he said it wasn't reassuring, since he still seemed unsure. But when Asa's pants dropped to the floor with his shoes and shirt, Austin followed until both of them were under the spray of water. She stepped back, trying to give them space, but when I stepped in, the space seemed to have shrunk.

I reached forward, grabbing the hem of her shirt and ignored her protest as I slipped it over her head. "I'll take off the pants too if you don't. We're running behind for class."

"I'm calling in sick," she whimpered, even as her hands went to the wet fabric at her waist and she pushed them down, letting them fall to the ground.

"Nice try, baby." I let my fingers weave into her hair as I pulled her head back, forcing her to look at me. "You're going, but we'll make sure you arrive with a smile on your face. Or at least, someone will." I looked over my shoulder. "Asa, remind us again how she tastes?"

"Like fucking heaven."

I looked back at her, her face red at the realization that it was Asa between her thighs when she was drugged up and tied down. "I concur." I smirked. "Best fucking meal to eat." I released her hair before kicking her knees out from under her, landing her on her ass. It took little effort. She was weak from all the running. "It's time for you to return the favor."

I reached behind me, grabbing Asa's shaft in my fingers and running them up his length, then down again, letting the hardness pulse as it thickened under my touch. Her eyes followed the movement as her arms covered her breasts, her body nearly shaking from the fear of what we would do to her. We'd never hurt her, she'd learn that, but there is a fine line between life and death, pleasure and pain, and if she didn't learn to walk it, she'd never survive with us.

"Touch him," I demanded, watching as she licked her lips, even as she played timid. She had no words any longer, no sassy remarks or quick comebacks, only nerves and fear, and they oozed from her pores, fueling the loss inside of me. "You scared, Vixen?"

Her chest puffed up, the perfect handful bulging against her palms as if I hadn't sucked on those tits less than twenty-four hours ago. It was cute, really, fucking adorable that she thought she could hide from us when her main job was to be consumed by us all. "No."

Her words came out braver than her body language portrayed, and I'd give it to her. She was an excellent actress, but not good enough to pass my test. "Do it. Prove to me you are a woman of your word. You signed up for this, have you forgotten? Screamed your approval for all to hear."

"Under duress." Her eyes burned.

I shrugged. "Do we look like men who care about the semantics? I said fucking touch him, Mac."

When she didn't move, I reached forward and

grabbed her hand, forcing her to release her breasts as I brought it to Asa's cock. His head fell back. The tiniest of touches from her had him nearly melting, and I was fucking jealous. I knew my time would come, but the way his eyes fluttered only taunted me about things I'm forced to miss until she apologized with that sassy fucking mouth.

I placed my hand over hers, forcing her to move against Asa's skin, squeezing her hand at the base, then at the tip as our hands glided over him. "You ever given anyone a hand job, baby?"

Her eyes looked enormous. She fought back the tears brimming them, and I wished she'd stop the fight and let them fall so I could lick up the salty trail and taste the sweetness of her defeat. She bit her lip before muttering, "No."

"What else haven't you done?" I asked, not letting go of her hand, making sure she felt every ridge of him. When she didn't answer, I asked, "Have you ever sucked cock?"

Again, with the teasing lip biting. It drove me mad. "No."

"Do you want my cock down your throat, baby?" She hesitated before a meek "Yes" escaped her. I didn't believe her, though. Not yet, at least, but one day she'd be begging for it. "You can't have my cock until I say. Ever shower with a man?"

"No." I caught her eyes as she tried to sneak a peak of us, tried to measure us up, and I bet it made her wet.

"Stand up. Let Austin clean you off," I demanded, and she struggled to her feet, trying to gain balance when I still refused to let go of her hand. When she was standing, I reached forward, not bothering to ask her as I dipped my fingers between her thighs. "You're fucking soaked for us. Do you want to cum?"

Of course, she wanted to cum. What girl didn't want to cum when they were in a shower with three males? She struggled to admit it, even to herself, but her eyes gave her away when her voice refused. I nudged her leg. "Spread your legs and don't fucking stop working Asa. He deserves a reward too, don't you think?"

She gulped and nodded. "Yes."

Austin moved behind her, loofa thick with suds, and slowly ran it over her body, massaging it into every inch as I let my hands work between her legs. She was soaked; my fingers had no resistance as they slid inside her body. She didn't even try to pull away, even though I knew she despised me. Love wasn't required with sex. In fact, without love, sex was so much better. Intense. Ravishing.

I slide my fingers in and out of her body, keeping with the rhythm she set as she worked Asa's cock. He was mindless, a useless participant in my game now that his dick was in her hands, but that was okay. I didn't need him to help me, only do his part and blow his fucking load, and he was close. I could tell by the familiar sounds he made, ones I've heard too many nights streaming into the bedroom when he was showering.

Her whole body shook. The hand that wasn't stroking Asa grabbed onto my shoulder, her nails a claw as they dug into my skin. Her chest moved in a frantic rhythm as I brought her closer to the edge and Austin brought the loofa closer to her core. When he finally reached it, he ground the scratchy material over her clit, tearing a whimper from her throat.

"Oh god," she gasped, the pace so fast now, her body so ready, that I could already feel it try to clench my finger, begging me not to leave it each time I pulled out.

"Fuck!" Asa cried out, his hand slamming forward to find a tile, a wall, glass... anything to hold up his weight as he shot his load, streaming cum against her stomach and coating our hands that still worked over him. When the cum no longer spouted from his dick, I released her hand and stopped pumping in her body, removing my fingers from her. She cried out in protest, her body chasing my fingers like a starving animal after a slice of food.

I raised our hands and held them up in front of us. "I told you, you'd be punished if you weren't in the gym on time, little Vixen. You don't get to cum. Now lick our hands clean. We're going to be late."

This time, she really did cry, letting the salty liquid spill over her cheeks as she obediently licked our hands clean of every drop of Asa's cum. I leaned over, letting my tongue glide over her cheek, collecting the moisture before I reached her ear. Her breath hitched, her chest pressed against my own as our naked bodies aligned with precision, my cock begging to be let in between her thighs.

Not yet though. She hadn't earned it.

"How did he taste?" I bit her earlobe. "Did you like it?"

"Yes," she answered, and I wasn't sure if she was lying or telling the truth. I didn't care.

I licked the shell of her ear and right before I pulled away, I whispered, "Good girl."

CHAPTER THIRTEEN

AUSTIN

"Pay attention!" I hissed. "You almost burned yourself."

Mac looked at the wall behind me, not looking directly at my face. "I am paying attention."

"Bullshit."

"Well, what exactly would you like me to do, Austin?"

"This fucking lab, so we don't fail before we start." I took the beaker from her hands and sat it on the table.

"It's not that simple."

"It really is. We've done many labs before. Each one was simple. We have the instructions right here."

"That's not what I mean," she told the wall behind me.

"What do you mean then, Mac? Because if you don't get your head in the game, it's going to fuck this up, and I don't want to explode the whole lab!" I put down the notebook I had in my hand and leaned against the cold cement countertop.

"It's nothing."

"It's something because you haven't looked me in the eye for a single second in the last twenty-four hours." I gripped onto the counter's edge, wishing I had all the strength to snap the concrete.

"In the last twenty-four hours, someone has drugged me, chained me up, coerced me into agreeing to join your secret society, one which I still know nothing about, by the way. Not to mention I find out my lab partner is a part of it, and he broke my trust by slipping me a roofie on our date, not an actual date."

"I would date you, if that's what this is about." I cut in.

"No. God no. Fuck no." Ouch. The way she said that sort of stung. "It's not about the fucking date. Or that I've now seen you naked and I can't unsee that. I can't even look you in the eye after seeing your penis." Another ouch. "Every time I close my eyes, all I'm going to see behind my lids are three perfect penises at eye level. Do you know how maddening that is?"

"Okay..." I drew the word out. "So this is about the shower?"

"No. Yes. God, I fucking ache, and do you realize

how much I hate that prick? I fucking hate him, Austin. I wish he fell on his face during that impossibly long five mile warm up and then strained all his muscles doing his weights and perfectly formed squats."

I was almost afraid to ask. "So this is about the mile?"

"Five!" she shouted and everyone turned to look at us.

"Sorry," I muttered. "I almost measured the wrong amount of sodium."

When all the heads went back to their projects she leaned in, whispering between clenched teeth. "It was five miles and no, it's not about the miles, though I doubt I'll ever move again. It's about all of it."

"Because you don't want to be ours?"

"I didn't say that."

"But you don't," I pointed out.

"It's not that I don't, it's that I don't even know what's happening." Her fingers flexed at her side.

"We're training you to be stealthy, strong, and the best in your class." I leaned in, forcing my head into her line of vision so she had no other choice but to look at me. "We're training you to be ours, Mac. And it might be harder than you expected, but it's worth it. And you know what?"

When she didn't answer, I forced her to lock eyes with my gaze instead of letting her look away, using my hand to guide her chin so that she couldn't tilt her head to the side. Finally, she gave in. "What?"

"We're also training to be yours. We've not touched another person since freshman year. Some of us even longer than that." I admitted, her knowing damn well I'm a virgin, even if she hadn't outed my secret to the guys. "It's not easy for us either, and sometimes Wick might not know when he's pushed you too far, and you're right to push back some. But I know he would never work you harder than he knows you're capable of. Use the push back, show us what your limits are, and we'll learn your boundaries just as much as you'll learn ours."

"Why didn't you tell me?" she blurted out.

"What?"

"That you were a part of this. You knew damn well that I was thinking of applying."

I hated how hurt she looked. "I told you not to," I reminded her.

"If you would have just told me the reason..."

"Would you have applied, anyway?" I asked, because we both knew she would have. Mac always liked to have her way, always did what she wanted even if I didn't like that. I learned that the hard way with my first round at being her lab partner, and yet, I must be a sucker for punishment because I signed up again, repeatedly. I couldn't stay away from her, and Wick was right. It was because I had been completely infatuated with her from day one, and even now that I had her, I wasn't even sure I wanted to share.

"I- I was curious. It's some big mystery, and I wanted to solve it. I didn't know it was for life."

"You said yes," I pointed out.

"I was tied up on a table, drugged, with my tits out, a stranger between my legs and an orgasm tearing through me, I clearly wasn't in my right mind." She looked up as she fought tears from the memory. "I don't even know if I can look you in the eye anymore after that."

"Because I've seen you vulnerable?"

"Yes," she hissed. "And took all my trust."

"Baby—" I brought my hand up to cup her cheek as I tried to offer comfort.

She batted my hand away. "Don't call me that."

"Are you embarrassed to be mine? Worried because all the eyes of this classroom are glancing sideways at us, itching to figure out what's going on?" Just mentioning the class, her back straightened and her face turned to panic.

"I'm angry, no, furious that you betrayed me." She turned, picking up a tiny spoon while scooping it into the glass container sitting on top of the scale.

"That's too much," I pointed out. "Did I betray you, or are you mad because you would have betrayed me? Or do you think it's more of I saw you, wanted you, and did whatever the fuck I wanted to own you?"

"You don't own me." She dumped the powder out and started again.

"I do."

"You don't fucking own me."

"Physically, not yet. But I will. You already agreed to it."

"I changed my mind." Her eyes closed, and she inhaled slowly before exhaling. "Fuck. I can't change my mind, can I? You guys would kill me. How would you do it? Slow? Fast? When I least expect it or bam! Jump right in with all the bloody details."

My stomach tightened at the thought. "We wouldn't do it. The organization would."

"Oh, gee, that's such a relief." She tossed the liquid into the beaker. "Thought I was dealing with monsters for a moment."

"You are." I took the tools from her hand because clearly, she didn't care what she fucked up on this lab, but I did. "Just because we aren't strong enough to kill someone we attach ourselves to, doesn't mean we aren't monsters. Wick didn't lie about the blade he cut you with. We all have one. Maybe one day, you will too."

Her face looked green at the thought of owning a blade made from a bone of someone she killed. I knew how that felt. There was a time I thought I could never do it. Now, I could dissect their limbs, then go eat a burger. I'd grown callous, for sure, but at least I knew I wouldn't hesitate if it meant protecting her.

"I don't think I could." I barely heard her voice.

"You will. But we will be there to help you through it. And Mac?"

"Yeah?"

"We weren't kidding about you being ours for life. You applied, you opened yourself up to us, and we picked you because you had everything we desired and more. Trust us to provide what you need, even if it goes against what you want."

"It's hard to trust any of you." She spat the words out with so much venom I felt the sting.

"Then pretend until it becomes second nature to lean on us. We won't lead you astray."

"Pretend." She repeated, "I can pretend."

The smirk she offered me was terrifying, and I knew I should be afraid of just what was running through her mind, but she was suddenly agreeable, and I didn't want to ruin that. "Good. Let's get this lab going. Take the attention off of us. The sooner we finish, the sooner we can be out of here."

"Why the rush?" She picked up the lab paper and read.

"I'm already getting texts from the guys, asking when we will be out." What I didn't mention was they were demanding we leave class early, spouting off about lunch before the next class and then taking her to dinner. Lucky for her, Wick cut our night run out, at least for today.

"Why?"

"Why not? They want food. Aren't you hungry? That protein bar we grabbed on the way out wasn't that filling, and you used a lot of calories today. Plus, we always try to eat meals together. We're a team."

"You've got some odd bromance thing happening

you're not telling me about, don't you?" She pretended to be concentrated on the lab work, but I knew that wasn't where her mind was.

"If you're asking if any of us fucked before, the answer is no." She flinched at the hardness of my tone. I leaned in to her, my voice low. "If you're asking if I've ever thought about it, the answer is yes."

Her chest hitched as she held her breath, and the blush on her cheeks told me that now that the thought had entered her mind, she'd be thinking about it just as much as I had. Maybe even more because now it surely would include her. Everything we would ever do now centered on her. She was our anchor we orbited around, and she may not have realized it yet, but she had more control in her pinky than any of us ever would in our whole bodies.

"Oh," the word breathlessly escaped.

"Yeah. Oh." I wiggled a brow. "Every fucking night."

CHAPTER FOURTEEN

MAC

Pretend. I could pretend.

If all Austin wanted me to do was pretend, then I could be an expert. Except, being around the three of them made it damn near impossible. He wanted me to pretend to lean on them until it became real, but it was fucking hard to lean on a guy, or three, when you couldn't trust a single thing about them.

I had trusted Austin once. I hadn't had friends here on campus. Hell, I didn't even have friends off campus. But what I had was a lab partner who I saw a few times a week and exchanged banter with. That was all. I didn't know him, not enough, clearly. But he didn't know me either. Now I felt like whatever fragile friendship I once had was built on a lie and I really had nothing.

"Ready?" Austin's voice tore me away from my dazed thoughts as I packed up my notebooks, laptop, and phone and shoved them into my backpack, which really could use some cleaning.

He held out his hand, offering it to me, and I wasn't sure what he expected, but taking it seemed weird. There were three of them; surely if I showed affection in public, people would talk. I didn't want the gossip. I preferred to go through life invisible. But I hesitated too long, and he reached over, grabbed my hand, and laced our fingers before taking my backpack and slinging it over his shoulder.

"We don't bite, Mac."

Funny he would say that because I was pretty sure Wick most definitely would. My nipples tingled just thinking about it, and I hated him for it. I didn't want to find his rough fingers or crass words a turn on, but despite my mind screaming that I hated him, my body craved the next time he touched my skin again.

"It's just new." I tried to make an excuse for why I didn't want to hold his hand.

"Don't lie to me. I know you better than that. You were never afraid of anything new."

"Yeah well, this is definitely a different new," I pointed out as he led me outside the classroom.

"New is new, Makenna. You're not fooling me." I hated that being lab partners for so long gave him the opportunity to get to know me. I hated how he was right. I wasn't afraid of the new, I was afraid of what I knew the new was capable of.

I made it two feet from the classroom before fingers grabbed my arm, pulling me to the side, slamming my body against a hard chest. Asa leaned close to my ear, "Where are you going? Planning to ignore us waiting for you?"

"I hadn't even seen you."

"Lesson one." His hand laid flat against my stomach. "Never stop looking at your surroundings. The only ones you can trust are us. Everyone else, assume they are an enemy."

"That's ridiculous," I scoffed.

"That's our reality." He kissed my neck. "We trust no one."

"You're paranoid." I rolled my eyes at him, even though he couldn't see it.

Austin and Wick could though, and Wick stepped forward, his fingers grabbing my jaw so he could lean in, sandwiching me between the two of them. He tilted his head to the side, giving me a display of his neck and the white scar that traveled down it, disappearing under his shirt. It broke the flawless flow of his body, and I was unsure how I had missed seeing that before, but it clearly was there now, and somehow, I found it oddly attractive.

"This wasn't given to me by being paranoid. Trust fucking no one, Mac, and maybe you'll have a better fate than I did. Maybe."

"I think you're being a little dramatic." I knew no one. I had no enemies.

His fingers squeezed on my jaw as he moved closer. "Dramatic? You joined the fucking Saints. What did you think would happen? You became a fucking target, and now we're all at risk. We wanted you. Don't question that. But it's a little easier to protect you if you fucking listened for one fucking time in your life instead of arguing and trying to gaslight my own experiences and warnings."

"I wasn't gaslighting. I was only—"

Wick's lips cut my sentence off, crushing against mine, and at first, I didn't know what to do. They were hard and bruising and refused to relent until my body gave in, softening under his, and my mouth worked back against his, even as I leaned heavily into Asa. Wick smiled against my lips as he kissed, a tongue slipping into my mouth to dance with my own, and I swear, just a simple fucking kiss felt like so much more. Explosions were igniting through all my cells, sending sparks bursting through me. All from one kiss.

He pulled back, not releasing my jaw from his grip. The corner of his lip tilted, and his eyes churned with lust. "That's our girl." His thumb grazed over my bottom lip for a second. "So fucking compliant when needed, practically begging me to take what I want."

I was not. But my mind and voice didn't cooperate, and I couldn't get the words out to argue that fact. He released me, stepping back, though Austin still held my hand and Asa still had an arm wrapped around my stomach. As if I wasn't nearly melted into a puddle on the floor, surrounded by half the college, Asa's hand squeezed my hip as he spoke. "We'll eat lunch at home."

"You're not to be alone outside of class." Wick picked up where Asa left off. "Each day you will have one of us with you or waiting outside the doors for you. Do not leave unless you're with one of us."

"That seems a little much."

"It's not," they all said in unison before Asa added, "It's not enough, if I'm honest. Let's go. I'm fucking starving and I've got English at 1:30."

"Probably starving because of all the energy you exerted in the shower," Wick smirked. "Because I'm not that famished."

My face heated, and I knew my cheeks were red. Asa released his hold on me before grabbing the hand that Austin didn't hold. "You're a fucking prick. You're embarrassing her."

"If the truth is embarrassing to her, that's her problem, not mine. I've no problem letting the world know I've touched your dick. What are they going to do? Talk? They fucking do that anyway."

I hated that he had a point, and I hated that the visual he brought up made my core clench at the memory. I didn't want to find him attractive. He was a fucking heartless dick, and he pushed me when I wasn't ready to be pushed. But damn it, my body hadn't gotten the memo.

We had taken a truck to class this morning since we were running late, so I was thankful I didn't have to walk the few blocks to their home. Our home? Hell, I wasn't sure what was going on. A day, not even a full one, with them, and my mind was a jumble of confusion. My muscles were screaming from the five-mile run this morning, and the millions of squats that sadistic bastard demanded I do, and if I had to walk back to the house, I'd rather sit on campus all day and skip lunch.

When we walked through the door, Wick put down the keys and turned to me. "I didn't have class this morning, so I got the rest of your stuff from your pigsty of a dorm room and brought it back here. My favorite piece was this one." He reached into his pocket and pulled out a deep blue lace panty. "You will model this one."

I swiped for it and missed as he pulled it up over my head and out of reach. "Bastard."

"Sometimes," he confirmed. "Come on, I made lunch."

Made? "You had time to make lunch?"

"I'm efficient." He walked through the house, and we followed, allowing me to see more of it than I had seen previously. "Plus, I had a batch frozen from the last time I made some, so really, it was just reheating."

We entered the kitchen, and he went through the motions of grabbing bowls and pouring a chili mixture from a slow cooker into a bowl before he leaned into the fridge and pulled out some toppings. He didn't bother asking what I wanted on top; instead he loaded it up with cheese, sour cream, green onions, and crushed up corn chips. Picking up the bowl, he looked at the table and then at me. "Sit."

It was an order, and I scurried to the table to sit down. I wasn't sure why I was in such a hurry to please him and follow orders, not when I hated him so fucking much, but I was starved, and the food really smelled delicious. He sat the bowl in front of me, then went back to a drawer and pulled out a spoon and handed it to me. "Eat."

On demand, I dipped the spoon into the chili, ignoring the sounds of the others serving themselves as I took my first bite. The rich notes and hints of spice hit my tongue, causing a moan to escape me. I closed my eyes, dancing in place as I happily chewed the rich food, and when I swallowed and opened my eyes, three sets were looking back at me. "What?"

"If you moan that much from a bit of chili, I can't wait until I'm inside of you." Asa reached up, scratching his forehead like he was trying to gather himself.

"It's good."

"I'm better," Asa promised.

"Two different pleasures, I can assure you. I was starving. This is fantastic, Wick." Which somehow shocked me. He was cruel and demanding, and yet, he was the one who sought to take care of me when he didn't need to. He got my things for me, cooked me a warm lunch, and served me, which was strangely thoughtful for a man who demanded I lick his friend's cum off his fingers just hours ago.

His Adam's apple worked as he swallowed. "It's nothing."

Except for me, it was something. I lived off ramen most of the time, if I bothered to eat at all. I couldn't always afford to stock up on food when I didn't get good hours at the student store. Which reminded me... "I work tonight."

"I'll go," Asa volunteered. "Wick's last class ends at seven and Austin can let the council know of our decision."

"Council?"

"We have to let the organization know that we've picked our housekeeper," Austin explained. "I wish we didn't, but we know they will hit twice as hard if we keep you a secret."

"Hit twice as hard?" I wish these boys weren't always talking in code.

"Yeah. When they send people after us."

"Why would they do that?" I didn't understand a thing I had gotten myself into.

"To prove our worth and yours?"

"Still not helping," I growled.

"You'll understand in time. Eat," Wick demanded as he stood back, arms crossed, watching me like he wanted to make sure I consumed every ounce of food he put in front of me. "We'll meet tonight at the diner."

"So fucking cryptic." I shoveled another spoonful into my mouth.

"Watch your mouth or I will fill it," Wick spat.

"You'd fill it regardless of what I said, Chadwick," I taunted, knowing he hated the name.

In seconds he was in front of me, his fingers threaded through my loose pigtail buns, pulling my head back so sharply that the air hissed out of me. "You've got a smart fucking mouth for a girl who volunteered to be our cock warmer. Do you want your mouth fucked right here, right now? How late are you willing to be for the next class because of your smart-ass mouth? Who would you pick, I wonder? Asa? Maybe Austin? Because I promise, you'd not be able to handle my cock fucking your nearly virgin mouth. Call me Chadwick one more time and you won't fucking make it to class with a voice left in your swollen throat."

The pull he had on my hair caused my eyes to well with tears, but I still refused to look away from him until he let go of my hair with a jerk. "Eat your fucking food. You need the calories."

He walked out of the room, leaving me with Austin and Asa. Austin sighed before he sat next to me. "He hates his name, you know."

"Clearly."

"Don't push him."

"Why? Because he's the deadly killer you keep reminding me he is?" I filled my words with sarcasm.

"No. Because he will follow through on his threat

and fuck your mouth hoarse. If you're not ready for that, don't push him." Asa sat on my other side. "We all have trauma. If we didn't, we wouldn't be here. We're orphans and rejects, just like you. With only each other as family, though some of us like to keep the details of that fact private. And sometimes avoidance is the only way to cope."

"It's just a name," I stated.

"And it was his father's too," Austin pointed out. "Try not to remind him of that."

CHAPTER FIFTEEN

ASA

She demonized Wick, and I could see why. He was a prick, and he didn't hide that fact. But what our girl didn't see was that Austin and I weren't innocent. We didn't get where we were by watching Wick and sharing credit for what he'd done. We each killed men. We each wore their blood and their regrets as we stopped their hearts. We each could be equally vicious, given the chance.

I sat on a stool a few feet from the register, watching Mac work. I hated that she worked here. We'd work on getting her to quit soon. The student store had been oddly busy tonight, like the universe was working against me, preventing Mac and me from sharing a single conversation. I despised how the universe insisted on constantly fucking with me.

A hand rubbed against my shoulders, and I nearly drew my knife and stuck it into the flesh before I remembered where I was. I turned, seeing a girl from my English class batting her eyes at me, a wide smile on her face. "Asa, what are you doing here?"

I stared, trying to remember her name, and came up blank. I never really bothered. "Sitting."

"I'm glad to see you outside of class. I've been thinking about your speech since last week. Such an amazing topic and so well presented."

I blinked a few times. "I'm glad you find the gastric system amazing."

She winced, clearly forgetting the ridiculous topic the teacher had me draw from his hat. All the topics were ridiculous. Mine just happened to be semi embarrassing to present and a ludicrous subject for an English presentation.

"Your speech had me on the edge of my seat." She nodded her head. "I loved it."

Why was this girl here? Talking to me. "Thanks." I turned my attention elsewhere, dismissing her. She didn't get the hint and kept talking. Finally, I stopped her. "I'm sorry. I don't remember your name."

"Julia."

"Julia." I paused when the mere act of me saying her name caused her to nearly swoon. "I just wanted to let you know before you continued that I'm not interested."

"What?" She held her chest like the admission that I didn't want up her skirt was offensive.

"I'm not interested," I repeated.

"I- I don't understand." The confusion was genuine, and I couldn't figure out how someone could be so dense.

"If you wanted to just chat, that's fine. As long as it's okay with Mac. But I'm not interested in dating you, fucking you, or entertaining you in any capacity that could make you think I would one day belong to you."

"You assume I want you?" Her hands fell to her hips.

"Was I wrong?" I quirked a brow at the question.

"No." Her lashes fluttered. "But if you'd-"

"Is there an issue?" Mac cut in. I hadn't heard her coming or even realized that the line that seemed to form all evening had dissipated, leaving only us, Julia, and some guy browsing the small selection of chips.

"No issue." Julia glared. "I was just having a private conversation with Asa."

I reached out, hooking my arm around Mac and pulled her close before burying my face into her stomach for a moment. My inhale was slow and satisfying. "This is nice," I muttered against her body, and it *was* nice. The hold was a comfort I didn't know I was missing, and I didn't want to release her. She didn't make me either, which felt oddly like a win for our team.

"About?" Mac questioned, and her hands came up, stroking through my hair. I hadn't realized she was doing it, but I didn't want her to stop.

"His speech for English," Julia replied with an attitude at the same time I said, "Rape."

Mac slapped my shoulder, and I laughed. But if Julia had her way, that's what she'd be doing.

"You two can discuss it in English class." God, those fingers working at the hair trying to untie it were heaven. "Not in the middle of the student store."

"You're an employee. You don't run this place," Julia snorted.

"That's true," Mac agreed as she looked thought-ful. Then she looked at me. "You're not allowed to talk to her."

"What?" Julia looked outraged, and Mac looked unfazed by her anger. "What gives you the right to demand him? He can do what he wants."

"He's mine." I loved the way she said it. The casual confirmation made my blood boil with want of her. I had to release her and pull away so I didn't do something stupid at her place of employment.

Julia laughed. "Asa doesn't date anyone."

"Funny, because he dates me." Mac stood her ground, daring the girl to challenge her on this.

"Asa?" Julia questioned.

"Ownership is a two-way thing. She owns me, I own her. If she says we can't talk, we can't. Thanks for the chat." I literally could not wait to text the boys and gloat that she placed her claim on me, in public, to a person.

"But—"

"I'll see you in English." I dismissed her, turning to Mac with a grin. With a huff, Julia stomped away. I waited until she was out of earshot before I spoke to Mac again. "You said you're dating me."

"Ugh, don't remind me." She rolled her eyes.

"You cuddled me."

"Gag." She stuck her finger in her mouth, pretending to heave.

"I think you like us," I teased.

"I think that you've made it clear I've no other choice."

"That's true," I agreed. "However, you could have told her to get lost without letting me snuggle."

"I thought you were being traumatized. I was trying to soothe the trauma."

"I don't believe you." I laughed before pulling her close to me again, widening my stance so she fit perfectly between my thighs. "You could have let us talk."

"She was annoying." The shrug she offered told me it was more than that.

"Were you jealous, Mac?" Oh, the boys would love to hear this.

"No."

"I think you were," I declared.

"Listen, I did not slurp down your cum off Wick's fingers just to have some other girl catch your attention. If I'm in this deep, I might as well commit fully."

Nothing could stop the ear-to-ear smile that took over my face. "You like us."

"Not particularly."

"You want to fuck our brains out," I taunted.

"I wouldn't know where to begin," she admitted.

"That's not a denial," I pointed out.

"No. It's a confession." She turned on her heels, acting as if she thought she'd really walk away from me, but I reached up, taking one of those damn pigtail buns in my hand and pulled her back.

Her body slammed into mine and she made the cutest sound when she stumbled. "You shouldn't run from us."

"I wasn't running. I was walking away. This still is my job, Asa."

"Running, walking, the same thing when you turned your back on me." I yanked her down, so that she was in my lap, then wrapped my arm around her chest to pin her to me. "And you should know, we're all predators, princess. We can't help but crave the chase."

I leaned forward, placing a kiss against the crook of her neck as I let my hand roam lower, skimming over her stomach before my fingers danced against the button of her too tight jeans.

"You like when people watch?"

Her words made my cock jump against her backside. "I'm not against it."

"Good, because there are people watching us

through the window, and if you choose to continue, you'll be putting on a show."

"We'll be putting on a show," I corrected. "You'll be the star."

"Asa," she warned.

With a sigh and one more kiss, I released her. "Fine."

I let her walk away. It was the hardest thing I'd ever done in my life. Especially since the taste of her skin was still coating my lips from where I'd kissed her neck. I picked up my phone when she returned to the register. I was midway through text messaging the guys when she asked, "What are you telling them?"

"What makes you think I'm texting them?"

"You are the hottest guy in the school and somehow you surround yourself with only two jack-asses. Just the two. Who else would you be texting?"

"You think I'm the hottest guy in school?" I was fucking beaming.

She threw a damn towel she had wiped the counter with at me. "You know you're hot."

"All that matters is if you think I'm hot. Do you, Mac?"

"Fishing for compliments is so unappealing." Her nose scrunched.

"My tongue will make it up to you," I promised, and her face instantly turned an adorable shade of pink.

"Of course, you're hot," she groaned as she

suddenly found a speck on the counter to rub at. "You've got this dark mysterious thing going and hair that every girl on campus is jealous of."

"You want to live out your biggest fantasy and braid it? Curl it? Maybe take out one of those vintage crimpy things and those tiny little butterfly clips that were all the rage in the 90s?" I reached up, running my fingers through the strands by my forehead before scratching lightly at the shaved sides.

"I said none of that," she glared.

"Shame. I'd let you." I'd let her and fucking love every second, though I'd not admit that to the guys. Having my hair played with and getting the attention of my girl is like living a double dream come true moment.

"You would?"

"I said it, didn't I?"

"Yes, but I didn't—"

"I *was* texting the guys," I finally admitted. "Telling them you're jealous."

"I wasn't jealous," she nearly shouted, and thankfully, the student store was practically empty.

"I'm taking it how I see it." I stood, raising my hands above my head, and stretched. "Are you closing down soon? I'm getting hungry."

"You're aware that we are surrounded by a literal store of snacks. If you're hungry, you have options." She spread her arms wide, sweeping it in front of her, displaying all the foods I could have picked from.

"I never said I was hungry for food." The moment

the words left my mouth, my stomach growled so loud she heard it.

A giggle erupted from her, a sound so cute that I wish I had recorded it. "No?"

"Okay. I'll admit, I'm starving. But in my defense, we're meeting the boys for burgers."

The hum of approval let me know she was on board for this idea. "Soy?"

"I'd rather die than eat soy burgers. Don't let that word leave your lips again or I'll punish you myself."

"Y'all like your punishments." Her arms crossed over her chest, but I didn't miss how even the thought of punishments got her nipples hard.

"I think maybe you do, too." I stretched a little more before strolling the small aisles. I grabbed a bag of pretzels before shouting over to her. "What's your favorite snack?"

"Popcorn. All flavors. Gimme." She did this little cute thing with her hand, like she was ready to grab all the popcorn bags.

I snagged one and brought it up to the register, typing in my student ID to pull up my pay account. "My favorite snack depends on if I'm going for all out junk or semi healthier options."

"All out junk?"

"Takis, doused in hot sauce." I rubbed my chest. "Heartburn for days, but worth every second. If I can't find those, flaming hot Cheetos."

"What's your favorite candy? And if you say Almond Joys or Mary Janes, I'm backing out now.

Nothing you could offer is worth the suffering of being in some sort of relationship with a man who loves those." She handed me my receipt.

"I love hearing you admit to a relationship." I picked up my pretzels before offering her the popcorn. "I don't mind Mary Janes. I love anything with peanut butter. Anything. So clearly, I love Reese's. Those peanut butter filled M&Ms, I could eat until I'm stuffed. Reese's pieces. Just give me all the fat loaded nut goodness and I'll be a happy man."

"Peanut butter cookies?" she questioned.

"With chocolate chips?" I asked before answering. "My absolute favorite type. I'd kill to have a warm one where the cookie is still gooey and the chocolate is melting."

"From what I've heard, you'd go through with it, too." She didn't seem to judge me for that fact, more of a resigned acceptance that she signed up to be with killers, and here we are, at her beck and call.

"There are worse things to be in this life than one who kills to protect those who couldn't protect them-selves." I popped open my bag and took out a handful of pretzels, shoving them into my mouth. "Besides, if you're going into this world without us at your back, you're going into it in danger. We're the safest people to be around, the best bet. You think girls can survive out there alone? It's not as easy as it looks. Know how many end up dead?"

"Don't spout statistics at me." She tossed a dirty

rag into the wash basket. "You're sounding like Wick."

"The best man to sound like, if you ask me." I leaned over, grabbed a fist full of her shirt and forced her to stand on her toes as she leaned over the counter. I'd like to fuck her like this. Her body strained as she leaned forward, her hands planted down for support. When she was close enough to me, I kissed her. It wasn't sweet like Austin probably would be, or damaging like Wick, but it was the perfect mix of ownership, showing her I wasn't fucking around. She was mine, and I may not be bruising her up and tossing her around, but if she tried to leave our control, I'd chase her until she fell to her knees, begging for forgiveness. When I pulled away, her chest was rising and falling rapidly. "Now, tell me what I need to do to help so we can leave this place faster?"

She hesitated, but after seeing I was serious, she handed me a broom and ordered me to sweep while she stocked a few low shelves. After the store closed, she counted the money before depositing it into a safe. One more round of sweeping, another round of wiping down counters, and a note for the person who would open the next morning, and I had her locking the doors.

"They are trusting," I mentioned as she turned the key in the lock.

"Well, there is campus security, and let's be honest, if the safe is short, they are going to know who's responsible." Mac had a point. If she was the only one working, the thief would be obvious. "The manager periodically stops in to check on us. He was just out of town tonight."

"Interesting. If I were going to murder you, I'd track the management schedule in addition to your own to know when and if you'd be alone. Keep that in mind. You need a new job. Actually, fuck that, you don't even need to work. We've got you." I grabbed her hand, lacing our fingers together, and it felt so fucking right to hold her hand.

"First, that was a creepy statement. Second, I need this job. It's my last year here, and I need to afford life after. I'm trying to get a head start."

"We're a team for life. Did you not get that?" The thought of my tongue gliding through her slits for the rest of our lives was too appealing not to salivate at the thought.

"You can't know that."

"Are you planning to die?" I sure as hell hoped it didn't reach that point.

"No."

I squeezed her hand. "We'll, I sure as fuck am not, either. Guess we're stuck with each other."

She squeezed my hand back, and from the corner of my eye I saw her lip lift a little in a smile. "I guess we are."

CHAPTER SIXTEEN

MAC

A few days ago, I'd never believe that I'd be here, walking with linked hands, with Asa. I hadn't lied when I said he was the hottest guy on campus. Every lady that passed by swooned a little at the mysterious cloud that follows him. Maybe he's the embodiment of a teen girl's rebellious stage, and that's the appeal. Still, holding hands with Asa Dominguez drew all the eyes to me.

I wouldn't admit I was jealous because I wasn't. But I took delight in squashing the girl's hopes when she clearly refused to listen to him. Austin told me I was theirs as much as they were mine, that I had the power to control them, too. I only needed to wield it, and I wondered how far I could push. What would they willingly let me do to show them I was the one in control?

If I wanted that story on the Saints — and I sure as fuck did now that I was stuck in this mess — I needed to stand my ground and not let them push me around. With Asa and Austin, that would be easy. It was Wick that I wasn't sure I could win against. He was so big, looming over me with his scowling expression. I doubted he had a soft tender spot in his whole body.

"We're just going to the diner tonight. But we'll take you somewhere fancy soon. I promise." Asa squeezed my hand, probably for the fifteenth time, and I don't know why, but I found the action sort of endearing.

"I like the diner," I reminded him as we approached the square of eateries. There was lots of outdoor seating and plenty of food to pick from, but the diner's burgers always seemed to hit the spot.

The closer we got, the clearer it was that Austin and Wick were waiting for us. Their colossal bodies were consuming the metal chairs outside as they relaxed casually. In the short time I'd known Wick, there was never anything casual about him. He was intense, strung tight, always alert, and for a moment, I let my mind ponder what he would be like in a moment where he wasn't in control, where he let go of the power he held so tightly to and just existed.

They stood when we got closer, their bodies dwarfing the two-person bistro table like it was a child's toy. When we stood in front of them, it was Wick who greeted us. "Took you long enough."

"I've got a job. I had to complete it," I reminded him.

"Yeah. So do we. And right now, our primary job is persistently annoying." Was he talking about me? That bastard!

"Easily overlooked with her beauty." Asa smoothed over Wick's comment.

"Are you hungry?" Austin asked as his arm came around to rest on my shoulder.

"Starved," I admitted. I was pretty sure I'd never had a longer day than this one. I wasn't sure how these men did it, but if this was their daily schedule, I was sure I'd be dead within two weeks before a single person tried to touch me, like they seemed to think would happen.

"Good." Wick gleamed. "I believe I promised to punish you this morning."

He pulled open the door to the diner as I asked, "For what?" My stomach was already balled in knots at the thought of what type of punishment a man like Wick could issue. "I made it to the gym."

"Late," he corrected. "We don't tolerate tardiness."

When we entered, the boys nodded their heads at the staff as they filed toward a booth in the back. The place was packed, and I wasn't sure if they called ahead, but somehow that booth was the only one that was empty. Austin slid in before Wick pushed me next to Austin and took up my other side.

When we were settled, I asked, "How am I being punished?"

I honestly didn't want to fucking know, but still Wick answered, "By teaching you control."

"I have plenty of control, thank you very much." At least, I thought I did. But the second a hand touched by my inner thigh, I jumped, nearly squealing if it wasn't for Austin's hand that slapped over my lips.

"Shh." Austin cooed, "You've got to be quiet."

"The thing about control..." Wick leaned in. "Either you have it, or you don't. Don't let it slip, little vixen, or the consequences could be dangerous. Pick up your menu."

I did as he demanded, even as my back was stiff, and my heart pounded. Something cool slipped against the denim of my inner thigh before touching my bare skin, and I wanted to look. I was so fucking tempted to do so, but I refused and gave all my attention to staring blankly at a menu of food I was too eager to eat. The cool air of the diner touched against my skin, and my eyes widened to saucer size when I turned toward Wick.

"Did you just–"

I swear I'd never seen the devil dance until I made the choice to look this man in the eyes. "Cut the crotch of these jeans. Yes. I think we need to put you in more dresses, don't you think, boys?"

They all nodded like they got a say in what I wore, but I didn't get to argue the fact because Wick's fingers were on my bare skin, moving up my thigh, dancing up the slit in my ruined jeans. The menu fell from my shaking fingers and Wick growled, "Pick it up."

I did as I was told, though I don't know how I found the strength to do so. My nerves were rapid firing, telling my brain that this was wrong. All the while, my thighs spread wider, practically inviting this man to touch me. I didn't know why I reacted this way. I couldn't stand the prick. But his touch made me see stars, and the attention was something I didn't know I craved until I was under his assault.

His finger pushed between my lips before slipping into my body. I gasped while he sat next to me, unfazed, looking over his menu. My breath came out in a pant as I whispered, "We can't do this here."

"And yet, I am." He didn't even glance at me as he removed his finger and pumped it back in, grinding his palm against my clit. He appeared completely uninterested in the fact his fingers were buried in my pussy as he gave all the attention to the menu. "The waitress will be here soon to take your order. I hope you're ready for it."

"Please don't." I was begging him without shame. I didn't want people to see us. The room was filled, stuffed with our peers and even a few families, and I was completely exposed. All someone had to do was drop a fork and tilt their head, and they'd see the full view of what Wick was doing to me.

"It's about control." He added a finger, stretching my body to accommodate his digits. "Can you control it? Can you fight the urge to break?"

I absolutely could not, and the fucker knew it. My body was already on fire. A thin layer of sweat had already coated my skin, and this angle was making it hard to concentrate on anything else but the feel of the monster sitting next to me. And he knew what he was doing to me. I saw it in the little upward crook of his lips as he reviewed the menu.

"I fucking hate all of you," I gasped as the agonizing grind of his palm took my breath away.

"We're all you've got," Wick reminded me, and damn it, it was painfully true.

"I did just fine without you before." My palm slammed against the table as I arched forward, my hips trying to guide Wick to the spot I wanted, without letting on that I fucking needed him to make me cum or I might die.

"You were lost, just like us. How does it feel to be found, baby?"

Right now? It felt really fucking good. I looked to Austin, then Asa, my eyes pleading to help, but neither of them was willing to step in. "I was doing fine."

"You were slowly drowning alone." Wick laughed. "I know, because we all were."

Austin dropped a hand, his fingers a warm ember

against my leg as he squeezed it and my body flopped back against the back of the booth, my eyes going to the ceiling as I tried to fight against Wick, even knowing he would win. They both would, because even though Austin wasn't touching me sexually, I felt every ounce of tension between us jolt from his fingertips and my body craved it. Begged for it. Wept for it.

"What can I get you?" I jumped at the sound of a woman's voice, my face red with mortification.

Wick leaned in. "If you're a good girl, I'll let you cum."

His voice was a whisper in my ear, so light that I knew only I could hear, but my body didn't care. The words sprung my nerves into action, my core already squeezing at the thought. He played it off like he wasn't palm deep inside of me, still gazing over his menu one last time, even as we both knew he didn't care what was on it.

Asa ordered first, Austin next. All the while, the pressure inside my body increased, the band wound tighter, waiting to release as I struggled to keep my breathing even and not moan right here in this booth with an audience. The waitress turned to me, expectantly, and I opened my mouth, but I couldn't get a single word out. Not when Wick's finger curved just right, rubbing seductively against my G-spot and stealing all thoughts from my head.

"I'll have the Ortega burger, double order of fries and an iced tea." Wick smiled at the waitress.

"Extra lemon. And you baby? What would you like?"

That fucking bastard. He couldn't just order for me, he wanted to make me suffer. He called it control, but the only person in control here was him, and we both knew it. I flexed both palms on the table and closed my eyes, trying to gather enough composure to get the words out. "I'll have-" Oh god, my voice was dry, barely scratching out as my chest rose and fell. "The Ortega. A side..."

Fuck him and his goddamn fingers because when he pressed his palm against my clit, his fingers curved, I nearly fucking lost my mind. "Go ahead, Mac. Order whatever you want, my treat."

Fucking god complex, he had.

"A side of fruit. Iced tea," I managed to say as my face burned with humiliation and my skin flushed with heat.

"She'll have a side of fries too." Wick smiled sweetly as he picked up our menus and handed them to the waitress.

The waitress's head tilted as she watched me. "Honey, are you alright? You're looking a little flush."

Every single one of the bastards snorted, their amusement clear. I gritted my teeth and tried to work through the sensations, ready to explode. "I'm fine. Just low blood sugar."

"It's her first day back at the gym, and *someone* clearly didn't eat enough to counteract that today."

Asa looked like he was scowling at me. "We'll take better care of her."

"Please do." The waitress's hand fell to her cocked hip. "Sometimes us girls don't do a good job taking care of ourselves when we're busy taking care of others."

"Don't worry," Austin added. "From now on, we've got her covered."

"I hope so." She tore the order off her pad of paper. "I don't want to see your friend here looking this flush again. It's worrisome."

Oh god. Please leave. I closed my eyes against the onslaught of sensations, knowing if she didn't leave in the next thirty seconds, I would orgasm right here in front of her and I'd never be able to eat here again. Hell, I wasn't even sure I ever would, anyway. "Thank you. I'm fine. Promise."

"Good. Your food will be out in twenty. I'll go get those drinks."

No sooner did she walk away that the orgasm took hold, rocking through my body like a wildfire, igniting every nerve and cell in its path ablaze. My body clamped hard against Wick's fingers, squeezing them tight and pulling them deeper into my body, as I curled toward him, burying my face into his arm as I gasped, trying to gulp air into my lungs as light danced against my vision and darkness crept in.

It wasn't until my body stopped pulsing and my muffled cries against him died that he pulled away, his hand leaving my body, causing me to miss them in their absence even when I knew damn well that I hated this man. He brought them to his lips, sucking them clean before he leaned down toward me. "Your control is still weak. You fucking bit my bicep."

I let my gaze fall to his arm and the teeth marks I left. I hadn't realized I was doing it, but I would have done anything to not moan and shout for the entire establishment to hear. I still couldn't process my thoughts, so instead I leaned my forehead down and closed my eyes, resting against the very man I couldn't stand.

A clank on the table brought me out of my daze as the waitress sat down our drinks. "Better drink up, honey, you're looking worse than before."

Then she sashayed away, while Wick's chest rose and fell with a silent laugh.

CHAPTER SEVENTEEN

WICK

Maybe I get high on power, I don't know. Is that even a thing? But each time I caused pleasure to rack through Mac's body, I felt invincible. It might as well have been my own release from the pleasure it caused me. Was that normal? Last week, this girl wasn't even on my radar. But the minute she said yes, the very second she became ours, she was all I wanted.

I forced her to watch as I ate my meal; her cum still soaking my fingers and adding the extra zing to the food that made me want to devour every crumb on my plate. When we finished, we took her home, stripped her body and placed her under the streaming water where we took turns cleaning her, washing her hair, drying her off and treating her like a proper housekeeper, like the lady that made our group whole.

"I'll show you to your room," I announced after I helped her get dressed, against her wishes, naturally, because the girl was as stubborn as they come. We couldn't possibly pick a girl who didn't fight us every step of the way.

"I have a room?" Her eyes widened in shock.

"Why wouldn't you?" Austin had her hair wrapped perfectly in a towel, the mound twice the size of her head.

"I don't know. I woke up with you this morning." Her brows scrunched together. "I just figured I had to share."

"Oh, you'll be sharing," Asa cut in. "But you deserve your personal space, too."

"That's..." She worked her lower lip between her teeth as she looked at us. "Considerate."

"It has no lock," Austin offered.

"She's lucky it has a door," I ground out. The thought of her shutting us out did not sit well with me. "I moved your things into it. We'll go shopping this weekend."

"No thank you." She spoke so quickly that I swear she hadn't even had time to think about the words I said.

"What do you mean, no thank you?" I growled. "I said we'll go shopping this weekend."

"I'm saving up," she admitted.

"Did I say you'd pay?" I reached up, toying with

one of those long strands of hair that had escaped her towel. "We're taking you shopping. Half your clothes are threadbare and ancient. Plus, we need a dress for the party."

"I..." That lower lip was going to bleed if she didn't stop. I let my thumb graze it before I pulled it free of its assault. "I'm okay. Really. My clothes are fine."

"It's almost winter. You've got two sweaters and no jacket. You're not fine. It's our job to take care of you, and if I remember correctly, you're down a dress. Consider it a replacement for the one I sliced up."

Her lips pursed thoughtfully. "Fine, I'll let you replace the dress."

"Okay. The dress," I agreed, knowing full well that we'd be replacing everything she owned, exactly to our liking, and she could argue all she wanted, but there would be no stopping us.

I took her hand, her palm warm in my own, and even though I squeezed hers tight, I didn't miss that she made no move to return the gesture. Was she mad about the diner? Because I could have sworn by the way her body milked my finger that she absolutely fucking loved the chance of someone catching her. Hell, I did too. Next time, maybe I'd have my cock out and her tiny little fingers wrapped around it for all to see.

After she fucking apologized.

I used my foot to kick open the door and my free hand to flip the light switch on, illuminating the room. She stepped in, her fucking mesmerizing eyes wide as she looked around her space. We'd worked hard on it, even before we knew she would be the girl living in it. With a black wooden four post canopy bed and a matching dresser, nightstand, and desk set, the room's mauve matte and gloss floral wallpaper popped as an accent.

We weren't ones for decorating. In fact, I would say we were all shit at it. But we'd tried, and we'd decorated minimally, hoping that she would put her own spin on her room. "If you hate it, we can change it. We just didn't want our housekeeper coming into a complete bachelor pad."

My stomach was in knots, and I knew Austin and Asa felt the same as we stood by, twisting inside, waiting for her to speak, to say something. Anything at all. Her fingers trailed over the velvety black bedspread before dancing over the mauve sheets. She touched a faux crystal lamp, turning it on and off before walking to the walk-in closet, then opening the door to the private bathroom that matched the room's color scheme.

"I've got a bathroom?"

"We all do." Asa put his hands in his pockets, probably to keep from fidgeting. "And the one you just showered in is shared, and for guests, not like we ever have any of those."

She spun around the bathroom , then took one more look at the closet before stepping back into the bedroom. She walked to the wall, her head tilted as her finger came up, stroking the lines of the black and grey roses. My heart might have stopped; my nerves were shot. When she finally turned around, she gifted us with a smile that was wider than any of us ever deserved.

"The painting is my favorite part." *Did I die?* "But I love it all."

"Wick ma—" I stomped on Austin's foot, stopping the words. I didn't want her to know that I painted that picture, that I did it just for her and had worked on it since the night of our first encounter at the student store, where her sassy mouth got me so riled up that I couldn't think. It took me three days, and yet I wish I spent three more because she deserved nothing but perfection. Austin corrected himself. "It's custom and our favorite, too."

"It's all yours, but if you don't like something, we'll change it," Asa reiterated. "We didn't know what you liked."

"Judging by her dorm room, she has no taste at all," I commented as I walked closer, way more comfortable with her scowl than her praise.

"That's unfair. You know they have strict regulations in there."

"You could have at least hung a poster," I pointed out.

"I- I didn't want to spend money on a poster," she admitted, and I hated the sad look that crossed her face, then the embarrassment that followed.

I never wanted her to feel that way, not with us. "Well, we'll get you whatever you like."

"At what cost?" she challenged, already aware that living with us would be anything but free.

I stepped closer until I was looking down at her. Her neck strained to look up at me. "A few orgasms here and there wouldn't hurt."

"I knew it would cost me.," she sighed.

"Your orgasms," I corrected. Her eyes burned with the possibility. I reached up, pulling the towel in her hair free before tossing it to the floor. Then I allowed myself a moment to let my fingers tangle with the wet strands. "I wonder how many I could draw out of you."

Her breath hitched. "I can't to—"

"Not tonight. We've got plans to make while you sleep. But soon. Soon I want to watch you wither from the pleasure and pain of too much, and beg for more. Who will give it? Austin? Asa? All three of us? Ever had three men at once, little vixen?" My voiced lowered. "Of course you haven't. You're practically a virgin still. Almost as pure as the day you were born, and ours to fucking corrupt."

Her eyes locked on Austin's and silently exchanged something. A glance at my friend told me he was guilty of something, and I didn't know what. "Was it him?"

"No. I've not had sex with any of you," she admitted.

"Then what was that?"

"What was what?" Austin asked.

"The look."

"There wasn't a look." He tried to lie to me, but he had forgotten I knew him better than anyone else.

"There was a fucking look."

"I saw it too," Asa confirmed.

"You both are delusional," Austin spat. "I can't even look at her now without accusations."

"You can look all you want. Fucking touch her for all I care. But there are no secrets among any of us, you fucking know that." I hated secrets. Secrets created divides, and we couldn't afford divides when our lives pended on trusting each other.

"It's nothing to do with us," Austin swore. "It's personal."

"There is no personal," Asa stated before I could. "We vowed that. Everything is always on the table. We haven't hidden anything from you. Ever. We'd like to trust you to do the same. If it's something that Mac knows, we all should know."

Austin looked like he might be sick, but I knew he'd confess. "Mac looked at me when you were talking about her being practically a virgin because Mac knows I am inexperienced."

"Inexperienced?" He couldn't mean...

"I'm a fucking virgin."

"You're lying," Asa shot back. "I assumed we all had fucked around."

"Have you ever asked me directly?" Austin was

getting antsy, clearly uncomfortable being the center of our scrutiny.

"No," Asa admitted. We had assumed Austin was like us, fuck boys tamed by the government.

"It makes no sense. You're hot. You're tall. You're lean, but the muscles are definitely there. Your cock is—"

"Are you writing his dating app ad?" I asked Asa.

This time it was Asa whose face turned to fire. I had wondered, more times than I'd like to admit, if Asa played both sides, and even if he never came out and admitted it, this cemented it for me. Asa definitely was into guys as much as he was into girls.

"You two will fuck," I announced. "And we're going to watch. Direct. Show you two how to have a fucking good time."

"Now?" Mac's hands twisted in front of her, nerves clear.

"No. But soon." I bent slightly, scooping her up to carry her into her bathroom, where I deposited her in front of the mirror. I reached for a comb in the drawer, then worked on the tangles in her hair. As silence drew on between us, I added, "I can't fucking wait."

CHAPTER EIGHTEEN

MAC

Living with the boys had been unexpected. A mix of sweet and tender tossed with sour and painful. Somehow, I craved it all, even knowing it was bad for me. The toxicity of the relationship was real, that was for sure. Wick controlled everything, and I pretended to fight it, but ultimately, I let him win because a part of me loved the control he had. Asa was the middle ground, a perfect mix of cocky and tender, whereas with Wick, I knew I'd get hard and demanding. With Asa, I never knew what mood he would be in. But Austin was always sweet, always caring, always concerned.

It had been two weeks, and I felt like it was the longest two weeks of my life. Like one big game of foreplay, taunting and teasing, bringing me to orgasm without fucking me to see how long before I would break and beg for it. I was close to breaking. I wanted to. But I refused to let Wick see any weakness in my desires. I refused to be the one to crumble first.

"Are you nervous?" Austin leaned against my door frame, looking way too handsome in a tux. I wasn't sure what type of event they were taking me to, but it had them on edge all day.

"Are you?" I turned, not hiding the fact that I was drinking in every inch of him. How had this become my life in two weeks' time? Austin Bruin, standing in my bedroom, practically eye fucking me. A far reach from sharing notes in the lab.

"I'm nervous because you guys seem nervous and that projects, you know."

He stepped forward. "Who said we were nervous?"

"Wick paced the living room for an hour, not even realizing I was there," I pointed out.

"Okay, we're a little nervous."

"When are you guys going to tell me what this all is about? What you guys are really?" I kept notes, though my notes were sparser than I wished they were. These guys hadn't given me much, but I was determined to come up with a story. Past the time I woke up in Austin's room the first night with them, I hadn't been able to explore their personal spaces or dig into their belongings, and it was frustrating, though I knew at some point I would have a chance.

I couldn't live in a place with three men and not snoop.

"Tonight," Wick answered for Austin as he appeared from the hallway, looking dreamy as his tux hugged the bulge of his biceps. "We have something for you."

"You always have something for me," I answered coyly.

"Your hair is down," Wick pointed out as he stepped closer.

His observation made my stomach tighten. I wasn't sure if he thought that was a good thing or a bad thing, but something in me wanted to please him. "I didn't think pigtail buns would work with this dress."

"I suppose not." His eyes roamed over me, turning to liquid. "I like it down. It's begging to be pulled."

Jesus.

He stepped forward, tugging on a curl of my long brown hair. "The dress is gorgeous on you, Mac, just like I knew it would be. It makes the green of your eyes pop and the curves it shows are begging to be touched."

"Thank—"

"Don't let anyone touch them," he cut off my attempt to accept a compliment.

"I wouldn't." I would be afraid to do so. Wick scared the fuck out of me, and I knew he would slaughter every single person who looked my way.

"They'll try. They will want to talk, pry information about us out of you. Be polite, but give them *nothing*." He enunciated his words, emphasizing that I needed to keep my mouth shut.

He stepped closer, his fingers completely intertwined with my hair now, his gaze on the locks that wrapped around his digits. "I'll behave," I promised.

A smirk curved his lips, even when his eyes weren't looking at me. He was always so mesmerized by my hair, always finding a reason to touch it. "Oh, I know you'll behave, little vixen. I just want you to understand that the stakes are high, and we can't afford for you to fuck up. If you fuck up now, you're dead by the end of the night. Do you understand that?"

He finally looked up into my eyes. His words pounded through my skull. "I understand."

"Good." Asa walked into the room. Asa, without a tux, was drop dead gorgeous. With a tux, nearly deadly on the eyes. "Are we almost ready to go?"

He stopped when he spotted me. "Mac." He breathed out the words in an exhale. "That dress is magnificent on you."

"You boys act like you didn't pick it out." I leaned against the arm of the chair I was standing next to. "I've never owned anything so nice."

The admission was hard to make, but it was the truth. Since my parents' death and entering the world of foster care, I was lucky to have a secondhand dress, never something new and of this quality.

Asa's hand wrapped around my hip, squeezing it before he pulled me, not asking but taking a kiss, devouring my lips and turning my insides to putty before he pulled away slowly. Speaking against my mouth, he said, "I'll buy you all the nice things. All you need to do is ask."

"I know," I whispered.

But I never would ask. They spoiled me enough as it is. They took me shopping against my will and loaded me up with things, not taking no for an answer, and I was fighting them every step of the way while deep down, I was loving it. Loving the attention they gave me and absorbing each one of their likes and dislikes, filing them away for later. My wardrobe was a mix of things they picked, and since that day, I'd made it a point to wear something from each of their styles.

Even now, the dress was picked by Asa. The color, a compromise by Wick. And the necklace and earrings that adorned my skin were hand-picked by Austin. My heels were an argument and compromise by all three, and I sat back and watched, fascinated at how well these men worked together.

Austin stole me away from Asa, his eyes burning hot. "Try not to separate from us tonight."

"I don't even know where we're going. How the hell will I promise I won't separate?" I sassed.

"Promise us." Wick pulled my hair, forcing me forward to kiss him.

These men were too much. "I promise."

"Good." Wick stood straight. "We've got you something."

"You got me a lot already, and I couldn't possibly accept more," I stated.

"You didn't accept what we got before," Asa pointed out. "This is no different."

"That's true." Wick reached into his pocket. "But this is a requirement."

"Requirement?"

He held out a mask, intricately painted, with crystal accents. "Wear this. We will all have masks on. This one will be yours. As our lady, it's an honor to wear a mask that matches ours." He held up his mask. Their masks were a more masculine version of my own. "Every event, you will need this one. We don't show our faces. We don't make friends. Understand?"

My fingers grazed over the details. "Did you guys make this?"

Wick ignored my question. "Do you understand?"

"Yes."

"Good." He gripped my chin, dragging me in for a kiss. When he pulled away, he forced my eyes to his. "We will keep you safe, I promise with my life."

That was a nice promise — an alluring, romantic one even. Except I didn't even know what they thought I was in danger *from*. So far, the only danger I'd been in were the workouts that Wick forced me to endure every morning and sometimes in the afternoon. There was no question how that man got so built, but I would prefer to stay a little on the chubby side. I wasn't built for these five-mile runs, even if they were getting slightly easier.

Austin drove while I was smashed between Asa and Wick in the back seat. They parked on a street lined with black cars and trucks in a part of town I was sure I'd never been. Wick's fingers gripped mine as I walked up, while Austin's hand guided my back, and Asa looked like a guard dog, ready to chew anyone apart.

"Church? You're taking me to church?" I asked.

"It's not that simple." Asa's eyes were everywhere but on me. "Religion is a falsehood created by men who wanted power. The biggest power is the power to persuade the weak minds of others. Churches are never just churches; they all have secrets they'd never let see the light of day."

"So, this isn't a church?" I was confused.

"It was," Austin offered. "Once." He leaned over, his lips so close to my ear that gooseflesh rose on my skin. "Now it's full of sins."

"You're taking me to a sex club?" I gasped.

"Worse." Wick's hand squeezed mine, and I was suddenly hanging on to his for dear life. "It's a club of death."

"Death?"

"Every man in that room has killed on contract," Austin offered. "And the women will one day too."

Killed? My mind raced, trying to take notes on what they had admitted. The men beside me, killers?

They had said as much, but I wasn't positive they hadn't made that up as some sort of scare tactic to keep me in line. I couldn't imagine Austin hurting anything, not when he was as gentle as they came. Hell, killers didn't draw bathwater, did they? Unless I was about to be their victim.

I panicked, suddenly digging my heels into the ground, refusing to take another step. "I can't go in there. You're going to kill me and—" I tried to shake my hand free of Wick's, but he was so strong, I had no hope. I'd only be released if he decided to do so, and he wasn't willing to at this moment.

"Calm down. No one is going to kill you." I swore he rolled his eyes at me, annoyed at my panic. "You're going to join us."

"Join you?"

"We needed a housekeeper, remember? You're part of the team now. But remember, talk to no one, give nothing away. If you make it through tonight, you're safe for another month, at least."

"Another month?"

"We'll talk about it later," Asa said. "I don't want to be late."

"Glad to know my fears are insignificant to you." I crossed my arms, trying to ward off the chill I felt, which had nothing to do with the weather and everything to do with the fear that wracked my body.

"Your fear is immaterial because we are confident we can and will protect you," Wick stated. "Stop being stubborn and let's go."

Easy for him to say. He's not the one who might be in danger. "Why should I trust you?"

"Why wouldn't you trust us is the real question." Austin's eyes burned into me. "When have I given you a reason to not trust me?"

"When you were part of a secret organization for our whole friendship, and I found out when you lured me to a bar, drugged me, then assisted in my abduction and captivity."

He pulled his lip between his teeth. "You know what? Maybe we have some issues to work through."

"You think?" My words were dripping with sarcasm.

"Little vixen, if you behave, I promise it will be worth it." Wick's lips were on my neck. My thoughts suddenly vanished. "If you misbehave..."

He didn't finish the sentence. He didn't need to. I'd learned over the last few weeks all the ways Wick could punish me for misbehaving, and each one of them was not discouraging me from acting out. But I had a feeling that this time, the sweet torture would be more intense, teetering on the brink of breaking me.

"It's about to start," Asa announced.

"They won't start without us," Austin reassured him before his gaze found mine again. "But being the last in puts a target on us. It shows weakness. An inability to balance our lives, and that means they will come for you first."

"He's right." Wick grabbed my hand, not caring

that I was practically stumbling to match his long strides. "I don't want to be the last in that room."

Funny, because I didn't want to be in that room at all.

We stepped through the double doors all at once, the black room warm with lit candles and crystal chandeliers. For a moment, I swore all eyes were on us, watching our every move until Wick moved first, squeezing my hand to reassure me as he led me through the crowd of men in tuxes. Everyone had a mask, but none were nearly as masterful as the matching set that donned our faces. In fact, aside from ours, few had decorative details at all.

Wick led me to the edge of the room, to an altar that was lit with dripping thick candles and scattered with rose petals. He dropped my hand and knelt down, before muttering a few words, tapping a statue and standing. The others followed, copying his motions, until all three had knelt and there was only me left standing in confusion.

"Kneel," Austin ordered, his hand pushing me. Then his voice rumbled in my ear. "On the lives I've sworn to protect..."

He waited, so I spoke the phrase. "On the lives I've sworn to protect..."

"I offer my loyalty, my love, my life, for one more day."

The whisper of his words danced against the shell of my ear, and I shivered before repeating, "I offer my loyalty, my love, my life, for one more day."

His hand grabbed mine, our fingers intertwining as he stretched my arm out, forcing me to tap the statue. It was a miniature replica of the Washington monument, a one-foot-tall obelisk made of granite. Before I pulled my fingers away, Austin whispered, "We're pledging our loyalty to the states, to our founding fathers, to those in need of protecting. Threats seen and unseen."

I was still kneeling when I turned my head to look at him; the candlelight making his eyes pop. "Why?"

"The world is cruel, dangerous, sick. Every day, people work to protect it."

"I don't understand." And I absolutely didn't. I understood that this world sucked. But that's why we had the first responders, police, firemen, the whole string of government entities.

"People in power sometimes abuse it. It's our job to stop them."

I was still confused, but Wick leaned over, his hand on his knee as he whispered into my ear. "We're the Saints, baby. Specialized Agents in Intelligence and National Tactics. The elite, recruited right out of high school to train to be the best, and we've passed all our training. Our reward? You."

My head spun, the shock of the information too much for me to handle. How had I been training with government agents while having absolutely no clue about their existence? And yet, here I was, pledging myself as they had, volunteering my life to the government because... why? Because I wanted to write a story? Or because I had no one in my life to tell me no? I trusted these men, even when all my senses told me I shouldn't.

I should be terrified about what I had signed myself up for, and I was. But I also recognized that I was in it too far now to back down. They hadn't been joking that if I made it through tonight alive, I would be okay. They genuinely believed that. No wonder they were on edge all day, pacing back and forth and acting short with their tempers. They were nervous, more so than I was.

I stood, turning to see the crowd of people, finally recognizing a handful of other girls who stood out in their own dresses, their eyes wide through the masks as fear took hold. Did they know more than I did? Or had they also walked in tonight, blinded by a truth they never once imagined?

I glanced at my men, each of them suddenly the only comfort I had around me. Ironic, since they once were the beings I trusted the least, and now they were all I trusted in. I opened my mouth, my lips gaping as I struggled for words. Just when I finally formed a sentence in my mind, a statement of my fear, and was about to voice it, a gong rang out, radiating through the high ceiling of the church, echoing painfully in my ear and causing the room to be blanketed in silence.

CHAPTER NINETEEN

AUSTIN

She knew the truth.

Knowing this meant I could breathe easier. I had stressed about it, worried that when she found out, she'd panic, run, turn and rush out of the church in search of sanctuary. Did she know that there was no sanctuary for a job like ours, though?

The gong sounded, and I took her hand in mine. Nerves danced everywhere she touched. We arrived on time, thankfully. Enough time to make our pledge, but not enough time for her to talk. We didn't want her to talk. Though I knew we couldn't avoid conversation forever. It would come soon enough, but not before the first sacrifice.

We followed the people, gathering toward the church's pews, though I knew Wick preferred to stand. Sitting made an easier target and gave less time to react to a threat. The room was nothing but threats to us, especially since Mac joined us. These men, our brothers, were temporarily our enemies, and by the end of these trials, some would die. I hoped none of them were us.

"We are gathered here this evening to honor those before us, those after us, and those men right now who risk their lives for the good of the people. We do not work for the government; we are the government of the people. Today, we welcome in our housekeepers and we wish you luck in the upcoming trials. Some of you may die, and for that, we honor your sacrifice."

There were gasps, all from the females, as the words sunk in. They would die, most likely, but Mac? If she was dead, it meant every one of us were dead because we'd protect her with our dying breaths.

Jones stood in front of the group, droning on about the organization and what to expect, and I listened to none of it, my eyes locked on Mac the entire time, trying to read her reaction, gauge her fears so that I could comfort her and ease the worry I knew she had. She watched in fascination, her brows scrunched together like she was trying to piece together a mystery that she didn't have all the clues to.

Beside her, Asa stood, his eyes hard as he scanned the crowd. He no longer trusted a single soul, and he had reason not to. We should have a month left of training, but that didn't mean people wouldn't cheat. It was the cheaters, the ones who didn't play fair, didn't follow the rules, that we needed to be cautious about.

"There will be a brief break before our teams bring forth their housekeeper and pledge their lives to them. But before we enter the break, I call forth Team Martinez." The team stepped forward, their housekeeper clutched between them like she was protected from the room full of assassins just by using them as a shield. "Today, you were late."

Martinez bowed his head but didn't deny it. "We were, sir."

"A part of our jobs is to be on time. Our schedule can be important. Miss a moment, a second, and it could throw off an entire mission. Are you aware?"

"Yes sir."

"Moore," the man shouted, and I flinched.

Wick stepped forward, walking causally to the podium, though I could see the tension in his shoulders. When he arrived, he stopped a few feet away. "Yes sir."

Mac's hand crept toward mine, linking our fingers together. Her hand shook, her fear clear. I squeezed her hand, hoping she understood Wick was fine. He would be okay. As long as our whole team wasn't called, everything was under control.

"You're the best in your class of trainees, are you not?"

"I'm sufficient," Wick replied.

"And modest," Jones said. "What happens when a housekeeper arrives late for their premiere ceremony?"

Wick's throat worked. "They die, sir."

"Good." Jones reached over to the podium and picked up a thick blade, handing it to Wick. "Do the honors."

"No!" Mac gasped, and Asa wrapped an arm around her, placing his chin on her shoulder, holding her stiffly in place.

"Shh," Asa hushed her, trying to stop the emotions. "He has no choice, Mac. If he refuses, they take you in her place."

"He can't," she began. "He wouldn't."

"He will, he has, and he'll do it again for the rest of his life because this was what we signed up for." I brought her hand to my lips and kissed her knuckles. "It's okay to close your eyes."

With little hesitation, Wick reached up, taking the hair of the girl in his palm as her body dropped, going limp. She screamed, crying as mascara dripped down her face, and though she tried to fight it, she was nothing compared to Wick. Her men argued, voicing their dismay, trying to fight through the bodies that suddenly appeared, blocking them from her rescue. We were helpless as we watched, not like we could stop it, anyway. They knew what was at stake, and they still arrived late. It was a risk. They took it.

Wick tilted her head back as another scream tore

from her, sobs so loud they vibrated off the cathedral ceilings and nearly hurt my ears. His movements were quick as he pushed the blade through her heart, cutting off the cries as her body slumped forward. He dropped her hair, and brought his hand to her shoulder, before pushing on her body while pulling the blade back. With the blade free, she fell to the floor, a slumped pile of flesh who would soon be forgotten by all but the team whose devastation replaced her cries.

The metal clinked against the stone flooring before Wick turned, not looking back as he stepped toward us, intent on joining his team. I didn't blame his haste. None of us liked to kill, despite how easily we could do it. But an innocent girl whose only fault was saying yes to a team who didn't prepare her for the possibilities was so much worse than an ordinary job.

We were guilty too. We hadn't prepared Mac enough for tonight, but she knew what was important. That if this night got fucked up, she'd die. She knew the risk enough. She had enough fear and sense not to question what just happened further. When Wick reached her side, she reached down, her fingers grasping the blood-spattered skin of his fingers, and brought his hand to her chest, hugging it to her.

It was the first time she'd ever shown him affection, the first time she was picking us, even though she spent so much time fighting against us, and Wick's face flickered with an emotion I didn't have time to read before he replaced it with something emotionless and neutral.

They dragged away the body, a streak of blood left in its wake before Jones approached the podium again, offering us refreshments and asking that we chat among ourselves before we present our females. I wasn't hungry, and I doubted Mac would eat, but still I turned to her when we were dismissed. "Would you like a drink? Some food?"

Her hand went to her stomach, like the thought of eating was too much for her to handle. "I think I'd rather get air."

"We can do that," Asa cut in. "Follow me."

We cut through the people, my hand not leaving hers and her hand not leaving Wick's until we had broken through thick double doors, coming out onto a nearly empty patio. When the doors shut behind us, cutting out the sound from within, Mac dropped both our hands before she turned to Wick. Her hands instantly went to his face, rubbing over his cheeks and turning his head like he somehow got injured instead of being the one who issued the death blow.

He batted her hand away. "I'm fine."

"I'm checking for myself," she whispered.

"I'm fine," Wick said again, stepping back.

"Not all injuries are visible," she observed.

She was right. Tonight, once the thoughts seeped in, Wick would hole up in his room and knock back his alcohol of choice, attempting to drown out what he did. It was expected and accepted among us because none of us enjoyed the kill. In the moment, the high was great, but alone, the images haunted us. We never forgot the look in the eyes, the feel of the blood, the smell of copper and death. It was the morbid reality of our lives, from which we could never escape.

Asa grabbed her arm midair as she was about to lean forward and coddle Wick more. He yanked her arm hard, pulling her back into his body, bringing her ear close to his mouth. "Not here, Mac. Never here in front of all the eyes that are no doubt watching through the windows. Emotions of the kill are a weakness. We can't show weakness."

Her hand dropped, instead wrapping around Asa's arm at her waist. "I didn't know."

"Now you do." Asa's voice was barely above a whisper. "What happened in there... Wick didn't take pleasure in it, I hope you know." Wick had taken a few steps away, pretending to straighten his tux, while he ignored the drops of blood on his shirt and the sleeve of his jacket. "It put a target on our back, too."

"I don't understand."

"In the next month, we've got to train you harder. We have to train you hard because those people in there, they're coming after us, intent on trying to take you from us. If they capture you, they do as they wish with you. Often, it's a kill. It's to weed out the weak choices because we can't afford weakness in our organization. Those men will want payback for Wick killing their girl."

"He had no choice." She turned in Asa's arms, outrage clear.

"That doesn't matter. He made the death blow."

"How long am I in danger?" Her hands came up to Asa's shirt, her fingers gripping the material so hard I wondered if it would tear.

"Until the organization calls off the sweep."

"And when is that?"

"When you've proven yourself, when you're able to stay alive, when the number of housekeepers has been halved. No telling." I explained, "It's always varied in previous years, but about a month, I'd predict."

Asa leaned down, kissing her forehead, holding her tight in his arms. "Don't worry, we'll keep you safe."

"And if you can't?" She was practically abusing her bottom lip with worry.

"We die together. We won't be the group of men that stand back and watch their woman die. You should know that much about us by now."

Wick joined our group. His suit was straightened, though he could do nothing about the blood. He seemed collected, his focus back. "Team Martinez is going to hit us hard. We need to secure our home, triple the measures. She goes nowhere without us. I don't fucking care if it's the ladies' room. We're going inside too. Once she's officially initiated, they can't touch her, so we just need to keep her away from them until then."

He spoke like she wasn't right in front of him, sandwiched between his body and Asa's. She was so short he easily looked over her head as he talked directly to Asa. Asa nodded. "I'll put a request in tonight and hopefully by tomorrow we'll have our place secured."

"Good," Wick agreed, his head nodding. "That's good."

"We'll take shifts as we've been doing, taking her to class. And take her on any jobs we're sent to," I added.

"Yes. It will be good training," Wick said.

"Do you think they will strike before the official start is announced?" I asked.

"I wouldn't put it past them. It's what I would do. If anything happened to our girl, and I lived, I swear there would be nothing to stop me from getting my revenge."

"It will be fine." Mac closed her eyes as she gathered herself. "It will be fine."

"It will be fine," I promised.

"I'm not fucking around, Mac. You go nowhere without us. You're sleeping with me from now on." Wick was close to losing it, barely holding on to his sanity. He was spooked, and I don't know what Team Martinez said to him while he was at the podium, but he was terrified they would strike any second. I could tell by the look in his eyes, that wild fear that was barely contained.

She turned toward him. Standing on her toes, she reached up, grabbing his neck to pull him down. She laid a kiss on his lips. "I trust you."

He stood frozen, afraid to move for fear of spooking her. She rarely willingly kissed any of us. But Wick, the one she hated the most, the one she fought with out of spite? It shook him more than the death he just issued. Maybe it was the words, the confession she spoke that went against all the actions she'd displayed until this point. Or maybe it was that, for once, she had made a move, not him. But his hand gripped the nape of her neck, holding her so tight that she couldn't move before he crushed her lips to his, devouring her soul right in front of our eyes.

He kissed her hard, nearly smashing her up against Asa as he closed in on her, not bothering to stop, or take a breath, until the gong sounded, calling us back inside. When he pulled away, his chest was heaving, and the space he granted her was hardly enough to move. He closed his eyes for a second, gathering himself before he spoke. "When we get in there, I want you to do as they ask. If you resist, you die. If you argue, you die. You know too much to let you go now. You understand, right?"

"What do they have planned?" she whispered.

Another gong radiated from within. He didn't have time to talk. I urged them on, not wanting her to be the next female with a knife to the heart. "We've got to go."

"It's just the initiation, Mac. Remember that. We've all done it."

Then Wick took her hand, pulling her through the patio and into the double doors, to the front of the church, where we planned to claim Mac as ours — and risk her life — because we selfishly didn't want to live our lives alone.

CHAPTER TWENTY

ASA

We weren't the last team to make it back into the room, and for that, I was thankful. Jones already proved that he's willing to start wars, take lives, and create divisions, even before the housekeepers were presented, making Wick set the example. He was shaken. It was clear. But I knew it wasn't the life he took, but more so what it represented. That girl could've been Mac, and we would have been powerless to stop it.

We lined up against the wall, our backs against the cold plaster. It was a protection, though it gave little comfort when the room was filled with men trained to kill in the most creative of ways. The third and final gong sounded, and with that, the heavy wooden doors slammed shut, sealing us inside.

"They're locking us in?" Mac's chest rose and fell rapidly, panic setting in.

"You'll be fine." I kept my voice low, hushed so that only we could hear.

"But—"

"We promised to keep you safe. Is that not enough? You said you trusted me," Wick pointed out, using her earlier words against her.

"And I do," she confirmed. "It's just... what if there is a fire? An emergency? A bomb?"

"Don't fucking say that word in here!" Austin hissed. "Do you want to set a room full of assassins off into savior mode?"

"It was theoretical." She hugged her body, her nerves putting us all on edge.

"You'll be fine. We're going up, taking an oath, doing their ritual, and we're out. We don't need to stay for longer than that."

"You promise?" She couldn't keep still. She was thrumming with energy.

"Pinky swear, princess." I held my pinky up to her, offering her the single digit like linking them would seal the deal. She reached up, linking her tiny finger with mine, only she didn't release it. Instead, she opted to hold it, bringing it down to her side and clinging to my finger for comfort.

Jones took the podium again, his mask consuming his entire face instead of the half mask we all wore. He tapped the sides of the podium, his eyes glancing over the crowd of people, and for a moment I swore he stopped, his gaze locked on Mac, before dropping it to the paper in front of him.

"Today we're welcoming in housekeepers in training. As you know by now, housekeepers aren't to be taken advantage of. They are to be utilized to the utmost ability and to be cherished with every ounce of our available emotions. They are a tool, like yourselves, and need to be treated as a deadly weapon, even when they appear to be anything but."

I glanced at Mac, trying to imagine her being a weapon like we were, and I couldn't see it. She was fierce, spicy with personality, but deep down, I saw the gentle soul. The one who tried to comfort Wick after they forced him to do something hard. The one who I had caught multiple times tutoring Austin, instead of sleeping. The girl who looked worried every time a female approached me, like they had even a minuscule chance of stealing me away. I couldn't use her as a weapon, even when I knew damn well that was what we were training her for.

"Housekeepers, teams, please come forth to begin the welcoming process." Jones spread his arms wide, gesturing to the steps in front of him, where people already gathered. I pulled Mac forward, following behind Wick with Austin trailing us, keeping her encompassed between our bodies as we headed down the sloped floor toward the front of the room.

The altar was lit with candles, the lights flickering and bright, casting shadows on the faces of those who already knelt at its steps. Wick found a place, his knees hitting the stone as he reached up, grabbed Mac's hand, and pulled her down. I took up her right, while Austin took her back, kneeling behind us and keeping her guarded.

Trust no one.

How I wished the mantra wasn't drilled into my head.

"Housekeepers, we gather you here before me because you are the chosen, the strongest among the applicants, the woman your team picked to join them. Have you agreed to be by their side?"

I forgot to breathe, my air refusing to escape the lungs that wouldn't contract as I waited for Mac to respond. There was a chorus of agreement, each one offered in succession until it reached Mac. She hesitated, sucking in her own breath before she finally let the word escape. "Yes."

The air whooshed from my body, my heart still pounding from the fear of her possibly denying us. When the last girl agreed to their acceptance, Jones continued. "It is an honor to join a team of elite operatives, an honor you should not take lightly. Their vow to you is stronger than anything you'd ever take in a church between spouses. It's sacred. It's sacrificial. It endures under the strongest of circumstances. Do you understand the severity of your integration with the men on your team?"

Mac's eyes were wide as she looked at me, then at Wick. If Austin weren't behind us, I knew that he too would have gotten the wide-eyed view. She was afraid.

Hadn't she realized we had her back, always? Figuratively, spiritually, emotionally... we would not let her fall.

"Yes." The word tumbled from her lips as the other woman agreed, and I wondered if they were scared like she was. They'd be crazy not to be. Hell, I was scared, and I wasn't the one in question here. I was already in too deep to back out. I'd already completed my training, already made my kills. There was no going back for me.

Jones walked the line of people before taking some metal goblets off a table, pouring wine into each of them. We all watched and, though we knew what was coming, Mac didn't, and I wished we had taken the time to warn her. Instead, we watched wordlessly as Jones placed a goblet in front of each team leader before taking to the podium again.

"Knife out," he instructed before addressing the groups. "The vow we take today follows us to death and shouldn't be taken lightly. If you wish to retract your agreement to join the men next to you, speak so now or hold your peace."

Jones waited, looking at each group until he got to Mac and I swore he stared, waiting, expecting her to back down until finally, his gaze passed from her to the next female in line. No one spoke up, prompting him to continue. "Please speak the words with truth in your heart, or you will fail before you've fully started on this mission in life. If there is no trust, one cannot be confident in the people you choose at your side. Trust them, and trust that you can provide them with what they need when it's needed."

He cleared his throat after a pause, then began. "I vow, with my life, to respect my family, the ones chosen not by blood, but by the power of my own self-worth."

We repeated his words, a chorus of men and woman speaking. We continued on, repeating every word he spoke, every vow, everything that would tie us to the girl at my side without a single regret in my heart. She was ours; we knew it from the moment we had her chained and at our mercy, and her vows now only confirmed it. We were hers too.

"Gentlemen." As the words were spoken, we all raised our blades we carried everywhere, slicing our palms. Some girls gasped, but Mac only looked on in shock as blood pooled in our hands. Wick picked up the goblet, dripping blood into it before passing it to Austin, who did the same. The goblet was passed to me, and I emptied my life force into the wine before holding it out, waiting.

Wick took Mac's hand, his eyes never leaving hers as he unfurled her fingers, displaying her palm. He held her gaze as he raised his hand, slicing into the tender flesh there. She flinched, but didn't look away from him. I took her hand, dripping the wound over the goblet, letting her blood join the mix of ours.

"With the consumption of this wine, you're agreeing to the bond between your team, putting them first, above all else. Agreeing to risk your life for theirs, to step into danger to remove them from it. You're giving your consent to remain at their sides, for the rest of their lives and yours, until death do you part. And it will come for some sooner than others. That is the cost of this job."

There were a few nods of understanding, but mostly everyone remained still.

"Drinking the blood signifies a new bond, one deeper than you were born with, and forged by your own making. Take them into your body, as they will do for you, accepting every part of them, without judgment or reservation. You may drink."

Wick was the first to lift the goblet to his mouth, talking a few gulps of the wine that mixed with our blood before handing the goblet to Austin. He sipped it quickly, handing it to me. Mac watched as I tilted the metal cup back, drinking the blood mixture, leaving just enough for her. I swallowed it, not caring that the wine did nothing to hide the metallic taste.

Wick took the goblet before putting it in her uninjured hand. "Drink."

Her eyes burned, an intensity I'd never seen flickering in them, before she tilted her head back, dumping the remaining contents into her mouth and swallowing it down, not even gagging like some of the other females around us were. She pulled the goblet away, a drip of wine slowly dribbling from her corner of her lip. I couldn't resist. I leaned over, licking off the droplet before capturing her lips, kissing her until Jones's voice forced me to pull away.

I couldn't concentrate on the rest of the ritual and what they said. The blood danced around in my system, making me hard, thrumming with energy I needed to release after seeing her drink our blood and claim us like we had so thoroughly been claiming her. I wanted to get her home. I wanted to get her naked. I wanted her to ride my cock, suck it, make me spill my cum until her whole body was sticky and painted with it.

When we were finally released, I was probably the first one up, but I wasn't as fast as Austin, who already had her hand, dragging her away from the altar and through the crowd of people. I had only made it three steps before Jones's voice interrupted Wick's and my departure.

"You were the only group to have a man sit behind your housekeeper. Why?"

Wick and I turned, our bodies giving nothing away even though nerves were eating us alive. "If we aren't protecting her back, we aren't protecting her at all. You and I both know the loss of Martinez's housekeeper put a target on our backs and hers."

"Your housekeeper understands what's at risk, does she not?" he questioned.

"Don't all of them?"

He nodded thoughtfully. "Never leave her back unprotected. They might get their housekeepers killed, but you will not. Understood?"

Wick tilted his head to the side, staring at Jones

in confusion but not voicing it. "We weren't planning to get her killed, sir."

"Good. Keep it that way. It's your job to protect her until the organization halts the attempts to assassinate and harm her. You will vow to do so at all costs."

Was that an order? It seemed so odd. Still, we both nodded before Wick spoke. "We will. As agreed on by our oath and our loyalty to her, we'll protect her at all costs."

"Good." Jones nodded. "Very good. Work on Mackenna's left hook. It's weak. Enjoy your night."

Jones walked away, and we stared after him until he disappeared through a doorway. I waited until he was out of sight before I turned to Wick. "What the fuck was that?"

"I've no clue, but let's get the fuck out of here."

I couldn't agree more. We found the exit, searching for Mac and Austin, finding them under a tree, waiting for us. *Smart, keeping her back to the tree, adding protections when we weren't there to help.* Upon approaching, they said nothing, only followed us to where we parked, all of us ready to fucking blow this place off, get home, and breathe again. Only it wasn't until we pulled away that I remembered we never gave Jones the name of our housekeeper, only her specs. Names weren't given until she passed her test, so how the fuck did he know the name of our girl?

CHAPTER TWENTY-ONE

MAC

I was terrified of what I just signed on to, but as terrified as I was, deep down I didn't regret it. It felt right. Which was odd since everything in my life had always felt slightly off kilter. As we pulled away, I looked back over my shoulder, peering through the glass at the people who still milled about the yard, chatting and talking, belonging.

I'd never belonged.

Never wanted to belong.

Until these men claimed me as theirs and stated I belonged to them.

This was an assignment. I knew that. I knew that from the start. I wanted to write my final paper on the Saints; I wanted to expose them, become the amazing journalist my mom once was, and tonight, I think I had gotten more than enough to get started on my piece. But in this moment, I didn't want to. Instead, I got this crazy urge to cuddle up to these men, to feel their skin against mine, and to get lost in all the pleasures I knew they could bring.

It was animalistic, I knew. Stemming from the blood of theirs that coursed through my body, heating me up and taunting me. Drinking blood was taboo, but when I gulped down the sweet metallic liquid, it felt nothing but right. My nerves came alive, and a slight thrum of arousal pulsed between my thighs. It awakened me, made me feel on edge, had me wanting things I shouldn't just because I'd tasted the most intimate part of them.

"You okay?" Austin asked from beside me, his hand on my thigh, making it burn and forcing me to fight the urge to squirm.

I swallowed hard, trying to force the lump in my throat away. "I'm..."

I let the words trail off because there was no valid description of how I was. Good seemed so under- whelming. Elated didn't quite capture how I felt. Instead, I leaned into him, letting my hand find his cheek before I kissed him. His body was stiff for a moment, his mind not comprehending that my lips were on his, devouring and sucking, begging for him to kiss me back. But then it registered, and a little growl escaped his lips before he turned us, pinning my body against the seat as he took control of the kiss I initiated.

"Fuck," Asa cursed breathlessly beside me before he leaned forward, hitting the back of the driver's seat. "Drive faster."

I faintly heard Wick ask, "Why? We aren't being followed."

"Because if this turns to fucking, I don't want to be exposed in the back of the fucking vehicle," Asa spat. There was a pause before the tires squeaked and the vehicle under us accelerated.

They spoke more, but I couldn't concentrate on what they said. All I could think about was the feel of Austin's body against mine and the softness of his lips. Had they always been this soft? I hadn't noticed. But I'd never really kissed him, not like this. Not so willing and all-consuming.

His hand skimmed up my thigh, the silk of my dress bunching up in his palm as he moved his lips to my neck. I arched into him, wanting to feel his whole body against my own, wanting the heat to consume me, wanting it to match the fire in my blood.

What was I doing? This wasn't like me. Hell, this wasn't like either of us. We were the innocent ones in the group, the ones who really had no fucking clue what we were doing and were just along for the ride. And when my hand skimmed against his crotch, that ride promised to be something fierce.

The vehicle turned, forcing my weight into Asa and breaking me away from Austin. I tilted my head up, my eyes meeting Asa's, and there was a pause, one heavy with indecision, before he leaned down and stole my lips. He kissed me with such ownership I nearly forgot Austin was there until his hand grazed against the apex of my thigh, causing a shiver to course through me.

"Fuck." Wick's curse broke through my thoughts. "We're almost fucking home."

Home.

I hadn't had a home in longer than I could remember, but somehow it felt right for it to be with these men. It was the blood talking. It had to be. Nothing made sense right now. Was I drugged again? I had to be. Maybe that wasn't really wine.

"I was drugged, wasn't I?" I muttered against Asa's lip. "The wine."

We pulled to a stop, and before Asa could answer, Wick was out of his seat and had the backdoor pulled open, lifting me into his arms. But he must have heard my question because amusement lit his face. "No baby, this is all you. You liked it, didn't you? Drinking down our blood like delicious nectar. Can you feel it? Feel the power it gives you, gives us?"

My eyes locked on his, my mind not caring who shut the car doors and who opened the door to our house. All that mattered was we were inside, and the lock turned and...

I reached up, threading my fingers into the short strands of Wick's hair before yanking hard, fueled by the growl that tore from his lips as I pulled his head to mine. "You're not fucking kissing me."

"Is that what you want?" he asked, taking the

steps two at a time and pausing at the top, looking at all the doors, not sure where to take me.

"Mine," Asa instructed, pushing open the door to his room.

"If I didn't want it, I wouldn't have demanded it." I pulled again, getting my point across by yanking on his hair, but he refused to budge. I paused, confused. Hadn't Wick been the one so open about what he wanted, so demanding, and now I couldn't even get him to kiss me? Something I oddly craved more than anything else.

He walked me to Asa's bed, a king size right in the middle of the room, covered in a black duvet. I should have known Asa's room would be shaded in black. It was fitting for the man who was dark and mysterious, the one whose dark soul drew all the girls in, having them begging to be his light.

Wick released me, dropping me unceremoniously onto the mattress, causing a squeal to leave me. I was about to argue, beg him not to do whatever he was plotting because my mind and body couldn't take it, not now. But then he barked Austin's name, calling him toward us.

"Take off your clothes," he ordered Austin, and when his eyes met Asa's, he told him, "Get her naked."

I didn't need his orders. I was perfectly capable of getting myself naked. In fact, there was nothing more I wanted to be in this moment than sans clothes in front of these guys, but when I shimmied my dress up my hip, Asa's hand batted away my own. "That's my job."

His hand replaced mine as he pushed my dress up, his lips trailing up my thigh and meeting the material at my hip as he did so. Such a gentle touch, and yet it had my core clenching and my chest heaving. My mind begging his lips to explore other places. The silk moved up my stomach as he teased me, his tongue swirling into my belly button before leaving a wet trail toward my breast.

My shoulders lifted enough for the material to be removed before he tossed it into a rumpled pile on the floor. How stark it was, the shade of green, vibrant in the sea of black decor. With my clothes gone, his palm lay flat on my stomach as his eyes devoured me. "You should go braless more often."

"Only when the clothes demand it." I gasped as his fingers danced against my skin before plucking at my nipple.

"I'll make sure they demand it," he stated before leaning over my body, taking my nipple into his mouth and toying with the sensitive bud with his tongue.

"Austin," Wick barked. "Why the fuck are you standing there? Get naked and show our girl what it's like to have all of us. Show her why she chose to keep three men instead of one. Let's show her what it's like to cum so hard she nearly passes out."

They all lost their clothes, faster than my eyes could track. The bed dipped as Austin's knee hit the mattress next to me and his head replaced Asa's hand. His mouth took the place of the fingers that had been strumming my nipple into a hard peak. My body arched into the warm heat of their mouths, not realizing that Wick's body was between my legs until his fingers grasped my thighs, forcing them wide before his mouth was against my skin, his tongue spearing into my body, making a cry leave me.

"We're making you ready, baby." Wick's words were broken up. His movement never faltered as he spoke against my core, the vibration causing delicious jolts of pleasure to bolt through me.

He moved his tongue upward, finding my clit and lapping against the bundle of nerves, letting the flat of his tongue glide over it in an unrelenting rhythm that made my body squirm, desperate for more, begging for less. I was delirious, confused about what I wanted, not knowing what I needed to make this pleasure peak.

"Are you going to ride him?" Wick questioned before I moaned so fucking loud, I hadn't even known I was capable. I'd never been loud in my previous limited experience, but I should have known that with these boys, I couldn't hold back. Hadn't they already proven that with the wild responses they'd already torn from me over the last few weeks?

"Answer me, baby, and I'll let you cum," Wick demanded, his fingers pushing into my body, already causing my muscles to contract. God, I loved the feeling, loved the fullness he brought to my body, and the sparks that the lips and tongues on my nipples pulled from me.

"Yes," I gasped as he pushed another finger into me, stretching my channel, prepping me for what was to come.

"Good girl." He bit my clit, the feeling tearing a scream of pleasure from me, causing me to teeter on the edge, placing me right there between pleasure and pain, dancing on the edge of release. And I wanted it. I was practically begging for it as I gyrated my hips against his face, using my hands to hold Asa and Austin's heads in place, not caring if they breathed or not.

"Again," I demanded.

"You like that, baby?" Instead of giving me what I asked for, his tongue gentled against me. "You dirty girl. You like it rough. You like the pain, don't you?"

I didn't respond. My only thought was how to get him to pick up his pace, to not lose the orgasm I knew was building. I tilted my hips, but he pulled away as I moved forward, refusing to give me what I needed.

"Did you like that, baby?" His words were hard this time, his breath teasing against my skin, and I was about to cry from the loss of him and his rhythmic tongue, coaxing pleasure from deep within my core.

"Yes," I gasped, a tear running down my cheek at the intensity of feelings that were overwhelming my body.

At my confession, he bit down again, and my body released, my thighs clamped up, holding his head hostage as the orgasm hit me with waves of pleasure, the intensity so strong that I hadn't even realized my nails were biting into Austin and Asa's necks until I felt the slightly sticky drops of their blood against my fingertips. But I didn't release them, I couldn't. All I could do was feel as Wick's fingers pumped into my body and my body clamped down, begging to keep them, begging to be filled with something more.

"That's it," Wick praised as he gave my clit another bite, this one slightly softer as my body relaxed and the orgasm ebbed. "So fucking beautiful when you cum." He whispered more words of praise and encouragement as I slowly came down from my orgasm, and my fingers relaxed, releasing the boys from my grasp and freeing Wick from my thighs. And right before blackness consumed me, he whispered one more time against my skin, "That's our fucking girl."

CHAPTER TWENTY-TWO

WICK

I nearly lost my shit in front of the whole fucking organization. But the thought of Mac's body falling on the floor, blood spouting from a wound, was too fucking much to handle.

It wasn't her.

I was thankful for that.

But next time, it could be, if we didn't get our shit together and work as a fucking unit. A unit that included Mac being trained to the best of our ability. Jones didn't need to warn us to watch her back. It was going to be the only view I had for the foreseeable future. Not like looking at her ass would be a hardship. Not when her ass formed the most perfect heart that called me to fall to my knees behind her and let my teeth sink into her skin.

I pushed my worry down, forcing my hands to steady as we knelt as a group at the altar, drinking down the mix of blood and wine, feeling the weirdly pleasant buzz under my skin. It couldn't be over soon enough. I just wanted to get our girl home, train her, protect her, breathe everything that is Makenna until I was positive that she could hold her own against any threat that might glance her direction.

I expected the possessive want in the boys after the ceremony. It was fucking natural. But Mac making the first move, practically devouring Austin in the back seat, wasn't what I anticipated. I couldn't take my eyes off them. I didn't want to. Just watching the innocent make out session between them had my cock so fucking hard I wished I could pull over and join.

They both were so fucking inexperienced, and that held some appeal to me, calling to all my controlling instincts to watch them fumble and find their way, learning how to take their pleasure and offer it too. It was irresistible, like a movie I couldn't help but replay, watching repeatedly. I filed the memory away for later, sure I'd call on it again, maybe in the shower while I stroked my dick, thinking of them both.

It wasn't enough though, not the memory of them kissing or the taste of her still fresh on my lips. I wanted more. I didn't care that she collapsed from exhaustion, that her orgasm made her lose conscious-ness, or that her body still shook. She was ours. She fucking said so. She'd do as I asked, follow my demands. She's Team Moore now, the strongest of teams, with the strongest of leaders. Me.

"Wake up." My fingers buried into her hair, pulling at her scalp hard enough to tear her from her sleepy, sated daze. "We're not done fucking you yet."

Her eyes opened slowly, the haze clearing when she realized it was my fingers digging into her scalp, forcing her eyes open. I looked over my shoulder at Austin, issuing instructions. "Scoot back against the headboard. Our girl is going to ride you, just like she promised."

Austin scooted back, his back hitting the black wooden headboard as Mac sat up, her face unsure as she looked between us. She'd clearly never done this before, but neither had he, so it was perfect for them both. "You agreed to be ours."

I probably didn't need to point it out. She knew what she agreed to. She's known this the whole time. "I know. I did."

"Are you on the birth control we discussed?" I fucking hoped so. I hated condoms.

"Yes."

She bit her lip, and it took every ounce of restraint I had not to lean forward and use my teeth to pull it free. "We're clean. You've seen our reports."

"I know."

"Then what's the issue?" I didn't want to pressure her, but the way she was going at him in the back of my car, I'd thought she wanted this. It had been weeks with us, and we'd made her come every way but with our cocks buried deep in her pussy.

She looked away for a moment, her eyes focused on the wall behind Austin before she finally admitted, "I'm just scared, that's all."

"Of us?" Asa's voice was gentler than I could have been. It was ridiculous. We'd proven time and time again that we were committed to her and everything about her. She had absolutely nothing to be scared about.

"I haven't done... that before?" Fuck. She really was the cutest, even when she was fighting me about every fucking thing.

"Good news." I smirked. "Neither has he. Remember, you held that secret for quite some time."

I was a little bitter about that. How had I not known one of my best friends was a virgin? Hell, it wasn't from looks, so it had to be by choice, and I couldn't fathom why a guy would do that to himself. The last few years in the organization excluded.

"Do you have to watch?" she asked, her hands ringing, nerves clear.

I laughed, the sound a hollow echo through the room. "Oh baby, we're not just watching."

"I... I don't understand."

"You will." I swatted her ass. "He's waiting."

She crawled over to him before swinging her legs over his hips and hovering over his erect dick. I knew she was wet enough for this. She was fucking soaked. Her juices still coated my skin. I may never shower again.

"Go ahead," I prompted as I reached between them, not giving a fuck as I held Austin's dick still so she could lower herself on him. His eyes closed, his breath came fast, and I knew he was nervous as fuck, but I wasn't judging shit. We'd all been where he was at before, even though I didn't have an audience.

She was slow as she lowered her body to his, trying to adjust to his width before bottoming out against his groin. I stretched her good, scissoring my fingers inside of her so that when this moment came, she'd have no pain, and judging by the look on her face, the pure bliss as Austin filled her, she was perfectly prepped.

I scooted forward, placing my hands on her hips as I straddled Austin's thighs, helping her move up and down as Austin's eyes closed tightly. I got it. The feeling of a wet pussy against a bare cock was unmatched. But he needed a distraction. I wouldn't have him coming in five seconds flat just because he had a near virgin, tight as fuck pussy sliding on his cock.

I knew I was pushing my limits. I didn't fucking care. I'd no clue how far I could push Austin, but I knew, or at least suspected enough about Asa that I hoped to not cross boundaries.

"Asa, by the headboard," I ordered. "Austin, open your fucking mouth. He can't suck his own cock."

Austin's eyes popped open and Mac gasped, but no one objected. Asa moved closer, his body tense, his eyes hesitant for a moment. There was a silent communication that passed between Asa and Austin, each of them unsure if they should cross a boundary that society had set for them. But fuck society. Hadn't society already told us the rules for relationships were one woman and one man? Yet here we were, rebelling against the normal and having Mac be all of ours, together.

Just when I thought I pushed too soon, maybe a little too much, Austin opened his mouth. His hand reached up to grip the back of Asa's thigh as Asa's hips jutted forward, his cock disappearing between Austin's lips. The sight nearly unraveled me, the moan that escaped them both practically my undoing.

Mac's body leaned back into me, her chest rising and falling as she watched them, and I knew that when I wrapped my arms around her body and dipped my fingers between her thighs, she'd be fucking soaked at the sight of them. I wasn't disappointed. "You're so fucking drenched, baby. You like watching our boys, don't you? Does it turn you on to see Asa shove his cock down Austin's throat?"

I am confident and uncaring enough to admit that the sight was hot. Explosive. A beautiful masterpiece in front of me. I let my fingers rub against Mac, teasing her clit, as my other palm skated against her stomach, traveling up to her breasts to give them a squeeze. "Don't fucking stop moving now."

I flexed my hips as she moved, using her ass to jerk myself off, stealing an ounce of pleasure that the three of them might be feeling. "One day, I'm going to take you here. You'll be screaming my name with every spasm your body makes."

"Oh god," she moaned. Her head lolled on my shoulder, her beautiful locks of hair tickling against my bare skin.

"You want that baby?" I teased her with my words, as my fingers teased her body, coaxing her closer to an orgasm as she rode against Austin's cock.

"Fuck," Asa panted, his head thrown back in bliss as Austin's hand disappeared, no doubt teasing Asa in other ways to get him to become this undone. His chest was heaving as he got words out. "I can't."

But he was, and he was doing it like they were used to fucking around together. I leaned forward, my hand grazing the expanse of Austin's chest as I spoke to him. "Suck him harder."

His cheeks hollowed as Asa's dick disappeared further into his mouth, making its home down his throat. Austin's hips bucked. The need to come was making him crazy, and I wanted to prolong it, to tease and torture him, but it wouldn't be fair, not when Mac's body was becoming tense and her breathing was more sporadic.

I increased my hips' movement, driving myself

repeatedly between the cheeks of her ass, making myself nearly dizzy with the lust, driving myself mad as my pre-cum soaked her backside, making the glide so fucking slick I slid effortlessly. The sounds of our pleasure mingled in the room, moans and grunts and words of praise, begs for more, until we were all strung right on the edge. A single pluck and we'd all stumble into bliss.

I reached up and dragged Asa by the hair to her mouth. Then I reached between Mac and Austin, pinching her clit, setting off the chain of orgasms. Her body seized up under my assault, her teeth biting into Asa's lip as her cunt milked Austin's cock, squeezing it so tight that he released his load on a gasp, one that Asa took full advantage of, shoving deeper into his throat and releasing. And when they were all coming down, their bodies loosening into limp limbs, I pumped my cock three more times before painting each one of them in my cum.

It was messy.

It was crude.

It was so fucking glorious I never wanted to forget the moment. I peeled Mac up, tilting her head to force my lips on hers, kissing her hard as my chest rose and fell, and when I pulled away, I couldn't help but take in every gorgeous detail of her, from her messy hair to the mascara that ran in black smears down her cheeks. Her lips were swollen. Her eyes were glistening, and I wanted to plunge my half hard cock into her body and work it to a steel rod again, but I resisted. Barely.

"You're so fucking ours. You're ours now, Mac." The words came out as a harsh grit of a statement. "Every fucking inch of you."

CHAPTER TWENTY-THREE

AUSTIN

"What are you doing?" Mac stood in the hallway, peering into the living room. Her hands were on her hips, her face pinched with annoyance.

"Cleaning." I hardly spared her a glance. I was in my zone, a place I loved to go to when my mind was overworked and my body was wound tight.

"You clean?"

"Who the hell do you think keeps this place looking so neat?" I shot her way. "Clearly not the housekeeper."

"I just..." She paused as her brows drew together. "I never thought of it, truthfully. I've been waiting for thirty minutes for you."

"I forgot," I muttered as I ran the sponge over the baseboard. I hadn't forgotten. I just hadn't wanted to be stuck in a room with Mac, studying, when all I could think about was the feel of her body milking mine and the euphoric taste of her skin. And that thought spurred thoughts of Asa, and what we did, what I allowed to happen and somehow didn't regret.

"Well, I'm reminding you now," Mac pointed out.

"How about you help me clean?" I grinned in her direction.

"How about you stop avoiding studying, like you've done all week, and just say what you want to say?"

I sighed. "I miss the simpler times when you were just my lab partner and you knew nothing about me."

"I still know practically nothing about you." She stepped into the room. "But I'm learning."

"Why is it so important I know this stuff?" I stood straight, my hands on my hips, my muscles in my back screaming thanks to Wick's workout he pushed on us this morning.

"Because we're lab partners," she reminded me.

"My grade isn't yours."

"But I care enough that I won't let yours be shit. Plus, I've got work tonight. We need to do it now or we won't have time."

"I seem to be busy now." I was hoping she'd give up, but knowing Mac, she wouldn't.

"Austin," she pressed, a warning in her voice.

"Mac," I teased.

"Please."

"When are you quitting your job?" I changed the subject.

"I'm not."

"Does Wick know that?" The mention of Wick's name had her face reddening.

"Fuck him." She spat the words out with venom. "He's not my boss."

"Only your protector." It was a gentle reminder. "He cares, you know that."

"In his own shitty way." She put her arms over her head and stretched. "My back is killing me, thanks to that prick."

Mine was too, but I didn't let on. "We have you taken care of financially, Mac. The organization should have you on the payroll as soon as you're permanent. You don't need that job."

But I saw the independent child in her rebel. The one who could trust no one but herself and couldn't believe the truth in my words. I saw this child because each of us had been the same way. Each of us had been let down so much in life that all we could count on was ourselves. I didn't want that for Mac. I wanted her to count on us. I wanted her to trust us instead of pre-planning the virtual strangers' couches she planned to surf for the next year once she graduated.

"I can't count on—"

"You can." My words were more forceful than I intended, and she flinched. I felt like an ass. I never wanted her to flinch away from me. Never wanted her to fear us. I closed the space between us, my palm nearly engulfing her cheek when I raised it slowly to her face. "Mac, you're one of us now. We'd give you anything."

She still looked doubtful when I leaned in and kissed her forehead. She jumped subjects quickly, using my vulnerability against me. "You've been avoiding me."

"I would never." I was actually.

"Was it because of what we did? Do you regret it?" Her voice was strong, but her words spoke of all the uncertainty. "You're my friend, Austin. And you're pulling away from me."

"I'm not pulling away," I reassured her, but my words were flat because maybe I was. "I'm just..."

"Ashamed? Regretful? Embarrassed?" She offered when I dropped the sentence, unable to figure out exactly which words I was looking for.

That she would think I felt any of those things blew my mind. "Never. Shit, Mac. I loved every second about what we did. I'd never be embarrassed or regret my time with you. Do you know I had a crush on you? The minute I first saw you sitting in that classroom with those fucking pigtail buns and all I wanted to do was hold them in my palms while I forced your head back to kiss you."

Her mouth formed a silent *oh*. "Then why didn't you?"

"Three years. That's how long we had promised to go celibate. Three years and ten bodies each got

us to this point. Endless training, endless team building. Learning each member of your team and
knowing them like you know yourself. No secrets.
We couldn't do any of that with the distraction of
sex. We couldn't even do any of that with the distraction of a female on the team because females, unin-
tentionally, are a distraction that we aren't strong
enough to resist until we've built up all our strength
together."

"Then what is it? If it's not me you're pulling away
from, why are you hiding?" I loved the fire in her eyes
when she confronted any of us. We could have her
writhing under us, crumbling to our will, but she was
still strong enough to give us shit, to push us. I
refused to let her join us at first because she was
mine, even if my infatuation was only one-sided. But
now I see what Wick must have seen this whole time.
Mac was made for us, and she was undeniably ours.

I closed my eyes and inhaled, then exhaled slowly.
No secrets. There should be no secrets between us.
Secrets break a team, but I wasn't fully ready to
address my feelings just yet, either. When I opened
my eyes and saw her blazing green eyes not backing
down from my own, I blurted out my truth.

"I'm confused."

"About us?"

"Never about you and I." I rushed the words out
as I let my eyes wander to the ceiling, looking toward
the room that I knew sat above where we stood.

"About Asa?"

I swallowed, wondering why the hell my throat was so dry. "I just, I guess I always knew he was bi."

"But you didn't realize that you could be too?" she finished.

She hit the nail on the fucking head. I'd never pictured myself with another man, but fuck, I couldn't even deny that I liked it. This was Asa, one of my best friends, and all I could think about the last few days, when I wasn't picturing Mac's body rising and falling against my own, was the salty taste of his cum sliding down my throat.

"He's my best friend," I stated.

"You can still be best friends."

"Not when every time I look at him, I think..."

I couldn't even voice what I thought, but she knew, anyway. "You think about what it was like and when you can do it again?"

"Yeah."

"I know the feeling." She stood on her toes, kissing my nose. "It was hot."

I felt her words ball into my stomach, lighting me on fire. "You thought so?"

"Mmhmm." She gave my nose one more peck. "Now finish this room, Mr. Clean, and then come study with me."

"Is that an order?"

"It's a demand."

She turned on her heels, stomping back up the stairs to her room, where I knew she had her note-books spread over her bed, the pages an explosion of colors. I loved that about her, loved that even her notebooks were color coded and the images inside were more art than graphs.

I waited until she was out of sight before I returned to my cleaning. My soul was a little lighter knowing that was off my chest and she didn't judge me for it. Though I knew at some point, I would have to talk to Asa. We'd have to discuss what happened between us. But I wasn't ready for that yet.

I finished the cleaning in twenty minutes, then I jogged upstairs to study with Mac. We spent twenty minutes going over scientific equations before the tension between us broke and we found ourselves naked, no longer caring about whatever studying we had planned for the rest of the night. No longer caring about anything but us.

CHAPTER TWENTY-FOUR

ASA

I felt it. Felt the stares following me around, the heaviness of avoidance, the words left unsaid, and I never thought I was a coward, until now. Until I spent every day for a week with my best friend and never once mentioned that my cock was in his mouth, and I didn't hate it. In fact, thoughts plagued me of when I could do it again.

"We've got an assignment," Wick announced.

He'd been up early, and instead of the grueling workout he usually forced us into, he had let us sleep. That should have been our first sign of trouble. Should have alerted me he wasn't being nice because Wick never was, but he had his reasons for not forcing us up and out of the house by six AM.

The scent of eggs and toast drew me downstairs,

along with hash browns and bacon. Like a sucker, I
followed the aroma and it led me right to the trap.

An assignment.

My heart sped up, worried about what that would
mean for Mac. "Are we taking her?"

"She needs to go sometime, get a feel for just
what it's like."

"And?" I sensed the words unsaid.

"I don't trust leaving her alone here. If it's a trap,
we'd leave her unguarded. Team Martinez wants her
head, and I know they would break the rules to
get it."

I suddenly wasn't hungry any longer. The thought
of Mac being in danger, the risk that was involved just
taking her on an assignment, it didn't sit well. She
wasn't trained for this yet. Sure, Wick worked hard,
pushing her, teaching her, demonstrating all the skills
she would need, but it wasn't enough. We'd had years
to learn it. The organization was giving her a month.

"I can stay behind," I offered. "Watch her. Keep
her safe."

"That's not how it works, and you know it." Wick
placed the plates of food in the middle of the table.
"We're a team for a reason. Teams work together, not
separate."

"I hate that you're right." I stared at the coffee,
wishing it was something stronger. "She's not ready."

"We'll test her," he stated.

"It won't be enough." Nothing would ever be
enough with her involved.

"What won't be enough?" Mac walked into the room, Austin on her heels, and I tried not to look at him, at them, at their rumpled state, but my eyes locked and refused to look away.

Mac abandoned Austin as she strolled toward me, and his arm stretched toward her, trying to prevent her from going. His eyes broke our contact, following her every move, and I knew by the look on his face and the smirk that he wore that those memories of last night flooded his mind. I wished I was in there with them. Instead, I was forced to listen to every agonizing moment through the paper-thin walls as they brought each other to orgasm. Thrice.

She stepped toward me, her fingers already poised to reach my scalp, and when the touch hit its mark, I shivered with pleasure. She loved my hair, loved playing with it, and I couldn't get enough of her fingers dancing along my scalp, rubbing against the prickly shaved sides of my skull, before untangling the long strands on top. I had it in a bun, strewed messily out of the way, but she instantly removed the band, before effortlessly weaving it into a master-piece. When she was done with the braid, she tied it off, letting the end drop to my neck.

Her arms braced against my shoulder as she leaned in, kissing my cheek. "Now you look sort of Viking-ish."

"And you like that?" I turned to her. I assumed she did, but I liked her facial features when she enjoyed something we did.

"Very much so."

"Then I'll keep it like this whenever you want," I confirmed.

"Stop playing Barbie and eat your food," Wick ground out, and I wondered if he was jealous of the way Mac openly showed affection toward us when, most days, he was lucky if she glanced in his direction. That could change, and probably would change if he weren't such a dick.

Mac sat next to me, and Austin took up her other side, leaving all three of us to face Wick at the table. She looked at the spread of food. "Thanks for breakfast. And letting us sleep in."

"I didn't let you sleep in. I got sidetracked by an assignment that came through. You'll work double tonight." Wick shoved potatoes into his mouth.

Mac sighed. "There he is."

Wick effectively ignored her comment. "Tonight, you have an evening class, correct?"

"I- Um, yes. English."

"If no one is there to pick you up, come straight home. Understand?"

What the fuck? He just said we'd not leave her unattended. "I can do that."

Wick stood, leaning over the table, his hand going to her neck as he pulled her forward. "Promise me."

Her eyes were wide as she looked on, and both Austin and I stood, ready to intervene. But she didn't offer him any sassy remarks, clearly seeing that he was already unhinged a bit this morning. "I promise I'll come home."

"If you don't, you'll be punished, Mac. I'm fucking serious." His fingers tightened a little, and I couldn't tell if she liked it or if it was the pain and lack of oxygen that caused her face to take on a shade of rose.

"Let me go," she stated, her eyes burning. "I'm an adult. I don't follow your rules. I said I promise, so save your fucking threats."

"Your team fucking Moore. You practically took my fucking last name, or had you forgotten that my blood and theirs runs through your body in a promise?" He adjusted his grip so that he forced her chin up, angling so that they were eye to eye. "Adult or fucking not, you follow my rules."

"I have no friends. Where the fuck do you expect me to roam after class? Want me to stumble my way into a classmate's apartment? Maybe have a few drinks and play naked Twister?"

His nose flared. Why did they always have to push each other's buttons? "You say shit like that again, and I'll keep you locked in the basement. Remember the chains that looked so fucking pretty on your wrists? They are waiting to meet you again."

"How could I forget?" She struggled to swallow against his palm. "I wake up in nightmares reliving that moment."

For a second, I saw his eyes soften at her admission, but it was quick. "That wasn't our intent, but we did what we had to."

"You talk a lot of bullshit for someone who is supposed to lead a group of men and keep them alive. I wonder if they buy all your lies."

"Mac," I warned.

"No." She spared me a glance. "I want to know. Did you convince them you had to drug me and chain me up? When you could have just asked me to go. I would have, you know. I trusted Austin and Asa."

"But not me."

"I still don't fucking trust you." She glared, her words hardly making it out through the tightening grip.

"Let her go, Wick," Austin cut in. "She's going to bruise."

"Good, she can wear my handprint as a collar to show the world she's mine, and she can't do shit about it." His eyes were blazing. "Do you hear that, Mac? Mine. Ours. The only way you get out of that contract is if we're burying you in the ground. You don't want that, do you?"

"Enough." I stood, placing a hand on top of Wick's. "She gets the point."

His hand released her, and she gasped as she fell back into her chair. "Sort of hard to tell when she acts like such an ungrateful brat."

"Fuck you," she shot back.

"I've already told you, not until you apologize." He smirked, and I knew that single motion caused fury to boil inside of her. I saw it in her eyes. Practically tasted the singed skin from the fire she was burning.

"The words will never be uttered from these lips. Enjoy your life of celibacy."

"I'll have you begging." His eyes roamed over her body, stopping for a second at her tits. "You will beg."

"Doubtful."

"We'll see." The promises and tension that hung in the air between them were enough to make me hard. For a moment, Austin's eyes met mine, probably thinking the same thing. "Eat. Go to classes. Get home. That's all you have to do today, and I trust, being that you appear to be a smart girl, that you can handle that."

"Do you talk to your mother like a jackass, too?"

"You know we don't have mothers." He laughed. "We're all orphans."

"Oh, so she got out while she could. Lucky girl."

I winced. Too far, but she didn't know that. She didn't know about his past or that his father was technically still alive. She'd never heard the story of our parents' deaths, and I personally didn't want to rehash it.

Wick said nothing to rebuke her statement. "Eat."

He pushed off from the table, choosing to walk to the sink and wash the dishes instead of sitting to eat. I reached over and grabbed a piece of bacon, shoving it in my mouth and chewing slowly. The tension was as thick as the slab of meat I attempted to chew. I wasn't hungry. I doubted any of us were. But we still ate in silence until Mac was done.

"We're going to class," Austin announced, and Wick turned around.

He must be itching for a fight because he let his eyes touch every inch of her before saying, "Not in that. Go change."

"Fuck off."

"Go change."

"I'm dressed fine." And technically, she was. She was covered.

"You have a whole new wardrobe, and you still wear that hideous sweater. It's cheap looking, old, it has a hole, it's beneath us."

"Beneath you maybe, but not me." She grabbed her bag from where she had sat it by the door.

"Makenna." Her name dripped with disgust. "Do as I say."

"Or what?"

"You won't get to class today."

"Fine." She crossed her arms in challenge.

Austin rubbed the bridge of his nose. "We've got a test today. Please, baby. I beg you... change."

"He can't tell me what I can wear." She tried so hard to hold her ground.

"Mac, I don't want to make up a test," Austin begged. "Please."

She rolled her eyes and turned on her heels, intentionally dropping the bag with all the books on

Austin's foot. He winced, but watched her walk away. When she was out of view, he turned back to Wick. "What the hell is your problem?"

"Nothing is my problem." He picked up the empty plate from the bacon.

"You're railing into her for no fucking reason."

"She's being combative for no fucking reason," Wick defended.

"Really?" I raised a brow at Wick, crossing my arms over my chest as I watched him. "Because I swore it was your fingers threatening to choke her out and not the other way around. I thought we were taking her on the assignment."

"We are."

"Where will we be tonight?" I hated when he formed plans and left us out of the loop. It was like pulling teeth without anesthetic just to get answers from him sometimes. Especially when he was in a mood. Like... Now.

"Trailing her. Watching her. I'll be waiting here, ready to handle her when she gets home."

"Handle her how?" Austin looked at Wick suspiciously, and he had every right to be suspicious. Mac was our girl, ours. All of ours. We took a vow to protect her, and sometimes Wick's methods were a little unorthodox.

"Depends on if she follows the simple instructions I gave her." God, I hoped she followed instructions, listened to him for once in her life with no more of a fight.

"You won't hurt her?" Austin's eyes looked up at the sound of her stomps hitting the stairs.

"What?" Wick looked genuinely offended. "She's our fucking housekeeper. Why the hell would I hurt her? She's ours. Mine."

"I just..." Austin bit his lip before continuing. "She drives you mad, and I want to keep her safe."

"I'm not going to fucking hurt her." Wick hissed, his disgust clear. "But tonight, Mac is going to learn all about lessons."

I swallowed my unease as Mac stepped back into the room, wearing a hoodie that I picked out. Black. My favorite color. She spread her arms wide. "Happy now?"

"Happier without the attitude."

She flipped Wick's back off, not caring that we saw. "Well then, you're always going to be miserable."

"Counting on it."

Mac took Austin's hand and grabbed her backpack from his other before dragging him to the front door. With a slam, the place went silent. Wick looked back at me, eyes blazing, and I scratched my neck and chin, looking anywhere but at him.

"What?" he finally asked.

"Nothing. Nothing at all." I shook my head, then sighed. "It's just, well, that went well."

"Oh, fuck off." This time it was me who received the bird right before he went back to washing the dishes.

CHAPTER TWENTY-FIVE

MAC

All day I was fuming. I couldn't help but be angry because who the hell did Wick think he was? Team Moore? They could all go fuck themselves if they thought they would take away all my freedoms. Telling me I couldn't stop on the way home when I've been by myself longer than I'd had them on my radar. It was practically asking for me to disobey. And I got it, I did. They worried about my safety after Wick took out one of their girls, but they said themselves we still had half a month until they could get payback and well, couldn't I enjoy that half a month before I was stuck with my boys every second of the day?

My boys.

It was hard to pinpoint the exact moment I started thinking of them as mine. But I did. Even if I only really could tolerate two thirds of them. That remaining third somehow still brought out a possessive streak in me. I know what people thought when we were outside. I'd seen the looks, the whispers, the nods of acknowledgement. They thought I was a whore, and maybe I was. But now that I'd had the attention of three men at once, shared a bed, slept on their chests with legs tangled, I didn't know if I'd ever be able to go back to the social norm.

"You're Wick's girl, aren't you?" The voice startled me from my thoughts. Class was over and everyone was cleaning up, but I hadn't seen the guy approach me.

"Ah, yeah. I am." It was fucking weird to say that. To claim him. Especially when I never missed the jealous looks of females wishing they were me.

His hands shoved in his pockets. "I'm Trey. I've been friends with Wick for a while."

Friends with Wick?

Warning bells went off in my head because Wick had no friends, not that I saw. But maybe I was over-reacting. Maybe he did, in fact, have friends, and I only knew a smidge of his life.

I held out my hand. "Nice to meet you."

He shook it. "Likewise. Any idea what your final paper will be on? I've been working on cattle in the meat industry, and I've never wanted to go vegan more in my life after seeing some of those conditions. It's an eye opener."

I hadn't realized I had other classes with him, but

he *was* familiar, and I paid little attention to my class-mates. "For journalism? I've not even started. I'm trying to narrow my passion down from a few topics."

That was a lie, of course. I already had a file going, a collection of things I'd learned about the Saints over the last few weeks since joining my trio. But that was none of his business.

"You better hurry. You'll run out of time," Trey warned.

"Good thing I work best under pressure and with a time restraint." I zipped up my bag and hoisted it up to my shoulder. Taking my action as a cue, Trey put on his bag, tilted up the hood of his sweater and followed me toward the door. When we were outside, I looked around, feeling a little hurt that I didn't see any of my boys. I knew they wouldn't be here, but after a day of roaming around without them, I strangely missed having them around.

"If you need help with that paper, let me know." Trey turned to me. "Where is Wick?"

"He couldn't make it today," was all I offered.

"He always picks you up from this class," Trey informed me, like I didn't know my own men's rotation.

"I'm aware. They couldn't make it." Why was this man making me feel unsettled suddenly?

"Interesting." His eyes roamed over me, and I grabbed the strap of my bag harder. "Well, send him my regards."

I most definitely would not. "Will do."

"Night, Makenna. Be safe."

Why the hell did that seem like both a caution and a threat? "Yeah, you too."

I refused to leave until he was fully out of sight and walking in the opposite direction that I was. When I was sure he had left, I walked toward the square. I will admit, I had gotten used to Wick cooking for me, and now that he was gone for the night, there was no way I was up to cooking for myself. I picked up a burger from the diner, knowing that Wick would be ticked I stopped here.

What he doesn't know would never hurt him.

I was halfway home when I got the first chill that started at the base of my spine and traveled upward. I looked around, searching, but I saw no one. Seeing no one meant nothing though, not when I felt the unease, felt the eyes against my skin, watching my every move.

I stepped faster, moving as quickly as I could while twisting my backpack enough to grab my keys from inside. I arranged my keys in my fingers, ready to use them as a weapon if needed, gripping them so tight my knuckles hurt. The unease followed me for two blocks until I saw the house in sight. I looked over my shoulder once before breaking out into a run.

How had I gotten this way? I once cared about nothing as I walked, using my independence as a shield. Now? I couldn't even spend a day by myself without having the paranoia that Wick installed bubble up. I was safe. It was all in my head. Nothing was after me, nothing was watching me, nothing was—

A rustle shook the bushes that I passed and I bolted, not stopping until I had run up the steps of our home. I reached for the door and panicked when I found it slightly ajar. Another rustle had me pushing it open, stepping inside. They'd just left it open, that was all.

But even I knew Asa was worse than Wick with the security of our place. He had cameras, locks, and enough safety measures to protect a fortress. His attention to detail was unmatched. He'd never leave the door unlocked.

"Hello?" I let my fingers search around, looking for a light switch as I took off my backpack, placing it on the ground. I placed my takeout next to it.

No one answered, and when I found the switch, flicking it up and down a few times, no light came on. Fuck. I would like to blame my paranoia, and maybe I should, but it felt off. It felt planned. It felt—

A body slammed into mine, the weight so vast that I stumbled, slamming into the ground. My keys skated across the wood floor, just out of reach. I opened my mouth, determined to scream when a hand slammed over my lips, silencing me.

I struggled against the weight, struggled against the hold. My head slammed back, meeting the nose of my assailant, causing him to grunt, but his hold didn't loosen.

Fingers shoved a cloth into my mouth, pushing it so deep that I instantly gagged. *Breathe through your nose,* I reminded myself. *If you die choking on your own vomit, the boys will be furious.* Though, I might die anyway. A large palm covered the width of my skull, grabbing a handful of my hair, and pulled, forcing my head back before slamming it into the ground.

"Stop fucking fighting me." That voice... it seemed so...

I couldn't finish my thought before the hand in my hair pulled again, dragging me out of the foyer. I struggled to claw at his hand, trying to get him to release me. My nails in his skin didn't faze him. My struggle was a minor inconvenience as he pulled me toward the stairs, forcing me to twist and stand or risk feeling every one of those steps in my hip and spine as I was dragged over them.

I stumbled as he stomped up the steps, falling to my knees twice before making it to the top of the landing. He stopped looking both ways, like he was debating before pulling me left. His foot kicked the door of Wick's room hard, the sound an explosion in the silent house.

When the fingers released me, I crashed to the floor, crawling on my hands and knees, determined to get away. I made it to the door before a band of steel fingers wrapped around my ankle and yanked me back. My fingers clawed at the wood, trying to resist the pull, but the flooring was too smooth and his strength too great against mine. Even with all the training I'd been doing, the bulk I'd been building, I was no match for a man this size.

When he had pulled me close enough, he leaned his weight on me again, straddling my hips and ass between his knees as he reached forward, grabbing my hands and yanking them roughly behind my back. He held both in one palm for a second, before he had the plastic of a zip tie wrapped around my wrists, pulling it until the plastic bit painfully into my skin.

The weight of his body left mine and silence settled in the air. Each step thrummed over the hard floor, and all I could do was pant for air into the cloth that obstructed my voice. I could beg, but it would be no use. All I could do was cry, but they were silent tears that streamed down my face. Tears of defeat. Tears of failure. Not the body-wracking tears of pain, soul shattering pain, that I knew would come if I lived through this moment. I wiggled my fingers, barely feeling them over the agony of the plastic strip cutting off circulation.

Fingers suddenly grabbed me, flipping me over so that my hands crushed under my back. He fell to his knees, straddling my hips as he ran a blade, a bone blade just like Wick's, over my collarbone. "See how easy it was for me to capture you?"

If he wanted a response from me, he wasn't getting one. Instead, I glared, my eyes fixated on the mask that donned his face. It was equally familiar and foreign. I'd seen something similar before, but my mind was hazy on the details. The blade traveled lower, tearing into the layer of my sweatshirt, slicing it wide open. If I wasn't tied up and gagged, I'd protest at that alone. Clothes were expensive, and Asa had bought this for me. It was something I'd never be able to afford on my own.

"Did you feel eyes on you? Following you while you disobeyed?" The blade slid slower, cutting into my denim, and I cried in objection, outraged over the destruction of the newest wardrobe I'd had since I was fourteen. I thrashed against his weight, trying to buck him off, kicking my legs under him to throw him off balance, but he didn't move. He was a solid stone, unwavering from where he sat upon my body. My efforts barely nudged him.

"You did, didn't you? You felt like you were being followed." That voice, I think I knew it. "Was it exhilarating? Running from danger? Are you ready to apologize?"

Mother. Fucker.

I was fuming when he stood up, releasing my body of his weight right before he grabbed my hair and used it as leverage to pull me up. I was on my knees before him, looking up at the towering height of the now familiar frame. He reached over and pulled the cloth from my mouth. The minute it was out, I spat out, "You son of a fucking bitch, you had some nerve..."

He yanked hard on my hair, forcing my head back so quick that my neck cracked. "You had instructions, and you didn't follow them. If this wasn't me, you'd be dead. You talked to fucking strangers. Men. You walked around campus, out of the fucking way for food, knowing you could cook at home. You ignored all the safety protocols we taught you until it was too late." He was right, I knew that. I just didn't want to admit it out loud until he leveled his eyes with mine and repeated, "You could have died."

"I'm sorry." The words stumbled from my mouth before I could stop them, causing those two-tone eyes to blaze.

He flexed his fingers that held my hair, before he slowly used his free hand to pop the button of his jeans, lowering the zipper painfully slow, until his cock pushed out. "What did you say?"

I refused to open my mouth. Refused to repeat the apology I never meant to give. But it was too late to take it back, we both knew it. He'd heard the words, the single simple statement he'd been trying to get to leave my lips for weeks. And now that they had, now that he'd heard them so clearly, there was no turning back.

He brought his blade up to my throat, teasing me with the coolness against my skin. "Say it again."

It wasn't just a demand; it was an order. One that stated if I didn't follow, there would be consequences to face. But there would be consequences either way. Only one would be far more bloody. I swallowed, my throat bobbing against the blade as I whispered, "I'm sorry."

The words hadn't fully left me before his hips

jutted forward, his cock plunging through my open lips, making me nearly gag as it hit the back of my throat. Another tug of my hair as he met my eyes. "If you bite me, I'll stab you."

It might be worth it.

He pulled back, drawing his cock out enough that only the tip remained between my lips, before he pushed back in, flexing his hips in such a way that I knew he had been desperate for this moment, desperate to be between my lips and have my tongue lap against him. At that thought, my tongue moved on its own, tearing a moan from his throat that ended in a curse.

I hated him in this moment, more than I hated him at any other time in our existence together, but I still couldn't stop myself from making the motion again, from drawing my tongue along the bottom of his dick, until the hand that held my head still trembled just the slightest. His pumps grew harder, damn near bruising the back of my throat, and I knew I shouldn't want him to follow through, but I craved to see the moment he lost control.

"I've waited so fucking long for you to apologize. Weeks, Makenna. Torturous weeks." His chest was heaving, his head thrown back as he looked at the ceiling. Without warning, he pulled out, his dick falling from between my lips as he released my hair.

It was a blink of a moment before he had me rising off the floor. My body turned so my bound arms were trapped between our bodies. His arm

wrapped around my stomach as he walked us
forward, stopping in front of the desk. His hand
dipped down, past my tattered jeans and into my
underwear. "You're soaked for me. So fucking wet
and responsive. Such a good girl response from such a
very bad girl."

I didn't deny it. I couldn't. My body reacted even
when my mind screamed for it not to. It liked his
touch, as much as I despised it. He pulled my body
back, dipping a finger inside of me as he whispered in
my ear, "I've been thinking about how good you
taste. The best dessert I've ever tasted. Euphoric on
my tongue."

Then he dropped to his knees, taking my cut-up
jeans down with him. He used his blade to cut
through my underwear, slicing through the material
like it was nothing before he demanded, "Spread your
legs."

My body's reaction was automatic, and my legs
spread wider at his command. His palm rubbed my
ass, squeezing the globes before he dove in, his
tongue working against my slit, lapping at my clit,
making my heart pound wildly. His palm slammed
heavily against my back, forcing my body to bend, my
shoulders and chin slamming into the desk, unable to
be caught by my bound hands.

I was helpless and exposed, completely on display
to him, and he used that to his full advantage. He
worked my body in all the ways he had learned I
loved over the last few weeks, driving me mindless

with pleasure and making my eyes blur. My body coiled and contracted until I was a weeping mess, begging him for more, asking for less. I wanted what I couldn't have, and shouldn't desire, because I was at his mercy.

I was on the edge, on the cusp of bliss, when he pulled back, stood up, and leaned against my back. His palms were warm as he trailed his hands up and down my body, his breath hot as it tickled my ear. "When you come, I want you to scream my name. Everybody on this fucking block is going to know whose cock you're riding, understand me?"

When I didn't answer, the hand left my back, finding my throat as he pulled me back toward him. "Do you understand?"

"Yes." My voice was barely a whisper, but he heard. He bent my body back down, holding my head onto the desk and jutted his hips, shoving his cock inside of me. My arms burned, my hands were practically numb, and the desk against my cheek was uncomfortably hard. And yet, every nerve inside of me screamed in pleasure, begging to feel more of whatever he had to give.

More pleasure.

More pain.

More rough, callused fingers roaming over my skin.

At no point did he become gentle as he used my body to steal his pleasure, setting every nerve I had into kindling, waiting to ignite into flame. But he wouldn't let me burst, not until I begged, pleaded guilty, asked his forgiveness for crimes I hadn't yet committed.

His teeth found my shoulder blade, biting into the skin, reminding me of the ache and pain of my arms that were still secured behind my back. "I told you to walk straight home. Do you know why?"

"No," I gasped. Each jolt of my body made my breasts push into the wood of the desk, my nipples dragging painfully over the surface.

"To protect you. To see how fucking well you followed instructions." He ground out, "You failed."

A hand came down on my ass, the sound radiating off the ceiling and causing a yelp of pain to leave me. Tears ran down my face, the pain awful, but I wanted more. "I'm sorry."

"If you can't follow simple instructions, you're fucking dead. Do you understand that?"

I thought I did, until this moment where he had me tied up, gasping for air, crying tears from the delicious pain he was causing. "I—"

"You clearly don't—" Another smack radiated off my skin. "—fucking trust us. Why is that so fucking hard for you?" His fingers bruised my skin as he gripped me tight, the desk slapping hard into the wall, causing an echo so hard it hurt my ears as he pumped into me.

"I—"

"Don't fucking give me a bullshit answer." He bit into my skin again, no doubt leaving a mark that would shine like a beacon tomorrow, announcing what we had done. Tomorrow, would I regret it? Pretend he didn't have me weeping under him when tonight it was all I ever wanted and more?

"I—" I tried again, but again, he cut me off.

"No bullshit answers." He yanked my hair, forcing my back to arch as he looked into my eyes. "Understand?"

"I've had no one to trust before," I admitted, and it was painful to look him in the eyes and say those things, admit what I never had out loud. But the last person I trusted, the last person I loved, my own fucking brother, turned eighteen and left me, never fucking looking back.

His hips slowed, the drag of his cock turning to a deliciously torturous grind as he leaned over, capturing my lips in a slow kiss. It was sensual, exploring, telling me of all the promises he planned to make and begging me to accept them. When he pulled away, his hand gently skimmed through my hair, the tiniest of smiles ghosting his lips.

"That's my girl." Then his palm ran a line down my spine as he pulled back, dropping me back onto the wood, letting my cheek press against it as I struggled to support my body without the use of my hands or arms. His fingers snaked around my body, delving between my legs to rub my clit in agonizing circles that had my ass bucking against him, begging him for more, begging him to let me cum.

His pace picked up. Each teasing pull out was met

with a delicious push back into my body until we were both moaning our pleasure, both seeking release, both willing to use each other to get what we wanted. My body tightened, my hands behind my back fisted, as my core contracted, balling until it released in waves around me.

"Wick." His name slipped from my lips as sparks shot through my body, the hum of electricity too much to handle and not enough.

My core squeezed his dick, my heated flesh withered against him as he spoke hoarsely. "Say it again. Say my fucking name again."

"Wick." This time I spoke the name through whimpers of pleasure, the name broken on my lips.

"That's my fucking girl," he groaned, giving three more sporadic pumps before he spilled inside of me, panting my name as he flooded me with his cum.

We stayed locked together long after our orgasms faded. The only sound was our combined breathing as we tried to come back to earth. Each of us locked in our own thoughts as our bodies locked together. He broke the spell first; his fingers ran gently up my spine as he pulled back, pulling himself out. He walked away for a moment, and I thought maybe this was part of my punishment, to leave me here, his cum running down my thighs and my arms tied up, but then he was back. A washcloth in hand as he knelt behind me, gentling traveling it up my thighs and in between my legs before he tossed it aside.

He picked up his blade, slicing through the plastic

that held my wrists together. When my wrists were free, he took them in his hands, rubbing them gently, stretching them to my side and over my head, trying to get circulation back into them. His voice was soft, barely above a whisper when he said, "You know I'd never hurt you, right?"

"Yes," I confessed softly. And somehow, even before I spoke the words, I knew I believed them to be true.

"I would die for you," he confessed, the words held not the roughness I was used to, but a vulnerability like he was afraid to speak them in this moment. "Step in front of any bullet that came your way and protect you with my life." His fingers toyed with a strand of my hair. "My girl."

CHAPTER TWENTY-SIX

WICK

It went too far, I'm aware of that. I hadn't meant to take her like I had, hadn't even meant to tie her up. I only meant to prove a point, and that point was that if she didn't listen to us, she could get hurt. If she talked to strangers like she had that fucking male she spoke to after class, she could get hurt. Walking alone in the dark, she could get hurt. Not paying attention to her surroundings, she could get fucking hurt.

When she walked into our home, she didn't pay attention to the shit around her. Her focus was only on the sound of Austin in the bushes outside or the possibility of being followed. We followed her. Asa was behind her the whole fucking way, reporting back to me with each step and detour. We'd never leave her unguarded, never alone. Not when our sole purpose for the foreseeable future was to protect her at all costs and train her to be as good as we were.

I never meant to take her bent over the desk, but I'd be fucking lying if I said wouldn't do it again. The sounds, the sweet heavenly sounds that fell from her lips were nearly my undoing. But it was nothing compared to the moment I heard my name sung in a sweet, husky voice. I couldn't control myself, not like I was trying that hard. But it had been over three years since I'd been inside a female and never had it been one so perfect for me.

I felt like an ass after, but I'd never admit it to her. Instead, I cleaned her up enough that she would not trail cum across the floor, cut her loose, then carried her to my bathroom where I ran a steamy bath. I didn't say a word to her. I didn't know what I'd say even if I did. Instead, I shed the clothing I didn't bother to lose earlier, climbed into the tub, and held my hand out to her.

The moment between my temporary offer of peace and her hesitation dragged on painfully. But then her little fingers were in my palm and she was stepping over the side of the tub and into the water, sloshing it gently before she turned and lowered herself down, letting her perfect ass grace my vision before it disappeared into the water. She sat between my thighs, her body stiff, her fingers fidgeting under the water until I wrapped an arm around her shoulder and pulled her back into my chest. I let my hand skim down her arm before linking our fingers and stopping the fidgeting.

We stayed like that, our fingers linked, through the whole bath, her not saying a word as I ran soap over her body. I only unlinked them long enough to lift her hair into a large messy bun on top of her head. I whispered words to her; praises and compliments I'd never admit in the light of day. But it was dark outside, my bathroom was dimly lit, and with her back turned, if I couldn't see her eyes, she couldn't see mine to judge my words.

When the bath grew cold and her fingers puckered from being submerged in water, I scooted her forward, stood, and got out to retrieve a towel for her. With my towel tied around my waist, I pulled the plug out of the bath, draining the water before I scooped her out. I dried her off slowly, making sure every inch of her was dry before I applied lotion and still, she hadn't said a word.

Had I ruined us, broken what fragile bridge we had built, before it was even stable? Maybe. But she had to know who I was. She had to know just how broken and fucked up I was before she got in any deeper with us. I wasn't a nice person. My father made sure of that. But I could try to be, at least to her, if that's what she needed.

Her body looked perfect splayed on top of my sheets, and I wondered if I should tell her I'd never done this before. Never had a woman in my bed longer than a quick fuck before I was pushing them out the door, shoes in hand, trying to rid them and their disgusting cloud of perfume from my space.

Mac didn't wear perfume. She just naturally smelled delicious, and I liked that about her. There was nothing overpowering, nothing that choked me to the point of gagging. I wouldn't tell her that though, at least not right now. Instead, I closed my eyes and flung an arm over her waist as I laid on my stomach next to her. I knew tomorrow would be different, back to the way it was when she hated me and I pretended to hate her, even if I wanted every inch of her body writhing under mine, begging for me to make her cum.

"Your room is colorful."

I startled awake, jumped at the sound of the voice next to me. Fuck, I hadn't slept that solid in ages, never allowed myself to sleep deeply for fear of things coming for me in the night. It was a valid fear. With the men I killed, and the people my father offed, retribution wasn't that crazy of a concept.

"Does that shock you?" My voice was rough, unused for hours as we slept.

"Well, yeah. I figured you'd have it all blacks and grays, like Asa. You don't strike me as a colorful man."

"Well, you don't know me much at all," I pointed out, and it was true. She didn't know shit about me. I liked it that way, even if I knew eventually it would have to change.

She shifted, her thigh moving further between my own. Shit, we were so intertwined. There was no way she would have escaped without me waking. I wondered how long she had laid there, awake, while I slept. I didn't move a muscle before asking, "Have you been awake long?"

Her lips curved up slightly. "Long enough to make sure not to wake you in time for the workout."

I glared, though I didn't really feel like getting up, anyway. "You're going to have to make that up."

She buried her head into my arm before acknowledging my demand. "God, I hate you."

It didn't feel like she hated me. "Feeling's likewise."

"Prick."

"I am what I am." I shrugged. "We need to get up."

"Why?" Her voice was muffled, her face still hidden.

"Because we've got shit to do. You can't sleep all fucking day. We've got three hours before we're on the road."

"What?" Her body pulled back; her words spoken dramatically. "That's like, not enough time to prepare."

"It's all the time you're getting. You don't need to prepare much. We'll be back home by tomorrow."

She sat up, her hair falling out of the bun I placed

it in last night, and strands fell messily over her face. She pulled her legs back. I instantly missed the feel of her warm skin against mine. Before I could stop her, she was climbing over my body, and my hands reached out to snag her waist, barely missing her.

She didn't hesitate as she reached to my floor, grabbing a shirt of mine and pulling it over her head, cutting off my glorious view. "You're messier than I thought you would be."

"What is that supposed to mean?"

She walked toward my shelves and my stomach tightened, but I didn't stop her. "I don't know. You're such a control freak. I thought you would be neater."

"Like Austin," I pointed out.

"Maybe, sort of. I guess. But you're messier than Asa."

"So?"

"It doesn't fit with the part of you that you let the world see." Her fingers ran over my art supplies, and I swear my heart picked up. "You're an artist."

"I was an art major. Before."

She looked over her shoulder. "But you changed because of the organization?"

"I changed because artists can't survive in our world. It was just a dream," I admitted.

"You painted my mask. And the roses on my wall." It wasn't a question. It was a statement. She didn't need me to confirm it; she knew it to be true.

"We need to get ready." I sat up, changing the subject. "Pack an overnight bag. Make sure it's light and with nothing of importance in case it has to be left."

"Do you need to leave things often?"

In our business, more often than I'd like, but I didn't want to scare her. "A few times."

"What are we going to do?"

Kill a man. Stage his body. Teach her that life is deceptive, and people are so untrustworthy. Everyone, but us.

"The assignment." I let my tone grow hard, putting on the mask of indifference I often wore to hide myself from the world. "And if you don't hurry the fuck up, we're going to be late. Go fucking pack."

Her head whipped toward me, her eyes clouded with hurt. But she dropped the paint brush she had been twirling between her fingers at the sound of my harsh tone and turned toward the door. When she reached for the knob, I called her name, not realizing I was going to until the word already left my lips. "Makenna."

Her hand held the knob tight, but her body twisted toward me. "Yeah?"

"Thanks for the fuck. It needs some work, but it got the job done."

I don't know why I said what I said. It was an asshole move, but an asshole was what she expected from me, so she shouldn't be shocked. Still, the deflation of her shoulders made me feel like shit. And when she didn't respond, only opened the door and walked out, I felt pretty fucking shitty. Especially since sex with Mac didn't need work. It was flawless. Raw. Charged. Unadulterated perfection. The best I ever had, and I fucked that up.

It was another few hours before I saw Mac again. She had one of Asa's black bags slung over her shoulder and my shirt she had been wearing was discarded in favor of Austin's. Why that bothered me so much, I couldn't say. But it did. Maybe it was because it was me who brought her to orgasm last night, my hands that washed the cum from her body and my legs that tangled with hers, yet it was them she clung to for comfort, as if they could comfort her more than me.

"Are you nervous?" Austin asked her an hour into the drive.

"No," she stated, though we all knew she was. The nerves clung to her like static, charging the air around us and making us all feel the buzz.

"You won't have to be hands on this round," Asa pointed out. "But you need to observe. Keep your wits about you. This job is ten percent action, ninety percent observation."

"I can observe." Her enormous eyes met mine in the mirror.

"The fuck you can. If you could observe, you wouldn't have been almost killed last night," I pointed out.

"I wasn't almost killed."

"If it wasn't me, you would have been," I reminded her. "It's a good fucking thing it was me."

She didn't respond to that, only turned her gaze to look out the window, ignoring us all as we drove for the next three hours.

It was evening when we reached the switch point. I parked our truck in the parking lot of a large truck stop and got out without a word to the others. What would speaking do when it seemed all we were good at was causing tension? Words wouldn't fix that.

Wordlessly, I left them, heading for the restroom, where I did my business before checking the stalls for a set of keys. I knew they would be there; it was just a matter of which one. I found them in the third stall, taped under the tank. I grabbed them up before meeting my team outside, dangling them in my fingers.

"What's that?" Mac asked curiously.

"Clearly fucking keys." I rolled my eyes. What type of dumb shit question was that?

"No shit," she shot back. "But they aren't your keys. Your keys have a metal M as a keychain since you're so obsessed with your last name."

"Trust me. I'm anything but obsessed with my last name."

"Why name the team after it then?" She cocked her hip. Her hands on the dip drew my attention for a moment.

"Because I'm the fucking best at what I do. I lead the team. Don't fucking forget it." I hardly spared her a glance as I looked back at Austin. "Drive to the end point. Then we'll assess."

Austin wordlessly took the keys as Asa and Mac walked away. I turned to them. "Where the fuck are you going?"

"To pee. Do you want to control that, too?" Her eyes traveled down my body. "Or maybe just tie me up and drag me to the restroom whenever you feel like it."

I glared at her, not bothering to respond as I grabbed my bag, walked the three spots over, and yanked open the door. I was still watching her as I slammed the door to the passenger side, glaring at the infuriating female the whole time.

CHAPTER TWENTY-SEVEN

ASA

"I'm sensing some tension," I joked as we walked into the women's bathroom.

"I don't know what you're talking about." She feigned innocence when she clearly hadn't realized everything that happened last night was playing on our live feed. A free show for Austin and I.

"About last night..." I began.

"I don't want to talk about it."

She wasn't getting off that easily. "Which part don't you want to talk about? The part where you bluntly disobeyed our orders to keep you safe, or that Wick fucked you so rough and so loud that it forced me to jack off while watching you two on the video feed."

Her face instantly went red. "You... saw that?"

"We both did," I confirmed.

"He was going to hurt me." She bit her lip. "And you were in on it."

"He never would have hurt you." How could she even think that? "And even if that was true, we've told you repeatedly that we aren't good people, Mac."

"I just thought..." She rubbed her eyes. "I don't know what I thought. For a while, he was different, and I could have liked the different."

"It's all the same Wick," I pointed out as I pushed open the stall door, allowing her to enter it before I pulled it shut.

"This is awkward." There was a rustle of material. "Can you like, I don't know...stand outside?"

"So I don't hear you pee?" I laughed. "Is now a bad time to let you know our bathrooms share a wall?"

"Oh god." I could hear the horror in her voice, and it amused the fuck out of me.

"Embarrassed, princess?" I let my amusement drip into my voice. "Hurry. I don't want him to bitch about time."

She did her business, flushed, and pulled open the stall door. She tilted her body, allowing her to walk past me. As soon as she stepped away, I grabbed onto one of those innocent-looking pigtail buns and pulled her back, slamming my lips to hers. Then I brought my hand to her cheek and ran my thumb along the surface.

When I pulled away, she was dazed. "Stop trying so hard to hide from us. We all see you."

"You should take your own advice, Mr. Dark and Mysterious."

"You think I'm dark and mysterious?" I couldn't hide how outrageously funny this was. "How are you supposed to know about me if you don't ask? It's that simple, Mac. Ask what you want to know."

She was silent as she walked to the sink. "What's your favorite color, Mac?"

"Purple. Any shade similar."

Our eyes met through the mirror. "Mine's green."

"But you have so much black."

"It's neutral and easy to match." Plus, nondescript on a mission. I can pack in seconds. Stains? Non-existent.

The door pushed open, and Austin stuck his head in. "We've got to go. He's getting agitated."

"He's always agitated." Mac wasn't wrong.

"We'll be out in a minute," I confirmed, and Austin just nodded, then the heavy metal door slammed shut.

"Are you going to address that?" Mac asked as I stared at the door.

"I don't know what you're talking about."

"I think you do," she pushed. "The tension between you is enough to make us all uncomfortable. It's like you're afraid to accidentally brush elbows for fear of what the other thinks."

"I'm being respectful." I reached and took her hand, pulling her toward the door.

"Like he was respecting you with your dick in his mouth."

My steps faltered. "That was different."

This time it was Mac who sashayed past me, dragging me along as she opened the door. "Was it? Because by not addressing the elephant in the room, it's making us all feel it."

"You're one to talk. You and Wick nearly burst the house into flames and still, you have him strung tight."

"It's his problem, not mine," she defended. "He's the jerk."

"He's not a jerk, he's just..." The defense was automatic, but even I could tell from the beginning it was a lie. When I failed to finish the sentence, she only raised a brow as she looked back at me.

"Just what I thought."

Our arrival at the new transport silenced our conversation. Through the window, Wick glared at us, his brows furrowed and his arms crossed. He didn't have to speak for us to know that when we got into that vehicle, silence would be the best policy. One wrong word would cause a world of drama, and I was not in the mood to fuck around and find out. Instead, I held open the door for Mac, ensuring she got in and buckled up, then jogged around the car, opened the door, and silently got in before closing it.

Austin hadn't even waited for the door to fully

close before he was backing up, and that was perfectly fine with me. The less for Wick to question and pull apart, the better evening we'd have.

"It's my kill," I announced, holding up the shorter of the three straws. Was it the best way of deciding who got to take a life? No. Was it effective? Absolutely.

Next to us, Mac looked pale. "Isn't there another way to do this? Why do you have to do it at all?"

"Are you concerned?" I goaded her, trying to get her to admit that she had affection for us. It never got old, hearing her concern for us all.

"No." Her face gave nothing away until it cracked just a little. "Okay. Yes. A little."

"We can handle it," I promised.

Her eyes flicked to the others before back to mine. "It's just—"

"It's just that this man is a killer," Wick cut her off. "Not like us. But he preys on women. Stalks them. Strangles them. Ends their lives, and he's protected. No one will touch him because his father is a powerful judge. People are afraid, but I'm not. We aren't. Do you know why?"

She shook her head. "No."

"Because I've lived on the other side. I've felt my way in the dark with a serial killer at my side, and each of them deserves to die."

"Are you not the same?" And I could see the blow

that was to him. He flinched, her thoughts reflecting what he'd feared most of his life.

"Good and evil." I tossed my straw onto the table of the motel we were sharing. "It's all about intentions, princess. We don't harm those who are innocent."

"Oh."

Austin leaned back in his chair. "We're going to need you to knock. Pose as a housekeeper, get inside the place."

He informed her of the plan we'd discussed earlier while she was asleep in the car. We wouldn't let anything happen to her, but we needed the distraction. He chased women her age, women who were perfectly formed and gorgeous. She was both, but she would appear to be unsuspecting if she asked to come in as the cleaning service.

"That seems cliché. He's going to be suspicious." She was squeezing her fingers so tight I had to lean over and grab her hand.

"You'd think." I pulled her hand into my lap, ignoring the glare from Wick. "But sometimes the obvious isn't so apparent when people are desperate. He's been getting sloppy for a while. It's how the organization was able to pinpoint him. Now it's our job to make sure he doesn't strike again."

"And you guys?" Her big green eyes looked at me so fucking trustingly. Damn it, they melted me.

Austin sat next to me. His knee brushed against my thigh. I jumped and scooted away. He ignored my reaction, instead concentrating on Mac. "Wick will be outside of the back window. You'll need to unlock it. Asa's going through the bathroom vent. He'll aim to slip in while you distract the target at the door. I'll follow through the door after I get the signal from either Wick or Asa."

"And if I can't get the window unlocked?"

"I'll break the fucking glass if I need to. If you're in danger, we'll know. Remember the self-defense moves I taught you?" She nodded her head, her throat working like she wanted to speak, but no words came out. "Practice them. Practice them until they are second nature."

"You guys are really going to do this, then?" Her poor little lip was so abused by the teeth she assaulted it with.

"They assigned it to us. So we are really going to do it." I wanted to clarify *we*, because she was a part of us now. We were in this together.

"By who?"

"By who what?" Wick picked up a piece of paper he had been writing on. Sometimes he needed to write out the plan, so he didn't forget it. Then he pulled out a lighter and burned it.

"Who assigns it to you? I mean us." I loved her correction. She was a part of us, and I didn't want her to forget it.

"The higher ups, and then Jones delivers it."

"And Jones, he's the one who did the speech at

the ceremony?" Her eyes were curious as she waited for a response.

"Yes." I squeezed her fingers. "One day Wick will have his spot. Well, hopefully."

"He's very..." Her brows wrinkled. "Had he gone to school with us?"

"No." Wick finished watching the flames and tossed the burning paper into the metal can to die out. "He's been out for a few years. Worked his way up."

She nodded her understanding. "I guess that makes sense."

"Get some rest," Wick demanded. "We'll work on your moves for a few hours later, then we'll hit about ten tonight."

She listened to his instructions, not asking any more questions. She picked a bed, pulled back the blankets and climbed underneath it while we all still sat around, softly discussing the finer details. It wasn't until we were positive that she was asleep that Austin finally addressed what we had been thinking.

"You were out of control last night." It wasn't said with anger or warning. It was more of a factual statement. The way Wick treated her was borderline too far. "We almost had to step in."

"I wouldn't hurt her."

Wick would never *intend* to hurt her, but the fact was, sometimes he didn't see things as a whole. It clouded his lenses with the anger he held, his wants, his desires, his need to always be in control. Anyone on the outside looking in could see that Mac pushed him, and sometimes it might be too far.

"We're not saying you'd hurt her on purpose," I continued for Austin. "It's just..."

"You were rougher than you should have been. She's our housekeeper; we can't be bruising her up. We are supposed to cherish her," Austin finished.

"She can handle the bruising." Wick didn't seem apologetic.

"She shouldn't have to." Austin glared.

"She liked it. You saw it. I know you both were watching the feed." Wick was correct on that. We watched it. We rewound it and watched it again. I even saved the video for later. I wasn't ashamed of that fact. They both equally fascinated me and got my blood boiling, but that was something I wouldn't admit to him.

Austin stood, stretching. "I'm just asking that you be more careful with our woman."

If Wick's eyes rolled any harder, they'd get stuck. "Fine. I'll treat her like a delicate flower."

"Good." Austin walked toward the bed Mac was on and peeled back the covers before dropping his pants into a pile next to the bed. "It was a long drive. Nap, then we'll work our shit out to the smallest detail."

"Since when do you give orders?" Wick huffed.

Austin just flipped Wick off, ignored him, and crawled in next to Mac, no doubt savoring the best spot in this whole fucking hotel room. But I wasn't about to be left out. Following Austin's lead, I squeezed into the small space between the bed and the wall and took off my pants, leaving me in only my boxers. Folding back the blanket, I sat down slowly, careful not to wake her as I lowered myself to the pillow. Instantly, her body curved against mine as her ass snuggled into Austin. Our eyes met over her head, a silent conversation played out between us, a temporary truce in the awkward communications we've been dancing around with, before he lowered his head to the crook of her neck and closed his eyes, letting sleep take him.

CHAPTER TWENTY-EIGHT

AUSTIN

We woke a few hours later in a tangle of limbs — mine over Mac's, Asa's over mine — and I didn't want to move. Not like I tried hard to do so. I knew it was almost time for the mission, knew that soon we'd have to break the bubble we were in and rejoin the real world.

But I wasn't ready yet.

I wasn't sure if I ever would be.

Mac must have sensed I was awake because her body stirred under mine, gentle movements as she tried to fight against the pull of lucidity. Wakefulness ultimately won when she opened her eyes.

I smiled, my voice hoarse. "Hey you."

"Hey yourself."

"We need to get up."

She turned away from me and buried her head inside the crook of Asa's shoulder. "No. Go away."

I laughed. "I'm not going anywhere. We have shit to do."

"No. And you can't make me."

"But I can." Wick's voice broke into our bubble. "We've got to be in position in two hours. Get up, do what you need to. Mac, I want you to practice self-defense. You need to be ready because if you're not, you're taking us all down."

"Don't place the blame on her," Asa muttered. "She's new."

"We were all new once," Wick reminded us as he loomed over our pile of bodies. "We were just as accountable."

"Housekeepers aren't meant for the dirty job of it." I tried to defend her, even knowing that house-keepers can be just as liable as any others. They didn't need to do the ten kills like we did, but they still needed to prove they were capable.

Wick pulled the blanket off of us, and Mac's hand tried to chase it, wanting to stay under the warmth as long as possible. "You two are going to spoil her into thinking she doesn't need to work as hard to be part of this organization. But what will you do in less than two weeks when people start coming for her, testing her training and seeking revenge for what we've done to their team?"

"It's not that serious." Mac sat up and stretched. But maybe she didn't understand the brutality of it because it *was* that serious. It was more than serious. It was about to be our reality. A reality I didn't want to acknowledge while her thigh was wedged between mine.

Wick grabbed Mac's ankle, pulling it as she screamed, dragging her out from between us and down to the end of the bed. He ignored her struggles as he leaned over her, his eyes blazing. "Tell me it's not that serious when we have your ashes on the fireplace mantel."

"I—"

"You can't fucking tell us, can you? Because it will be serious. Losing you will be serious to us. Not having a housekeeper is fucking serious. We opted to take you on as a liability. I wouldn't change that. We are the best team out here for being fresh out of training, but even we can fuck up. I don't want that fuck up to mean your life."

"I don't want that either," she admitted as she looked at him, wide-eyed.

"Then do you think you could cooperate a little? Do what I ask? Not fight me every step of the way?" Wick's face was close to hers now. Only an inch separated them, and I waited for him to capture her lips. It's what I was aching to do.

But he didn't. When she nodded her head, agreeing to his terms, his hands grabbed her hips and lifted her up, tossing her over his shoulder and carrying her to the bathroom.

The door slammed behind them, and I turned my

head to look at Asa. His eyes were already on me, watching me wordlessly. My stomach tightened, my nerves suddenly on edge, reminding me I had spent days avoiding moments like this, moments where I was alone with Asa and forced to confront what I couldn't admit out loud.

That the one moment of intimacy between him and I had unlocked something within me, and I was afraid he wouldn't feel the same.

I opened my mouth, then closed it. Unsure exactly what to say. Then I opened it again, only to be cut off by his words.

"We should talk."

"We should," I admitted.

"You're avoiding me." He didn't say it with feeling. It wasn't an accusation. Just a fact.

"I just..." I turned my head and stared at the ceiling as I looked for the words I needed. "I just don't want to cross a line and ruin our friendship. Especially after what... what we..."

"You sucked my cock," Asa filled in. "Own it. There isn't any shame in that."

He's right; between us all, there is no shame. Being with him, what we did had nothing to do with shame and everything to do with confusion. "I'm not ashamed of it."

"Then?"

"I'm confused."

"Been there." Asa's throat worked around in a swallow. "But then I realized the world cares a lot more about my preferences than I do, and it's none of their business. All that matters is my happiness. Don't you think?"

"Are you happy?" I asked, not sure why because it didn't really solve how I was feeling.

"With you and Mac in bed with me?" I turned to look at him, not expecting that statement, but eager to hear what he had to say. "I've never been happier."

It took a moment for his words to sink in. I had been afraid to admit what I was feeling this whole time, which was ridiculous when he looked at me the way he was, with burning eyes and a cheeky grin.

"I'm afraid," I admitted.

"Love and affection are scary," Asa pointed out. "But you suck dick like a pro and I could get used to that. So instead of avoiding me like a pansy, why don't we see where things go?"

"It could fuck up the team dynamic."

"Regardless if we're fucking or not, the team dynamic is already wonky," Wick shouted from behind closed doors. "So fuck or whatever. Just leave the rest of us out of the suffocating tension."

"He acts like he didn't create this tension when he demanded you to open your mouth."

The reminder heated my body, making it nearly impossible to remain under the blankets. I kicked them off, struggling with the blankets that tangled around my feet before they fell to the floor.

No sooner did I free myself than Asa's body rolled on top of mine. His arms braced his weight on each side of my head as his lips found mine, devouring me and taking away all the doubts I had spent days building in my head.

His tongue was gentle as it coaxed my lips to part and let him in, but his teeth were sharp as he bit my lip, tugging it between his and making unspoken promises of what could come, what would come, if I just let him in.

After kissing me thoroughly, making me breathless and my body on fire with the need to follow this through, he pulled away, giving my lips one more tender peck before he pulled back. "We've got work to do."

"But—"

I tried to argue because damn it, I didn't need to prep for the work that was coming. I wasn't the one doing the kill this time. That was on Asa, and he'd never needed prep time. But he stopped me, a single brow dancing in a seductive taunt. "But if I kiss you much longer, I'll get carried away and not stop, and I think Mac and Wick would like to leave the bathroom at some point."

"Let 'em watch," I joked.

"Oh, they will. Just not tonight." He smacked a hand against my thigh. "Let's go. We've got predators to off and a woman to please."

The thought of pleasing Mac was the only motivation I had to get off my ass. I rolled to the side, finding the carpeted floor under my feet before standing. With a stretch, I walked toward the bath-room, knocking. "You can come out now."

I heard a gasp from the other side before Mac replied, "I'd rather not."

I blew out a breath. So it was like that in there then. Got it. I walked to the table and picked up my wallet, then looked at Asa, who was sitting on the edge of the bed, the broad spans of his muscled back on display and making my mouth water. When had I ever thought that about another male?

"I'm going for a walk, maybe grab a snack before we have to bounce. Get my thoughts in order. If you need anything, call." My voice was too fucking gruff, but no one questioned me as I opened the door and stepped out, walking into the chill evening air and disappearing from sight.

CHAPTER TWENTY-NINE

MAC

"You can do this." Austin, always my biggest cheerleader, squeezed my hand as we walked through the parking lot of the hotel. "Wick picked the lock of the supply room, said there is a cart you can use in there."

"Great." The words held no enthusiasm. "Fantastic."

"Good news is, practice makes perfect." He was beaming, already proud of whatever we were doing here.

"How did my life get me here?" I groaned.

"You mean with three men that worship you, I assume."

I let my head fall limply on my shoulders, allowing me to look at him. "Yeah. Exactly what I meant."

He pulled me aside, forcing me into an open door the minute we approached the building. His body caged me in as he gave me a kiss that made my toes curl. When he pulled away, he smirked. "Your cleaning cart, housekeeper."

He nodded toward the cart. "Thanks. Just what I always wanted."

"Room 105. Remember, the minute you disappear inside, I'll already be approaching the door. Leave it unlocked if you can, but if you can't, it won't stop us."

"I know." How could I not know? They'd drilled in what the plans were nonstop for the last two hours. I knew they wanted to keep me safe, but I'd rather not do this. Even if it meant taking out a predator.

"You've got this," he urged me on, trying to build me up.

"I know."

"Then why aren't you moving?"

Amusement danced in his eyes, causing the gold flecks to nearly make the blue of his eyes glow. I cursed, realizing he was right. I had my assignment and the tools I needed to operate my part of the assignment already at my disposal. I grabbed the cart, pushing it out the door, but before I exited, Austin's hand snagged my hip, pulling me back so he could kiss me one more time.

When he pulled away, he looked me up and down. "You'll be saving that maid's uniform."

"Typical male," I grumbled as I stepped out into the pathway, walking five doors down to room 105.

When I reached the door, I stopped and gathered myself. I could do this. It was easy. Simple. Just knock, get myself in, figure the shit out. Easy. The boys would be in there, they'd protect me. They wouldn't let me down. Except there was a part of me that didn't know if I could trust them, didn't know if they would leave me in this vulnerable position.

They wouldn't betray me.

They cared for me.

I was theirs.

They were mine.

They wouldn't let me die.

I raised my knuckles to the cheap wood, rapping against the door. Time seemed to slow as I waited. On the other side, it was silent. I raised my hand, knocking again, this time a little louder. A slight shuffle on the other side of the door alerted me that the room wasn't empty like I had secretly hoped it was. Another minute passed before the door opened, and cold eyes peeked out.

"Housekeeping," I declared.

My skin crawled as his eyes roamed over me, drinking in the short skirt and low-cut shirt, exposing my cleavage. I wasn't his type, according to reports. He liked them with fuller breasts and less curvy, but Asa assured me that men were opportunists, simple as that, and though I may not be his type, I was like a present one didn't expect, but adored anyway.

I was sure that was a compliment, but I couldn't wait to get an assignment where we got to objectify them instead of my assets.

His eyes stopped at my breasts, not bothering to rise as he talked to my boobs. "I didn't order house-keeping."

"Didn't you read that sign?" I swallowed, hoping he couldn't tell how nervous I was or notice that I was sweating way more than was attractive. "It's complimentary. We clean daily. How are your towels? Need fresh ones?"

"My towels are fine." His eyes dipped to my legs.

"Sheets?" I patted a fresh stack that was on my cart. "I can't say for sure that those are fresh. I wasn't the one who cleaned this room last."

"I'll take the risk." He moved to slam the door, and I stuck my foot in between the crack. My heart pounded, the nerves inside of me doing somersaults.

"I can see the dust on your window from here. At least let me wash it down. Make it sparkle for you."

He was silent for so long I thought I blew my last chance at getting inside, but then he pulled the door open wide, inviting me in. "If you insist. If this is what you really want. Then, by all means, come inside."

I hesitated as our eyes locked, and I could see the soulless look in the depth of his irises. Evil. He was pure evil, and maybe there was a part of me that hadn't believed it. That wanted the boys to be lying that this man deserved to die. But I could see it now, see how the wheels turned as he thought of all the ways he intended to cause harm to me, all the ways I'd die.

I grabbed the window cleaner and a rag, closed my eyes for a moment as I reminded myself that my boys were close by, that they wouldn't let him harm me, then I stepped through the threshold. The door slammed the minute I was inside, and the turn of the deadbolt was deafening. I turned, giving the wall my back and not the man whose eyes glinted with malice.

I wasn't sure how long I stared at him, but he broke the silence first. "Well, are you going to clean the windows?"

"Um, yes. Sorry." I backed toward the window, still trying to keep him in sight. After pulling back the blinds, I sprayed it down, wiping its glass like I'd done this a million times in my lifetime. While I scrubbed along the seam, I flipped the lock because, though this wasn't the window Wick would enter, I wasn't sure if I'd be able to unlock the door for Austin. He was guarding the exit something fierce, and I doubt he would let me walk back out that door.

"The other window?" He prompted when I turned to him and gave him my best fake smile.

"Oh. Sorry. Yes." Shit, I was a crap housekeeper, clearly. Ironic, since I joined the boys as their housekeeper. Not like they actually wanted me to clean. Seemed like Austin had all the cleaning under control.

Walking to the furthest window meant I had to

give him my back. Something I absolutely didn't want to do, but I had no choice. If I strained my ears, I thought I heard a noise in the bathroom. But maybe it was hopeful thinking because this guy was giving me serious creep vibes.

Each step I took, he took a step to follow. He was close, near enough that I swore I could feel his breath against the back of my neck. My back was stiff when I reached the window, my palms slick with sweat as I swept aside the curtains and squeezed the blue liquid to spray the clear glass. I leaned forward, the rag touching the window when I felt the first touch.

I jumped, attempted to turn around, but he had me smashed into the glass before I could even think about any of the self-defense moves that Wick tried so hard to drill into me. His face moved close, smashing against my cheek. "You picked the wrong room."

I could scream. It wouldn't help my situation at all. They would come. They would. I knew it. Even if I didn't see a single face outside of the window.

I dropped the cleaner and the rag, letting the distraction of them falling to the floor take his attention away from the window so I could flick the lock. No sooner did my fingers move the latch than he was pulling at his neck, removing his tie. He used the tie to wrap around my throat, cutting off my air as he pulled me back by the material.

I stumbled backwards, my hand going to the silk around my neck, trying to pull it loose. His fingers were bruising as he grabbed my arm, twisting it to a nearly painful position as he dragged me toward the bed. He tossed me onto the bedding, his face a sneer of disgust.

"Look at you, you whore. Come in here, insisting on teasing me with your disgusting little cunt. You do this to all the guests, don't you? Tease them with that slutty little skirt, not letting them get a glimpse of the pussy it covers."

"I—" I gasped out the word as his fist wrapped around the tie, tightening it more.

"I didn't tell you to speak."

He crawled over my body, straddling my legs with his own, dropping his weight on my thighs to prevent movement before he reached for the seam of the dress, effortlessly tearing the material down the side. His fingers grabbed my thigh, digging in so tight, I knew that I'd have a bruise, but still I tried to struggle. Tried to prevent him from tearing into the material that still separated his skin from mine.

He reached for his belt, pulling it free from his slacks as he grabbed the hands I was using to push against him with, the hands I was fighting and flailing against the attack, using them as my only weapon. He grabbed my wrist, nearly snapping it as he jerked it toward him, wrapping the leather around it before he grabbed my other one, tying them together and rendering my arms useless.

Then he unbuttoned his pants, letting his fly open and his cock bounce out. "Do you know who I am, whore? Do you know whose room you walked into today? You wanted this. You were practically begging me to let you in so you could feel my giant dick inside your body before you die."

I cringed. Words like that were no wonder he couldn't get his ladies organically.

His fingers grabbed onto my underwear, the movement anything but gentle. He had just tugged when Asa's voice broke in, his knife pointed at the side of his neck. "If you move another inch, I'll kill you right here."

His hands left my body, and he held them high. "I wasn't going to hurt her."

"I don't know who you think you're fucking lying to, but I can see the bruises and the welts already peppering my girl's skin."

Asa grabbed onto his hair, digging his nails into his scalp as he dragged him back, tossing him on the ground as Wick stepped through the window. One look at me and his eyes were blazing. Fury rolled over his face in an array of emotions before he went to the man on the floor.

"Fucking prick," Wick spat. "Josh Martin, did you think we wouldn't figure it out? Did you think because your dad had power, you'd get away with it forever?"

Wick's foot met Josh's teeth. He swayed and collapsed, only to fumble to a sitting position again and spit a mouthful of blood at Wick. "Fuck you."

"Look at her," Wick growled. "Look at what you did to my girl."

Austin's fingers were working the belt off my hands. I hadn't even seen him enter, but I was glad he was here. I was thankful they all were.

"That whore?" Josh laughed.

He never finished his display of amusement before Asa pushed a blade through his eye. He pushed it in at an angle so that it didn't kill him, didn't disable him, but he felt every ounce of pain from the injury. I winced, nearly gagging at the sight of a grown man howling in pain, a blade sticking out of his eye socket. When Asa pulled it out, the sickening sound of the blade breaking the suction from his eye, I fought a heave.

Austin rubbed the bruises on my wrist before bringing it to his lips, kissing the raw skin. "The windows were old. The front one wouldn't open, and the door was locked. I had to go around back."

"I almost got stuck in the ventilation. Next time, Austin goes. His shoulders aren't as wide," Asa tossed over his shoulders as the man in front of him begged.

"Why didn't we think of these logistics?" Wick pondered.

"You're the team leader," Asa huffed as he sliced into an artery of the man's leg, near his groin. His eyes fell on me. "The femoral artery. It's bloody but effective. Come here."

He beckoned to me, and for a moment, I was frozen, my eyes fixated on the blood that pooled around the guy's body. But Austin nudged me forward, and I stumbled off the bed, avoiding the blood as I met Asa at his side. Wick watched me. "You'll be punished if you pass out."

Like I could fucking stop it. The prick. "I won't."

"Good." Asa nodded before he grabbed my hand and placed his blade in my open palm. "The carotid arteries are here." He used his fingers on the man as his body grew limp and pointed out the location on each side of the neck. "The best place to stab is here and here."

My fingers trembled around the bloody handle of the weapon Asa had so casually handed me. "Okay."

"Now stab him." I knew the order was coming, but hearing Asa say the words so emotionlessly was shocking. It was Wick who would do things so heartlessly, not Asa. Not my guy who observed every detail and touched so gently. "Now."

He pulled the limp head back, the good eye of the man at half-mast. He was almost gone, his life almost ended, and I knew it was for the best. I knew the harm he'd done and the girls he'd killed. But to take his life, to snuff it out myself... "I can't."

Without waiting for further argument, Asa's hand wrapped around my wrist and he jolted me forward. He forced me to push the blade into the neck. Then used his other hand to push on Josh's head, bringing his skin to the hilt, splitting the flesh and tearing through his tendons, allowing me to feel every single thing. Then he pulled back, dragging the head from the blade, releasing the pressure and weight before dropping him to the hotel floor.

"I didn't think you'd do it," Wick mused.

"I told you before the raid. If they order her to make the kill, I can't change that."

"What?" I gasped as I dropped the blade, the sound of it falling cushioned by the outdated carpet.

"Yeah." Wick patted me on the back. "Last-minute changes from above. You understand, right?"

Then he walked away, leaving a one-eyed bloody mess staring back at me.

CHAPTER THIRTY

WICK

I was an asshole.

It wasn't a new development. We all knew it from the start. Still, not disclosing the fact that Mac needed to make the kill made me feel slightly worse than expected. I knew I was holding onto this secret, knew I should have said something, but instead of speaking up, I scooped Mac up and took her to the shower with me earlier. Stealing a moment just to be with her before the hell of emotions from the job got unleashed.

The disgust on Asa's face when he had to carry out the order, had to help her take a life, made something in my chest twinge. I didn't tell him, didn't tell them. I held that information close to me until Mac was out of earshot and already taking up position to infiltrate.

Asa was furious; I'd never seen him so mad. Usually, he was even-tempered, and it was Austin who occasionally had the outbursts of anger. But for a moment, I thought Asa would drive his knife through my heart and take her out of there, carting her off to some secluded place that was off radar with no electricity.

That was how much this girl infatuated them. I could admit, just not out loud, that after having her pussy squeeze like a vice over my cock, I could see the appeal.

Asa left her, the guilt of what he forced her to do already eating at him. I wasn't as weak as Asa. Whatever guilt I felt, whatever disgust, was overshadowed by the need to please the organization. We were the best team of fresh trainees they had. We deserved the best housekeeper. If she couldn't perform a simple killing, she wasn't for us.

It was Austin who moved to her side first. He used his body, the width of his shoulders as a shield, blocking her view of the body that lay in front of her. "You don't have to look."

"I killed a man," she muttered.

Asa truthfully did her a favor. He was dead regardless, close to bleeding out. The blow she issued only sped up the process. Last injury, last breath, the organization would count it as hers.

"He was already dead," Austin reassured her,

though through the eyes of an innocent, she'd not see it that way.

"I killed a man," she repeated.

"She's in shock," Austin observed.

"She'll get over it." I wasn't going to coddle her. It wouldn't be the last death she'd see.

"She didn't know she was going to make the kill," Austin pointed out.

"Had to happen at some point." I shrugged.

"It's just—"

"Look. She needs to be tougher than this. Our life isn't for the weak. Let her thicken her skin."

"You're a jackass," he growled before he bent over, picked her up, and walked out the door.

"I'll call clean up," I said out loud, not like anyone was here to hear me. They were both ticked at me. It was better this way. If I hadn't held that secret, they wouldn't have let her come. Would have made her wait back at our hotel room. Kept her in the car. Held her up somewhere away from any traumatic experiences.

I made the call, figured out the cleaning arrangements, and waited in the room for the crew to come. After that, it was out of my hands and not my problem. When the crew came, I wasn't shocked to see my team had left me without a ride back to our hotel. They were petty mother fuckers; I'd give them that.

I walked the few blocks, not willing to call a cab and give more traces of our whereabouts. Generally, the organization had us covered. But that didn't mean

I could be careless. The walk wasn't awful; the air was chilled, and it gave me time to think about what the hell we were about to do. How the hell were we going to protect Mac when the world inevitably crumbled down on us?

Asa stood outside the door of the room, looking like a guard dog, his teeth bared at me as he snarled, "You're a fucking ass."

"I did what I had to." I shrugged it off, hoping the guilt would roll off my shoulders with it.

"You did what you *wanted* to," he stated.

"I didn't want her to make the kill." Which was my truth. But I would not go against agency orders to prevent it.

"You may have not wanted her to make the kill, but you did nothing to prepare her. Did you ever fucking think that if you had told her she'd be doing the kill, she might have been in a better mental state? Catching her off guard with something this big, this life-altering, wasn't fair. We had over a week to prepare for our first kill. Months of training, and a week to prepare for the first assignment. You gave her thirty seconds and counted on me to force the follow through."

"You claimed the kill was yours this round," I pointed out.

"We drew fucking straws while this whole time, you knew none of us would follow through. She won't even fucking look at me." Asa pushed me. His palm hit hard against my shoulder, and all I could do was stumble back in shock.

"What the fuck?" was all I got out.

"You had me do it because you were too weak to do it yourself," he accused.

"I'm the team leader."

He pushed me again, this time with more aggression, but I refused to let it bother me. Refused to give into the urge to fight back. It wouldn't solve anything. "You're a fucking coward who didn't want to do it yourself, didn't want to be the villain in her story, so you forced me to do it."

"I'm already the villain!" I shouted. "She looks at you both like you're fucking gods and I'm the scum on the sandal of Zeus's foot!"

"And why the fuck is that?" He stepped closer again, his face close to mine, his eyes burning, and I'd never in my life seen Asa like this. I hated that I turned him this way. That I was the reason his temper surfaced. When I didn't answer, he continued. "It's because you're selfish. You only care about what you want and how it will benefit you. Fuck everyone else."

"That's not true," I tried to defend, but even the words tasted like a lie.

I cared about my team. No one questioned that. But I wasn't above manipulating and ordering them to do as I pleased, how I pleased, so that I came out on top.

"You're really shit at this teamwork thing. Why can't you just admit that you went about this order all wrong? But you can't, can you?" Another push and I stumbled off the curb, putting us eye to eye. "The great Chadwick Moore never could do wrong. He's a fucking saint. He cares so much about his team; he'd protect them with his life." He paused. "As long as it favors himself."

"That's not fucking true!" I shouted. "I would protect you all with my life. How fucking dare you question my loyalty?"

"Oh." Asa laughed humorlessly. "I forgot. You will protect us physically. But fuck our mental stability. That belongs to you to fuck with as you please. Rest up in the fucking car. We don't want you anywhere near her. We'll pull out in two hours."

"Are you giving me orders?" I growled.

"Well, I'm sure as fuck not in the mood to take them from you."

He turned, giving me his back, and I reached up, my hand on his shoulder, intent on stopping him, but he whirled around so fast I hadn't even realized his fist had balled until it met my eye, the force so strong for a second, I thought I'd crumble. I shook out the pain, knowing for sure my eye was about to be swollen shut.

"Feel better?"

"Not quite," he admitted.

"Want to hit the other eye?" I offered, breaking the tension, which was funny, until he reminded me he literally had his blade in an eye socket mere hours before.

"With my blade? Gladly." He inhaled deeply, then exhaled, the fight leaving him. "Give us a few hours. Please. Keys are in the ignition."

This time, when he walked away, I didn't stop him. I let him go, granting him the one request he rarely voiced. I didn't move until he was inside the room. The door slammed, and the lock clicked into place. I knew that lock was to keep me out, and the sound echoed uncomfortably loud in the night, disturbing me more than I thought it would.

The keys were in the ignition, like Asa said they would be, and I was thankful for that. I didn't want to have to sit in front of the hotel room door, moping, swollen eyed, looking like a couple's spat gone too far. I would rather lie in the middle of a busy street than outwardly appear so desperate to be in that room with the rest of my team.

But I *was* desperate. Maybe even a little sorry. And I couldn't gauge just how mad Austin was, or how well Mac was taking the situation from out here.

I tilted the seat back as far as it would go, then got comfortable, knowing that I was in for a long couple of hours. It took me thirty minutes to fall asleep, and when I did, I was in so deep, my mind reeling with memories and thoughts, bringing me back to my childhood and the feel of the first time my knife sunk into flesh.

And I'd forced that on Mac.

I was tossing and turning, my mind a jumble of images, of feelings, of blood, when a knock on the window jolted me awake, tearing me from the fitful sleep and into the eyes of the girl who was haunting me.

CHAPTER THIRTY-ONE

MAC

I was stunned at first, shocked, horrified that I had done something so ruthless, so heinous, so final. He was dead; I knew that. As much as I wished he would come back from that, return to this earth and open his eyes, I knew that wasn't possible. The blood, god, the amount of blood that coated every surface around the body, filling the air with the scent of copper, made me retch every time I thought about it. And it was that blood that only confirmed the truth for me. He couldn't be saved.

After the initial shock wore off, the regret seeped away slowly. He was a bad person. I saw with my own eyes, felt with my body, heard him speak the words that only confirmed the truth. He was a predator. A killer. A psychopath. And if we didn't stop him, how many more deaths would be brushed under the rug because of his links to power within the government body?

I did the right thing.

He deserved it.

Still, after days spent pondering the life I took, I still struggled to accept it in full. I was glad I did it, but I couldn't believe it was me.

I brushed my hair, parting it on each side before sweeping the long strands back and twisting them into two buns. I had class today, and the more time I spent with these guys, the harder I found it to force myself to go, even though Wick insisted. After pulling on a dress and a pair of thick tights, I found some combat boots in my closet and slipped my feet into them.

The dress might have been something Wick picked out; I wasn't sure. But the boots, a hundred percent Asa. He wore the matching pair daily and somehow, I found that fact endearing. The boots clonked loudly on the stairs as I made my way down to breakfast. Each step I took down the stairs made my thighs scream with pain from all the squats Wick forced me to do this morning.

"What are you doing?" Wick's voice boomed from the stoop of the stairs.

"Dying from leg day," I grumbled.

"You can't wear that outside."

"Watch me." I flipped him off, knowing damn well I was provoking him. I liked him best provoked.

"It's raining," he pointed out.

"Then I guess you better not let me get wet, Wick. Shouldn't be hard with that mood you're in."

"Mac." The words were a rough growl, and though I taunted him, acting like his moods didn't turn me on, they did. They very much made me as wet as a broken fire hydrant. "Put on something warmer."

"I've got leggings. I've got boots. We've got umbrellas. You're driving. I'll be fine." I ticked off all the reasons his demand made no sense.

Austin appeared in the doorway of the living room, his eyes gleaming as they checked me out from head to toe. "She's fine. It's hardly drizzling, anyway."

The growl of displeasure echoed off the walls as Wick stomped passed me, practically shoulder bumping me into the wall. I waited until he was out of earshot before I whispered, "He's in a mood."

"Again," Austin added. "He's just... sorry. He's sorry he forced you to do it. He didn't want to. None of us did. But the agency—"

"Does he think I blame him?"

"Don't you? He's the team leader."

"By that logic, I'd blame Asa more. He handed me the knife, gave instructions, and helped me along." I pointed out the obvious.

"He's worried." He changed the subject as his fingers toyed with his hair, a nervous habit I found he did often.

"Because it's almost time," I guessed.

"Any day. Any day they could come barreling in here, and your life depends on our ability to protect."

"I trust you. All of you," I told him, and it was true. I'd trusted no one more than I'd grown to trust these men. I hardly knew them, but I was discovering more about them each day.

"We're going to be late," Austin pointed out. "Hurry and get breakfast."

I walked past him, tapping a single finger on his nose before I disappeared into the kitchen. They had a plate made for me, a spread of French toast, eggs, and sausage that looked amazing. I knew Wick had cooked it. It's what he did. He replaced all his hardness with soft gestures. Just like Asa filled the voids with every detail about everything he could, and Austin liked to offer all the gentle touches and softness the other two lacked.

I took my plate to the table, practically inhaling the cinnamon goodness of the French toast and humming with happiness from the greasy sausage. When I finished, I washed my dish and met Austin by the front door. Asa and Wick were already waiting for us. Though they weren't going to campus this morning; they had other things to take care of.

They dropped us off a little early, a fact I minded little, and when class was over, and everyone filed out of the room, there was still no Wick or Asa in sight. "They're late."

"They texted me they would be," Austin announced, and sometimes I hated that I wasn't involved in their group chats. "I've got to find something at the library, a book for history, and then we can walk home if you want."

I agreed, trudging toward the library while looking at my phone screen. I pulled up all three of their names on my messages app and typed one out.

How come I'm not in your group chat?

Wick's response came fast. *We can't talk about you if you're reading it.*

What the hell do you say about me?

Austin took his phone out of his pocket, feeling the vibrations. Then he read the messages, his face turning red as a grin took over. "You really don't want to know, Mac."

"Whatever happened to my sweet lab partner?" I grumbled, crossing my arms as the phone rumbled in my grip.

How detailed do you want? Fucking Wick. I felt like he was taunting me.

Clearly all the details, asshole.

Careful what you ask for, sweetheart, Asa chimed in, and I groaned.

"I hate you all."

"Do you though?" Austin pulled open the library door, and I stepped through. "Because I can list a million reasons you love us, and none of them involve clothes."

"I could probably get naked with a female and have the same outcome," I taunted.

He raised his fist to his mouth and bit his knuckles. "Oh, I'd pay to see that."

My phone buzzed, and I knew without looking that it was Wick. I looked anyway. *Today's text rundown comprises how your boobs look amazing, the tights are delicious on your thighs, you whine too much about squats, you used up all the hot water this morning, and you're two days out from shark week. Oh, and Austin gets your company all day long while we losers have other shit to do. It's still early. I'm sure by the end of the day, the list of topics will grow.*

I opened my mouth, then closed it. Opened, then closed. Looking like a fish out of water as my mouth gaped at the text. How did they even know that? *I* didn't even know my period was two days away. I mean I guessed soon, but two days? That's insanity.

How do you even...

I left the text at that because I truly had no words. They knew what I was asking though because it was Asa who replied before the others could.

You know I like to track everything. It's for the best. Information, no matter how small, is fucking useful in our job. And for the record, it was Austin who complained about you using all the hot water. I'm perfectly okay with freezing, if it means you're happy.

"Fucking suck up," Austin spat, earning him a glare from the librarian at the counter as we passed. "I wasn't complaining, I swear. But it was so cold my balls ached."

"Sounds like a complaint. You could have joined me," I pointed out.

"I didn't know that was an option, and also, you take showers like you're at the entrance of hell and ready to jump into the pit. I don't know if I'd survive."

"Sounds like a you problem," I whispered as we passed two people studying. I didn't know where we were going, but he let me lead the way. I assumed the history section since I vaguely remembered a mention of history class, so I weaved my way through the tables and shelves until we were buried in the back corner.

Austin's fingers ran over the edge of some books before he informed me, "I'm doing a report on the Roman Empire."

"Sounds fun. We can watch some documentaries if you'd like," I offered.

His head turned. "You'd do that?"

"I mean, I can't promise I'd stay awake, but I would definitely try," I clarified.

He was silent for a moment as his eyes took me in, crinkling at the corners, though he didn't smile. After a moment, when I figured he wouldn't talk at all, he licked his lips. "I'd like that."

"Good." I nodded before raising a hand, running my fingers over the rows of dusty books. "Me too. Any specific book you're looking for?"

He still hadn't moved, even though I had walked a few feet away. When he didn't answer, I turned to find his eyes on me, burning liquid pools of blue that made my skin flush. "What?"

"It's just you're so fucking beautiful."

I wasn't hideous. I knew that. I was average. But sometimes these guys made me seem like so much more. "Are you trying to butter me up for something?"

"I've never been the buttering up type," he asserted, and that was true. Mostly everything with Austin was straightforward. He was kind. He always thought of me and never asked much in return. He wasn't like Wick, who went out of his way to be a dick, or Asa, who sometimes got into moods that I couldn't decipher. He was Austin, and always perfect.

He stalked forward, his eyes still blazing. "Wick was right. You should have changed this morning."

I looked down. "I think I look fine."

"It's not about looks, Mac. It's about how tempting you'd be to us, and with that dress, you're a fucking dream."

I took a step back when he got closer. "I'm wearing thick leggings."

"We know what's under them."

"Then why buy it?" I questioned, not understanding these boys at all.

"We are suckers for punishment. Clearly."

"Clearly," I mocked.

He looked over his shoulder before he glanced back at me. "Call them."

"Excuse me?" My brows pulled together in confusion.

"Video the team," he ordered.

"In the library? That could be too loud."

"Put in headphones." He pulled out his ear buds from his pocket before placing one in my ear. "Call them."

"Okay?" I was so confused, but I followed orders and pulled up Asa's number. After hitting the call button, I waited for the phone to connect.

After a minute, Asa answered, his worried face taking up the whole screen. "Mac, what's wrong?"

"I- Austin said I needed to call you," I explained as Austin took my phone from my hands, putting it up on a shelf so that nearly my full body was in the screen's frame.

"Did he now?" Asa smirked and leaned back in the seat. He glanced at Wick. "Pull over."

Wick listened to Asa without question, but I argued, "No need. I can call back if you're busy."

"You better fucking not hang up that phone because I swear to god baby, I'll punish you." Wick spat out. I could hear him, but his face was out of the screen as he drove the vehicle to the side of the road.

I don't know why, but whenever Wick used a pet name, it hit hard, always heating my body with lust. I almost wanted to ask what my punishment would be this time, but my mouth went dry when Austin dropped to his knees in front of me, his fingers reaching up to grip the waist of my leggings before he shimmied them down my hips. His eyes met mine, blazing.

"What are you doing?" I gasped before hissing out, "We're in the library."

"That explains the books." Asa was amused as he watched us.

"I told you not to wear that dress," Wick taunted as his face came into the frame, sharing the video call with Asa.

He told me. I didn't listen. But damn it, I didn't know not doing so would mean this as an alternative. "I didn't know."

Cold air hit my skin as Austin pulled off my panties, his lips kissing my thighs before he nudged me. "Widen your legs."

"Why?" My heart was beating so erratically, I was positive this might actually be the death of me. I might die here. In the middle of the library. With my soaked panties around my knees.

"Makenna, I think you know why." Wick's sultry voice filled the earbud, making me shiver.

If I had a single question about what was happening, it dissolved when Austin's nose brushed against my clit a second before his tongue probed inside of my body. My mouth opened, but before a moan could escape, his hand came up, clasping over my lips.

"You're in a library, Mac," Asa reminded me. "Control yourself."

"Fuck off," I panted as Austin's fingers left my mouth in favor of digging into the skin of my thigh, holding my stance wide while his other hand went to my pussy, parting my lips to give him better access. His tongue lapped inside of me while his nose brushed my clit and the sensations, the angle, made it nearly impossible to think.

"Don't stop talking. Or he stops," Wick ordered.

I didn't dare question if he was serious. I knew Wick enough now to know that he would withhold all the pleasure from me for his own sadistic satisfaction. With my chest heaving, I muttered, "Where are you?"

Wick's nose scrunched. "About an hour away. You knew I wouldn't tell you my plans today. Why ask?"

"I—" Fuck. I reached back and grabbed a shelf, knuckling it tight as a finger was added into my body. "I need to talk."

"You do," he praised. "Like a good girl. Why are you in the library?"

Why were we in the library? My cloudy mind couldn't remember. All it could think about was the man between my thighs. My hand reached down, tangling in the messy mop of blonde hair. "I- I don't remember."

Austin bit my clit and I turned my head, biting into my shirt to stop the moan the feeling was drawing from me. Wick wasn't letting me dismiss the answer that easily. "You know, and Austin won't move a single muscle until you answer me."

Austin's thick finger froze, unmoving in my body, his teeth still held my clit in their grasp and it was too much to handle. I needed him to move. I needed to feel. I closed my eyes, trying to remember. With my chest heaving, I licked my lips. "The Romans."

Austin's finger pulled out, before pumping back in, making me gasp before biting my lip to stifle it. Wick's gaze was wicked, scheming, amused, as he watched me. "I knew you knew it, little vixen. You just needed a little incentive. Next question..."

"Oh god," I panted half from pleasure, half from fear of whatever this man was about to torture me with.

"If someone were to attack you right now, how would you defend yourself?" Asa's hand moved, and the sound of his belt jingled, making my eyes burn into his, daring him to join me.

"I'd let them kill me. Just fucking let me die," I whimpered. "There would be worse ways to go."

"Mac." Wick scowled. "I'm serious."

"So am I." Another whimper escaped me as Austin bent his finger, teasing me, rubbing against that bundle of nerves that was pure pleasure to counteract the pain of his bites.

"Real answers, Makenna."

"My back is covered," I stated, trying to think when it was clearly an impossible task. "I'd only need to worry about my sides and front."

"Okay good. Continue." Wick leaned forward, His eyes on the screen but not on my face. Instead, he was concentrated on the spot where Austin's head was squeezed between my thighs and his hand held my dress up, exposing my bare skin for anyone who walked by to see.

"Left is a dead end." My body was wound tight. The need to cum outweighed nearly anything else. "There is a shelf behind Austin."

"Okay," Asa groaned on the other side of the line, but Wick didn't spare him a glance.

"My right." My chest rose and fell heavily.

"What about your right?" He knew I was close, his lips tilted up, amused at my torture and the struggle I was battling.

"It's the only angle of attack," I answered.

"And what the fuck do you plan to do about it?" Wick prompted. "A man's running at you, ready to take you out. Do something, Mac."

"If I have a knife, I could throw it," I offered.

"You're a shit aim at knife throwing and we all fucking know it," he pointed out.

"I'm getting better," I argued. God, my body was on fire, my nerves were building up with the burn, ready to crest, but each time I got close, Austin would pause, ruining it all.

"Not enough to stay alive," Wick insulted. "What else have you got?"

I wracked my mind, trying to grasp what to say. "Move low. Duck. Make myself a smaller target. If they are within reach, groin shot. Throat if I'm upright. If they've already got me, nails to their eye sockets."

There was a long pause while Wick mulled over

whatever I said. I hadn't even remembered what answer I gave him. I just wanted this to end so I could cum. So the tension that held my body tight would release me from its hold.

Finally, Wick nodded. "Good enough. Let her cum."

With that, Austin sucked my clit into his mouth, and I exploded at the same time as Asa's moans filled my ear. My hand pulled at Austin's hair, gripping it so hard I knew it had to hurt, but I couldn't control it, while the other hand covered my mouth, stifling the screams of pleasure I knew wanted to release.

When I finally came down from the high of pleasure, Austin stood, not breaking eye contact as he pulled up my leggings and brushed down my dress. A devilish smile spread shamelessly across his innocent boy next door face. He licked his lips, his eyes falling to mine before he leaned down, kissing me. I tasted myself, the musky sweet flavor mixed with a taste that I only associated with him.

With a quick pat of my ass, he pulled away. "Mac?"

"Yeah?" I answered breathlessly.

"You've been blocking the book I need this whole time."

I shoved at his shoulder as he reached behind my head, grabbing a book that was indeed about the Roman Empire. He laughed, not caring how loud he was as I spat, "Asshole."

CHAPTER THIRTY-TWO

MAC

"Ten more."

"I'd rather die," I ground out. And if I did ten more pushups, I just might. I wasn't made for this life. Why hadn't he realized this by now?

"You can and you will," Wick ordered.

"No. Really. I don't think I can do it," I groaned as I nearly faceplanted.

"Eight more and I'll carry you home," he offered and fuck, that was an appealing offer. An offer I knew he'd follow through with because Wick never went back on his word.

"Fine." I dipped, my arms nearly giving out as I tried not to touch the ground. "Can I do it on my knees?"

"Like a lady?" He raised a brow. "With that mouth?"

He had a point. "Please."

"No knees. Six more. Come on, baby. We've got places to be tonight and can't wait around all fucking night for you to finish your set."

"Just leave me here." To die. But I left that part out because he already accused me of being overly dramatic.

"You know I can't do that." He put his hands on his hips, raising his shirt just enough that I saw a delicious patch of tanned muscle. I dipped down one more time to distract myself from the eye candy in front of me.

"Why are you guys so obsessed with me?" I joked.

"The obsession probably goes back to that mouth of yours." My spaghetti arms nearly gave out with his words as I lowered my body one more time. "Halfway there, baby; you've got this."

"You've got a fair point," I grunted. "What's the plan tonight?"

"If you shut the fuck up for once, you might have an easier time working out. Ever think of that?"

I rolled my eyes. This man loved getting under my skin. I swear, I had a love-hate relationship with him. I loved when he touched me, but hated him every other moment of the day.

Another dip and I thought I'd die. Finishing the other reps nearly took me out, and when I was finished, I collapsed onto the gross gym floor, a pile of sweat and flesh. "I'm done and I'm dead."

"Look at you. You did it. Good girl." He reached down and offered me his hand to pull me up. It took longer than it should have and more effort than I liked just to reach up and place my palm in his. He yanked, using all his strength to get me to my feet. It was a good thing because I'd doubted I could do it myself. "Jesus, Mac, you're like an overcooked green bean, just flopping around. Stand the fuck up."

"I'm dead. You've killed me."

"I've not killed you." Wick shook his head. "You've still got your clothes on."

"Unfortunate," Asa added as he walked up. "Almost ready?"

"We'll never be ready if Mac doesn't stop fucking around." Wick's eyes roamed over me, though he was talking to Asa. "She's gotten skinnier. I prefer her with meat on her bones. Maybe up the carbs and protein?"

"What if I liked this new skinny?" I glared at them both as they examined me with thoughtful expressions.

"Maybe stop with the five-mile runs." Asa winked at me, knowing I hated them.

"She needs to be able to run and have some speed if she's ever in danger and needs to escape," Wick argued.

"Good point. We'll pull back slightly and increase the calorie intake."

"I'm right fucking here," I nearly shouted.

"Believe us, we can't forget when you're never fucking quiet," Wick insulted me.

"Be nice to my girl." Austin walked in, his sweaty locks of hair sticking to his forehead as he ran a towel over his face. The sight of his sweaty abs flexing made me temporarily stupid, my mind short circuiting.

"Your girl is never nice to me," Wick huffed.

"Because you're a dick." Austin came forward, his musky scent encasing me as he leaned in for a kiss. "Ready to go home? We've got a surprise for you."

I perked up. "Really?"

"Yep. It's why Asa and Wick left town without us." He reached forward, sweeping a stray hair out of my face. "It's getting late. We've got to go home and get ready."

I wiggled my fingers in front of me toward Wick. "Wick promised uppies."

"Uppies?" Wick quirked a brow. "You know what, I don't even want to know." He turned around. "Hop on."

"No bridal style?" I joked, though I was thankful he was carrying me at all. Why did looking fit have to hurt so badly?

"No offense, but you reek. A shower would not kill you before we leave."

I climbed onto his back, adjusting my arms around his neck, not caring that I nearly strangled him from my grip as he stood. "You made me do a million push-ups, of course I'm not the freshest."

"A million? Please. You hardly did thirty."

"Thirty was enough."

I pulled my arms tighter, enjoying as he gasped for breath before he hiked me up higher. Austin got my water bottle and Asa picked up my bag, and together they followed behind us as we left the gym and walked home. Wick never let us drive to the gym. Claimed driving defeated the purpose of a workout when a walk could be considered a stretch. I thought he just liked to see me suffer and this was the most efficient way.

"Any tighter and you're going to kill me," Wick gasped as I nearly strangled him going up the stairs.

"It would be deserved." I leaned into his shoulder and smiled before giving him a gentle bite.

"I'm a little afraid to give her the surprise," Wick admitted. "Maybe we should hold off until she realizes I'm not the worst person in the world."

"I never said you were the worst." I loosened my hold, marginally. "Just not the best."

"That makes me feel so much better." He leaned against the wall of the house. "Austin, get the door."

Austin jogged forward, using his key to unlock the front door before pushing it open and allowing us through. Wick's grip on my legs loosened as he slowly released me, bending slightly so that my feet could touch the ground as I slid off his back. When I was off, he turned to Asa. "Get the package."

"Is the package my surprise?" I was nearly bouncing on the balls of my feet with excitement.

Growing up, since my parents' death, I rarely got surprises, but with these boys, I felt like they were always shocking me, even if their offers were as simple as my favorite candy or a coffee ready and waiting when I got out of my shower each morning.

"It is," Asa confirmed.

I squealed with delight as he handed over the poorly wrapped bundle with a big pink bow. "Can I open it now?"

"No." Asa rolled his eyes, but the tilt of his lips gave away his amusement. "It's only to look at."

I ignored his snark and tore at the ribbon, letting it fall to the floor as I tore into the paper, letting my hand find the coolness of a hard object inside. I pushed the paper aside and looked up in shock. "It's a—"

"It's a bone knife, just like ours, made from your first kill," Austin explained.

I didn't know whether I should drop the object or hold on tight. I was still struggling to come to terms with the fact that I killed a man. Even though I knew the world was a safer and better place without him.

"It's bleached and hand carved. Processed uniquely just for this purpose, so there is no DNA left on it, in case you're wondering. No traces of his vile self left except the modified bone. It's a gift from the agency, sort of a welcome to the team special."

Inside, I was cringing. The thought of touching someone's bone wasn't all that appealing, but I'd admit, it had a pretty sheen to it. And the carved handle, combined with well-conditioned leather, begged my fingers to run over its surfaces.

"It won't hurt you," Wick informed me as I hesitated. "He's already dead."

I knew. I was there. I killed him. I watched the flash of shock in his eyes and felt the blood pool over my fingers in a sticky coating that I thought would never leave my skin, even days later.

Still, this was the life of a housekeeper. I signed up for this, and if I wanted to write that paper, expose them for who they were at the very core and become the journalist I'd always dreamed of, I couldn't let myself hold back.

I reached between the layers of tissue paper, letting my fingers graze the unnaturally cool bone before I took hold, grasping it in my fingers until I fully wrapped my palm around the surface. It was light. I didn't know why I expected it to be heavy. And under my fingertips, it felt nothing like bone and everything like the deadly weapon I knew it could be.

"I want you to wear it on your thigh tonight in its holster. Wear a dress. I want to know it's there when the material flirts around those thighs," Wick instructed me.

"Where are we going?" I asked, not taking my eyes off the weapon, as I realized they never told me of tonight's plans.

"Fundraiser. All the clubs are taking part," Austin supplied.

"Oh, that's cute. You think you're a club," I mocked.

"We've got pledges, don't we?" Wick raised a brow in challenge, and I hated that he was right. They had a whole slew of mysterious members, pledging loyalty, and I'd only seen a handful. "We've got to leave soon, or we'll be late."

"Late?"

"Yeah. Asa is our sacrifice this round. We volunteered his services." The amusement dancing in Austin's eyes told me I wouldn't enjoy what they volunteered him for, and judging by Asa's face, I knew he wasn't thrilled.

"For?"

"The kissing booth." Austin laughed.

"That's so... unhygienic. Asa would never." I nearly gagged at the thought of kissing a bunch of strangers for money. But Asa? He hated people. He'd never willingly sign up to lock lips with any that tossed money his way.

"He is. He drew the short straw."

My head whipped in Asa's direction. "Tell me he's lying?"

"Unfortunately, drawing the short straw seems to be my habit."

"What? No. I don't like this. I don't want him kissing any ol' woman who walks up. He'd have too many to count."

"That's the idea. Everyone wants to make out

with him, anyway. Might as well make money on it," Austin pointed out.

"But... He's mine." The declaration of ownership sounded deflated, even to my ears.

"That's our girl. We like you jealous. Just don't use that weapon on any of us, or anyone else tonight, okay? And remember, it's for charity." Wick's palm came up, squeezing the back of my neck. "Get dressed. You've got twenty minutes."

I turned, stumbling up the steps, knowing the moment he issued me a time frame that he would have his timer ticking away, stealing my moments. If I was late, I'd be punished, and I never knew if that would be good or bad. When it was good, I fucking begged for it. Craved it even. But when it was bad, I hated every moment and wished he'd fucking die, even as I thought about the next time he would have me on my knees again.

His laugh echoed through the house as I pushed open my bedroom door, slamming it behind me before rushing to the shower. I wrenched the knob, turning it on, hoping it would heat as I tore away my sweaty gym clothes from my body. I grabbed a scrunchie and tied my hair into a messy bun before stepping under the lukewarm stream of water.

I scrubbed quickly before taking my razor and shaving every visible part of me. I wish he had given me more time if he expected me to wear a dress. Prep takes work, but I did what I could in the rush of the moment. I shut off the water and jumped out of the shower without even bothering to dry off. After tying a towel around my body, I stood in front of the mirror, debating on what type of make-up to wear.

With limited time, I opted for natural skin, a touch of mascara, and a dash of blush, the way Asa liked it. But instead of tossing on lip gloss, I took out a deep red lipstick, applying it generously before brushing out my hair and styling it in a twist.

I was down to the last minutes, and my heart was pounding in panic. I hadn't a clue on what I'd wear or the time to figure it out. I went to my closet, letting my fingers skim every dress I owned, all picked by the boys, but nothing really screamed at me. Everything was too dressy or not dressy enough, and I needed a dress somewhere in between.

I glanced at my dresser, spying a hint of blue peeking out, and an idea formed. I opened my drawer, pulling out a blue silk slip. I knew that when Wick purchased it; he hadn't meant it for the outside. But having me wear it as a dress would drive him crazy, and I loved to see him come unraveled. Plus, I wanted Asa to think about me as he kissed all the other girls and remember who owned him.

I pulled the silk slip over my head, not even bothering to put on underwear or a bra. It would leave lines after all, and I didn't have the time to figure out what undergarments would work best to combat the lines. After a spray of perfume, I smoothed the silk down my curves and then grabbed the holster and a pair of strappy heels that Austin had picked out, then ran out of my room. My steps thundered down the stairs, only stopping in front of a freshly showered and dressed Wick.

"Forty-five seconds to spare," he announced. "You're getting good at this."

"You've forced me to," I reminded him.

"Being able to do things in an allotted time is a solid life skill and will come in handy on assignments." His eyes lifted to my face and traveled down my body. "What the fuck are you wearing?"

"A dress." I pretended like I didn't know the difference.

"That's not a fucking dress. That's lingerie."

"Are you saying you don't like it?" I pouted.

"I didn't say that," he stuttered, a reaction he'd never had.

"I think she looks beautiful." Austin stepped slowly down the stairs.

"I didn't fucking say she didn't!" Wick spit out. "But this is highly inappropriate."

"I like it," Asa confirmed. "It reminds me of promises she's not yet made."

"Aren't you fucking poetic? I don't want her wearing this out." Wick looked seconds away from losing his shit.

"Why? Because it's made for the bedroom or because I've got nothing underneath?" I wagged my brows.

"Jesus." They cursed, then Asa spoke. "Tell me you're lying."

"I'm lying," I stated.

Asa dropped to his knees at my feet, his fist pulling at the silk as he bunched it up toward my hip. When the cool air exposed my bare pussy, he cursed, his fingers tightening. "You're fucking bare."

"I didn't want lines," I admitted.

He leaned forward, his head resting against the junction of my thigh. "Are you trying to torture me?"

"I will not deny that you deserve torture." His fingers released the silk in favor of touching my bare thighs.

He pulled back, his eyes meeting mine for a moment as he took the holster from my fingers. His eyes burned, his gaze unwavering as he strapped the holster to my thigh, before patting the knife it held securely, hidden under the silk of the slip that flared out from my hips. Then, he took my shoes. "Put your foot on my thigh."

I followed his orders, watching as he strapped on one sandal, then the next, his concentration only on me. When they were secure, he stood up, pulling me close to him by my hip as he whispered into my ear. "When you ride my cock tonight, you'll be wearing this dress and these heels. Do you understand?"

My throat was dry. I was used to orders from Wick, but Asa never demanded of me, though maybe this dress pushed him too far. I swallowed past the lump that formed in my throat as my head nodded. "I-I understand."

"Good." He turned to his friends. "Get her

soaked for me while I'm not there, but don't let her cum."

Then he walked out of the door, and like the desperate woman I was, I followed him. I wanted to keep him in my sights as long as possible, hoping he'd give in now instead of the torture of waiting for him to fulfill his promise.

CHAPTER THIRTY-THREE

AUSTIN

I might die before the night's end. In fact, I was sure of it. Walking next to Mac, knowing that under this dress was a knife and bare skin was the closest to torture I'd ever experienced. I held her hand tightly, unwilling to separate myself from her, connecting us so she wouldn't get lost.

"Why couldn't he do the dart toss?" Mac leaned into me as we walked along, her heels adding a few inches to her height, placing her at my chin.

"Come on Mac, seriously? Look at that guy?"

She eyed the guy at the dart toss, his crooked teeth on full display as he smiled and ran a hand through his greasy hair. She cringed a little. "I'm sure he has a great personality."

"I bet his mom told him that, too." She punched

me in the shoulder, the sharp burst of pain radiating upward. "What the hell was that for?"

"My mom used to tell me that." She scowled, and I knew she meant to intimidate, but it only made her cuter.

"Your mom was a liar, Vixen. Your personality is shit," Wick cut in from her other side. Her head whipped his direction in disbelief, but before she could get a word out, he continued, "But that ass? Top-notch, grade A, perfection."

"Jerk." She leaned away from him, holding me tighter.

"Got to be a little more creative than that if you want to hurt my feelings, baby. This skin is as tough as it comes." Wick gave her a smile that spoke of all the sins that salvation could never save him from.

"Don't call me baby." I snorted, knowing she loved it when we whispered pet names. If she thought that would hurt him, she was wrong, and she'd clearly didn't know anything about the man next to her.

"Because you don't like the name or because it reminds you that your actions are that of a child?" He fucking loved to get a rise out of her, but I really wish he'd pick a less public place to do it because fuck, it always ended the same way – someone coming, someone screaming, and the other walking away victorious.

"Fuck you." Her voice was so loud, heads turned.

"Can't you see I'm fucking trying?" His tone matched hers.

I yanked at Mac's arm. "Let's go try to win you a goldfish or something."

Her eyes widened as she turned to me, her bickering with Wick forgotten. "They still give those away? I haven't seen that since I was a child."

"How often do you go to carnivals, babe? Last I checked, you were penny pinching your way through life, barely having fun in your thrift store pants." Maybe it made me a jerk for pointing that out, but it was true. Even now, we struggled to get her to have fun and there was absolutely no way she bought anything. In fact, we had to buy it for her, sometimes sneaking it into her drawers.

"You know what? I'm not a fan of any of you tonight. I'm sleeping in my room with the door locked." Her lower lip came out in a pout, and I reached up, pulling it between my fingers.

"You wish that was an option," Wick snorted.

"We'll soften you up," I promised. "Plus, we've got keys."

I doubted she could even sleep without one of us near her. She might fall asleep solo, but there hadn't been a day that went by where she hadn't woken to one of us taking up space and breathing her air.

"I'll push the dresser in front of the door."

Wick grinned at that. "I've seen your upper body strength, baby. You're not pushing anything over five pounds." Before she could get more annoyed than we already made her, Wick took her hand. "Come on, let's go win you a fish to kill within the week."

"You have little faith in me."

"You hardly remember to feed yourself." I used a hand to guide her back. "What makes you think you'll remember to feed something else?"

"I can cook."

"That's yet to be seen." We held close, fighting through the crowd that threatened to tear us apart.

"Okay. I can't cook. But I could figure it out." She admitted as my hand fell to her ass. God, the globes covered by silk were perfection.

"Good. You'll make dinner tomorrow. We'll go grocery shopping in the afternoon," Wick informed her.

"I didn't mean—"

"It's happening now, Mac. No turning back. Look, a fish." He pointed his finger to a big sign in the shape of a fishbowl, showing it was the booth that let people toss ping-pong balls into fishbowls to get a prize. "There are your victims now."

"You have no faith in me." Her heels clicked against the pavement as she practically dragged us toward the fish. She was overdressed, but damn, was I glad she was.

"We know you," I pointed out.

We stopped in front of the booth and Wick took out some cash, handing it over before a basket of balls was sat in front of us. We each took some, tossing them, angling them, strategizing, until finally

I got my ping-pong ball to float on top of one of the little bowls. I leaned over Mac's shoulders, my lips close to her ear as I whispered, "Wick likes to be superior, but it's clearly me who has the hand-eye coordination."

She smirked, her hand poised as she tossed a ball, right as two girls sidled up next to us. A blond pulled her hair over her shoulders as she tossed down money. "I would have paid more, but he refused."

"It's a shit type of fundraiser if they think they'll make money if he won't even kiss their lips."

Mac's body straightened under my touch, her interest piqued.

"Yeah well." The brunette responded. "They're clearly making money from simple kisses on the cheek. Did you see that line?"

"He's probably paying them." The bitter blonde took her ping-pong ball and tossed it toward the glass bowls. She missed, not even coming close.

"He doesn't need to pay them," Mac muttered under her breath.

"Excuse me?" The blond tilted her head, eyes locked on our girl. Shit, I wasn't in the mood for a catfight. If I was, I knew Mac could take them both.

Mac inhaled slowly. "He has them lined up because he's hot. We all know it."

"Ten bucks for a kiss on the cheek? Not worth it. I don't care how hot he is."

"It's for charity," the brunette reasoned.

"I don't care. Ten bucks is ten bucks. The least Asa could have done is give me a peck on the lips."

Mac shrugged, though I clearly saw the satisfied glint in her eyes. "I can get a kiss for ten bucks."

The blonde's eyes roamed over her. "Doubt it."

Wick stepped forward. "In fact, I bet even *he* could get a kiss for ten bucks." He pointed at me. "Maybe it's you. Brush your teeth lately?"

Her mouth fell open, clearly offended. "Prove it."

"I don't think we need to." Wick stated, but fuck, I knew him well enough to know he was about to issue a challenge. He baited them and they fell for it.

"I'll pay a hundred each to charity if they can get a kiss from Asa Dominguez and his sorry excuse of a kissing booth." The blonde smirked. "You lose. You owe me two hundred bucks."

"A hundred, each? Doesn't really seem worth it. It's charity after all. Why not make it five?"

"Each?" Her mouth gaped, and Wick just shrugged.

"Total, if you can't afford it."

"I can afford it," the blonde huffed.

The brunette stuck her arm out. "Ashley... I don't think this is a—"

"It's a great idea," Mac cut in. "Five hundred... each. And we'll kiss him."

The blonde held out her hand, ready to shake, and the brunette shook her head. "I wouldn't."

"Come on, Jen. Have you seen him kiss a single person today? This is a sure bet."

Wick's eyes spoke measures about what was about to go down. If only they bothered looking. "Yeah, Jen," he mocked. "It's a sure bet."

For us.

I was a hundred percent confident that Asa would kiss us if we walked up there. He never turned down a chance to kiss Mac, and though we'd had little time alone since we talked in the hotel, I was sure he wouldn't reject me either. Especially not for charity. Their hands locked, setting their deal in motion, and even Mac's eyes sparkled with mischief as they squeezed Wick's hand.

"Don't forget your fish." The man at the booth stopped me as I took a step away. He held up a bag, offering me a limp-looking goldfish as my prize.

My fingers grasped the bag, even as Mac was pulling me away, clearly distracted from our original goal. The fish sloshed within my grip as I followed behind them, not sure where we were going, but confident that the girls who fell into Wick's trap knew the way.

"There!" The blonde's finger pointed, and I followed the direction, seeing the painted sign for the kissing booth. Just as they had said, the line wrapped around a gate, meshing with a line to the Ferris wheel. "I don't understand why it's so long if he isn't even going to give out real kisses."

Did she really want to share kisses with all these people? Combine spit with the masses? It was bad enough poor Asa was subjected to kissing cheeks all in the name of charity, but to kiss them on the mouth? Disgusting.

"People like to donate," I pointed out because, well, I honestly didn't know why the line was this fucking long. Asa was hot. I got that. He had the mysterious, rebel vibe going for him and fuck if I wasn't a victim of that, too. But I'd never wait in line for him if the circumstances were different.

"Isn't that your friend?" Mac asked Wick, pointing to a man in a hoodie.

He brushed her off. "I have no friends. Can you get us to the front of the line faster? I don't have all night to waste on this stupid bet."

"You could just give me the money now and be done with it," Ashley suggested.

"You honestly don't know who I am, do you?" Wick silently laughed.

"No fucking clue. I don't care either." She would if she knew how many men he'd killed. If she knew he was a member of the illusive Saints, and Asa was one of his closest allies.

"You would." His words were nearly a threat.

"Doubtful." Blondie rolled her eyes. "Look, there's Christy."

"Oh joy." Wick mocked. Still, he tugged on Mac, causing her to nearly fall in those fucking heels that had me hard just looking at them.

Twenty bucks later, Wick had Christy bribed, and we stood in line, waiting to kiss the man that I could kiss for free at any other time. This close, I could see just how over it Asa was. Between each kiss, he wiped his mouth, and I swore I saw him gag a time or two. Understandable, considering the circumstances. Ten people became nine. Nine became eight and before I knew it, we had one person in front of us.

She turned to Mac. "I've dreamed of this moment ever since he gave me his napkin sophomore year."

Did these people not see Mac hanging on our arms throughout campus, or were they just choosing to ignore it?

"Yeah? I've been thinking about kissing him since this evening." Mac was mocking the girl, but she didn't even notice.

"I heard he had a girlfriend, and he's off the market, but if that was true, why would he be doing the kissing booth?"

"Yeah. If that was true, why *would* he be doing the kissing booth?" Mac repeated the question while glaring at Wick, knowing damn well he probably had something to do with it.

"He's probably gay," Ashley added from behind me. "There is no way he would turn me down. Have you seen my boobs?"

Mac looked at Ashley's boobs, then at her own, a frown turning her lips down. I leaned in. "Yours are the perfect size, if you ask me."

"Next," Asa called, not even looking in our direction, and the girl in front of us walked down the aisle toward him.

"I don't think he's gay," I corrected Ashley. "Just

knows what he wants." And what he wanted was us, Mac and me. I left that part out though, not wanting to ruin Wick's fun.

"He didn't even glance at me," Ashley huffed.

"You try kissing this many people." Jen stood up for Asa. "I bet he is just tired and wants it over with."

Even if he wasn't tired, Ashley clearly was a miserable person. Not Asa's type at all. He liked them with fire and spice, thick hips and a grabbable ass, just like Mac. He never was a fan of bottled blondes and big boobs.

"Next," Asa's uninterested voice called, and we stepped forward together, the group of us heading toward him. When we reached the booth platform, he didn't even glance up as he said, "One at a time, pick who goes first."

"I'll go first," Mac announced.

Asa's head popped up, and his back suddenly straightened as they locked eyes. He didn't speak a single word as he reached out, grasped the silk of Mac's dress and pulled her in. His lips locked on to hers like he needed them more than air, and as she stumbled forward, her hands falling to his chest, she kissed him back hard, devouring whatever he had to give. The gasp that left Ashley was satisfying. But not nearly as satisfying as when Asa's eyes locked with mine, and his hand reached out, gripping my shirt to pull me in, only parting from Mac to crash his lips to mine.

Faintly I heard Wick gloat, "I believe you owe me

money. Well, the charity. In the name of Asa and his sponsoring club."

Asa's tongue danced with mine, teasing me, drawing me in, nearly killing me on the spot with want before he pulled our lips apart, only to capture Mac's again, pecking her lips lighter than before as he whispered, "What are you doing here?"

"Making money for the sorority donation, clearly," Wick answered for her. "And following through on making our girl desire us, without giving in to her demands."

"This is unfair." Ashley stomped her foot. Literally stomped her foot like a toddler throwing a tantrum. "I didn't know he was with..." She waved a hand, not knowing which he was with. "Them."

"Didn't the girl in front of us warn you he has a girlfriend?" Wick pointed out.

"But it was a trap. I didn't know it was her." She glared at Mac, and I pressed myself in front of her and Asa, who were still in their own little bubble of foreplay, his hand skimming up her thigh as loose strands of her hair distorted my view of his face as she leaned over him.

"They told you they could get a kiss. You didn't believe them."

"You lied by omission," Ashley accused.

"You didn't ask," Wick stated. "Pay up or well have you kicked out and banned from any future school-sponsored events."

"You can't do that."

"Watch me," Wick threatened and, well, he could do worse without a single consequence, but he was being nice.

Ashley crossed her arms, while Jen stood by, not sure if she should insert herself. Finally, Ashley let out a huff, breaking under Wick's intense stare. She pulled out her wallet, tossing a handful of hundreds into the bucket of money Asa was collecting. "There. That's all I have."

Wick leaned over, doing a quick count. "We'll bill you for the other two hundred." He took out his own wallet, spotting her the money she was missing.

"I—"

Wick's assertion of authority cut her argument off. "We'll bill you."

"Fuck you," she growled as she spat at his feet before grabbing her friend's hand and storming off.

Wick waited until they were out of sight before he stepped forward. His fingers reached out, grabbing a handful of Asa's long hair, and tugged his head back. Without warning, he crashed his lips to Asa's, whose body stiffened in shock. After a few seconds, Wick's hands released him and he pulled away. His nose scrunched up as he surveyed our team member.

"I wanted to see what all the fuss was about." He stepped back. "I'm not impressed."

Then he walked away, leaving Mac and me to scramble after him, the taste of Asa still a ghost against our lips.

CHAPTER THIRTY-FOUR

WICK

It was hotter than I expected, feeding into some sort of taboo urge that always waited under the surface, begging to be unleashed. But it wasn't my thing. Asa's lips were made for kissing, just not by me.

"You kissed Asa," Mac stated as she caught up to me.

"It didn't even make my dick hard." Which was true. Not even a fucking twitch.

"But you still—"

"Dropped two hundred bucks for a kiss I probably could have gotten for free if I asked? Yeah. You better fucking believe I'm going to redeem a kiss for two hundred bucks. I don't care who is on the other side of it. For that price, it could be the fucking Pope and I'd slip him tongue."

"I might pay another two hundred to see that." She laughed, and that sound, that rich melody, wrapping around me like a comforting blanket, that was what made me hard.

I spotted a bench not far off and I plopped down on it, pulling her into my lap as she sat. When Austin sat next to us, I spread her legs, placing one of her legs over his so that she was sitting on both of us.

"Can you see him?" I asked.

"See who?" She looked around, confused. "Your friend?"

I didn't know who the fuck this person was that she thought was my friend, but the only friends I had lived under my roof and shared this angel that warmed my lap. "Asa."

"Yeah. I see him." She smiled.

"Look at the way his cheeks still are flush from touching your lips," I pointed out. She squirmed on our laps. "Imagine the plans he has for you tonight."

Her chest picked up pace as it rose and fell. "I can't wait."

"Do you enjoy watching him kiss other girls?"

"I-I hadn't watched," she admitted. "I can't."

A girl stepped up to his platform and my hand reached up, taking Mac's jaw and forcing her head in that direction. "Do not close your eyes."

For a moment her eyes fluttered, but then she came to a resolve and she held them open, refusing to close them, even as the girl grew closer to Asa. Her breath held as she watched Asa's lips graze against the female's cheek and pull away. The female stood straighter. A look of disappointment crossed her face as she stepped down from the platform.

"Watch her," I ordered as I held her still. "You see the way her nipples pebbled, already turned on by a single kiss to the cheek?"

Mac's head nodded, and I held firm as the next girl took her spot in front of Asa. He went in for a kiss. Mac's chest rose and fell. The girl tilted her head, a failed attempt at stealing his lips, but he tilted away, not giving in to her desires.

"How does it feel?"

"What?" Mac's voice was a whisper as she spoke.

"Seeing another woman want what's yours?" My voice purred into her ear.

I grabbed Austin's hand, placing it on the bare thigh of our girl, encouraging him to touch her. Her whole body shivered under the touch. "Possessive."

Her admission made me smile, though she couldn't see that. "Explain."

A little whimper left her throat as Austin's hand skimmed her inner thigh. "I'm proud that I can have what they want. That he picks me instead of them."

"Look at her," I ordered. "Do you think she'd drop to the ground right now and suck his cock if he asked?"

I let my hand fall from her face. The back of it trailed her body, skimmed over her breasts and stomach until I reached lower, only dancing over her sensitive skin for a moment before using the hand to unzip my pants and pull out my cock. I rubbed my dick with my palm, knowing she could feel it sandwiched between our bodies.

"Well?" I prompted when she didn't speak.

"Yes."

"Would you?" I asked as I put both my hands on her hips, moving her over just enough that, though one of her legs was still on Austin's, her body was aligned with mine. Without warning, I flexed my hips, pushing my cock inside her body, fucking loving the gasp of shock as I filled her wet pussy up, stretching it with my length. I groaned my satisfaction. "Would you suck his dick if he asked you?"

"He wouldn't have to ask," she confessed, and beside me, Austin swore, the image too much for him to hold back on.

"You are a good girl sometimes, Mac. Do you know that?" I cooed, letting my cock just rest inside of her, letting the pulse of her pussy and the squirm of her hips send pleasure through me.

"Move," she begged, her eyes still on Asa. "Please. I need to feel you move."

"I'm not doing that, Mac." I tsked my disappointment at her begging. "What would people think?"

"Fuck what people would think," she whimpered.

"That's my girl." I nuzzled into her neck, proud that she said something so very like what I would have said. "But I'm not moving. Squeeze around me. I want to feel you grasp my cock."

At my order, her body squeezed mine, gripping

me tightly, tearing a moan from my lips that I couldn't stifle. I sat up straighter, forcing my cock deeper into her body as I leaned into her ear. "Watch them. Watch every person who steps up and wants a piece of what's yours, and every time you feel jealous... Turned on... Possessive... Squeeze my cock. Look at all of them, Mac. Look at how full her breasts are with want. Look at her rosy cheeks. He did that to her. And you'll do it for me."

She tried to move, to force her body up and down, to bounce against my length, but I held tight, refusing to let her go. Even when she begged and cried, big tears running down her cheek as her body squeezed my cock, seeking pleasure that wouldn't be enough, I refused to move. I was going crazy. I was over the edge and frantic with want. It was the hardest fucking thing I'd ever done, refusing to give her what she needed.

She looked at Austin, the tears used as a weapon. "Austin, please."

Even as Austin's hand ran up and down her thigh, he couldn't help her. I leaned forward, the position driving my cock deeper than I thought possible, making her gasp as she reached back, clawing at my body. "He can't help you, little vixen. No one can fucking help you. Do you want to know why?" When she didn't answer, I let a hand travel up to her throat, squeezing slightly before using my fingers to push her chin in my direction. "Do you?"

"Please."

She never looked more beautiful than when she begged. "He can't fucking help you because when my cock is buried in your cunt, you're fucking mine."

"Oh god." Her words were gasped out directly into my mouth as her lips parted an inch from mine.

"I should lift your dress, shouldn't I, baby? Show everyone who owns you. Show them how perfectly your cunt parts for my cock, and how much your body weeps for me."

"Don't," she pleaded and fuck, but the pleas only made me want to do it more. I wouldn't, but fuck if it wasn't tempting.

"Eyes on Asa," I ordered, pushing her gaze away from me. "Look at the ass on that girl walking up to him. Do you think he wants it?"

"No," she whispered.

"You sure? I can almost picture his hand on her creamy pale skin."

"No." She spoke more forcefully.

"Why?"

"He's mine." She squeezed my dick like a vice with her admission and it was close to bringing me over the edge.

"Fuck. Do that again." When she didn't squeeze my cock, I leaned forward, close to her ear. "Squeeze my fucking cock like I told you to. Do you want to be punished?"

"Aren't I already?" Her voice was weak, but she did as I told her, her body gripping me so tight I couldn't hold back. My ass arched off the bench, my cum shooting inside of her as I struggled to maintain a look of composure, acting like I wasn't balls deep and shooting my load inside my girl.

When I could finally speak, my heart racing, my hands shaking, I smoothed down her hair. "No baby. This is a reward. You just can't claim your prize until tonight." I placed a kiss on her neck before lifting her off my cock and smoothing down her dress. "When he fucks you tonight, it's going to be my cum that's coating your thighs. Don't you dare wash it off."

CHAPTER THIRTY-FIVE

MAC

It hurt. It hurt so fucking bad in the most delicious of ways, and I hated Wick for it. I was a sobbing mess, a needy, sobbing disaster, and it was all because of him and the sweet torture he delivered. I don't know if I could live with the buzz between my thighs. It only intensified when I held my legs tight, giving me a faint flutter of what it would feel like if he just let me cum.

"Stop squeezing your thighs together, baby. You're only going to make it worse." Austin's fingers did gentle circles on my knee.

"You think *I'm* going to make it worse? Like your finger toying with my sensitive skin isn't driving me mad," I snapped.

Wick snorted. "She's a little testy right now, Aussie. She doesn't mean the things she says."

"Speak for yourself. I mean every fucking word," I seethed.

"She's gorgeous when she's denied. Don't you think?" Wick smirked. "Open up."

I opened my mouth, letting him fork in some funnel cake. "I'm going to use my knife on you."

"Always threatening with a good time, too," he informed Austin, like I didn't just threaten to kill him.

"I hate you," I growled as I crossed my arm, chewing the funnel cake, which made everything slightly better.

Austin leaned forward, nuzzling my neck. "You smell salty. Like Wick. It's making me jealous that I didn't get in on the action."

"We're at a carnival. Might as well treat me as a ride," I grumbled.

"Baby, don't be like this." Austin's hand flattened my hair. "You know Asa said you couldn't cum."

"I forgot. Was he in charge of my body?"

"Baby. Stop."

"No. Let her be sulky. I would be too," Wick cut in. "If I was denied an orgasm."

"I hate you," I growled.

"I hate you a little less." He looked so damn proud of himself. Meanwhile, I could barely walk. It was unfair. I was always suffering at their whim, while they always got everything they wanted from my body.

"Come on, I'll buy you a corn dog," Austin offered, encasing my hand in his warm one and pulling me away from Wick. Wise choice because I might have killed him. It was always a possibility when they insisted I wear a blade strapped to my thigh. When Wick was out of earshot, Austin offered, "If Asa didn't order it, he would have let you come."

"Doubt it." I truly was acting like a child, but Austin and I were the closest out of the three of them, so I didn't care.

"He would have. There is nothing he loves more than bringing you pleasure. I know, because I can see the rapture it causes him." Austin squeezed my hand like it was going to help, but all it did was remind me of the way my body squeezed against Wick's cock, begging him to move inside of me and not getting fulfilled. The thought had my core pulsing, and I cursed, because even that simple squeeze felt like unobtainable bliss.

"When was the last time you had a good roll in the hay with Asa?" Austin continued, completely oblivious to my suffering.

"When was the last time you've had one?" I countered.

"We've...not," he admitted. "I'm not sure I'm ready for that. Asa is one of my best friends. We're stuck together for life."

"It appears I am stuck here, too," I reminded him.

"You're different. You were made for us."

"I think I was made for a man who would give me orgasms at will without making me suffer being unfulfilled. But okay."

Austin smiled and shook his head, before glancing a few feet behind us at Wick, who was strolling casually along. Of course he would be. He just came hard, and it was now coating my thighs uncomfortably. "You'll get yours tonight."

"Now would be nice."

"Now is not an option," he declared before squeezing my hand and lacing our fingers together, stopping us in the corn dog line.

Austin bought me a corn dog, and while I ate, he and Wick made all the lewd comments that would have ruined the buzz from the delicious treat on a stick, if I wasn't so starving from the workout and skipping dinner to come here. Then, when it got late and all the lights flickered on, we walked along the border of the carnival, playing all the games at least once before riding the Ferris wheel.

"I should have made you cum up here," Wick breathed against my ear as we stalled at the top and damn, that thought was enough to make my breathing pick up, anticipating the possibility of him taunting me. "Calm down, baby, it's not going to happen."

I reached for Austin's hand and lifted my dress, knowing not a damn person could see up here.

Letting my legs fall to the side, I dragged Austin's hand to my clit, and mimicked the motion I craved. He didn't pull away, but he didn't stop me. "I'm not participating."

"You're only going to make it worse for yourself," Wick sighed, but his eyes were fixated on my bare skin that I knew had to be glistening with moisture. "He won't let you cum, either."

"Austin." I let my eyes go wide as I watched him, pleading for him to disagree, but he didn't.

"I'll give you anything you want, sweetheart, but not this. I'm not going against what Asa asked. He never asks for much, you know that."

This was true. Asa was a saint. The only one who ever demanded was Wick, and I was happy to ignore as many of those demands as I could. But damn it, my whole body was on fire, every step painful as I denied it the pleasure that was so fucking close, then ripped away. Even now, as I tried to force Austin to touch my clit, the gentle touches made my eyes roll back.

His free hand reached over his body to touch my jaw, pulling my face toward his so that I was looking into his eyes. I could hardly bring myself to look away. His eyes burned; the blue smoldered as he absorbed every inch of my face, taking in the need in my eyes and the blush of my cheeks. "You're fucking beautiful."

"I hurt," I admitted.

"It'll be worth it."

"Just once," I begged him, and his finger slipped low, dipping into my body and I jolted, a needy sound leaving me before he formed a hook and dragged it along my inner wall, causing a cry to leave me just as the Ferris wheel jolted into movement. His finger was slow as he removed it from my body.

Then, keeping his eyes still locked on mine, he brought the finger, coated in my need and Wick's cum, to his lips and sucked it clean. He pulled it out, the pop of its release echoing in my ear. "No."

"Put your dress down and be a good girl," Wick ordered, ignoring the exchange between us. "It's almost our stop."

He pulled the dress down as far as it would go and forced my knees shut, before placing a hand of ownership on my thigh, resting it lightly. The weight alone was a tease, a promise of what could come and what they were denying me. When the car jolted to a stop and our bar lifted, Austin stood first, taking the bag with his fish off the seat and stepping out of the cart before turning to me, offering me his hand.

Every petty ounce of me wanted to resist it, and for a moment, I tried, except the moment I stepped past him, Asa's voice broke in. "Don't you dare." My gaze jolted up, tearing away from the glare I was giving Austin to find Asa leaning against a poll. "They are only doing what I asked. Stop acting like a spoiled brat and take his fucking hand."

Asa? Talking to me like that? I was shocked. So shocked, in fact, that I froze in place until the attendant had to remind me that he had other cars to clear out. I mumbled an apology before taking Austin's hand, letting him drag me off the ride's platform and back into the crowd.

When we were away from the Ferris wheel, Austin's hand still holding mine, he turned to Asa. "Bad mood?"

"The worst." Asa closed his eyes as if he was trying to escape it. "I need a shower."

"Me too," I piped up.

"And some fucking food." Though he looked slightly pale at the mention of food, probably still grossed out from the booth.

I smirked. "I could feed you."

He didn't even crack a smile at my joke. He must really be in bad shape. "Some food with nutritional value."

"I'll grab you something," Austin offered.

"No."

"Make you something?" Even Wick was sweet enough to offer, which only goes to show that somehow, he was in this four-way relationship with us, even if he wouldn't admit it to himself or to them.

Asa pursed his lips before shaking his head. "No. Maybe I just need to go home and wash the skank off of me."

"That's..." I know my face showed my disgust at his choice of words. I just didn't really know what to say.

"Disgusting," Austin finished. "But valid. We watched them line up for you. It was wild."

"I can't even tell you how many times someone reached for my balls. Some were successful. It was disgusting. The only thing making it mildly worth it was you two..." He froze before continuing. "Three, showing up for a kiss."

"We watched you," Wick informed him. "Made her watch. Do you know how jealous our girl gets each time a female touches you? Squeezed my cock so fucking hard, and I refused to let her cum."

Asa's eyes heated as they fell to me, and at Wick's admission, my body tensed, squeezing and clutching at something that wasn't there. God, I just wanted to be filled. Fulfilled. The same damn thing. "You liked it, baby?"

"No," I admitted.

"Don't fucking lie to him" Wick growled.

I swayed to the left, barely missing a little kid who was wandering aimlessly, licking his ice cream cone. Bet I could lick that better, but that seemed a little inappropriate to say to a kid. "I didn't like that they were touching you. I liked that they wanted something that was mine. That they couldn't have."

"Are you staking your claim?" Asa's voice was low, almost deadly as he spoke, his desire to hear the truth making his voice thick.

"I don't need to stake a claim. You're mine."

"That sounds like staking a claim," Austin observed.

"You've never claimed it before." Asa's arm wrapped around my waist, pulling me tight to his side. "Officially, I mean."

"Isn't me being here a claim enough?" I leaned my head on his shoulder. "I mean, you three are a lot to handle. I mean *a lot*. Wick is insufferable, won't let me wear anything I want, always insisting I work out, even when I have cramps. Then there is Austin, who insists we study together, only we never fucking study. I always end up naked, and my grades are slipping."

"That's me studying, baby. I'm studying you."

"It doesn't work that way." I sighed. "And you. Do you know how freaking hard it is to go anywhere when you're trailing behind me like a puppy? And behind you? The swoon of females wishing to suck your cock. It's all so..."

"Perfect?" Wick supplied.

"Not what I was going to say," I huffed as Asa guided me out the front gate, away from the crowd. "What I was going to say was—"

"How lucky you are," Austin cut me off this time.

"That wasn't it." I grunted my annoyance. "I was going to—"

"Talk about all the ways we suffocate you, make you want to fuck us more." I looked up at Asa's profile, his chiseled jaw flexing as he fought not to smile.

"Yeah." I inhaled deep, before letting it out. "That's exactly what I was about to say."

CHAPTER THIRTY-SIX

ASA

I was going mad every time I gazed in her direction. Damn near closed down the whole charity booth as her eyes watched me while Wick fucked her slowly. If you didn't know any better, you'd not notice that his cock was buried deep inside her. But I knew. I knew them both, and though I pretended I hadn't known about it, the images were lasered into my memory for the rest of the night.

I couldn't leave that fucking place fast enough. Touching all those women, and a few males, really soured my mood. When I left our place this evening, all I could think about was when I could have Mac's body writhing under mine. Now? All I could think about was washing every inch of the grime off my body and trying not to gag in the process because my lips against all those strangers' skins had officially made me nauseous.

I found them at the Ferris wheel, a place I knew they would be based on Wick's update text. Then I subtly guided them toward the exit, needing out before I went crazy. I was overstimulated, mentally done with all these people, and if I had to stay here a moment longer than was necessary, I doubt I'd survive.

We were already on the road when Mac turned to me. "You made a lot of money."

I let my fingers graze along her inner thigh, glad she opted to sit next to me. "At least a quarter of it was from you guys."

"Easy money," Wick explained, not taking his eyes off the road. "She was mad she didn't get any tongue. I only made her madder. It's what I'm good at."

"I noticed," I answered dryly.

"I don't think I've ever seen Asa in such a mood," Mac observed.

"Fix it," Wick ordered.

Mac met his eyes in the mirror, her pink little tongue darting out to lick her perfectly bowed lips before her shoulders rose. "Okay."

I had just enough time to process her agreement before her fingers were unzipping my pants and diving in. Pushing aside my boxer briefs, her fingers wrapped around my semi-hard cock. I looked down at my lap, already getting hard just from the image of her fingers against my skin and the feel of her palm sliding over my shaft.

"Wait until we get home. I need a shower," I told her.

"Their skin didn't touch your dick. Let Mac have a taste," Wick argued.

Upon his suggestion, Mac's head bowed low, her tongue already teasing against the tip of my cock. "Fuck."

I couldn't stop the curse as it fell from my lips, my hand automatically going to her hair, bunching it in my fingers and owning it, owning her, as I pushed and pulled, forcing her to work my cock the way I liked. I was lost to the feel of her mouth and the suction she'd created when Wick pulled into our driveway. He cut the engine before reaching into the back seat, taking Mac's hair from my hand and pulling her up.

"He needs a shower, remember, baby?" Wick pointed out. And I could fucking kill him.

I leaned over, found the blade at Mac's thigh, and unsheathed it, holding it to Wick's neck quicker than he could blink. "Don't fucking touch her."

Mac's eyes were wide as she looked between us. But fuck. I was so close to coming I could already feel my spine tingling. I *had* wanted a shower. But now all I wanted was Mac. Mac shook out of Wick's grip and reached forward, pushing the blade down so it wasn't threatening Wick before she leaned close, her breath tickling my skin as she spoke. "All night they left me wanting and waiting for you. I've got cum dried on my thigh and every movement I make sends sparks of need shivering through my body. You told them to do this to me. It was your orders."

"Princess." I softened my voice.

"Fix it or I'll use that knife on you before you even have time to slit his throat."

I loved the wild side, the sparks of her that were sassy and demanding. The ones that reminded me she was perfect for us because she didn't just let us control her. She controlled us right back.

"I wanted you for myself," I explained. "I didn't want to have them taking it all from you when I was spending my evening wishing I was with you."

My cock was still in her hand, and she squeezed. "Take me to bed." When I didn't move, she tacked on, "Now."

Wick's crooked smile was the only sign he gave that he knew what he was doing, torturing her the whole time. "You heard her."

After fixing my pants, I pushed open the door of the vehicle, stumbling out before I reached in, grabbed her arm and yanked, pulling her toward me and giving her no room to escape. She was weightless as I tossed her over my shoulder, and she hardly fought, even as I jogged up the steps. The door was locked, and I didn't have keys, so I slammed her body into the wall and crashed my mouth to hers. I couldn't wait a second longer. I needed the release as much as she did. Her tongue danced with mine, her nails clawed into my shoulder as her ankles crossed behind my back.

Keys rattled to our side, but I ignored them, giving my woman my sole attention. My fingers grazed over her breasts, hating that the thin silk slip covered them. The thought of her in this outfit drove me mad, made me wild all damn evening, knowing she didn't have a bra on and anyone who looked could see her nipples.

The squeak of the door's hinge had me tearing my mouth away from hers, my chest heaving as I admitted, "I thought about your nipples through this silk all fucking night."

The confession had her back arching, tilting her tits toward me. My palms fell to her ass, and I squeezed it before I lifted her up slightly, carrying her through the doorway. I made it five steps before we pitched forward, her body falling to the stairs, her fingers holding tight to my shirt, keeping us connected. My lips crashed onto hers, devouring the moans she gave me as I rubbed against her, not caring that the stairs at her back were uncomfortable. I just needed friction. I just needed her.

The door behind us slammed.

Footsteps walked away.

And I didn't care about a single thing that went on, not when Mac's body was writhing under mine.

It was she who pulled away first, fire blazing in her eyes. "Upstairs."

I didn't want to take the time to move. I'd take

her right here, right on the stairs for the others to watch. Lord knew they would like the sight. But she asked to move, she wanted us alone, and I'd always, no matter the circumstances, give my girl what she wanted.

Using will I didn't know I possessed, I pulled my body off hers and scooped her up, carrying her bridal style to my bedroom. I used my foot to kick open the door, then used it again to slam the door shut behind us before tossing her on the bed, letting her bounce on the soft surface while I looked down at her.

Her hair was a mess.

Her face rosy.

Her lips puffy.

Her chest heaved.

She was so fucking gorgeous, a fucking master-piece staring down at me, and I could hardly handle the view. I grabbed onto her ankle, pulling her down to the edge of the bed as I dropped to my knees before her. My hands were rough as they gripped her knees, yanking them apart to gift me a view of her bare pussy, already glistening with want for me.

"Look how pretty you are. All this is for me. Have you been this wet all night?"

"Asa," she begged, "please."

I moved my lips closer, letting my nose run along her inner thigh. It drove her wild, her body pushing up toward me, begging me to touch her. "You smell like Wick. And you. And it's so fucking delicious I need a taste, princess."

That was all the warning she got before I let my tongue graze her thighs, tasting the remnants of Wick, salty against her skin. It coated my tongue, a deliciousness that burst alive in my mouth and tore a moan from my throat. I couldn't get enough, even as I was lapping it up, cleaning her of all that remained. I wanted more.

I cleaned up both thighs before I even dared venturing to her folds and diving my tongue inside. A single swipe had her wild. Her fingers clenched so tight to my sheets that I swore the threads tore. If I had thought the flavor of her thighs was divine, it was nothing compared to the heated remains she had tucked into her core, and I wanted it all. Diving my tongue into her body, I lapped it up, my groans of satisfaction vibrating through her as I showed her how much I enjoyed what they had saved for me.

"So fucking good," I growled as a hand landed on my scalp, her fingers grabbing a fistful of my long hair and tugging on it.

She tried to guide my head, but I wouldn't budge, not even when she was practically a puddle in front of me, the silk bunched around her hips, her hair looking chaotic, and her being every bit the goddess I knew she would be from the moment I laid eyes on her.

"I'm so close. God, Asa, I'm so fucking close."

I pulled away at that, not willing to give her what she wanted. I let my tongue guide me up her body, not stopping until my lips were locked with hers.

Then I bit down hard, enjoying the cry of pain she released before I sucked her lip into my mouth.

I released her lip and pulled back. "Haven't you realized by now?"

"What?" Her body squirmed under me.

"Today, this evening, not letting you cum. It's been one giant game of edging. But baby, when you finally get that release, I promise there is nothing like it."

"I can't handle any more," she admitted, and the torture in her voice only confirmed her confession.

I let my finger skim her slit before dipping inside of her body. "How many times have I had you alone?"

Her body gripped my finger, pulling it deeper inside, and when I pulled it out, I pushed back in with two. Her nails dug into my skin as she gripped my biceps, trying to hold tight to the arm that was bringing her pleasure. "A few times."

"A few." I stopped my movement, refusing to pump my finger until she looked at me. When her eyes connected with me, I corrected her. "Once."

"Once?" Her breathing was picking up. "That can't be true."

"Once. Every single other time I've had eyes on us, people watching. Ordering. Observing. And I don't mind, baby." I confessed, "I fucking love when they watch. But sometimes, I want just you. Just the sweetness that only your body can offer."

Her body relaxed at my words, nearly molding to

mine as she hooked a leg behind my thigh. "You said nothing."

"I don't fucking mind. You know that." I leaned down, letting my tongue lick her neck before I nibbled the skin there. "Your body wants me so fucking bad, doesn't it, princess? I can feel every pulse as it begs and weeps to come."

"Make me come," she demanded.

"You're not ready," I stated.

"I am," she whimpered. "I'm so fucking close."

"Are you?" I knew she was. I could feel it in every squeeze of my finger. She was drenched from wanting me. Her body was screaming for a release that I could give her, but I refused. Each time she built up, I pulled back, letting her get just to the edge but not fully there.

"I'm going to cum," she gasped, and I pulled back, not letting her get there, causing her to plead. "Please, Asa. Let me cum."

"Let yourself." I pulled my fingers fully out of her and rolled, taking her with me until she was straddling my hips.

She leaned down, her hair a curtain around us as she stole a kiss from my lips before she pulled back, raising to her knees just enough to push my pants and boxer briefs down my thighs before she grabbed my cock and aligned it with her core.

She sunk down slowly; each excruciating inch was delicious torture. I wanted it to end. I hoped it never did. Every fucking time I was inside of her, I was floored by how tight she was, how perfectly she was made to fit my body. She was mine and fuck, after so many years of solitude, it was crazy to wrap my mind around that fact.

When she was seated, her flesh tight against mine, her head tipped back, bliss escaping her mouth before she rocked her hips slightly, using the friction to rub her clit before she rose to her knees again, staying up only long enough to drag against my tip before slamming down again.

My fingers gripped onto her thighs, and curses fell from my lips, unfiltered and uncaring as she used my body to find her pleasure while giving to me what I'd spent the evening denying her. My need and want rippled up my thighs, and I had to grit my teeth and focus on anything but her just to keep from coming.

The sounds, the moans, the pleas, my name spoken in a harsh whisper as she lost control, were nearly my undoing. I held tight, my vision blurring, until her body pulsed and squeezed around me, gripping me so hard I couldn't control my body any longer. I couldn't hold off if I tried, and my orgasm rushed forward, spilling into her cunt as she screamed her pleasure, her nails gripping into my chest so hard that I knew I'd have crescent-shaped patches of blood. I'd wear them like a badge of honor, prideful that it was me who brought our girl to the brink of pleasure and over the edge so hard that she lost all control.

It was an eternity before her body relaxed around

my cock and her jerky movements slowed, until she allowed herself to collapse forward, where she laid her head on my chest, panting. My fingers came up, stroking her hair, loving the feel of the strands in my fingers as I whispered gentle praises into her ear.

When her breathing leveled and she could speak again, she tilted her face to look at me. "That was ..."

"Incredible?" I offered. "Fantastic?"

Ignoring my fishing for compliments, she continued, "The hardest I've ever cum in my life. That could become addictive."

"So sex with us hasn't been addictive thus far?" I teased her, knowing the answer. She couldn't get enough of us. Even when she pretended to hate us, she adored us all too fucking much to walk away from this. Whatever this was. Not like the Saints would let her leave. It was too close now. Any day the announcement would be made, and we had to be alert in protecting her.

"It's been okay."

"Okay?" I huffed before shoving her off my body, separating us from where we connected. When she fell to my side, I rolled, caging her in with my arms on each side of her head so I could lean down and kiss her lips. She kissed me back slowly, kissing like time stood still for this single act and the world didn't matter. I forced myself to pull away. "For someone who isn't addicted, you sure beg for what we offer."

"I like to orgasm," she simply stated.

"We better be the only ones who ever get you to

orgasm." I narrowed my eyes in warning, even knowing that she'd go nowhere else.

"Don't bore me and we'll see."

I pinched her side. "You think we'll bore you?"

She smirked. "I mean, I'm already bored."

"Why is that?" I pinched her again.

"Because your mouth keeps talking when I want it against my skin."

I kissed her chest, smiling against her skin before I spent the next two hours showing her just how much this mouth could entertain her.

CHAPTER THIRTY-SEVEN

MAC

I woke with a startle, my heart beating fast, nearly pumping out of my chest. It was dark still, not yet reaching dawn, and the source of what woke me was unknown. But something felt off. Something shook in the night or whispered in the wind, and that something didn't belong.

My head tilted to the side, where Asa was fast asleep, his beautiful face slack and relaxed, with his arm tossed over me. On my other side, Austin slept, having joined us as we faded off into sleep, inviting himself into the bubble of bliss that Asa and I had spent the night creating.

A creak of the floorboard had me sitting up. Asa's arm fell to my waist, not even stirring after our night together. He was exhausted, the sex only adding to the weariness he held until he crashed hard. I listened carefully, trying to find the source, but the house was still. Not a single sound echoed and not a person stirred.

"Probably Wick," I muttered as I let myself flop back down, snuggling deep between the men I adored as I made myself comfortable. I closed my eyes, inhaling their soothing scent and letting myself drift. I was almost there, almost to the point of dreamland, when the wood on the stairs creaked again.

I shot up, using both my hands, one on each of my guys, to shake them. "Wake up!"

Austin jumped up first, panic and confusion clear as he looked around for a threat. His eyes settled on me and relaxed as Asa stirred. "What's wrong?"

"Someone is out there." I pointed to the hall.

"No one is out there. We'd hear them." Austin stood with his hands on his hips, his pajama pants slung low, and even in my state of panic, I couldn't help but drink him in. Every inch of him was under my scrutiny, my vision memorizing every dip.

I blinked a few times, willing myself to forget images of him long enough to explain. "I heard a floorboard squeak. Twice."

"It's an old house," Asa mumbled. "Settling happens."

"It was the stairs. The fifth and second step. I can

tell," I rushed out. "I know, because I always avoid those spots."

"Wick probably got thirsty."

"He avoids them, too."

"Princess." Asa pulled me down. "Calm down. You're fine. We're fine. There's nothing out there."

Austin's knee hit the edge of the bed as he leaned over me, offering me his mouth as he kissed me gently. I willed myself to relax into him, letting him run his fingers through my hair as Asa's hand lazily stroked my thigh in his half sleeping state.

"Fuck, you taste good, baby. A mix of you and Asa. My fucking favorite," Austin proclaimed against my lips, as a hand reached over to steady himself, using Asa's abs as his anchor.

My fingers reached for his waistband, diving in, not caring that he was only trying to distract me from my own created hysteria. It was working. I no longer cared about what threat could have created the noise. All I cared about was his hard length against my fingers. He was right, I'm sure. The house was settling. It was old. It–

I pulled my lips away, but continued to stroke. "Okay, but what if it's not the house settling?"

"Baby. One of us would have woken up."

"I woke up. I'm one of you," I reminded Austin.

"No alarm went off," he pointed out.

"Did you set it?"

He reached for the back of his neck and

scratched before giving me a sheepish smile. "Well, no, but I'm sure Asa or Wick..."

"Asa was with me the whole time," I reminded him. "Wick came in the door before you and went straight for the kitchen."

"Okay, but—"

Asa sighed. "Would it make you feel better if we checked?"

I squeezed Austin's cock more aggressively than he deserved, and he winced, then nodded. "Okay then. I'll go check."

"It's all a girl could ask for." I batted my eyes innocently at him, knowing he didn't believe in my innocence. Not after the things we'd done in the dark.

With a sigh he hefted himself up and dragged himself backwards until his feet hit the floor and he stood up. With a salute, he took a step backwards, then another, watching me the whole time as he made his way to the door.

"Do you believe this mockery?" I asked Asa, but when I looked at him, he was already dozing off to sleep.

"You know, a relationship with me came with mockery prior to signing up. Being my lab partner was only a glimpse into my greatness." Austin beamed, his smile wide, the tiniest of cleft at his chin making its appearance and making me nearly swoon.

"Or lack thereof," I deadpanned, schooling my expression so that he couldn't read just how much I wanted to drag him back and force that smile between my thighs.

"Lies," he spat.

"You lie. Now hurry," I urged. "My right side is freezing without your body heat."

"The amount of demands you make to us is astonishing, baby." He shook his head. "And here I thought you were this time obsessed, nerdy, science girl."

"English."

"What?"

"My major is English, remember? Science was just a requirement to graduate."

"I'd never know it with the number of times I've gotten my ass handed to me because I was late to the lab."

"I hate tardiness." A fact he couldn't argue with.

"I've noticed." He smirked.

"Go," I groaned. "Hurry."

I looked to Asa's silent sleeping form and back to Austin just as he said, "Bossy."

And that's when I saw it. Him. Eyes that were black as coal peered through the ajar door and backed away, hoping I didn't notice. I had. I swallowed up my fear, even as my hands trembled. "Austin. Give me a kiss before you leave."

"What?" He laughed. "I literally just gave you a kiss."

"I need another one," I pushed. My heart beating so loud it shocked me he couldn't hear it.

"I'll only be a second, Mac."

"*Now*," I demanded as I let my hand roam under my pillow, searching for the blade that I knew was somewhere.

"Okay." He held his hands up in surrender as he walked back to the bed.

When he leaned down to kiss me, I veered my head to his cheek and whispered into his ear. "There is a man in the hallway. I saw him look into the room when you–"

I never got to finish my warning before the door flung open, right as my fingers contacted the hilt of my blade. I gripped it, not hesitating as I lifted it up, throwing it hard over Austin's shoulder and straight into the chest of the man. The blade made contact with a sickening thud, throwing him back into the doorframe, where his legs gave out and he slunk to the floor.

"Fuck," Austin growled as he whirled around just in time to see the second man step into the room. "I fucking knew it."

"You think we were going to wait around and let someone else take the kill that's rightfully ours?"

"Fuck you, Martinez." Austin growled and before the man could get a word out, Asa, who I thought was asleep, rose. He flung two blades at once, the action so swift that I hardly saw them fly through the room before each one landed in opposite shoulders.

The man, the one I assumed was Martinez, hissed out a breath, but before he could reach up, Austin was on him, pulling the blade out of his shoulder and jamming it into his abdomen. The grunt of pain was all I heard before Austin took it out, pushing the guy out the door. He reached back, grabbing the hair of the man with the blade in his chest, and pulled, dragging him out of the room with him.

"I- I- What was–" My breath was coming rapidly. The fear was consuming me as I fought not to panic. But it was too late. "Did I kill him?"

"That guy?" Asa rose a single brow. "He'll be fine. It's Austin he needs to worry about."

Asa pushed back the comforter, then crawled over me. He didn't glance back as he picked up a pair of boxers and put them on. I stumbled after him, grabbing his discarded shirt and tossing it over my head as he led the way out of the room.

Wick was in the hallway when we emerged. "What the fuck happened?"

"Martinez."

"Shit," Wick cursed, running a hand through his hair. "It's a week early."

"He's aware. Said he wanted to be the one to make the kill. Mac got a guy in the chest. It was glorious to see our girl protect us."

"Yeah?" A smile spread over Wick's face. Such a rare thing. "You did that, Vixen?"

"I–"

"She didn't even hesitate," Asa continued.

"I knew you had it in you." Wick leaned down, stealing a kiss before he pulled back, already taking the stairs two at a time before I even opened my eyes. "Martinez, you fucker. You broke the fucking rules of the game and now you'll fucking pay."

"I'm not fucking afraid to die," a pained voice spat.

"It's a good thing I'm making you live first." Wick's voice was sinister, and I knew he had plans that would make this guy wish for death. "You know the rules. I caught you; we can pick the punishments."

"Fuck you." Martinez spat at Wick's feet, barely missing him.

"Asa," Wick called. "Is that an option you're willing to explore during his remaining time on earth?"

A look I'd never once seen crossed Asa's expression, one of hard calculation and soulless endeavors. It was a look that made me believe Asa could be as cold as Wick and maybe more calculated. It reminded me that these men who drew me baths and fought for my attention were remorseless killers.

Asa stepped forward, his hand in Martinez's hair, pulling his head back so that they were eye to eye. "I wonder, Martinez, will you beg for forgiveness when my cock is inside of you or moan your repentance as pleasure brings you to your knees?"

"You're fucking dead, Dominguez. Dead."

"Probably." Asa's eyes roamed around him. "But at least when I go, I'll be taking your virginity with me."

Martinez snarled. "I'm not a fucking virgin."

Asa laughed. "I wasn't talking about pussy."

Martinez struggled against Wick's hold, cursing and calling Asa every crude word in the dictionary before Wick's elbow came down, slamming into his skull, and Martinez's body went slack as he slumped forward, knocked out.

CHAPTER THIRTY-EIGHT

AUSTIN

The meeting was called on short notice, but that didn't stop fellow members from milling about the old church, dressed in solid black, their sinister half masks in place, eager for the event. The masks hid little. I'd learned long ago who hid behind them, which monsters were working at my side. It was best to know who you could trust, and who might turn on you in a blink of an eye.

It was why we were here.

We knew it would happen, but we hoped it wouldn't. Still, that didn't stop Martinez and his men from attempting an attack on Mac's life, on our lives.

A ball of regret lodged in my throat as I thought about it. Thought about how I hadn't believed her and that almost cost us our lives. Thought about how she hadn't hesitated to throw her blade, hadn't apologized to the man who was now tied up at the altar, still barely alive after the perfectly thrown blade sunk into his skin. Another inch over, she'd have had his heart. Her hands shook by the end of the night. Thoughts of what she had done slowly seeped in until her eyes had that glassy, glazed look, and I'd had to wrap my arms around her waist and pull her back to my bare chest before whispering words of praise for what she had done for me. For us.

"Are they going to kill them?" she whispered as her arms wrapped around mine, holding onto me so tight that it made my chest puff out, feeling the superiority of her love rush over me.

"They deserve greater than death for coming for you," Wick answered for me as he guided her through the people, his hand at the small of her back.

"They had their girl killed," she pointed out.

"No excuse to go after mine." Wick raised his chin in greeting to a friend. Or were they foes?

"That one, the one I got with my blade..." she muttered. "He said you were friends."

"I'd never been his fucking friend and I never fucking would have," Wick growled. "I never needed more, or wanted more, than what I have right here with Asa, Austin, and you. Don't forget that, baby."

"He had been following us for a while," she admitted. "I kept seeing him."

Memories of her mentioning Wick's friend at the carnival flooded into me, and I could have stabbed my heart for ignoring the warning signs that were presented right there in front of me. But we couldn't have known that this was the guy who she had met in her class, couldn't have known that this guy was watching our moves, trying to find a right time to get to us, knowing that the opening of the kill season, the housekeeper sweep, was next week.

"After tonight, no one will see him," Asa muttered under his breath, but I knew Mac heard him. She flinched, her fingers digging into my bicep, using me as an anchor. I hoped she left a bruise. Hoped that she left her own mark of ownership upon my skin so the world would know that she possessed me.

A gong filled the church, our signal to file into the pews and offer ourselves to our government for the greater good. The crowd pushed their way through the thick wooden doors, eager to get an update on whatever drama had called this last-minute meeting. People never changed, despite the aging. People loved to take in the drama and woes of others, loved to hear gossip to discuss among themselves. Tonight, we were the gossip and the example. Tonight, we'd shed the blood.

We didn't go for the balcony that Wick usually favored. Tonight, we took our steps carefully as we followed the line of people, servants of the states, through the aisles of the pews. We did not stop at the empty spots, did not shove our way into a favored space for a good view. We walked until we were in front of the crowd, taking a spot on the first row of pews, reserved for no one, but never touched.

Another gong sounded, the vibrating ring so much louder from where we stood, only feet away. The noise made Mac cringe as she dropped her hands from my arm only to find my hand that was dangling at my side. She laced our fingers together, squeezing tightly as she searched for Wick's.

"I knew you liked me," he teased her as he took her hand, bringing it up to his lips to kiss her knuckles.

"As much as I love a root canal," she whispered back, though it was clear that wasn't true. They might fight a lot, but that tension fueled their sleepless nights. We had a lot of those.

In front of us, Jones stepped up to the podium, his back straight as he looked out to the crowd. It was a full house, not like we expected anything different. When they called, we answered. When orders were given, we obeyed.

His fingers gripped the side of the smooth wood as he leaned forward slightly, relaxing into a stance. "Ladies and gentleman, it's nice to see you here tonight. Thank you for answering our call." No one dared speak, but the truth was undeniable. No one would miss this. "Repeat after me…"

The traditional words were spoken. The pledges made. Everyone was on edge, waiting for the moment to come, the ball to drop, the betrayers to be slaughtered. Their time was coming to an end, and we could see the fear in their eyes as they watched their supe-rior proceed with a meeting that would end with their blood on the slate floor.

An eternity passed before the final words were spoken. "This meeting was called today because of a violation of our code of conduct, a stain on the ethics we live by. In a world where rules are bent and broken, we must hold strong, stay unwavering in our beliefs. Do you agree?"

The crowd all cheered, hollered, and praised Jones for holding steady in the rules they taught us from the very beginning of our time with the organization. The rules weren't hard to follow, even if they were strict. And the consequences of disobeying them were dire. Severe punishment was in place to deter such rule breaking. Clearly, it didn't work.

"It is with great sadness that we are gathered here today." For dramatic effect, Jones hung his head for a moment before raising it, letting his eyes meet the crowd and travel the length of the room before finally settling on us. "This morning, during the early hours before dawn, members of Team Martinez broke the rules and went after not only our own people, Team Moore, but also their housekeeper."

There were gasps, but I couldn't imagine why. We all knew that Team Martinez was coming for us, even if no one thought they would be brave enough to attack our team. But for us, it was a matter of when. If they had succeeded in our slaughter, tonight would have ended differently. There would have been no meeting or consequences, for they would have proven us a weak link in the organization. But they were caught, we lived, and now they must be punished.

"Tradition states that we give their fates over to the team they wronged." Tradition also declares that they be killed, but that went without saying because no one would let someone they can't trust live. "In the time since the attack, Team Moore has shown Team Martinez why they have gained their reputation."

All eyes were on the bound men at the altar. The blood, the cuts, the scars, the broken bones. Wick showed them just how brutal he could be, and they suffered. They deserved the suffering after the threat to Mac.

Jones turned to the team. "Team Martinez. You are missing a member."

They refused to speak, but their eyes gleamed with hatred, hard with defiance. They wouldn't give up the location of their last member, that was clear. But if found, he was as good as dead. The organization left no loose ends untied.

Jones paused, but the team refused to speak. "From this moment forward, we shun him from our program. He is a wanted man of the United States."

The swollen eyes of their team leader met Jones's before he spat at him. "Fuck you."

When a man was going to die, he had nothing to lose, I guess.

Jones, to his credit, didn't react, only adjusted his

suit before he turned back, addressing the members of his society. "Let this be a reminder that our rules are in place for a reason, and no matter how pointless they may seem, they test the loyalty of the men at our backs. To act on impulse and anger is selfish. Remember that, and the consequences, any time you wish to betray the men you vowed to always protect."

A choir of yes sirs broke the silence, then Jones's eyes were on us. "Team Moore, will you honor us with your presence up on the altar?"

"Yes, sir," Wick answered before he positioned Mac between himself and Asa, leaving me to guard her back.

I couldn't be sure, but I swore I saw a slight nod of approval from Jones before his mask of indifference slid into place again. Our steps were slow, measured, a tactic I was sure Wick had expended for the dramatic effect. When we reached the front of the room and stood in front of the mangled bodies of the men who tried to take us out, Jones turned toward the people. We followed, facing the crowd.

"As is tradition, punishment for the transgressions of Team Martinez falls to you to issue. Do you accept responsibility for the harm they have caused and vow to correct all that's been wronged?"

"I do." Wick stood tall, his posture relaxed, though I knew otherwise. I could see the little signs that gave him away. The light tick of his jaw, the barest movement of his pinky finger. He was on guard, ready to spring into action in case that single missing member of Team Martinez appeared with threats in his heart.

"Then it shall be done."

In traditional fashion, the chamber echoed the words of our leader, and in unison, all those present muttered, "Then it shall be done."

Jones turned to Wick. "How do you wish to proceed?"

"Death."

It shouldn't have shocked anyone. Death was how it always ended. Still, there were some sharp intakes of breath as the words were spoken.

Jones nodded before unfolding a cloth that covered a large sword. Cradling it in both hands, he stepped toward our group. "Team Moore, I honor you with the weapon responsible for the deaths of many of our past men. May you swing hard and not miss, ending the suffering swiftly."

I hoped he missed. I prayed to fucking god, who clearly didn't exist, that he missed and instead the sword came down dully, hitting bone and not his neck. It was what they deserved, after all.

Jones went down the line, nodding once to each of us, pausing longer on Mac to offer a slight tip of his lips before he nodded and stepped toward Wick. With a half bow, he presented the traditional weapon, a sword used in this organization since its formation. The blade sparkled in the light of the bulbs, taunting us about what must be done.

Wick's hands reached out, the weight of the

weapon placed in his palm as he nodded his thanks back to Jones. "With honor, I will swing true."

Nothing more needed to be said after that. Wick never missed. His aim was never off. And if there was anyone in this room that was to be my executioner, I could only hope it would be him ending my life. He stepped forward. The blood that had already pooled from their injuries squelched under his shoes.

He stopped in front of them before circling around their kneeling bodies. "Team Martinez, there is no joy in the taking of a life." He swung before they could register that his words were a distraction, severing the head off the body, letting it roll slightly when it dropped. The team leader was in shock, not fully able to comprehend what had happened, when Wick raised the blade again, slamming it down true, snapping the bones in his neck before his head departed from his body. Wick cleared his throat, the words hoarse as he breathed heavily and finished his words. "There is no joy in the taking of a life, but the satisfaction of removing a threat brings me peace tonight."

He let the sword lower, the blood already flowing over the stone as the bodies of the dead flopped forward. The metal hit hard against the slate, echoing through the silent room, announcing for those who dared not look that it was done. They were dead, and those who dared come for our housekeeper, who dared threaten Mac, would join them.

CHAPTER THIRTY-NINE

WICK

It was a party, not like I was in the fucking mood for a party. But tradition called for honoring the dead, and wouldn't you know it, we're the fucking hosts. Our house was packed, both Saints and civilians crowded in, funneling beer through tubes and taking shots, all on Team Moore's fucking dime, and there wasn't shit to be done but wait it out.

I'd rather be asleep.

I'd rather be alone.

I'd rather be balls deep in Mac's cunt.

But apparently none of those were an option.

The music was giving me a headache, making my temples pound and my eyes ache, and through my torture, these fucking freeloaders were oblivious to me not wanting them here. I was a lit fuse ready to ignite. An explosive urge danced under my skin and, if they weren't careful, if they were in my path, that explosion could be directed at them.

"Great party man." A fucker I'd never seen before patted my back as he passed, and I ground my molars.

He didn't know. None of them knew. But the murderous tendencies, the reason I was so fucking good at being a member of the Saints was because it ran in my blood. I'd been doing it since I was a child, holding the bloody knife, burying the dead bodies, and maybe then they weren't my kills, but I'd own them just the same.

Tonight sparked a particularly bad memory I had fought years to forget of a young woman kneeling at my father's feet, her hands bound behind her back. The begging and the crying still woke me at night. The sickening sound of the saw and the screams as he slowly parted her head from her body was the worst of it.

That was his mistake.

He had forgotten that we had neighbors by then and were no longer surrounded by vacant homes. He had forgotten that our basement wasn't soundproof. He had forgotten that evil only prevailed for so long before the greater good stepped in.

I wanted to be the greater good my whole fucking life, and sometimes, if I tried hard enough, I could convince myself that I *was* the greater good. That killing for the Saints was saving us all, saving the innocent who couldn't fight, saving my soul. But it was a lie. It was a fucking lie because I couldn't be the greater good when the warmth of blood against my skin made me fucking hard, and the sound of a final breath sent shivers of lust through my body.

A clawed hand snagged my bicep, and I knew in an instant it wasn't Mac. I shook it off, disgusted at the touch. Once I would have loved the attention. Now? All I wanted was the back-talking brunette that made my blood boil and fought me every step of the way. The painted fake nails and loads of perfume did nothing for me.

"Baby? Why are you pulling away?" I nearly gagged at the use of a pet name. How uncreative. I cringed, thinking about the many times I'd called Mac that.

"I'm taken," I spat.

"She doesn't have to know." The purr in her voice was made to seduce, but I felt no attraction. Mac would never purr. In fact, I was sure Mac did not know how to fucking purr.

"Well, I fucking will." I stepped away, turning my back and walking off in the opposite direction.

I needed to find Mac, and I knew she was here somewhere. The last remaining member of Team Martinez wouldn't be a threat tonight, if they were at all, so Mac was free to roam our home, even though it was stuffed with people. There were too many Saints' eyes on her, willing to protect her until the call to kill was made.

I pushed through the crowd, forcing my way through the people that were bouncing along to the music that was playing in the poorly lit room. Somewhere along the way, someone brought out black lights and glow sticks with a smoke machine. The smoke machine, combined with whatever shit people were smoking, was making the air thick and unbreathable. My fucking eyes burned.

I practically shoulder checked everyone in the kitchen on my way to the backdoor, stumbling through it into the fresh night air. I gulped it down greedily, letting the cool crisp air replace the stale smoking wisps that resided in my lungs as I leaned against the deck railing. It was nice out here, and I wished we found more time to take Mac out, maybe a moonlight picnic or some other shit that usually drove women wild.

A laugh echoed into the night, the sound so familiar my back straightened, and my head whipped around, following the sound. Mac. I'd know that laugh anywhere. It rang around me daily, even if I was never a recipient of its melody. I gazed at the lawn below, searching, not finding her until the sound broke through the night again.

I spotted her down the stairs, standing close to a guy who was familiar, but I swore I'd never fucking seen before. The rage came quickly, not giving way to logic as I took the steps two at a time, not stopping when I reached the ground. My feet carried me angrily forward and before I could register it, his collar was in my hand, his eye already meeting my fist.

She wailed, begging me to stop, as she practically jumped on my back. I felt nothing. Nothing but an all-consuming rage. "She's fucking mine!" The man in my grip was practically limp, but he didn't dispute the fact. "No one talks to her."

An arm wrapped around my throat, pulling me back before my next punch could meet flesh. Asa's lips were close to my ear when he spoke. "Calm the fuck down. We were right here watching her."

"Not well enough if she was talking to this fucker." I still tried to swing, not caring that Austin stepped between us while Asa pulled me back. He pulled at my fist, forcing me to drop the guy to the ground before pushing me backwards, away from the heap of a human.

"It wasn't like that." Asa was breathing heavily, the exertion from keeping me back taking it out of him. "They were talking about a school assignment. A journalism piece. We were three feet away from them, and you were too fucking blinded by rage to notice."

"You let her talk to others," I growled.

"She isn't a prisoner."

"She's mine." I ground the words out, letting them know there was nothing else to it. It was a fact.

Mac stepped forward, leaning over her friend that had since sat up, and Austin pushed her back. "I wouldn't touch him, baby. Wick's a little unhinged at the moment."

"At the moment?" Her voice was high and squeaky, nearly frantic as she repeated the phrase. "There hasn't been a moment with him when he *hasn't* been unhinged!"

She wasn't wrong in her assessment. I couldn't help it. It ran through my blood. I was a fucking monster, like my father. Still, she took Austin's advice, stepping back from the guy as Austin helped him up. She refused to look at me, her focus only on him, and if I hadn't already beaten him to a pulp with a single punch, I'd do it again.

"Mac." I said her name, and she ignored me. I tried again. "Makenna."

She looked Austin in the eyes. "Do you hear something?"

"I wouldn't be like that," Austin warned. At the same time, Asa asked if he was good to let me go.

"It's fine. Get your arm off me." I grunted, shaking him off. "Mac."

"No." She spoke to Austin, not me. "I don't need to talk to him."

"You have to understand..." Asa began.

"I don't have to understand shit. Look at what he did to him. Fucking look." She pointed to the guy whose eye was definitely swelling. "If he wants to act like a barbaric monster, he'll be treated like one."

She turned on her heels, not giving me a chance to explain before she pushed through the crowd of people who had gathered and stomped away.

CHAPTER FORTY

MAC

I knew walking away from him wasn't the right move, but I did it anyway. He was so fucking used to getting what he wanted, issuing orders, and not having consequences that me not obeying him shocked him. But I knew he wouldn't remain in shock for long.

I was almost to the steps of the deck when his hand slammed down on my shoulder and forced me to turn and gaze into his furious eyes. "Where the fuck do you think you're going?"

"Away from you!" My words dripped with loathing, and I hope he felt every ounce of disgust I was feeling for him.

"You're not going anywhere."

"And who is going to stop me? You? What are

your plans? Give me a black eye too? Beat me to where I can't stand either?" I knew it was a low blow. Never had I ever felt threatened by him, at least not to where I feared for my life. Not since the first day when I'd woken up in chains, but even then, I think I knew he wouldn't harm me.

He reared back at my words, clearly feeling hurt that I would even say such a thing. "I would never."

I made it a point to look past him to my friend, who was leaning against Austin for support. "Never, huh?"

"Not to you, you know that. I'd protect you with my life."

"Oh, yeah. Protection. Is that what you were doing? Protecting me by beating up one of the few friends I have?" I didn't let my gaze waver as I stared at him, letting him feel the heat that bubbled inside of me.

"You don't understand." He spoke the words, his teeth grinding. "You can't trust him. You can't trust any man but us."

"Is that so?" I laughed. "And why is that?"

He stepped closer as I stepped back, forcing my back to hit uncomfortably into the rail. "Men are dangerous."

"No." I laughed. "*My* men are dangerous. *You're* dangerous. Most of them are average, non-threatening beings."

"Do you realize what we have to do to protect

you, to protect what's ours from the men of this world? We made you quit your job because we couldn't stand the thought of them lurking around you. Did you even realize how many of them lurked and watched you until we intervened? No man is friendly just because they respect you, Makenna. None."

"That's... That's not true." My heart pounded wildly at the look in his eyes. Did he actually believe this bullshit he was spouting?

"It is." He looked around, taking in all the eyes that were on us before he decided he didn't give a shit. "Ask any of these fuckers and they'd tell you."

"No." I was shaking my head.

He leaned forward, his lips tickling against my ear as he demanded, "Ask me how I know."

"No." I refused to fall into his trap, to be a part of whatever game he wanted to play.

He pushed forward, smashing me against the rail and pinning me between the wooden post and his hard body. On instinct, my fingers came up, digging into the material at his waist. Our exchange turned him on, or maybe it was the adrenaline from whatever outburst he just went through, because his dick sat heavy between us, a weight pressing into my stomach as he leaned in. On instinct, I gasped.

"You feel that, don't you? Even when mad, you're fucking drawn to my cock." His smirk was infuriating, but maybe it's because it was so fucking true. I hated him in this moment, but that didn't stop my core from clenching in want, wishing to be filled by him. He must have read my thoughts, must have known, because one hand held me in place while another went to his waist, releasing his belt before going for his button.

"What are you doing?" I hissed.

"Whatever the fuck I want."

His free hand gripped my skirt, pulling it up, revealing my bare ass for all to see. "Stop."

"No." His eyes were cold. "Let them fucking watch. Let them know who owns you."

"I–" I couldn't protest further. In a blink, he hiked up my leg and jutted his hip forward, impaling me with his dick. I cried out, my body not ready to take his size, not ready to be on display for a yard of party goers to witness.

"You're fucking mine. Do you understand that? Do you understand what type of fucking monster you tied yourself to?" His voice got softer, allowing only me to hear. "Don't you get what tonight has done to me?"

I didn't. I mean, I could assume it wasn't fun. No one liked to kill, but everything I knew about Wick proved he didn't let shit affect him. He let nothing affect him. He was a stone pillar, standing strong, and nothing could break him.

"I didn't ask you to kill them."

His hips moved, the post at my back painful, and even though I didn't want this, didn't want him in this moment, I sensed he needed me. Without thinking, I wrapped my leg around his hip before he hefted me up and forced my other leg around him.

His voice was strained. "You didn't have to ask me. They were a threat to your life, and that means they needed to die. Whoever thinks they could harm what's mine deserves nothing but death. But..." His breathing was heavy, already he was close to the edge, losing the control he worked so damn hard to cling to. "But the demons."

He stopped talking, leaving his words heavy in the air. I reached up, letting my fingers toy with his hair before I clutched a handful and pulled, forcing his eyes to mine again. "What demons?"

His eyes were glazed over, a million miles away from this moment, even when he was right here, his skin against mine. "They were always tied."

"What?"

"It's so they can't fight back."

"What the hell are you talking about?" I sputtered, my fingers digging into his scalp while the other hand held tight to him, practically hanging on for dear life against the assault on my body.

"Fuck." He grunted, his eyes squeezed shut for a moment as if he was trying to fight something, a memory, an image, the pending orgasm. When he opened then again, he mumbled, "The women."

"What women?"

His hips jacked into my body so fast that the railing creaked against our combined weight, groaning with the pressure we pushed upon it. "It's why you can't run from me. You can't walk away."

"God," I groaned, the feeling building deliciously between us, almost ready to spiral. "You're making no sense."

"I'm making tons of sense," he shouted, his hand came out, and out of reflex, I flinched. His face softened as he continued its descent to the rail behind me. Quieter, he whispered, "I'm making tons of sense."

"Wick. Have you been drinking? You're sounding insane."

His throat bobbed as he shook his head, his eyes staring off into the distance before the hand still at my hip tightened, bruising the skin. He leaned in again, his mouth close to my ear as he slammed my body down hard, impaling me almost painfully on his cock. "Chadwick Eugene Moore..." I gasped as his name spoken fully for the first time registered. The name of the most notorious serial killer to hit local streets in decades. The name of the man who snatched girls off the street, tortured them for weeks, then forced his child, not even a teenager, to help murder them. After a pause, he tacked on a fact I'd already connected. "Junior."

He groaned into my neck as his head fell to my shoulder, his hips pivoting unevenly as he finally lost his battle. With a curse, his fingers reached between us and he pressed down, circling my clit hard enough to make me scream before my orgasm slammed into me. A few more pumps and he was releasing inside of me, gasping for air as he clung to me tight.

His cock jerked one last time as spoke into my neck. "You can't fuck with me, sweetheart. My soul can't always fight the demons. I'm barely hanging on."

CHAPTER FORTY-ONE

ASA

"Don't feel bad for him. He'd hate that," I stated as I pulled Mac out of the shower.

I was furious with what Wick did, displaying her body, fucking her in front of everyone on our lawn. But I knew his control was on the edge. He got like that sometimes. Got a little crazy when memories of the past mixed with the present.

"Is- Is it true?" she asked. Her arms were wrapped around herself, a shield from us.

"It doesn't change anything." Austin was sitting on the edge of the tub, his legs stretched out in front of him. Wick was nowhere to be seen. He fled shortly after he handed our girl back to us, and no one had seen him for hours.

"I suppose it doesn't," she admitted. "But what I know, what he went through as a child, it's- It's so-"

"Horrific?" I asked.

"Yeah."

"He was already so fucked up when social services got to him, he was nearly impossible to contain. The minute he turned eighteen, the Saints recruited him. It's helped him, believe it or not. Gave him a purpose. Made him replace his evil with whatever good was left inside of him. Gave him something to use his energy and urges toward. It's why he's so fucking good at it. He's been doing it for most of his life." I didn't want Mac to be afraid of him, though I suspected that in some self-sabotaging way, that's what he was trying to do. Trying to force her away because he was caring too fucking much for our girl.

Austin pushed himself up from the bathtub. "Are you okay?"

"Why wouldn't I be?"

"Because you stabbed a guy, watched Wick kill two, and then got fucked in front of half the college." Austin gave it to her bluntly, but she didn't need it sugar-coated.

She winced. "Oh yeah. That."

"I'm sure people will forget about it tomorrow." She was nodding her head as if to agree with herself.

"I wouldn't bank all my money on that." Austin adjusted her towel, pulling it tighter around her body before wrapping her hair into a pile on top of her head. When he finished, he looked over his work before adding, "But it will be alright."

"You think they'll talk?" Her lip quivered, and I couldn't help but lean over and steal a kiss.

"Oh, they'll definitely talk." I stole another quick peck. "But no one could hear what you guys were talking about, and from the outside view, it was fucking hot. I mean, your broken up friend didn't think so, but everyone else..."

"Is he okay?"

"He's fine. His ego, now that's damaged." Austin smirked.

"It wasn't like that," Mac explained.

Austin's face scrunched up and if that expression wasn't adorable, I didn't know what was. I'd die before admitting that out loud, though. "I think maybe you might have been a little blind to the circumstances. We were close to you, Mac, listening. We let you guys talk, but if he even attempted to touch you, it was game over for him."

"It was game over, anyway," I tacked on.

"That's not funny." Mac glared.

I shrugged. "I mean, it sort of is."

She growled under her breath before stomping away, leaving us to follow her. When we reached her, she was in her room, digging through drawers of clothes before pulling out a pair of black leggings — my favorite — and a shirt I recognized as Wick's. After slipping into a pair of underwear, she pulled on the leggings, then tossed on the shirt sans bra.

With a sigh, she turned to us. "Give it to me straight. How bad is downstairs?"

"Austin will be in his happy place for a while," I confirmed.

"I'll help."

"You'll sleep," Austin demanded.

She was tired. Not only was it nearly dawn, but last night she hadn't slept well either. Not by choice, of course. Having someone invade your home intending to kill you does sort of put a damper on the desire to sleep. But now that she was safe, she needed rest.

"Seriously. I can help. It's not fair that you have to clean it up on your own."

"I won't be on my own. I've got Saints to help me," Austin assured her. "And you've got Asa. He won't leave your side until this place is cleared of everyone but the four of us. Understood?"

"I— "

I knew she was about to argue. Our girl literally argued about every fucking thing, so I cut her off. "Mac. Do you understand?"

"I understand." She understood, but I could tell she didn't exactly agree with it.

"Then it's settled." Austin clapped his hands together, and for a moment, I was sure he was about to announce, 'Go team!' But he put his hands in his pockets, then gave Mac one more longing look before kissing her forehead and strolling out the door.

I waited until his feet had touched the bottom

floor before I stepped forward, closing the door and locking it. Then I turned back to her. "My room or yours?"

She looked at her bed, not bothering to answer me, before she stepped forward and pulled back the sheets, climbing in. Normally, I'd prefer her in only a t-shirt, but with strangers still lagging about and around the house, I was glad she had the sense to put some pants on. I trusted the Saints, but the truth was I didn't know every single one, and I'd always err on the side of caution when it came to my girl. But me? I didn't care who saw my ass and let my pants drop to the ground before climbing in next to her and pulling the covers over us.

It was another thirty minutes before her eyes fluttered, and an additional ten before her breathing evened out. It was only then, when she was fully asleep, that I let my eyes close and allowed myself to drift off.

Hours later, we woke to the sound of Wick in the hallway, his voice low and sloppy, clearly drunk. "Where the fuck is she?"

"She's asleep, man. With Asa. You can see her when she's awake." Austin's voice was level, soothing even, as he spoke to our leader.

"I want to see her now," Wick demanded.

"You're drunk."

"I've had a few drinks. I'm not drunk," Wick's words slurred.

They were the famous words of literally every drunk person. Austin sighed, "Well, still. She's had a rough few days. Let our girl sleep."

"I need her."

"It can wait."

Wick took a step, then stumbled against the wall. "It can't wait."

Beside me, Mac stretched, her arms going above her head as her short little legs straightened. "I should go out there."

"He's fine. He's drunk," I assured her as I shifted, turning to my side before wrapping my arms around her waist.

"He needs me."

"He needs a good therapist, but they always quit," I laughed.

"Are you making fun of the fact that he's been through shit? Because it's not funny." She scowled.

"Honey, if we can't laugh at our trauma, we can't laugh at anything." I tightened my hold, even as her fingers came to my arm, trying to pry me off of her.

"I just... I want to talk to him."

"It's probably not a good idea." I sighed, knowing damn well that she was going to get what she wanted. She always got what she wanted. "He's not that stable after the night he's had. And he's been drinking."

She squirmed free and rolled away. I tilted onto

my back and looked at the ceiling as she spoke. "He wouldn't hurt me."

"That's the thing, sweetheart... he might."

"You're wrong." She huffed before stomping toward the door, and I was on her, jumping out of bed, nearly tripping over the bedding to get to the door before she opened it.

She unlocked it and twisted the knob when my hand slammed down against the frame. "Just... be careful. That's not too much to ask now, is it?"

"I'll be fine."

She nudged me to move, and I did, but not before adding, "I didn't ask you to be fine. I asked you to be careful." I released my hand on the door and stepped back. "Don't push him too hard, okay?"

The hall was empty when we left her room. Neither Wick nor Austin was in sight, but it didn't take long to find them. Following the curses and the groans to Wick's room, Mac stopped in the doorway and looked in. Wick was passed out, face down on his mattress, while Austin struggled with his boots. Mac said nothing as she stepped forward, meeting Austin at Wick's feet before kneeling down and unlacing his other shoe.

"He isn't normally like this," Austin tried to explain.

"I know."

"He can get violent," he attempted again.

"I know."

"He—"

Mac turned to Austin. "I said I know. If you're not going to be helpful, you can get out."

I loved it. Loved every ounce of fire that thrummed in her veins. She wasn't afraid of us, wasn't afraid of anything we could do. She knew what was at stake. Knew that no matter what, we couldn't or wouldn't hurt her.

"Don't be like that, Mac," Austin cooed, and I could tell it only made her more annoyed.

"Be like what? A caring partner taking care of one of her men? How dare I?"

"That's not what I meant," Austin tried again.

"I know what you meant. I know what Asa meant. And I'm telling you that right now, he doesn't need to be coddled. Is he a fucking asshole for what he did earlier? How he treated my classmate and me? Yes. And he'll deal with that later. Don't doubt me about that. But he's telling us what he needs, and you're not listening."

"We're just trying to protect you." I stepped closer to her, sure that there was no way she'd be able to pull that boot off herself. Yet she did it. Three strong tugs and she stumbled backwards to the floor.

After she pulled herself up, she glared. "I don't need protecting. Not from him. He's not the one who tried to kill me. He's not the one who's going to set a target on my back any day now. He may have been out of control and wild. He may have more trauma than I want to even think about. But one thing I know for sure is I was never in danger once tonight. I was the anchor keeping the demons at bay, if only for a little while. So, if you aren't helping me, you can leave."

Her back turned, her concentration on Wick. While she wasn't looking, Austin and I exchanged a silent conversation. After a few moments, I gave in and joined her, helping her pull him up to the pillow before I followed her lead and made myself comfort-able, passing out in a pile of bodies and letting much needed sleep pull me under.

CHAPTER FORTY-TWO

MAC

"Someone stole my shit," Austin fumed as he stormed into Wick's bedroom, tossing things around, looking for whatever was missing.

"It's not in here," Wick grumbled, his arm slung over the side of the bed as he buried himself into the pillow. "Go the fuck away."

I sat up, pulling the blanket with me. Wick and I were the only two still in bed, and I didn't want to be anywhere else. I liked it here. The entire area smelled like Wick and that scent relaxed me, threatening to drag me into sleep for another hour or two. "What stuff?"

"My laptop," he mumbled, lifting a pillow on the floor.

"It's not fucking in here," Wick shouted into his

pillow before his arm came up and practically clotheslined me backwards to lie with him.

"Did you check your backpack?" I asked.

"Yes, mom," he mocked. "That was the first place I checked. But my doorknob was fucked up. I think someone broke in during the party."

"The fuckers," Asa chimed in from the door. "Anything of value on it?"

"Not really. My history paper was almost finished, though."

"Anything on the organization?" The pillow muffled Wick's voice.

"I'm not fucking stupid. I put nothing on there to give away the organization."

"If your history paper is on the cloud, I'm sure we can recover it." Asa leaned against the door frame, looking delicious. "In the meantime, try tracking it."

"It's off or dead. I tried." A growl left Austin. "It's not important, I know that. But fuck if it isn't frustrating."

"You can borrow mine," I offered. "I only use it occasionally for English. Everything else is handwritten."

"You can use mine for porn if that's what you're really worried about." Wick's body shook as he silently laughed into the pillow.

Boys.

I didn't know what the hell I was supposed to do with them, but damn it, I strangely wanted to keep them. It was never supposed to happen this way. I was only going to stay long enough to get my paper written for journalism, that was all. Now? Shit. I didn't know. I'd started the paper, but I wasn't sure if I could go through with it.

"Fuck off." Austin used his thigh to nudge Wick as he walked by. He was annoyed but clearly losing his steam. "It has all the school sites up. I'm going to campus to report it just in case anything fishy is sent from my account. Maybe see if I can get a reset."

He didn't wait for us to acknowledge him. He just walked out. Asa stayed a few minutes longer, giving me eyes that I guess I was supposed to interpret, but I was clueless. Then he tilted his chin toward Wick, before pushing off the wall and announcing, "I'll go with him."

In seconds they left me alone with Wick, who still hadn't looked up from where his head was buried. The weight of the room felt heavy, suffocating the longer we went on without speaking. It was clear he would not be the first to break the silence. That left me.

"So, are we going to talk about last night?" I finally asked him.

"Nope."

"I think we should." Okay, well, I didn't exactly think we *should*. I just knew we had to. If I could avoid this conversation, I'd do it. Probably should have gone with Austin and Asa.

"I was drunk." He still hadn't looked at me, and I allowed my fingers to trail along his spine, tracing it.

"You weren't drunk until after you threw a tantrum and left," I reminded him.

"I was halfway there," he insisted.

"Wick." I threaded my fingers into his hair and pulled, then forced him to look at me.

He licked his lips before swallowing hard. "Mac."

"You beat up Mason for no reason," I accused.

"Mason? What kind of name is that?" He scoffed before admitting, "I had a reason. He was talking to you."

Why was that statement both sweet and infuriating? I loved the possessiveness these men had. Loved that they would rather stand close to me every second of the day than live a second without me. It wasn't love; we hardly knew each other. But being wanted after so long without a single person was addictive.

"Your reason isn't substantial."

He twisted so that more of his body faced mine. "How about he could have been dangerous?"

"He wasn't." That, I was confident of.

"You don't know that, baby. Angel. Vixen. Fuck, how do people even come up with names?" he snarled, but before I could even figure out what the hell he was talking about, he continued. "I'm going to be honest with you, Mac. When it comes to you, everyone is a danger. Everyone is a threat. You think we know the faces of everyone in that church? We don't. I know a few, only people I've been able to make out, plus the team leaders. That's all I've got to go on for protection. That's for their protection and ours, so if we get caught, we can't identify them. But it hinders us because every person at that party could have very well been a threat, scoping you out to prepare for your kill."

"That's..." Fuck, that was terrifying. "It's not like that. I've known Mason since freshman year."

"And how long have you known Austin? Known of me? Asa?" he pointed out.

"That's different." It wasn't. I knew that. I opted to change the subject instead. "When were you going to tell me who you were?"

"Would it have made a difference?" He brought his head down to the pillow again, but this time he turned fully, so our bodies were facing each other. "Most of the Saints hadn't learned a damn thing until they were recruited. Me? I've practically breathed death my whole fucking life. I was born into it, you know. My mom was just another one of his victims, one he liked a little more than the rest. One he wanted to keep around for a while longer."

I tried not to let him see me wince, though I'm sure I couldn't really hide it. I didn't know what to say. 'I'm sorry' didn't really seem adequate. Instead, I let my hand travel up and played in his hair, gently toying with the strands. "I don't care about your upbringing."

"Good to know, because I can't change it."

I continued, ignoring him. "What I care about is that you acknowledge you were out of line."

"I wasn't out of line." He tilted his head, nuzzling into my caresses, and I didn't want to say anything and scare him away, but I couldn't remember a single moment in my time with him where he was this soft, this unguarded from the world. Maybe it was because he had no more secrets to hide from me. Or maybe it was just that, for once, he wanted his guard down. Whatever it was, I didn't want it to change.

"You fucked me in front of a yard full of people!" I raised my voice slightly to get my point across.

"Oh. That." Shrugging, like the fact that half the school campus saw him maul me against the railing had slipped his mind. "Yeah. No. Sorry. I just don't think I was out of line. I wanted people to know who owned you. No, I needed them to know. Now they do."

"Why?"

"Why what?"

I was tired of his bullshit, and we'd only been awake for fifteen minutes. "Why did you need them to know?"

"Isn't it obvious? If they know you're mine, they won't fuck with you. And..." He stretched his back a little before looking at me again. "And I need to know you're not being fucked with."

"I wasn't being fucked with before you came along. I'm sure I'll be fine after."

He turned so fast, rolling over me, pinning me to the mattress. "There will be no after. This, us, we're for life, Mac. Have you changed your mind? You know what getting out means."

"I haven't changed my mind." Which unfortunately was the problem. I took these vows, accepted this life, to write a story I would be proud of, to answer questions no one knew. In the process, I somehow got sucked in.

"Good." His eyes roamed over every inch of my face before he leaned down, kissing me gently. It wasn't like Wick to do anything gentle. "I'm not sorry I fucked you in front of a crowd. I'm not sorry I lost control. And I'm not sorry you got a glimpse of the skeletons in my closet, because even telling you my secrets, you weren't afraid. You liked it, didn't you? You fucking loved knowing that you rode the cock of a monster."

Ah, there was the asshole I'd somehow grown fond of. And yet, he wasn't wrong. There was some sort of thrill that went through me when I thought about it, some sort of understanding that Wick was the ultimate, most unapologetic asshole, and somehow, I got off on that. Even when I begged him, tears running down my cheeks, I fucking loved the taunts and teases he offered me. We were both fucked in the head. That much was clear, and maybe it was that damage that complimented each other. That broken unwanted piece of us that made us click so well, even when we were repelled away by our own stubbornness and control.

When I didn't answer him, he leaned closer, our

noses touching, his breath tickling against my lips. He dropped his voice, the barest of whispers as his eyes flitted between mine and my lips. "You're like my little North Star."

I shifted my hips, widening my thighs to allow his body to be cradled between them. "Hmm?"

It was half a question, half a moan as his thick length pressed into me, even with our clothing in the way. Amusement danced over his face before he grew serious again. "Sometimes I get lost. My mind is a jumble of things I can't decipher, and it threatens to take me down. But you keep it clear. I just look at you and my focus shifts. You are the one true direction. The only good thing that I've ever had in this entire lifetime. Were you meant to always be mine, Mac? Because I can't possibly imagine you anywhere else."

Maybe he was still partially drunk? Or it was his artist's heart coming out to play. At least that's what I told myself because he was here, baring his soul in the most uncharacteristic way, and I was a fraud. A betrayer. A liar. I just hoped that they never found out. Because if the time came, and my lies caught up to me, I'd never forgive myself for crushing their trust and breaking their souls.

CHAPTER FORTY-THREE

AUSTIN

I was steaming. So fucking angry that someone had the nerve to come into my house, break into my room, and steal my shit. I had nothing about the Saints on there, and for that I was thankful. But I was almost done with a history paper, and I had been working on something for English. Plus, I had just transferred all my science notes digitally. Mac would flip if she realized I tossed out all my paper notes for our labs.

I felt like it was a whole day wasted dealing with this shit. I reported it to the agency just in case it had to do with the challenges coming up. Then I reported it to the campus, in case it appeared in another student's possession or was used for something nefarious. After that, it was a mess. I needed a new password and to be logged out of all devices for my campus email and online learning application. But I couldn't remember my original password. It took me four different administrators just to find someone with knowledge enough to guide me on a reset. A reset I couldn't do, because it needed to be done by... the administrators.

"This is a fucking shit show," I complained to Asa, who thankfully followed along with little annoyance.

"Could be worse. Could have Saint docs on there," Asa said. "There's a reason Wick makes sure we delete anything related to missions after each one is finished."

"I had my door locked," I reminded him. "And deleting doesn't always work."

"Well, if you're not looking for Saint information, the info won't make any sense to you, anyway." He pulled open the door to the diner, where we were going to eat lunch. I'd texted Mac and Wick to join us, but I hadn't heard if they were showing up.

We walked past the hostess, giving her a slight nod before claiming our usual booth in back. Asa sat with his back to the wall, while my back was toward the door. Which was the only reason that a few minutes later, when hands covered my eyes, I was surprised. My hand flew up, instantly recognizing the soft skin of Mac. That her scent engulfed me, taunting me into instant lust, didn't help.

I curled my fingers around hers as she leaned in and whispered, "Boo."

"I'm terrified." I kept my voice monotone, showing no emotion.

"I'd be too." She leaned in and kissed my cheek before taking a seat next to me. Wick forced Asa over, claiming his own spot. "Any luck on your laptop?"

"No." The aggression over the matter left me with a sigh. "But I got the password changed for all of my school-based programs."

"That's something." She smiled widely.

"It was a bunch of bullshit, but I'm glad we got it taken care of." I leaned back, the faux leather squeaking with my movement. "I'm still ticked about it, though."

"Understandable. Any suspects?" Her body heat against mine was deliciously soothing, and I couldn't help but raise my arm and place it on the booth behind her head, before slowly creeping it down to her shoulder, pulling her in. "That was such a juvenile high school move."

"Did it work?"

Leaning into me, she answered, "It did."

Picking up where we left off in the conversation, I continued, "I used Asa's computer to check the cameras this morning. It seems somehow, they were offline at the time of the party. I think maybe the Wi-Fi was down."

"Fucking technology," Wick hissed. "We need to figure shit out. That can't happen again."

"There are good things and bad things about

technology," I pointed out. "It's an assistant, not a crutch."

"Doesn't make it any less annoying." Wick hmphed his displeasure.

The waitress picked that moment to come by, taking our drink orders and asking if we'd like the usual. We came here enough that she knew us. She also knew that when Mac wanted a salad, she needed to bring Wick a side of extra fries or onion rings because Mac would pick off his plate.

The food came, and we devoured it. Each of us consuming our meals, lost in our own thoughts, but enjoying each other's company. We chatted about nothing, needing to have some normalcy after the week we'd had, and it was nice. For a moment, I had the brief thought that maybe this was what our life could be like, and I knew I could get used to it. Used to having the people I loved around me, relaxed and happy.

Ding.

All our phones went off in unison. But we weren't the only ones. Several phones on the other side of the diner all vibrated with an alert, too.

Our eyes locked, and I licked my bottom lip before the word escaped me in a rasp. "No."

"No, what?" Mac asked. Her head jolted between us as we silently locked eyes with each other while avoiding her gaze.

Wick's eyes fell to the table, where each of our

phones sat, and I stopped him, leaning forward with my hand out. "Don't do it."

"Don't do what?" Mac's fingers were on my bicep, her nails digging into me.

"The thing is..." I swallowed hard. "If we read it, we can't avoid it."

"We can't avoid it either way." Asa was right. But I wanted to live in bliss a little longer. I wanted to pretend our world was perfect, and we were just a normal family, enjoying a normal evening of food. Chatting among ourselves because we had not a single worry in the world. Not—

Ding.

"Fuck." The word gritted out of Wick as he reached for the phone, and I closed my eyes. Tried to close off the attempt to acknowledge what was coming, but it was no use. We all knew it. When I opened my eyes, he had his fingers wrapped around the cell, picking it up slowly, keeping his eyes on us.

He turned at the last second, his face unreadable as his eyes scanned the screen. Then, as slowly as he had picked it up, he reached over and placed his phone screen side down. He didn't speak. The suspense, even knowing the probable outcome, was heavy among us. His eyes grew blank, but the muscle in his jaw ticked.

The moment stretched, became unmanageable, and finally, it was Asa who demanded, "Just fucking tell us."

Wick swallowed hard, his throat working through

a lump that clogged it as he stared off behind me. When he finally spoke, our world crashed into inevitable shattering pieces. "It's begun early. The entire organization will be after our housekeepers. It's us against the world, and I fucking hope we are strong enough to survive. If not, she's dead."

CHAPTER FORTY-FOUR

MAC

My blood roared to life, my heart pounding, the need to flee outweighing any other feelings I had. Yet my boys sat around me, as calm as could be. My hands were shaking as I reached for Austin's thigh. "What do we do?"

"We wait," Wick answered for him. "No use drawing attention to yourself. Besides, you've trained for this."

"You've trained for years. I've trained for a month and a half," I hissed.

"And you're phenomenal." Wick didn't blink as he issued the compliment. "They will not attack tonight. They need time to group, figure out which house-keepers they want to hit, if any. And that's assuming they can figure out the teams and their members. It's hard to see through the masks in meetings. There could be not a single team coming for you, and that would be a wise fucking decision for them."

"Or they could all come for me because you strut around like a fucking peacock and preen with the power and skill you possess," I accused him.

"Or there is that." He nodded. "But we needn't worry tonight."

"I heard it," I reminded him. "I heard the other alert chimes. They are here."

"And that's unfortunate." Why was he so cool? How could he be so calm when my life and theirs were literally in danger? "But I'm not searching them out or broadcasting our presence. We'll be going to the back door."

"Why are you so fucking calm?" I leaned across the table, kicking his leg to get his attention, forcing him to look at me.

"I've no other choice." His voice was soft, barely audible as he spoke. "You know what's coming. We all do. If I panic, if I let my fear take over, I risk you. I can't..." He swallowed. "I can't risk you. I-I didn't know it was going to be this hard when we signed up. I'd never wanted to be attached."

The statement was probably as vulnerable as Wick would ever get with me in public. More than he was ever willing to give in front of Asa and Austin. He was the strong one, the team leader, the impenetrable Chadwick Moore, and I was just the poor discarded girl who signed up for no fucking reason but to write a paper and gain acknowledgement, and now here they were, willing to die for me, and I... I wouldn't be able to survive if that happened.

Austin's hand reached down and wrapped around my fingers. He squeezed. "Wick and Asa will go out first. We'll follow."

"I think we should go out together," I protested.

"We've got to clear it, Vixen." Wick had never been so docile in his life. "Make sure you're safe."

"I'm safe when I'm with all of you."

"You're safe in here around all these people. Once you walk out, you're in danger. For all we know, they could be waiting in the parking lot. Waiting for us to leave so they could swoop in and get the job done."

"I thought you said they wouldn't attack tonight!" My voice was so high pitched, it was nearly painful as it tore from my throat.

"I mean, I wouldn't. It wouldn't be logical. There is no correct way to assess your protection unless it's assessed during the time of the games."

"The games." I huffed. "Because that's what our lives are to you men."

"Your life is more to us than that." Asa leaned in. "But sometimes you can't let your emotions get involved. Sometimes, you've got to pretend like there isn't a shit load of males hunting the female you've been infatuated with, and go about your business."

"Just another Tuesday," I stated while waving a hand nonchalantly.

"Speaking of Tuesdays." Wick's eyes were

assessing the surroundings, and I knew he was planning our exit. "The games don't cancel class. If we
aren't going about our everyday activities, the organization deems it a cheat."

"Idea." The word came out cold. "Why don't we
put their lives on the line, then they could decide if
trying to stay alive is a cheat or not."

Wick stood and tossed down some cash before
leaning over the table. "How do you think they got to
where they were? They started at the ground, just like
us. One day, I'll have Jones's job, he'll move up, and
the cycle will continue. Don't dilly dally, we don't
have all night to get you home."

In a blink, he was gone, and I was left to absorb
the information he offered. He was after Jones's job,
and maybe one day, he'd get it. He was the best, after
all. At least that's what I heard. And even though this
job started as a temporary endeavor for me, I wanted
to be there and watch as all his dreams came true. I
ignored the pain in my chest at the thought of not
seeing him succeed.

"Did he say dilly dally?" I murmured to Austin.

He slowly nodded. "It's not even the weirdest
term I've heard come out of a serial killer's mouth.
Up you go, baby girl; we've got our beds calling us,
and we will make it there tonight."

One day, I hoped to have just a fraction of the
confidence that these men had. But that day wasn't
today, and as I rose from the table, I couldn't stop my
fingers from wrapping around the butter knife and

sliding it up my sleeve. Just in case, I told myself, though I hoped, like fuck, I'd never use it.

"I'll always be at your back, remember that. They are waiting for you." Austin's fingers tapped against my waist as he urged me forward.

"Are you scared?" I whispered because fuck, I was terrified. I'd continue to be terrified. My life was on the line, all because I wanted this damn story? What the hell was wrong with me? I didn't need to follow in my mother's footsteps. Maybe I could have found a nice freelance office job like my father instead.

Austin chuckled, but it seemed fake, a false sense of joy. "Baby, we're the Saints. Nothing scares us."

"There is nothing saintly about you boys." I bit my lip as I stepped forward, acting casually as I inched my way down the hall.

His voice was low, seductive, as he leaned in. "We are so fucking saintly when we sin. I've heard you evoke the gods more than once."

My skin heated with the memory and a blush crept up my skin. "If you're trying to distract me, you're doing your job well."

"I'd never try to distract." The innocence in his voice was false. I'd been around Austin long enough to know he was nothing but a distraction.

He reached in front of me and pushed open the door at the end of the hallway, holding it open so I could exit. The minute my foot touched the pavement, the surrounding energy shifted. My head whipped to the side at the sound of a gasp, only to see Asa's arm wrapped around the neck of a man, whose eyes were bulging as he lost his battle for air. Blood coated Wick's shirt, and he growled to Austin, "Get her the fuck in the truck."

Austin's hand grabbed my wrist, his fingers so tight we nearly fused together as he dragged me toward the vehicle. No sooner did he have the door open than Asa's hands were on my waist and lifting me up.

"I've got a cleanup crew on the way," Wick announced as he slammed the door. "That was just fucking inconvenient. A little heads up would have been nice." He reached over his shoulder and pulled the seatbelt before clicking it into place. "It's just our fucking luck to be in the middle of a meal and bam! Target on our back."

"Oh god," I muttered, "I won't be able to go anywhere."

"You'll be fine. That was just bad luck. We'll be prepared when we leave the house next time." Austin pushed a lock of hair behind my ear and squeezed my hand.

"We should have been prepared this time." Asa looked at me through the rearview mirror. "That was our mistake. They cut off some time. We usually have more time."

The engine roared to life, and Asa pulled out, not a hint of the fact that he choked a man to death moments prior. Hell, he didn't even glance toward the bodies that they'd dragged to lean up against the wall of the building. His fingers just tapped lightly against the steering wheel as if he was humming along to a song.

"You two just killed men, and you're acting like you're on your way to a Sunday picnic," I broke the silence.

They all looked at me, but it was Wick who spoke. "It's our job, Mac. We kill people, and so do you now."

Only I didn't want to kill people. I didn't want to feel flesh give underneath my blade ever again. I didn't want to intimately know the warmth of blood gushing on my skin. I wasn't this person. Was I?

And yet, you've got a butter knife up your sleeve, prepared to do just that.

I ignored the voice in my head. "I don't know if I'm made for this."

Wick laughed, and goosebumps rose up on my skin. "It's a little fucking late for that now, don't you think?"

I didn't know if I ever really thought about when this moment would come. I always had just one more day, a week, a few weeks, and I never thought it would happen. And now? So close to the other attempt on my life, and it was all too much, too close together. Hysteria bubbled inside of me, the panic clawing at my chest, causing my breathing to speed up.

"Oh no, you don't." Asa watched me through the mirror. "Fucking breath through it, Mac, because you're not about to lose your shit now, on the drive back home. Absolutely not."

"I—" I tried to speak, but my throat was closing in, the feeling too tight to force words past.

"Listen to me right fucking now." Asa slammed on the brake, jolting my body forward until I was forced to brace myself on the seat in front of me while my boys grabbed onto whatever they could to stabilize themselves. Asa turned, forcing me to look into his eyes as I panted. "What was one of the first things we said to you, then repeated again and again?"

"I—" My mind was blank. I was stumbling to grasp any concept right now, simple or complex.

He continued anyway, "If someone gets to you, then we're all dead. They would have to get through us first, and we are going to need you to trust that we can keep you safe. Trust that in instances we can't, the training we could provide is going to be enough for you to keep yourself alive. Now suck it up. We're five minutes out from home. Unless they break the rules — which I won't lie, is a possibility — they can't touch us there."

Asa never talked to me like that. He never raised his voice. My eyes pricked, burning behind my eyeballs.

"What is it now?" Wick slammed his head back into the leather headrest.

"I..." Asa's words and his tone replayed through my mind, and I latched on to what I thought was the most important of them. Death. Them dying. The thought of them dying because of me was too fucking much. I couldn't handle it. Not after the week we had. My eyes welled with tears that fell before I could stop them. "I don't want you dead."

"Jesus," Wick cursed. "She's crying. Why the hell are you crying?"

Austin rubbed his hands over his face. "We won't die."

"But Asa said—" I sniffed.

"I don't fucking care what Asa said," Wick cut me off. "Use what we fucking taught you, and we'll have no problems." There was a pause before Wick whispered to Asa, "Shark week?"

"Any moment," Asa confirmed.

"Just great. Exactly what we need. Mac emotional. Perfect fucking timing."

I used my shoulder to wipe away the tears. "I'm not emotional. And you guys shouldn't track my body cycles. It's creepy and an invasion of privacy."

I didn't want to mention that even I didn't know my period was close. I clearly liked to risk it all and live on the wild side, then act surprised when she showed up. They hardly spared me a glance, as Asa continued like I wasn't there. "We've got this handled, right? We can keep this under wraps without too much drama?"

"Are we talking about the housekeeper sweep or Mac's period? Because honestly, we can handle one at a time, not both." Wick flipped the visor, and when a pack of gum fell down, he leaned forward, retrieved it, and popped a piece in his mouth.

"You guys are assholes." I threw myself back into the cushioned seat.

Wick turned to face me again. "We may be assholes, but you're not panicked anymore, and we've vowed to keep you alive."

He offered me a cocky grin, and I fucking hated that he was always right.

CHAPTER FORTY-FIVE

ASA

It had been two days since the housekeeper sweep orders had been issued. Two days of Mac pacing around anxiously while the rest of us assured her it would all be okay. Could we promise? Sure, but it might be false. We didn't know if it was going to be okay. We only knew that we were the best, and if she was going to live through this, we were her best bet.

"We've lost two housekeepers," Austin announced, and I winced, not wanting to imagine the pain their teams must be feeling. The announcement had brought the reality home. This was a dangerous game we played, a dangerous life we lived, and Mac, the innocent girl who once worked the student store, got dragged into it because we were selfish and we wanted to own our own fucking female. We wanted her as part of our team and not some disposable cunt we picked up for a night along the way.

"Two?" Mac's eyes grew wide with panic, and I wished Austin would have kept his fucking mouth shut until after she'd left the room.

"That's not a lot." Wick gazed at his sketch pad, uninterested in the conversation. Except I knew him. I could see the slight tick of his cheek from the tightness of clenching his jaw.

"It's two lives," Mac stated.

"And neither of them was yours. You didn't know them. We didn't know them. It's insignificant," I reminded her.

"Asa." She scowled as she put down her laptop. "When did you become the heartless one?"

When I needed to protect my heart from possibly breaking. "I'm not heartless, it's facts, princess. This happens every year, and we can't let ourselves get emotionally attached."

"So you'd rather forget their names?" She looked so fucking beautiful when she was getting riled up. Her cheeks turned the perfect shade of red, and I couldn't help but lean over and steal a kiss from her, even though she was clearly angry at me.

When I pulled away and leaned back into the couch, I stated, "I'd rather not know their names at all."

Austin leaned forward and pushed her laptop closed. "How about a movie?"

"With you three? No thanks. You'll probably all

pick some slasher movie and set me on edge some more."

"We've all got class tomorrow. Might as well enjoy today in our cave," I reminded her.

"I'll make popcorn," Wick offered before standing, already stretching his limbs.

"I said I didn't want to watch a movie." She glared at us all.

"That's your period talking." I barely dodged the pillow that was thrown at my head. "You *do* want to watch a movie."

When she missed with the pillow, I was shocked she didn't hit me with her knife next. I knew the comment would tick her off, but I loved the fire that flamed inside of her just as much as I loved the sweet. "Assholes. All of you."

"What did I do?" Austin pouts.

"Suggest a movie." She moved her laptop to a side table and curled her legs up onto the couch.

I stood and took the folded blanket that was on the back of my chair with me. I carried it over to Mac and spread it over her lap before plopping down next to her. Even though she sulked, she didn't object when I picked up the remote and turned on the TV. I picked the movie — nothing that involved blood, guts, or death of any kind — and waited for Wick to enter before hitting play.

"What are we watching?" he asked as he placed a bowl of gourmet popcorn in Mac's lap. I knew he couldn't just toss popcorn into the microwave. He had to take out the iron pot and make popcorn in a fancy way, complete with his own seasoning blend.

"Some rom com." I smirked, knowing Mac was about to harm me. "I didn't want to make Mac cry."

She pinched me so hard I knew I'd bruise. "Jackass."

I pulled some of the blanket onto me, sharing her heat underneath as I leaned against her shoulder. "You know I'm only saying shit because it gets your attention, right? Maybe I just need more attention from you."

She pushed my head off her shoulder, and I laughed. "Negative attention."

"Negative attention is still attention, princess."

This time when I laid my head against her, she didn't push me away, and when my fingers laced with hers, she didn't object. During the movie, she let me lay my head in her lap, her fingers playing with the strands of my hair as she lazily watched, the motion lulling me to sleep.

It was dark when I woke again. Each of us was passed out with the screen of the television black, the word Samsung bouncing around the screen as it idled. I rubbed my face with my palms, trying to figure out how long we'd all been out. It was daylight when the movie started, but that had to have been hours ago.

I shifted my body, and a creak timed perfectly with my movement. But I froze, knowing damn well that movement on the couch never created such a sound. Nudging Wick with my foot, he jolted awake, his eyes frantically looking around until he spotted me. When his eyes focused, I mouthed the word, *Hall*.

He understood instantly, his body tight as he silently rose. Each step he took was muted as he crept toward the pocket doors of the hall. Austin had closed them, even though we usually kept them open. The glare from the hall's light bounced off the screen and had made it impossible to see the movie. Not like any of us watched it long, clearly, since we all passed the fuck out, but now I was thankful for the space between us.

Wick shook Austin as he passed him, forcing him awake while we left Mac sleeping. I didn't move. I kept my body in front of hers, a shield, if need be, from whatever dangers could be lurking. With silent, practiced words, Wick instructed Austin through the kitchen, and he'd go through the hall, and hopefully together, they could close in on the threat.

Austin nodded, his bulky frame jumping over the couch in a swift move before landing soundlessly on his feet. I followed him with my gaze until he disappeared through the doorway, then I looked back at Wick, as he parted the door slowly, careful not to make a noise before he slipped out through the smallest of cracks.

I let my ears strain, listening to every sound that spread through the dark, hearing absolutely nothing. I moved slowly, pulling and detangling my body from Mac's sleeping form, trying not to wake her but allowing my body to come to a full stance, ready to defend and protect. I palmed my blade as I kept my attention alternating between both entry points, but not discounting the use of the windows. I was lucky that the couch was shoved against a wall, offering protection, but I hated that not once, but twice, our home wasn't as secure as it should have been.

I could pull up the cameras, but with us all in different places, that only tore my attention away from where it needed to be, and that was on Mac and her safety. I pondered the options while I stood on guard in the deafening silence of our house. For a moment, after I'd been standing for far too long, I questioned everything, wondering if the noise was a figment of my hazy half lucid mind, but as soon as that thought hit, a solid mass slammed against the kitchen cabinet a room away.

My body swung in the direction, my stance prepared, ready to fight should the scuffle come through the doorway. But it seemed contained, the grunts and huffs echoing into the dark as things shattered, but nothing seemed to wake Mac. After the week we'd had, the lack of sleep seemed to catch up to her, and she was out cold.

A hand slapped onto the wood, breaching the entry into the living room, but it was already too late. The body crawled into view, and I made it one step forward before Austin's foot came forward, slamming a head into the ground. He grabbed the dark mop of hair, yanking the hair until his neck arched, forcing a vaguely familiar set of eyes to stare at me as Austin reached forward, drawing his weapon across his neck and tearing his life from him.

He let go of the hair; the body hit the wooden floor with a sickening thud as Wick came in, blood splattering his shirt. His chest heaved. "The entire team came along. Is there no place fucking sacred anymore?"

"They kill us. They move to the top team. Plus, taking out housekeepers? The bonuses and perks involved are top notch." Austin's chest was heaving as he pointed out the obvious. "We've done it."

"I hate fucking rule breakers." Wick ignored Austin as he fought to catch his breath, his hands on his hips as he looked at the body by Austin's feet. "I've got a clean-up crew on the way. Got one in the back, right through the heart, in the hallway. Another's guts are all over the stairs. Think we should move her?"

"We've got to. I don't want her waking to this shit show. They don't offer therapy in this program, and I think she's one dead body away from breaking." She was strong. Stronger than I thought she'd be. But even the strong struggled with this life. If we didn't have each other, we never would have survived it.

Wick stepped forward, pulling a syringe from his pocket before kneeling onto the couch beside Mac. "That's exactly what I was thinking." In a blink, he had the sedative plunged into Mac's skin, the prick hardly causing a stir from our girl. When the liquid emptied into her body, he pulled back. His eyes searched ours, for once needing our approval over what he just did. "It was for the best."

I swallowed hard, feeling like somehow, we had just betrayed her. "For the best."

"No one mention shit about what happened tonight. Deal?"

"Deal," I echoed as Austin said, "Deal."

Lights of a vehicle outside our window alerted us that the crew was here. Wick reached over, brushing a strand of hair off Mac's forehead. "Get her to bed. Stay with her."

I nodded before leaning down and scooping her into my arms. I'd have no problem staying with her. Next to her is the only place I ever wanted to be. As I carried her out of the room, footsteps on the porch rumbled through the house. I took each step slowly, avoiding the guts Wick had spilled. It wasn't until I was in my room, the door almost closed, that Wick unlocked our front door and let the organization into our home.

The one place we were supposed to be safe from them.

CHAPTER FORTY-SIX

MAC

It had been two weeks of constantly looking over my shoulder, and though my boys seemed tense, I finally felt like I could relax. In two weeks, not a single soul had come for me. At least, not since the first night at the diner when they were waiting outside the door, knowing I'd come out. The boys made it seem like it was a big deal. That people would come left and right, and as much as I'd like to believe them, so far, it seemed calm. Safe even.

Every day, we'd go to class. The only difference was that now I'd have one of them sit in my sessions with me. Science was the easiest since Austin was already my lab partner. Nothing changed in those classes, making it easier to concentrate. But the other classes, when they sat sulkily behind me, wishing they were anywhere but there, well... those weren't as easy to focus. Especially when Wick had wandering hands, Asa had outlandish texts, and Austin, well... he just took to organizing my backpack, causing a whole shit ton of distractions.

When not in class, we spent more time at home, opting to skip the gym and the runs. Though Wick would never let me skip a workout fully. Instead, he's created a convenient, at home workout that required no weights, but still made my muscles burn like I'd dipped them in acid. Only there was no carrying me home when I was ready to collapse. Instead, he forced me to walk up the steps myself, nearly crying from the strain.

Dinner was home cooked. Groceries either bought by one of them or ordered in. They were risking nothing, and for that I was thankful because it was my life. But I was going crazy. I'd grown fond of these men, attached really. But twenty-four seven surveillance was becoming too much.

"Please," I snapped, while in the bathroom on campus, "let me pee alone."

"Absolutely not." Wick smirked as he held open the door for me to enter.

"Can you at least let me have a solo stall?" I asked.

"I've seen you pee. It's no big deal." He shrugged.

"It's no big deal unless you want privacy, which I am severely lacking," I argued.

"We need to make sure you're safe." The door

slammed hard behind him, and he flicked the lock so that no one else could enter while we were in here.

"The flimsy bathroom stall door will not make or break my protection. Check, there is no one in here."

He would have checked anyway, but still he pushed each door open. He stuck his head inside like simply peering into the two by four space would cause him to miss something vital. When he had checked every square inch, he turned back to me. "It's clear."

I could have told him that. I stepped into a stall and tried to close the door, but his hand stopped me. "Seriously, you just cleared it."

"There are windows above the stalls," he pointed out. "Keep it open."

"That no one can get to," I reminded him.

He put his hands on his hips and looked up at the offending window in annoyance. "I've gotten through smaller places in worse locations."

"Ninety-nine percent of the population wouldn't even know how to get up there." I turned away from him, hanging my bag on the hook in the stall.

"We're trained killers," he reminded me. "We aren't like most of the population. In another few months, we'll be sitting cushy at a desk job, blending in with society, but you want to know what's different, Vixen?"

I sighed. "What?"

"Two to three days a month, we'll be called to do the society's bidding. We volunteered to be owned, signed up to be part of something that no one can see. We will be invisible to society when we're so much fucking more. Everyone around us can go home on the weekends, but we don't go home until there is blood on our hands. We aren't ninety-nine percent of the population. We are the one percent, and I'm going to take every precaution possible to protect you, even if it seems absurd."

I didn't care which speech he was giving me this time. It *was* absurd. Still, to avoid further drama, I did my business, collected my bag, and washed my hands. It wasn't until we were roaming the campus halls, searching for the other guys, that I finally got the nerve to ask, "Can we eat out tonight?"

"It's not safe."

"I'm feeling claustrophobic at home. I just need some fresh air."

"No." He crossed his arms, ignoring my protest until Asa snuck up behind us.

"I don't see how just food will hurt. We'll all be there." Asa, for once, took my side.

"You know the danger." Wick's eyes burned with betrayal, and I knew that if we weren't in the middle of the school hallway, he might have laid Asa flat out.

"What if we just do a drive thru with the windows down?" Austin offered. "It's a compromise. Maybe take her on an evening drive."

"It's dangerous."

"Everything is dangerous with you, but we've not

had any issues yet." The boys all exchanged a glance that was unreadable, but I let it slide. "Please."

"I don't like this."

"I haven't found a single thing you do like," I pointed out.

"I like you." His hand tightened against me, his fingers flexing. "Alive. In my bed."

His fingers tickled me slightly, and I giggled. I loved when he was playful. He rarely was. "If I was dead in your bed, that would be creepy."

"I've seen creepier."

My face pulled in disgust. "Eww. Please, Wick. You all will be with me. What's the harm?"

"I think we all know of the harm." He led us toward the exit that opened up to the outside. His eyes were already roaming every direction, searching for threats.

"Asa. Austin. Help me out here," I begged.

"We'll all be there," Asa pointed out. "You can drive, and she can sit between us in the back. Perfectly protected."

"Or a moving target," Wick grumbled, but I could already see he was giving in. His body relaxed some, and the fight in his voice wasn't nearly as intense. "Thirty minutes, tops. Drive through, and a twenty-minute drive. By minute thirty-one, if we aren't in our driveway, I don't give a fuck who you are, you'll be punished."

"I like punishments." Asa winked, but Wick wasn't amused.

"Your punishment wouldn't be nearly as fucking enjoyable as Mac's."

I stopped and stood on my toes to kiss his cheek. He may not have wanted to agree to it, but he did, for me, and that had to be a big step in the right direction. Plus, he admitted I'd get punished enjoyably, and I almost hoped we were late. It gave me something extra to look forward to.

When I pulled away, he yanked me back, stealing another kiss before dragging me to the outdoors. Once outside, all of their demeanors changed. They still clung tight to me, but now they watched all that surrounded them suspiciously, questioning everything. They'd invested so much of themselves into keeping me safe, and I was standing here, the jerk of the bunch. The dishonesty made my stomach knot, but I closed my eyes tight and fought against it. They weren't as angelic as my mind tried to convince me they were.

And for the rest of the afternoon, as they locked me away in our home, I convinced myself of that as I worked on my journalism project, ignoring the knots in my stomach.

"Let's get that cute ass going." Austin nudged my leg with his foot.

I looked up at him from where I had sat with my laptop for hours, having a war between myself, my wants, my needs, and the possibility of hurting those I thought I might care about. "What time is it?"

"Time to get some fucking sustenance." Asa walked into the room, looking delicious in his black jeans and shirt. His dark hair was pulled back, forming a knot on the back of his head, and I wanted to remove the tie and run my fingers through the strands that I knew felt like silk. "I'm so fucking hungry."

"Burgers?" Austin looked down at me, his hand outstretched, waiting for me to take it.

Closing my laptop and putting it aside, I reached up, curling my fingers around his, then he pulled, yanking me up. "I could do burgers."

"We always get burgers," Asa complained.

"If you're as starved as you stated, it wouldn't matter." Austin pulled me in, giving me a kiss on the forehead, like he needed it after hours of not touching me.

"Tacos?" Wick asked as he walked in, clearly hearing the disagreement.

"I could do tacos," I agreed. I literally could eat anything if it meant I got out of this house.

"I could eat Mac's taco." Austin smirked.

"That was so very cringe." I laughed.

His face told me he agreed. "Yeah, I regretted it the second it left my lips."

"Mac's taco aside..." Wick stood in front of us, his hands on his hips, a scowl in place. He meant business. Even if that business was just food. "There is a taco joint a few miles down the road that has a drive thru. We won't have to get out, meaning she won't be at risk."

I doubted I would have been at risk, anyway. However, he was letting me get free... sort of... and who was I to ruin this moment? "Let's get us some tacos!"

I moved toward the door, but none of them moved. Behind my back, Austin spoke to the others. "She's too agreeable. It's suspicious."

"Way too agreeable," Asa confirmed.

"I'm desperate to be out of this house," I reminded them. "I'd ride in the trunk if that meant I could make that happen."

"Was that an option?" Wick mused.

I whirled around, taking a page from Austin's cringy book of statements. "You get me some fresh air and food and I swear, I'll let you do whatever you want to my trunk."

The keys were in Wick's hand in a flash, and somehow, he passed me, getting to the door and holding it open. When I reached his side, he leaned down, his voice a seductive whisper that made my skin pebble with want. "Vixen, I sure hope you aren't in the business of making promises you can't keep, because the plans I've got for you tonight...'

He let his words trail off as fire pulsed in my veins, heating me up and making me want things from these men that only they could offer me. "Is that so?"

He licked his lips as he watched me. His eyes trailing the length of my body, starting at my toes and slowly traveling upward. "I never break a promise. If you don't know that by now, tonight's the night you learn."

Then he shouldered past me while I stood back, a blubbering mess of lust and want as I watched his ass move perfectly in a pair of worn-out jeans. "Jesus," I muttered to myself, but it was Asa who replied.

"Jesus will not help you with that one, Mac. You're on your own."

CHAPTER FORTY-SEVEN

WICK

I wasn't thrilled about this whole outing. The danger far outweighed the experience, but Asa and Austin were suckers for Mac's big eyes, and with three against one, I hardly had a chance to win. We should have told her. Should have told her about the bodies that had piled up that she'd not seen coming. Should have told her that the stitches on my side weren't some freak accident and came at the cost of a knife fight just outside that bathroom window she swore was harmless.

But we couldn't. We wanted her to be lulled into the false reality that she was safe with us because fuck, if she couldn't trust us to protect her, she couldn't trust us with anything. We were her fucking teammates; she was our fucking housekeeper. It was our job to keep our girl safe without worry.

"This is nice." Mac beamed in the backseat, and I couldn't tell if she was being sarcastic or if she really thought that sitting here in our truck, in the drive thru of a taco shop, was really an enjoyable experience.

"I feel like you're mocking us," I grumbled, my hand slung carelessly over the steering wheel as we waited to order.

"I'm not mocking you," she reassured me. "I'm just happy to take what I can get. I would have taken the gym at this point."

I turned around to look at her. This must be serious if our girl would willingly go to the gym just to get out of the house. "You mean there were other options?"

I never would have taken her to the gym. Too many people. Too many weapons. Too much room for an accident. But she didn't have to know that. She hated the gym with a passion. Every morning, rain or shine, when I forced her up to work out, she would grumble and curse my existence, like the early morning workouts weren't doing wonders for her ass.

She changed her response quickly. "Yeah, actually no. The gym was never an option."

"Damn. Could have had a good morning," I taunted, knowing she'd fall for the bait.

"We still can!" she rushed out.

"Too late."

Her lip instantly came out in a pout at my rejection, and Austin reached over to rub her thigh, always the one to soothe. "He never would have taken you, baby."

"He's right. It's too dangerous." I pulled the truck forward, inching closer to ordering.

"Spaz." She spoke under her breath, but I still heard her.

"Hardly."

They chatted in the backseat, ignoring me as I pulled up to the window. I'd bought them all food enough times to know the orders. After ordering way too much food, enough to be breakfast too, I pulled forward and paid. Another five minutes passed before I had a bag stuffed with Styrofoam boxes filled with tacos and burritos, plus paper bags of chips.

After placing all the food on the floorboard of the passenger seat, I pulled forward. "Are we eating at home or now while we drive?"

"Home," Mac decided for everyone. "Asa eats like a slob."

"Not what you were saying last night." I looked in the mirror just in time to see him wink at her. She reared her arm back and punched his bicep.

I guess every statement is sexual when you're with a bunch of guys. "Alright then, a drive it is. Then we eat."

I pulled out into the main flow of traffic and headed toward the industrial district. I figured if I got us to a place where there was little to no traffic, doing a few donuts and playing around for a few minutes might bring our girl some joy. Crossing the railroad tracks, I passed an invisible line that separated the inhabited part of town from a less savory area. The buildings were all the same, with galvanized metal sidings and matching roofs. Some lots were full, smoke rising from chimneys and vents announcing the productions inside. While others sat rusting, with abandoned parts and overgrown weeds.

I pulled into an empty lot and turned to look at my girl. "We've got five minutes."

"Five minutes for what?"

I didn't answer her. Instead, I pressed down on the gas, gunning the engine forward, fucking loving her scream as I jerked the wheel, causing the truck to spin out. The more I sped and drove erratically, the more delight came from the backseat. I never wanted to stop. Never wanted to stop hearing the joy and seeing the grin placed on her beautiful face.

But time always passes way too quickly, and as much as I wanted to push forward, to continue absorbing every moment of the happiness that had been stolen from us over the past few weeks, I couldn't. We were more than past the halfway mark of the housekeeper sweep. Even so, my heart knew I couldn't keep her safe out here too long.

As if my heart was attached by a string that pulled me toward danger, I tilted my head to the left as I yanked on the wheel, only to see a Jeep, its lights cut, barreling toward us. "Fuck!"

Without warning, I yanked the wheel in the opposite direction, but it was too late. The Jeep clipped the back of the truck, pushing us into an uncontrollable fishtail. Her scream of fear was the only thing louder than the blood that pulsed through my body, thrumming in my ears. The moment the spinning stopped, I pressed hard on the gas, jolting our bodies forward.

"I didn't fucking see them!" I shouted.

"Out of fucking nowhere," Asa confirmed.

A sharp left had us back on the main street. Behind me, tires squealed, and I knew without looking back that whoever the fuck they were would follow. I'd kill them. I'd kill them all for this, even after the housekeeper sweep was over. They'd pay for putting her in danger. They'd pay with their fucking lives.

"Put your fucking seatbelt on," I growled out, my anger not directed at her, but I knew she felt it just the same. They had taken off their belts during the donuts we were doing, but now the action seemed like such an unnecessary risk.

They gained on us too quickly, their vehicle butting ours until we almost plowed into a ditch, but at the last moment, I turned, cutting us across the street, nearly hitting a light post in the process of avoiding a ditch.

"They have their fucking housekeeper with them." Asa cursed. "How the hell are they going to put her in danger like that? They should be worried about keeping her alive."

My tires squealed as I turned into a full parking lot, hoping the jumble of cars would confuse them. "They what?"

I'd never dream of taking Mac out during the month of the sweep for a job. She was precious to us, but if they took their housekeeper out on this job, that only meant it was sanctioned or... people wanted us dead more than I thought. Both were a possibility. Both made my stomach sink in disgust.

I sped down the aisles of the parking lot, praying there was a single spot I could pull into before they were back on my tail. I was about to give up when Mac gripped the back of my seat. Leaning forward, she pointed. "Second spot on the left. It's empty."

I squinted at where she was pointing and sure enough, the spot was barely visible between two large vehicles, but it was there, and it would be a tight fit. I could do it, even if it meant scraping the hell out of the other vehicles. I whipped the car into the spot, yanking the steering fast and hitting the brakes, barely missing the car to the side.

Cutting the lights and engine, I slunk down in my seat. "We are sitting ducks here. If they don't find us, they will hang around until they do."

"It would give us enough time to fight," Austin observed. "Come up with a game plan."

"And put Mac in more danger." Asa looked at our girl where she slunk down next to him. "I can't fucking believe they would risk their woman like that. It makes no fucking sense."

"There has to be a reason," I mused. "Stay down."

In the mirror, the reflection of their vehicle slowly crept through the lane, stopping periodically. When it stopped behind our truck, I held my breath, fear clawing up my throat at the unknown. If they got out, that would be it. We'd fight for sure, but there would be no way to escape. We would be boxed in.

I held my breath, fearing that breathing might somehow trigger them, then they pulled forward, and I exhaled, taking a moment to relax. When I gathered myself, I looked back at the others. "They're gone."

"We need to get home." Austin stretched up to peer through the window. "If we were at home, we'd have all our weapons and a way to secure her."

"If we were at home, this probably wouldn't have happened," I reminded them, furious that I somehow let them talk me into taking Mac out when it was clearly dangerous for her. For us all, really. In the distance, the faint sound of a train echoed, the horn blaring, alerting me to the fact that if we didn't cross the track soon, we could be stuck on this side for an unknown amount of time as the train passed. "We need to cross the tracks."

"Clearly. That's where we fucking live," Asa spat, his frustrations dripping from every word he spoke.

"I meant before that train comes, dickwad." I cringed even as I called him by the name. Clearly, it was the stress talking. "I hear the horns. If we get stuck, we could be on this side for over an hour."

Mac spoke up for the first time, even as her fingers trembled against Asa's thigh. "They passed us already, right?"

"Yes?"

"Pull out. They changed who was in charge when they put their backs to us," she explained.

"I don't understand."

She leaned forward, the seat squeaking with her movement. "They gave us the power to control the situation. Now we are behind them, so we can control the chase."

I blinked a few times as the meaning caught up with me. "If we're behind them, we become the aggressor."

"That's right." She licked her lips, and even though the situation was high stress, my eyes followed the movement, jealous I couldn't follow her tongue with my own. "Pick a spot, ram them from the back, but make sure it will trap them enough that it can give us a head start, then hopefully we can be out of here and on the other side of the tracks before they catch up."

Austin was already unbuckled and shoving his body through the sunroof, searching for them. "Almost to the corner of the light. Going right."

He slunk back down, and I looked them over, thankful that I had them as my family. "Buckle up.

Hold her tight in place. If she gets hurt, I'll kill you both myself."

We were on the move in seconds, our tires squealing, as we backed up. Using Austin's directions as my guide, I headed toward the right corner of the lot, stopping before I hit the curve. If the information he gave was correct, they would be approaching this spot any second, and my body was already tense, waiting for the impact I knew would come.

"Hold her tight. Be ready," I instructed as a dirt cloud billowed toward us.

Mentally, I counted down. Verbally...I was frozen. Any words after my order to protect were stalled in the lump in my throat as I waited to attack, hoping I didn't harm my family in the process. The cloud grew closer, making it impossible to see.

Austin, knowing the issue, unbuckled his seatbelt, and I cursed. I demanded that he get down, not that he listened. Instead, he shoved himself through the sunroof again, shielding his eyes as he looked over the lot of cars. "On my count of three."

"Fuck. Get in," I growled, my hands gripping the wheel so tight I could feel the plastic and leather mold under my touch.

"One."

Mac squealed, her arm wrapping around his legs and holding on tightly, refusing to let him move.

"Two."

Fucking bastards. Adrenaline was kicking in, pure panic making me sweat.

"Three. GO!" He shouted the order, and without another thought, I pushed down on the gas and released the brake, gunning the truck forward. If Mac hadn't been holding Austin, I knew by the impact on the other vehicle, he would have been a goner. Instead, his body pitched forward, his hands slammed against the roof, but somehow, he got himself mostly in the truck's cab seconds before we slammed into the other vehicle.

The crunch of metal against metal was deafening. The impact, jarring. I didn't let off the gas, even as I smashed into the front of their car and pushed it against the parked vehicles. My tires squealed, smoke pouring up from the strain of them moving and not going anywhere. When their vehicle stopped budging and no amount of pushing would jolt them further, I reversed, peeling out of the parking lot before they could register our departure.

"Everyone okay?" I panted as I looked into my mirror, seeing them pull out of the parking lot, dragging their bumper.

"Perfect." Mac's voice wasn't convincing.

"Hold on. We aren't free yet."

The train was coming; the arms with their lights flashing moved down, trying to stop traffic, but I couldn't stop. We couldn't afford to slow down. I pressed harder on the gas, hoping that, despite the damage I'd just done, our truck would keep trudging along until we were safely home.

"We won't make it." Asa's hand was gripping the

handle on the ceiling, while his other arm was firmly over Mac's chest.

"We have no other choice." My teeth hurt from grinding them. Every muscle I had was strained with tension.

"Don't," Mac begged, but I ignored her. Instead, the truck jolted forward, disregarding the blinking barriers as I tore through them, scattering their pieces over the tracks, making it to the other side just as the train whooshed behind us with speeds so strong, the whole truck shook.

CHAPTER FORTY-EIGHT

AUSTIN

"Just breathe," I instructed, as I pushed Mac's head between her knees.

We made it. Barely. The adrenaline still pulsed through my veins, even though I knew that for the moment, we were safe. Safe was such a deceptive fucking word. No one is ever really safe. No one ever really has the security they brainwash and gaslight themselves into thinking exists because it could be gone in a blink.

We could have died with one well-placed ram to the back of the truck.

We could have died in that parking lot.

We could have died as our truck broke through the barriers, stalled on the tracks, and ended it all.

But we were alive, and that was fucking freeing.

"I am breathing," Mac whimpered.

"I'm fucking not," Wick admitted as he rose a shaking hand to his forehead and brushed his hair away. I'd never seen him shake before, but then again, we'd never been this close to death. With a breath out, Wick's hand found the steering wheel and gripped tight. "We need to go."

No one bothered to dispute his statement. We knew that the best place for us at this moment was at home in the safety of our own walls. With each mile that ticked by, the more I could relax. We were checking behind us constantly. But the train was long, and so far, no one tailed us.

It wasn't until we were inside our home, Mac over Asa's shoulders and the doors locked, that we finally could let ourselves feel the full spectrum of relief. We almost fucking died tonight. For what? A moment of carefree living in an abandoned lot? I wouldn't take it back, because the joy on Mac's face would always play on repeat in a reel in my mind. But we needed to be more careful. We needed to support Wick when he said no and not let those pretty eyes and lush lips manipulate us into doing something we all knew was a bad idea.

"We shouldn't have gone." Wick stood in the foyer, his hands on his waist, stress clearly etched into his expressions. We had secured everything, locked every door and window. Set the alarms. Checked the cameras. After the place was secure, we readied our weapons, placing them strategically around the house. Now it was time to relax and let whatever happened happen. As if we could truly relax. "I knew we shouldn't have gone, and I allowed it to happen."

"I pushed." Mac owned her mistake. "I didn't realize—"

"Of course you didn't fucking realize," Wick shouted after cutting her off. "You think you've been safe this whole time while they have mowed house-keepers down left and right?"

"I—"

He didn't let her answer. "You've been their number one fucking target." He laughed as he shook his head, a humorless laugh sending chills up my spine. "Stupid girl."

"Wick," Asa warned. Then he turned to Mac. "He didn't mean that, he's just angry. Scared."

"Fuck you. Who are you to say what I did and didn't mean? I meant every fucking word of it. She knows she's with me; she knows our team's reputa-tion. She fucking knows every time Jones has us go up front and slay a member, we become targets. We are fucking targets without her here, but with her? She can't be that naïve to think that everyone has left us alone."

"I just thought—"

"You thought fucking wrong." He stomped away, and Mac dumbly followed him toward the kitchen.

"Mac, leave him," I instructed. "Your life was in danger enough tonight. You don't need to add to it."

"He's not a danger to me," Mac insisted as she entered the kitchen.

"I'm the son of a fucking serial killer. I'm the biggest danger you'll ever fucking face." Wick spun around. "He's right. Get the fuck away."

"I'm not afraid of you." She spat the words out.

"Mac." I reached forward, but she shook me off, already prepared to go head-to-head with Wick, and maybe it was time to get whatever anger they had out so that they could both focus on keeping her alive. Still, I wouldn't let him hurt her. Not like I thought he would. I stood close, ready to step in, if need be, while Asa already had his blade in his hand, ready to end it to save her.

"You see them, Mac? So fucking concerned for your life that they would kill me, one of their best fucking friends, to save a slut like you."

Her eyes blinked a few times. "Slut?"

"What did you think everyone would say about you? The whole campus knows you're sleeping with the three of us." Wick smirked. "Have you not heard the whispers behind your back?"

"He's angry, Mac. He's trying to hurt you."

"You think I want to hurt her?" Wick laughed, and I could see it, see the edge of one of his manic episodes creeping in, see the lines of his crazy chiseling away at his sanity from the emotion of almost dying and almost losing the one good thing in our lives. "I don't need to want to hurt her. The truth is enough. Guess how many people died because of that fucking addictive cunt we fuck?"

She bit her lip as she held a hand up, clearly seeing his mood was unstable. "Wick—"

"Fifteen. Five fucking sets of three in the last two weeks since the sweep started. Fifteen pairs of eyes that went into a blank void the second our weapons pierced their skin."

"Fifteen? Fifteen people came after me." She gasped, then she turned toward Asa and me, wanting confirmation.

Asa groaned. "It's true. But Mac, understand, it's the game we signed up for. It's the—"

"And the others?"

"The others who?" My eyes roamed over her face, so fucking distraught because she couldn't let Wick be. She just had to chase him and his demons.

"Housekeepers?"

Asa's tongue darted out, toying at the corner of his lips, and I fucking knew it wasn't the time, but I still watched in utter fascination. "Any housekeeper that got taken out died in their first attempt. The ones still living haven't had an attempt. They must have formed an alliance for protection."

"But there was a housekeeper tonight." Mac's brows scrunched up. "Why?"

"Because clearly her life was worth the risk," Wick muttered as he violently pulled open the fridge.

"That makes no sense." Mac lost her steam at

fighting against Wick and now was focusing on the problem.

"I'll check the forums. There could be a change in rules," I offered.

"It doesn't fucking matter if there is a change of rules. They came after what's mine and for that, they die." Wick slammed the fridge door, a cold water in his hand.

"What am I? Campus slut? Or yours?"

"You're fucking mine *and* the campus slut. One and the fucking same." Wick tore the cap off and downed the entire bottle in three gulps. "They came after my family."

"They deserve to die then," Mac stated matter-of-factly. "And we're going to do it."

Why did that statement make my cock hard? Wick froze in his stewing anger. "We're...?"

She stalked forward. "Did I stutter on my words, mighty Chadwick Moore?"

"Don't fucking call me that," he growled.

"Or what, Chadwick?"

"Mac," Asa and I both warned together.

The girl never listened to warnings, especially from him. In fact, I think if it came with a warning, it was more tempting to her. Where was the lab partner who obsessed over me showing up and doing the work? She was so quiet and timid then, before we really knew her. She was gone, replaced with this infuriating woman who always pushed the buttons of the one man she shouldn't.

"I'm not in the mood to be taunted." Wick tried to shrug off her goading.

"Can only handle taunting when you're the one doing it, right? Can't fucking deal with other people giving you the bullshit you so readily hand out."

What the hell is she doing? I thought. *Can't she see he's already on the edge?*

Wick tossed the empty bottle in the trash as he stalked forward, his eyes not leaving Mac. "So you want to kill them, huh? Suddenly you're as blood thirsty as the rest of us? Think you're big enough, strong enough, powerful enough to take on a team now? What's your endgame? Get me angry enough to let you?"

"You don't *let* me do anything." Oh, boy. "I'm my own damn person."

"Okay." I reached for Mac's arm. "It's been a night. Let's talk about how we want to go about seeking our revenge on the team we met later."

"No." Mac pulled away. "Let's talk about it now."

They were facing off as Wick stepped closer, getting in her face so she had no room to escape. I knew he wouldn't hurt her, but fuck, that didn't mean everything around them was safe. His voice was low, menacing. "Tell me how you'd do it."

For the first time, she stuttered. "I-I'd..."

"Kill them in their sleep? Approach them in an alley?" Wick questioned. "Chase them to their death like they tried to do to us?"

"I-I could kill them in their sleep."

"The coward's way." Wick stepped forward, and she stepped back, her back slamming against the counter.

"Then I'm a coward. But if I had to guess, a female my size taking on four people, three of which were men, wouldn't work so well. I'd be outnumbered. The only way I could successfully do it would be to outsmart them."

"Then outsmart them." Wick leaned closer. "What do you have in that little brain of yours?"

"Nothing I'd want to share with you."

Wick's hands slammed down on the counter behind her, caging her in. "Tell me."

"This is going to end with them fucking," Asa muttered.

"No doubt." I crossed my arms over my chest and watched. I was perfectly okay having a front row view of their hate fuck. I'd seen them go at it, and never once were they this angry at each other.

"They are going to celebrate on the last day of the sweep. Not the day after when it's all over with."

"What makes you say that?" Wick leaned forward, his face closer to hers.

"Well, for starters, they like the challenge. It was bold of them to take their girl and go after us. It was bold of them to do it where there could be so many witnesses."

"Some of the teams have balls. I'll give them that," I added, and both Wick and Mac glared at me, like I was interrupting their moment. I held my hands up in surrender, even though they were the ones in the fucking kitchen and not a bedroom.

"That doesn't explain why you think they will celebrate success early."

"They're cocky. They will assume they are home free. After all, would you strike in the last hours?"

Wick brought a hand up to his jaw. "Nah. Too many things can go wrong, and if we are a minute after midnight, our heads will be on a stake."

"Exactly." Her eyes tracked the movement of his lips. "They won't expect it. That's our time."

"Then what?" He inched into her space.

"Find where they are celebrating."

"Okay, but that's public," I pointed out.

"Drug them, help them out to their cars. From there, it all depends on what you want to do. The agency will clean up anything not in the public eye, right?"

"They will," Wick confirmed, his chest heaving as he watched her. "Fuck, you're so fucking pretty when you scheme."

"For a slut and a stupid girl," she tacked on to his statement.

"Vixen."

"Oh, fuck off." She ducked to go under his arm, and he practically clotheslined her back to the counter.

"Where the fuck do you think you're going?" His body hovered so close; I knew she felt the heat burning off his skin.

"To bed."

"I was mad," he stated.

"I'm *still* mad." She glared up at him, having to crane her neck just to meet his eyes.

"Any second now." Asa stepped up next to me, knowing the tension between them was about to snap.

"I went against my gut for you, and look where that put us," he gritted out.

"It put us in a position to intimately know who a set of enemies are and what we need to look out for." She pushed at his chest.

"Fuck." The word left him as a curse and a plea, before he reached out and grabbed a fistful of her hair and pulled her head back, slamming his lips to hers.

CHAPTER FORTY-NINE

MAC

He was trying to hurt me. I knew it; he knew it. Everyone in this fucking room knew it, and I would not let him. He could spout words and names all he wanted, but we were all responsible. I begged them. That was true. But they were just as guilty as I was because they withheld the truth from me. Let me be comfortable pretending a threat to us hadn't existed when it was there the whole damn time.

"I was mad," he finally confessed after a push and pull match in the kitchen.

"I'm *still* mad." I glared up at him. Mad at him for the names he called me, mad at the situation, mad that all I wanted was to be a journalist and instead I was deep into something I was not a hundred percent sure I was prepared for.

He pushed against me, pushing me back into the counter, and all I wanted to do was wrap my arms around him, squeeze him against me, and remind myself that he was okay, we were all okay. Because this evening could have gone so much differently.

"Any second now," Asa whispered, and I refused to take my eyes off Wick to see what he was whispering about.

"I went against my gut for you, and look where that put us." Wick's words were low, spoken through gritted teeth, and I could feel his anger. Feel just how today's events affected him. It radiated off him in waves, making the air around us suffocating to breathe.

"It put us in a position to intimately know who a set of enemies are and what we need to look out for." They wouldn't come for us twice. I knew that. The first time was brave enough, but now, now I wanted them dead for the risk they put on my men's lives.

I pushed at Wick's chest, trying to earn myself some space so I could breathe. Instead, he didn't waver. The torture of what he was feeling and words he'd never dare express played out over his face, saying too much and too little all at once.

"Fuck." Wick gasped the word out, practically using it as a plea before his hand dug into the hair at the nape of my neck, pulling tight as he flexed his fingers closed around the strands. I hardly had time to register the pain in my scalp before he slammed his lips to mine, dragging my body against his as he consumed me with a kiss.

I stood up on my toes, straining to get closer to him, wanting his body touching mine. My body pulsed; fire flamed inside of me, erupted from a single touch of this man's lips on mine, and I wanted more of it, all that I could get. I wanted to feel the blaze and let it consume me.

It was always like this with him. All or nothing. He didn't kiss for fun. He kissed to steal all the oxygen from my lungs so that all I could do was breathe him in to survive. His fingers in my hair pulled hard, cranking my neck back at an uncomfortable angle that was only soothed by the deepening of his kiss.

"You're so fucking infuriating." His chest rumbled against my breasts as he spoke into me, causing my nipples to pebble painfully hard.

"You're a fucking jackass," I got out, even as my thigh raised up, my calf pulling his body toward my own to bring him closer.

He stopped for a second, his eyes staring into mine intensely, showing a world of turmoil under the surface. His voice was a broken rasp when he finally spoke. "I almost lost you."

"You didn't," I reminded him before tugging on his neck, forcing his lips to mine again, letting him devour my soul through the single touch.

He may have spent his whole life thinking he was just like his father. That he was a monster in a man's skin. But he'd never be like his father. He was so fucking protective of what was his, so loyal, that I couldn't imagine him ever causing harm to anyone he cared for. His protection had no limits. He'd burn the world for me, and I had the power to hand over the match.

I moaned into his mouth as hands ran up my stomach, sliding until they cupped my breasts, and my mind may have been slightly muddled from the intensity of the kiss, but it took me a moment to realize that they weren't even his hands that were touching me, not when his fingers dug into my hair while the other held my ass firm against the counter-top. Lips grazed against each side of my neck and the touch, the sensations, set me on fire, making every nerve in my body light up, forcing me to whimper.

"Do you like that, Vixen?" Wick grunted as he flexed his hips against my core, dragging his length against the seam of my jeans.

"Yes!" I nearly cried out the words, overwhelmed by the sensations.

We'd all fucked before, separately. Sometimes two to one. But never since those first days, the days when I was getting to know them, as they were getting to know me, had I ever experienced all of them with me together. A lot had changed since then. They'd grown, I'd grown, we'd all grown together, and now I knew their bodies as intimately as I knew my own. I knew what touches set them off, and I savored the sounds they made when their bodies were overwhelmed with pleasure.

"Do you want us all, baby?" He bit my bottom lip, drawing out pain as the taste of copper entered my mouth.

"God, yes," I gasped out when his tongue flicked against my own.

I let my hand fall from his waist, but kept the one holding tight to his neck. I reached out, grabbing Asa's waistband before tugging him forward, breaking apart from Wick long enough to allow my lips to meet Asa's. The kiss with him was slow, not rushed and bruising like with Wick. Still, it didn't dampen the want that clenched in my core, begging me for the relief that I knew they could offer me.

Hands found the button of my jeans, flicking it open, before shimmying them down my waist, past my thighs, and letting them fall to the ground. I didn't question who was tearing off my clothes. It didn't matter. They all knew how to work my body like experts at this point, and all I wanted to do was feel the bliss that I knew their fingers, hands, and mouth always promised.

Austin dropped to his knees before me, his hands wrapped around my thighs as he parted my legs, his tongue and teeth biting and licking as he traveled up to my core. I let a hand fall, digging my fingers into his scalp and tugging, trying to force him to the spot I wanted him the most. He didn't budge, didn't move, even though I was ready to beg.

"You think you can control us?" Wick laughed against my lips, but there was no genuine humor behind the sound.

"I just—" I tried to tell him I needed them. I had to have them right this very second or I would physically die, my body would explode from want as need consumed me and left me as a pile of incoherent mush, but then Asa's teeth found my nipple and he bit down, tearing a scream from my lips that was swallowed up by Wick's kiss. "Fuck."

Wick pulled his lips from mine, a wicked gleam in his eyes. "I think she likes when we use our teeth."

I couldn't deny that. There was something inside of me that craved the pain that they unknowingly tore from my body with each nip and graze. My core flooded, and I knew Austin would lick the remains of my need off my thigh before Wick ever let his tongue flick between my legs, and somehow, that only added to how turned on I was.

Wick's lips traveled down my neck, abandoning my lips in search of my other nipple. His teeth teased against the sensitive tip before he bit. Ignoring the moan that left me, he pulled back, using his tongue to soothe the ache. They repeated their actions, alternating between nipples, him and Asa working in sync to cause me pain and pleasure that was so intense, literal tears ran down my cheeks and sobs of want and need escaped me.

When Wick dropped to his knees next to Austin, I was shaking. My legs were hardly holding my weight, and if it wasn't for Asa's body leaning his weight against me, pinning me to the counter, and Austin's shoulders wedged between my legs as he teased the sensitive flesh of my thighs, I'd have crumbled. Wick nudged Austin, forcing him over a few inches as they spread me wide, displaying my dripping core to them.

"Your cunt is soaked," Wick announced before licking along the slit, barely letting his tongue touch. "It's so fucking delicious."

"Oh god," I gasped, my hand shooting to his hair to balance myself.

"What do you want us to do princess? We'll do it." Asa's voice vibrated against my skin.

God. I did not know what I wanted them to do. I wanted it all. I wanted to feel every bit of them, every touch, as they wrung the pleasure from my body. I could barely form a coherent word, let alone a sentence, to answer him. Instead, with Austin's teeth clamped down against my sensitive skin, the only words that I could think of were, "Touch me."

"You want us to touch you, princess? Are we not doing a good enough job now?" Asa teased, his tongue darting out to flick my pebbled nipple.

"No. Yes." I gasped as he bit. "I mean, I need more."

"How much more?" Wick demanded.

"All of it," I whined, and I was never one to whine. Not before then. Not before I knew there was so much pleasure to be had, and all I needed them to do was stop dangling the possibility in front of my eyes and show me some action.

"You're so fucking greedy, you know that. Every fucking night you have us bruising up this pussy, and you always want fucking more." Wick slapped my cunt as he stood, before cupping it in his hand, burying the tip of his middle finger inside me as a little tease of what was to come. "Do you ever get tired?"

"No." I wiggled against him, wishing Asa and Austin would give me some room. Let me move so I could sink his finger further into me.

Wick leaned in, his face so close to mine that I could taste the remnants of the cinnamon gum he had been chewing in the truck. "So. Fucking. Greedy. So. Fucking. Perfect."

I tilted my head, moving quickly so he couldn't pull away, and bit his lip, pulling it into my mouth before releasing it with a pop. "Make me cum."

His lips tilted up in amusement. "So. Fucking. Demanding."

Before I could utter another word, he flipped me around, forcing my hands against the counter, holding them there as he caged me in. I ignored the rustle of clothing behind me, my body able to focus on one thing and one thing only: the hard length that was rubbing seductively against my ass.

"How do you want it, baby? How do you think you'd feel if we took this sweet ass of yours, claimed every part of you as our own, right here in this kitchen?"

"I—" Wick's hips thrusted forward, making me mindless as the word tumbled from me. "Yes."

He reached forward; his hand fumbled with the lid of the coconut oil, and at first, I was confused. Then, when the lid was finally freed, he dipped his fingers in, lubing them up as he whispered in my ears. "You want them to eat your delicious little cunt while I work your ass?"

His question to me was a demand for my men, and before I could plan a response, Austin and Asa were between my spread thighs, their tongues battling against each other, their hands grappling at each other's bodies as they ate me out so thoroughly that I didn't realize that Wick's fingers were dancing against my ass until he slipped a finger inside, pushing against the band of resistance.

My body jolted forward, my thighs trying to squeeze shut, but unable to move closed past the bodies that were wedged between them. I didn't know whether I should pull away, or chase the foreign feeling of having Wick touch me more intimately than ever before.

Wick's hand moved up my hip, traveling up until he brushed some hair from my face, whispering against my cheek as he pulled his finger out and pushed it back in again. "You're doing so good."

"I don't know if I can do this," I panted. My fingers were gripping the counter so hard my knuckles were white, and I swore at any moment my legs were going to give out.

"You will," Wick promised as he laid a sweet kiss on my cheek. "You're my little vixen, remember? Fierce in every way. Show me how good you can be."

A hand traveled up my leg as Wick worked his finger in and out, stretching the rim of my ass painfully while also offering me a weird edge of pleasure that I didn't think I'd ever get enough of. Fingers danced against my inner thigh before parting my lips and plunging into my body.

"Fuck."

"Not yet, baby," Asa cooed, before his tongue danced against my clit and his fingers pumped into me, leaving Austin's mouth to nip, suck, and lick at all the sensitive spots that drove me nearly as wild.

I couldn't handle it, couldn't handle the overload of sensations that were sparking through my body, tearing whimpers and moans from my throat without my control. Three more pumps and a well-placed crooked finger later, and my body exploded. My muscles squeezed and contracted against Asa and Wick's fingers as cries of bliss left my lips.

Wick used the opportunity to slip another finger into my ass, the sensation heightening my pleasure, and I couldn't handle it. My vision grayed; my body weakened. Each jolt of pleasure, every wave, was too much and not enough. I wanted more. I couldn't handle more. I wanted to feel them. I felt too much. I needed air. I couldn't breathe.

When the orgasm ebbed, a strong arm wrapped around my hips and pulled me backwards, tearing Asa and Austin's mouths from my body as a hand swept through my juices and pulled them back, coating my ass in my cum. "It might hurt a little baby, but then it's going to feel so fucking good."

That was all the warning I got before the head of Wick's cock pushed through the stretched ring of muscles. Wick moaned. The reflection from the glass window gave me a perfect view of his head tilted back, his eyes closed in pleasure as he slowly pushed forward, giving me time to adjust to his size before stretching me further.

With a huff, he forced his eyes open. His palm landed on my back while his other hand reached forward, digging into my hair. He pulled my body upright, the shift in position really driving home that his dick was tightly lodged in my ass and I couldn't even move on my own. We spun, his back slamming against the counter to hold him up as he held me tight against him, forcing me to remain upright.

"Spread your legs wider," he demanded.

"I can't." Tears were dripping down my chin, and I didn't know if it was pleasure or pain that was causing them. Both equally delicious.

"You can. Do it," he ordered, and even though I was terrified to move, an inch at a time, I pushed my legs wider, spreading them.

Asa stepped up, standing so close that my breasts crushed against his chest as he leaned in for a kiss.

Where Wick was rough and hard, Asa was always controlling but gentle, never leaving a bruise, never needing to get his point across. His fingers danced along my thighs, relaxing me enough so that Wick could move, and though it stung, with each pull out and push in, my core tightened, begging for another orgasm that I knew I didn't have in me.

When I was relaxed enough between them, Asa gripped my thigh and pulled it up to his hip. "Give me your other leg."

"I can't." I knew my eyes were wild, my mind crazed. But there was no fucking way I could have Wick inside of me like this without having my feet on solid ground.

"You can and you fucking will. Stop fighting us every step of the way," Wick growled into my ear, his fingers so tight against my skin I knew I'd bruise.

I whimpered, but I followed orders, trusting Asa and Wick to hold me up as I lifted my other thigh to Asa's hip, wrapping my legs around seconds before he flexed his hips, pushing inside of me.

My vision grew gray for a moment, nearly taking me under as he gritted his teeth and ground out. "So fucking tight." Wick flexed, tearing another moan from Asa before he added, "I can fucking feel you moving."

Like any other team building exercise, they were always in sync, each one moved with the other, taking each push and pull slow as I cried, and begged, pleaded with them to help me, to make me cum, to end this and make it last forever.

"Shhhh." Austin leaned over as he reached for the coconut oil. "We've got you. We've always got you."

Austin pressed in, his lips fleeting against Asa's neck and shoulder, while he used one hand to cup my bouncing breast and the other to work against Asa's skin. I'd been close with these men, but never had we all been skin to skin, touching so intimately, and I didn't know how to handle it, didn't know if I could take much more.

Austin's hand disappeared as Asa tipped forward, pushing me into Wick, forcing him to tilt back. Asa's eyes closed. A moan rumbled from his chest, and Wick's chest heaved behind me before he spoke through pants. "This is way too fucking hot."

I would have to agree, even though I wasn't sure what set him off suddenly. What had his chest rising and falling and those sounds of bliss leaving him? At least I didn't know, until Austin thrusted forward and Asa plowed into us. His breath hitched as his head fell to my shoulder, his teeth biting down as his cock jumped inside of me.

The simple movement was more than I could take, and my body gave in, clenching at the cocks buried inside my body as my orgasm tore through me. Asa's skin was a mess, my nails digging and scraping his flesh as I begged them to stop moving, pleading until the screams that tore from my body stole my sound and replaced it with a scratchy replica of my voice.

When my orgasm faded, I was nearly limp, but they didn't let up, each man pounding into my body harder now, sure that I could take it, while Austin clutched Asa, flexing his hips, pushing him into us, forcing us to fuck at an angle that made Asa's cock rub against the sensitive bundle of nerves inside of me while Wick's teased every bit of sanity from my mind.

My body was so sensitive everything sparked with pleasure and I couldn't take it anymore. I was too sensitive. So sensitive that it was nearly painful. "I can't come again."

"One more." Asa's jaw was tight. "Just one more."

Wick's hand wound around me, his fingers toying with one of my nipples. His voice strained. "I'm almost there, baby; just give me one more. Can you do that for me?"

I shook my head no, even as my voice broke. "Okay."

"Good girl." His hand traveled up from my nipple, stopping to cradle gently against my neck to hold me in place, then he let loose, pouring every ounce of his want and need into me. His hips slammed against me while Asa pushed. The sound of skin moist with sweat and need echoed through our kitchen. Our pleasures mixed, curses and praises falling from our lips, until the tightness wound at my core snapped as a scream tore from my throat. The second my core contracted, Wick lost it, a roar of bliss leaving him as he came, spouting ropes of cum inside of me.

Asa's head fell forward, his teeth digging into my shoulder. "It's too fucking much. I can feel him and you."

His fingers tightened against me as his cock swelled, spilling into me while my cunt milked him. Wick's dick jerked, and I whimpered, the slight movement already pushing me to the edge of insanity. We stayed locked together while Austin gritted his teeth, rocking gently against Asa, until Asa slipped out of my body. The moment I was released, Wick's legs gave out, and he sunk to the kitchen floor with me in his lap, his semi-hard dick still inside me.

Austin used the opportunity to push Asa against the counter, forcing Asa to hold on to the countertop while Austin positioned Asa's hips where he wanted them. With a hand wound through the strands of Asa's hair, and a hand on his back, Austin bucked into him, jolting his body so hard that his knees knocked against the cabinet at each thrust.

Wick's hands roamed over my body, soothing my sensitive skin as we watched, kindling a fresh wave of fire over my skin. I hadn't realized how hot it was to just watch them love each other, appreciate each other's bodies, until now. Now I couldn't get enough, my eyes taking my fill of them panting together, pushing and pulling, grunting and groaning while

Wick's chest heaved against my back, the sight making his cock harden against me.

And when I thought the image in front of me couldn't possibly get any better, Austin pulled Asa's hair hard, forcing his back to bow. Another two rough jolts of his hips, and Austin's head tossed back, his mouth wide as he came, triggering Asa's second orgasm. They rode out their pleasure until they couldn't stand any longer and both men fell to their knees, collapsing beside Wick and me.

Long moments passed where no one spoke. The only sound that could be heard was breathing as we each tried to come back to earth. It wasn't until the room grew uncomfortably quiet that Wick finally spoke. His head turned to the side, looking at his two teammates. "Y'all better be cleaning that cum off my cabinet. I cook in here."

Then he scooped me up and stood, carrying me out of the kitchen and up the stairs to the shower, where he somehow wrung another orgasm out of me. Twice.

CHAPTER FIFTY

WICK

I rubbed my palm over my hard cock as I hit replay, watching the video of us all fucking in the kitchen again. It had become my obsession over the last week. The play of her face as she came, the sounds that poured from our team as we connected, the way Austin owned Asa during sex when he was so nonchalant any other time... it was all so fucking hot. Skin against skin, moisture dripping down Mac's thigh, claw marks scrapped against Asa's skin. It was all so fucking beautiful.

A text pinged on my phone, and I looked down, seeing a message from Asa. *We leave in ten.*

Fuck.

I was so damn ready for this. I'd been craving this revenge since the moment they tried to take our girl.

But fuck, I was nervous. We'd never had Mac lead a mission before. Hell. She'd only taken part in one. And now? She was the one issuing us orders and making demands. I'd follow any demand she made if she promised to let us fuck like we did in this video, so uninhibited and needy.

I slammed my laptop closed, cutting off the video, and stood up, stretching. Then I tossed on black clothes and slipped into my boots. I was the driver, Mac's orders. Apparently, my face was too recognizable; everyone in the organization knew who I was, and that prevented stealth.

I think they just liked that, for once, I wasn't in control.

I fucking hated that I wasn't in there with them the whole time. Fucking hated that they ordered me to stay put in the back corner until I got orders to get the car and be ready to pick them up. Uber. I was their fucking Uber, and I'd never been more angry at a plan and more turned on that my girl thought of something I'd never have thought of.

I met them downstairs in the foyer. Mac looked incredibly sexy in a black, long sleeve dress that went down to mid-thigh and a pair of heeled, knee-high boots. I knew these were from the shopping trip she had done once with Asa, and usually I would argue her outfit, deem it as inappropriate, but even I could admit that tonight, she would blend in perfectly with the crowd's attire, even if I'd hate the thought of her being watched.

"You look good." I nodded to my teammates, acknowledging them next to her. "You do too."

Fuck. What was I doing?

Crossed the line one time and watched them fuck and now I was giving them compliments.

"You remember the plan?" Mac asked, her nerves clear.

"Do you?" I wagged my brow.

"I created the plan, dumbass." She nudged me.

"Got your blade?"

"Both!" She smiled proudly.

"Both?"

"My bone blade and my butter knife." She held up a butter knife proudly.

"Where the fuck did that come from?" I asked, before holding up a hand. "You know what, doesn't matter. No one is dying by a butter knife blade."

"Protection is protection," she stated, as the hand holding the butter knife cocked on her hip.

"Famous last words, I suspect." I grabbed her hip, dragging her to me before taking her mouth and owning it, working it until she was a soft molten puddle that melted against me. Only then did I part our lips. "Get in the fucking car before I change my mind."

She grabbed a tiny beaded handbag, and I smiled as I followed behind her, knowing that the tiny bag was a piece of me, something I hand-picked for her wardrobe. Her hips swayed as she walked, and when she reached the car and pulled open the door, I couldn't take my eyes off her thighs as her dress snuck almost up to her hip as she climbed in.

It was going to be a long night. An impossibly long ass night.

I climbed into the driver's seat of the car, pushing the seat as far back as it could go to accommodate my body. I preferred the truck. This right here was not the most comfortable drive, but rarely did you see an Uber that wasn't a car, and Mac insisted we needed to play the part.

Beside us, Asa and Austin took my truck, and I grumbled about it under my breath. Mac looked over. "Relax. I wanted to ride with you, but if you're going to be a grouch, I'm sure they will let me in."

My hand shot out, gripping her bare thigh. "Don't you dare."

She smirked, the look full of promises for the future. "If you insist."

I reached forward and adjusted the steering wheel before putting my key into the ignition. I let the truck move out of the driveway, then I pulled out, following the boys. We had spent the last week making plans. All of today, Asa had watched, listened, learned until he finally caught pieces of what their plans were for tonight.

"Capture." I sighed. "I wish they'd picked a better lit bar. It's going to be impossible to keep eyes on y'all."

"You'll manage."

"If anyone touches you, I'm chopping off their

dick, I swear to god." I gritted my teeth, my jaw tight at the thought of it.

"What if they don't have a dick?" Her voice held laughter.

I paused, thinking about it. "If they don't have a dick and are touching you, I'll probably watch if I'm honest. I love me some female-on-female action. The best of the best of porn."

She shoved at my shoulder. "You're a fucking pig."

"Can't deny it." We let the silence between us grow comfortable for a moment before I turned to look at her. "You will be careful, right? Remember all I taught you?"

"Eyes on the road," she ordered, and I turned my gaze back to the road. "I'll be fine."

"It's so fucking risky. They took their housekeeper out, and look at what's about to happen. But we are taking you out. Our housekeeper. We're making the same stupid mistake to get back at them. Hours before midnight. It's going to be a shit show if this goes wrong."

"Do you trust me?" She looked toward me, her long lashes batting expectantly as she waited for an answer.

"Trust has nothing to do with it." I was gripping the wheel so hard my fingers hurt, but I couldn't bring myself to loosen up. Not with the tension that was thrumming through my body. Not when my mind was racing with everything I knew could go wrong and probably would, because my luck was that fucking awful lately.

"Trust has *everything* to do with it." Her hands flew out in front of her, gesturing around us. "If you can't trust me when I say I've got this handled, then we might as well stop this farce right now because our relationship, whatever relationship this is, can't go any further."

"I'm appalled that you would even try to pretend that what we have isn't real." I tightened my grip further.

"Well then, how hard is it to fucking trust me, Wick? It's always like this with you. Asa and Austin accepted my plan as good. But there is always a push-back from you, always thinking that no one but your-self is good enough to follow through with plans and make shit happen."

"Are you really going to start a fight now, when we are five minutes out of an operation, and we should have a clear head?" I pushed back, because she was right. If I wasn't doing shit myself, then it wasn't good enough. I couldn't trust it to be done right. I questioned every detail until I drove myself crazy with worry and nerves.

"No." She threw herself back into the seat before she let her head loll toward me. Her eyes took in every inch of my profile, but I refused to return a look. I kept my eyes straight, staring at a road that I had practically memorized since I drove down it so many times. "I just... can you just trust me? Please. I want retribution as much as you do. I promise you that."

I swallowed, feeling the lump of discomfort lodged in my throat, but I nodded. "Fine. I trust you." I paused for a moment. "Just don't let me down."

"Never." This time it was her turn to swallow, looking uncomfortable. "Never."

A few minutes later, we were parked on a side street, Asa and Austin parked behind us. The minute Mac stepped foot on the sidewalk, they were already sidled up to her, arms around her waist to pull her in for a kiss. It was a fifteen-minute drive, tops. They couldn't have been that desperate for her, yet they acted like it had been days since they felt her pillowy lips on theirs.

"Finished yet? We have a mission tonight, and I don't want your lust for her to ruin this," I barked out.

"Calm the fuck down." Asa glared, and I'd give it to him. He was the only one who didn't back down when I get into moods. Well, him and Mac, but she didn't count. She was mine, regardless. "We're just trying to psych ourselves into going in."

"Psych yourselves?" I laughed, though there wasn't genuine humor behind it. "You've had all damn day to psych yourselves up for this. We got the call for the end of the sweep last night."

"It's just..." Austin looked around before taking a step closer, lowering his voice. "After this is over, after tonight, it means that this is all real. That she is ours... permanently."

"Like there was any doubt." I rolled my eyes as I walked, putting distance between us, following orders to keep away from them. But then I turned and stomped back toward her, slamming my lips hard enough to hers that I hoped they bruised. I hoped that when I was through, her lips would be red and swollen and there would be no doubt that, tonight, she was getting so thoroughly fucked. No questions, just facts. When I pulled away, I leveled my eyes with hers, laying my forehead against hers. "I trust you and your plans. I trust your decisions. I trust you won't steer us wrong. But trusting doesn't make it any easier to see something... someone... I care about stepping into danger."

I stepped away from her before she responded to my admission. I didn't want to see the softness in her eyes, see the pity at how weak I could be.

I left them without another word. Walked away and abandoned them on the curb in a shady neighborhood as I made my way to Capture. The line was out the door, not like I expected it not to be. The place was always packed, the dark ambiance a sweet spot to those who wanted some privacy for whatever risky activity they wanted to partake in public. The lights were dimly lit on the outside of the building, the attempt to create an intimate atmosphere before even entering only making the club appear seedy. Stale beer and vomit scented the outside, the cement sticky with things I wouldn't dare to think about. And all I could think about was that I would have never taken Mac here, never exposed her to the scum that surrounded me in this moment. She was too classy for this, too precious for such trash.

Did they truly not care for their girl? Capture? That was the best they could do to celebrate with her?

It took all of twenty minutes to get through the line. Behind me, I knew my team was waiting, anticipating the plans we formed while sitting at the same table I fucked Mac on last night. I walked carefully down the dark hallway, letting my eyes adjust to the dimly lit space before I stepped into the crowded room. I pushed past drunk girls, clinging to the wall for support, ignoring the ones who reached for me lustfully.

No one interested me. No one except Mac.

I kept to the outer wall as if the wall could pull darkness further around me, making me invisible. It didn't, but it helped ensure that there was no threat at my back, making me able to relax slightly as I kept the bar in sight, waiting to see my team, my family, enter. While I waited, I let my gaze bounce around, searching for the crew who tried to end us. It didn't take long. Their obnoxiously boisterous laughs drew my eyes to them. Their care waning with each drink they took.

They didn't deserve to have their housekeeper. If I had any doubt, it was eliminated at this moment. And she, who did not put her foot down, did not talk them out of going drinking, did not deserve the position.

Were we much better? Letting Mac talk us into this adventure, this scheme, all in the name of revenge. Maybe not. But I'd be damned if I put her in such careless danger while she was here.

I spotted my family, Mac flanked by Asa and Austin as they reached the bar, and even though she was out in the open, their eyes were alert, looking everywhere around them, unlike the drunken team in the middle of the dance floor. They were going to make it easy, too fucking easy.

And I was right.

Less than twenty minutes later, Mac had two drinks in hand, the powder already placed inside. When she shimmied herself onto the dance floor, the liquid sloshing over the edge slightly, I watched as she executed her plan flawlessly.

She leaned in, whispered something to the girl as Asa ground against Mac's ass, seemingly unaware of his surroundings. An act, a ploy, because we both knew Asa was more aware than anyone on that dance floor. She was effortless in her act, the team so fucking trusting of a stranger, that when they had the drinks in their hands, the liquid downed, all I could do was look on in awe over the magnificent creature that belonged to us.

She fucking got an entire team to drink drugged liquid without batting an eye. Fucking outrageous. Fucking ballsy. Fucking beautiful.

I watched for a few moments longer, waiting until the team in front of me swayed a little too much. Their steps faulted, their movements jerked, and only then did I bother to slip out of the crowd, squeezing through the back exit of the building. I took my time getting to the car, knowing that my crew still had to work those fuckers outside of the building, and it wouldn't be easy. Not when the drugs kicked in and they realized their fatal error. Not when the urge to fight it off, to defeat the desire of sleep that pulled at them, wanting to take them under, finally took hold. And definitely not when they realized that this night would be their last one on earth and their death was their own fault.

Finding the car, I pulled open the driver's side and sat, waiting patiently for the text I knew would come. The text calling for help. The text for that team's last Uber ride.

CHAPTER FIFTY-ONE

MAC

My nerves were in knots the entire drive over here, even with Wick's nonsense distracting me. Fear of what could go wrong and what just might coiled inside of me as I fought off self-doubt in favor of mantras of accomplishments.

I can do this.

I will do this.

I can be successful.

I will be successful.

After all? What do I have to lose? Besides my life and the lives of the three most important beings I know.

I don't know if I can do this.

I can't.

I—

"Relax," Austin reassured me as he squeezed my

hip in line. He was always so reassuring, always so supportive, that it almost offset the waves of doubt that Wick always instilled in me. Almost.

"This could go wrong," I muttered.

"Or it could go right." He nuzzled against my neck. "Besides, if we get in there and decide to change our mind, we can. Nothing is set in stone."

Except I couldn't. I needed to do this. I needed to follow through on our plan to get my revenge for what they tried to do to us, for what they tried to take from me. I couldn't let them walk away at the end of this sweep into blissful peace without at least attempting to play the game of cat and mouse that they started between us. Only, I was so much more than a simple cat. I was Team Moore, and our roars could be heard for miles away.

The line went quick, and I was thankful for Asa and Austin distracting me, attempting to ease some of the worry that had me wringing my fingers together, twisting them to the point it was nearly painful. When we were admitted through the entrance, I stopped for a moment and took a calming breath. It was now or never. I could do this.

Walking the path through the dark musty hallway toward the double doors, which held music and laughter that was so loud my senses screamed, made my stomach knot. I pushed through, forging my path through the crowd as I entered the room, until I spotted the bar.

We relaxed against the edge of the bar for a while,

all three of us pretending like we were in some sort of deep conversation as we scanned the surroundings, looking for the team that offended us. I tried not to look toward the wall, made it a point not to look for Wick because if I found him, I might crumble. I might give up on this crazy scheme of retribution and take him home, have those eyes — full of disappointment — look up from the ground where he'd kneel as he feasted on my pussy to cheer me up.

Asa's lips came to my neck, his body warm against my bare arms as he leaned in. "To the left, middle of the dance floor."

I followed the direction, my eyes fighting through the haze as I searched for what he saw. It took me a moment, but I locked on to the familiar faces, the images of mug shots I studied ingrained into my mind, making them recognizable.

"I see," I mumbled, as his palm flattened against my stomach.

His tongue licked up the side of my neck, making me shiver. "You want me to order some drinks?"

"I've got it." Austin waved a hand up, getting the attention of the bartender.

He ordered five drinks. Three to get us started, to ease our nerves, and two to share, because we were a generous type. Four minutes later, five drinks were set on the bar in front of us. Asa turned slightly, grabbing a drink and handing it to me, while keeping his eyes on the group.

"For courage." He smiled, the wicked gleam of his

eye dancing, and I knew he enjoyed this. This was his element.

He tossed back his drink, and Austin and I followed, drinking up in five gulps before slamming the glasses down. "Ready, boys?"

"You know we'll follow you anywhere, baby. Just say the word." Austin sat his glass down, waiting for me to take action.

I leaned over the drinks while my boys guarded me, making it physically impossible for anyone to see what we were doing. Then I let the powder drop in, trying not to think about the time when my own men betrayed me and did the same thing. With a swirl of my finger, I mixed it up, hoping it would be dissolved before we reached them.

I picked up both glasses, holding them in my hands. The condensation made my already wet palms slick as I glanced at Asa and Austin. "Want to dance?"

"Thought you'd never ask." Asa palmed my hip as he walked behind me, his body loose as he rocked slightly, but I knew him. I knew that the relaxed demeanor was a lie. I knew his senses were in over-drive, and I'd bet that a single pin drop would tear his attention away from me.

We approached slowly, not making our intentions known. They didn't need to see us coming. In fact, it was best they didn't. The song changed, an upbeat tempo stealing over the dance floor. My hips gyrated with the beat, wishing I had other plans tonight that involved this song and naked men, and not murder and mayhem.

Too late now.

They picked their fate.

I reached up, tapping the girl on her shoulder. Her head turned, her eyes already hazy from whatever liquor they'd consumed. "Excuse me." I slurred my words. "I-I see you thinnnk three is better than one, too."

I used my head to gesture to the men dancing with her. "Definitely."

I smiled, knowing that I would agree to that statement, too. Especially after the out of this world sex we had in the kitchen. I held up the drinks. "We ordered too manyyyyy. Want themmm?"

I practically shoved the drinks at her as Asa kept his head down, his body nearly humping me on the dance floor. Austin's back was to them, but he acted as if Asa was his focus. Their team eyed the drinks, and just when I thought they would reject them, they shrugged and reached for the glasses. She downed half a glass and handed it over to one of the guys, while the other two shared the other.

"Thanks." She licked her lips.

"Not a problem." I smiled. "Enjoy your night."

Then, we danced. Asa close against my skin, Austin closing in on us both, acting like we didn't give a fuck about the world when, in reality, we were just waiting for their world to fall. The weight of Wick's gaze sat heavy against my skin, and I couldn't see him through the crowd of people, not in this poorly lit club, but I knew his gaze was on me, taking in every move of my hips and categorizing them for later.

I'd be punished, I knew.

Punished for the way I moved in front of strangers, the way eyes fell to me. Punished because it was Asa's hands against my body and not his. But I'd never let on that I hoped for the punishment. That I knew the second I assigned him to be our Uber that he'd be stewing and categorizing all the ways to get back at me.

The girl was the first to stumble, nearly falling into Austin, who reached out to catch her, ignoring the glares of her men. One reached out, his hand missing Austin as he fell forward. Austin grabbed his shoulder. "Whoa there. Looks like you've had a few too many tonight."

The guy blinked a few times. "No."

The girl held her head, her voice faint. "I'm feeling a little dizzy."

"Alcohol. Am I right?" I laughed it off. "Why don't we go sit down?"

Another of her men stepped forward. He was lanky, and I bet he would be stealthy as fuck if this was a mission. "She's fine." As soon as the words were spoken, he shook his head, looking suddenly disoriented. "We're fine."

"I'd never question you. I just know that sometimes us petite girls get hit hard with the liquor. One second, we are fine, then BAM, the alcohol takes hold, and it takes us hard. That's all." I explained it away like I didn't just drug them.

"Maybe we should go, man." One of them slung his arm over the lanky guy, looking more confused by the second.

"Let us help you. We'll call you an Uber." I smiled brightly, ignoring the fact that we were standing still on the dance floor while the crowd of people danced around us. I took my phone out of my purse, already texting Wick before they could even dispute it. Then I tossed it in my bag. "Done."

"We don't need—"

"It's already done," the girl said. "Let's just take it. I'm not feeling well."

The men eyed us suspiciously, but it was becoming rapidly clear that none of them could drive. Hell, the one closest to us could barely stand, let alone operate a vehicle. Finally, the one farthest away brought a hand up to his head, probably trying to soothe away the fuzzy feeling. "Fine."

I took the girl's hand, turning away as I dragged her slowly out of the crowd. Behind us, my men walked next to hers, righting them when they stumbled. Time dragged, their steps slowed, and right about the time when the drugs really kicked in, we burst out of the door and into the fresh air. By this time, everyone was heavily leaning on us, their limbs not cooperating, their thoughts slowed by cotton.

"They good?" a random guy asked as he walked by. "Need any help?"

"The drinks." Asa laughed. "They were strong tonight. I'd be careful if I were you. We've got it. We're just waiting for their Uber."

"No problem, man. Have a pleasant night." He walked away, and Asa smirked, always the fucking charmer.

Two minutes later, Wick had pulled up to the curb, the barely used black car blending in with the surroundings. When he stopped in front of us, I reached forward, pulling open the door. "Uber?"

"Yes ma'am." I smirked. I kind of liked the sound of that. "Where to?"

One of the men pushed and stumbled his way forward as he fell into the front seat. If I had to guess, it wouldn't be long before the drug pulled them under, at least keeping them knocked out long enough for us to get them to a location we planned and drag them out of the car. His words were slurred when he demanded, "Twenty-first and main."

"Got it." Wick turned, looking uninterested as we piled the other three into the back seat.

In minutes, they were on the road, and we were practically power walking to the truck to catch up. In their state, they wouldn't harm Wick, that we knew. It was dark. They probably didn't even recognize him. But I hated the thought of him being left alone with the enemy for any amount of time.

My boys waited until we were secured in the truck's cab before talking. "You fucking did it, baby. Your plan was flawless."

I knew it would be. From personal experience, unfortunately, I knew how quick that stuff worked. I also knew that being given less than a full dose meant they'd come around quicker, and that was what we hoped for. We were running out of time. Less than two hours before midnight, and we needed them dead. A second after midnight meant if we called in a clean-up crew, we'd be punished.

"You doubted me?"

"Never," Austin replied, his hand hot on my thigh. "How does it feel? Your first operation planned by you and executed by us?"

It felt fucking fantastic. From here, I knew it was easy. From here it became Wick's operation, and my part was done. I pushed down the excitement and disbelief. "It feels... right."

"Fuck yeah, it does," Asa's voice echoed through the cab.

I leaned into him and closed my eyes, savoring the feeling of their solid bodies against mine as we drove the rest of the way in silence. It wasn't a long drive per se, but we were short on time. Forty-five minutes seemed like an eternity when the clock ticked down, reminding us of the looming deadline. It was after eleven when we pulled into the field in the middle of nowhere.

"He seems to have arrived with no problem," Asa pointed out, using his chin to gesture towards the field that was only illuminated by our headlights.

I exhaled, not even realizing I'd been holding my

breath. I worried for him, which was ridiculous because Wick was the most capable of us all. Still, three enemies in the same vehicle seemed a little much, even as I planned it. I tried not to let my hands shake as I watched Wick drag an unconscious man from the front seat. His hands were tied, his head lolled to the side as Wick dragged him.

Asa parked and cut his lights, before opening the door and shouting to Wick. "You don't even need us!"

"This one woke up, tried taking a swing." Wick dropped him, kicking him in the side as the body jolted. "Had to knock him out."

"And tie him up," Austin observed.

"He almost clocked me."

"Wouldn't be the first time someone almost clocked you." Asa was fighting a laugh while Wick glared.

"You're so fucking funny." He growled out, "Now get the fucking ice water. We've got people to wake."

Austin and Asa each took a handle on the ice chest and carried it toward Wick, placing it on the ground at his feet. We glanced at the unconscious bodies piled on top of each other because Wick just didn't give a fuck. Austin put his hands on his hips, staring down at them. "We sure about this?"

"They wanted a chase," Wick pointed out.

I was suddenly second guessing my idea. "Maybe we should just do it now?"

"Really Mac? Are you afraid of a little blood?"

Wick strolled to the truck and pulled out a duffle of weapons. "Because I'm not doing this shit alone."

"I-" I was fucking panicking. "I thought you would do the kills, and I'd lure them here."

"Change of plans." In the dark light with only the glow from the cab of the truck illuminating us, Wick's face was sinister. "Their deaths are on your hands, regardless. Might as well enjoy it."

He turned a knife in his hand and offered the handle to me as we locked in a staring contest. I didn't even need this knife. I had my own. But when it became apparent that he would not falter from our locked eyes, I relented and grabbed the hilt. "You think I won't do it?"

"I didn't say that."

"You didn't have to. I can tell you think I'll fold."

He crossed his arms in front of him. "Prove me wrong, then."

"Maybe I will," I spat.

"Good." He turned to the others. "Pick your weapons and dump the water. We're about to hunt, boys."

Then the water poured over the lump of bodies, starting thirty minutes of chaos.

CHAPTER FIFTY-TWO

ASA

The water hit their skin, the cool droplets splashing back and wetting my boots. When it was empty, we tossed the ice chest aside as the four bodies at our feet came to life. They sputtered as they choked on the liquid, their bodies twisting and turning, trying to get away from the damn near freezing water.

"Why, hello?" Wick taunted, and I already knew he fucking loved this. He loved this plan to taunt and tease them, to let them run and let us chase. It brought back aspects of his childhood, the sinister memories of times living with a serial killer parent. "Know who I am?"

They were all too disoriented to even respond, the drugs still running through their systems, making their heads fussy and their limbs not work. We reached over, taking arms and pulling, yanking them to a standing position, forcing them to be level with us, even as their bodies swayed.

"What the fuck!" One guy, a vaguely familiar face of a former classmate named Doug, blinked a few times, trying to figure out the situation.

Wick patted him on his shoulder, being anything but reassuring. "Remember a few weeks ago, when you chased our truck, putting my housekeeper in danger?"

"No, I don't know what you're talking about." His voice was a rasp, the words barely coming out.

"Funny, because your license plate listed your name, and that girl next to you is the exact face in my rearview mirror. You put my girl in danger, my whole fucking family, and for that—" Wick's words were cut off as the situation registered.

"It was all fun and games, man!" He was in a full-blown panic while the other three members of his team struggled to catch up. "You know the rules. And he said he would pay us extra to take you out."

"Who?" I stepped forward, my hand on the collar of his shirt as I waited for an answer, the material fisted tight in my grip.

"I don't know his name. Team Martinez... he... shit. Man, look, it was all for fun and thrill. The game..."

"Isn't over until midnight," Wick pointed out. "Run."

"Come on, man," another chimed in.

"If I were you, I'd run," Austin taunted.

"You wanted a chase," Wick reminded him. "Time to run."

The female wailed hysterically as Wick took a step forward, and that step was all that was needed to push them into action. They stumbled backward, each of them grabbing at each other as they tried to get their heavy limbs to work, but that was part of the fun. They barreled through the open field, stumbling, falling, crashing into each other, before they finally realized that being a team wouldn't save them and separated.

We'd never separate.

Put a fucking target on our back. We'd gladly take the hit, rather than put ourselves over our team.

We watched for five full minutes in silence, an amused grin tugging on Wick's lips as he kept his eyes trained on them. When the minutes were up, he turned to us, excitement nearly ready to bubble over. "Time to hunt, boys." He turned his gaze to Mac. "And girl."

Then he stomped forward, no hurry in his pace, and we followed.

They wouldn't escape. Wick made damn sure of that when he picked the location. It was miles and miles of openness. There were no trees to hide behind. No brush to duck under. Just freshly plowed dirt and a promise of upcoming rain. I took a deep breath, anticipating the moment before the sky broke and water pelted down.

What a glorious night for them to die.

Beside us, Mac kept up, her barefooted stride not faltering. "You should have brought other shoes."

"Pardon me. I hadn't planned to be a part of this event," she tossed back sarcastically when I referred to her only having the heels she left in the car.

"It builds character," Austin offered.

And it was funny to me. It was all so fucking hilarious that this team was moments away from dying and all we could do was chat casually, like we didn't intend to kill them. Like their lives weren't in danger and we weren't on their heels, hunting them.

Wick kept his stride as he moved his duffle bag to his chest, digging around until he pulled out a bow. Seconds later, arrows followed. He removed the duffle from his shoulder and handed it to Austin before he stopped, positioned the bow against his chest, notched the arrow, pulled back, and let it fly.

A girlish scream tore through the night, but somehow, I suspected it wasn't the female. Another three arrows sailed into the night air before he began walking again. We were closing in fast, their drunk and drugged steps no match for our completely sober ones.

Another stop, more arrows in the air before Wick mumbled, "I think I accidentally got one of them."

"That wasn't your intent?" Mac gasped.

"No. My intent is to toy with them like they toyed with us. Think of the arrows as an equivalent of their vehicle hitting ours, nudging us into panic."

"You're a fucking monster," Mac proclaimed. I'd never seen Wick look so proud. "I think I like it."

"Good." Even in the faint light of our flashlights, I could see the enjoyment on his face. He reached into the bag again, pulling out some fireworks. "Here."

She took the fireworks and held them. "What am I doing with these?"

He didn't respond. He took one from her fingers, pulled a lighter out of his pocket, and lit it. Then he wound his arm back and sailed them forward, and as they fell, the pop, the flash of light, the screams... they fed his soul. Mac nodded, understanding evident as she reached for his lighter. She flicked it on, lit an explosive, and sailed it through the air. Her throw wasn't nearly as powerful, her aim off, but somehow it still landed on the ground next to one male, exploded as it touched the soil.

His curse echoed, and Wick turned. "Him first."

Without asking questions or even wondering why, as a unit, we turned in his direction, closing in on him. One would have thought it would have been Wick to make the first kill, but it wasn't. In fact, if I had to guess, I would assume he was saving the death, waiting for the very last person to take the final life of the crew who tried to take ours. Austin reached the guy, his hands still bound and a giant goose egg protruding from his forehead from when Wick knocked him out.

"If we had all the time in the world, I'd make this

last," Austin explained as he grabbed his hair and yanked his head back. Then his knife was through the exposed skin of his neck, blood bubbling and gurgling out in thick dark rivers as his eyes rolled backwards and his body fell back.

"One," Wick counted as he sailed another explosive into the air. The pop and following curses alerted us in which direction the next victim would be.

It didn't take long to find him. He was stumbling, falling, and grappling as he struggled to keep himself upright. Wick shined his light in the man's direction, keeping him directly in the beam, reminding him we knew where he was and we were coming. Our steps slowed as we progressed closer, but my heart sped up. No one had to say it. I already knew. This kill was mine.

He tried to run, only tripping over his leaded feet as he looked over his shoulder and into the beam of light. He couldn't see us, he couldn't see our faces, but the terror on his would be etched into my mind, catalogued with the other lives I'd claimed.

"Please," he sobbed. "It was just a job."

"And so is this," Wick's voice boomed.

"I wouldn't have killed her," he sputtered, and fuck him. We all knew that was a lie.

Wick laughed. "People will lie about anything when they face death. It's sad really. When I go, nothing but the truth will leave my mouth. Run a little faster now, rabbit. The big bad wolves are coming."

He taunted him, and it worked. The guy tried to run, only not very successfully. His chest heaved, the sound of his labored breathing filling the night as his mud and dirt covered body worked to escape the inescapable. Above, a flash of lightning sparked across the sky, followed by a rumble of thunder, before the night went silent again.

"Oh god," he whispered, but the words carried forth to us, the pitiful resignation clear before he stopped, falling to his knees in the soil, his back to us, and waited.

Ten strides later, we were at his side, his hair in my hand as I leaned forward, whispering in his ear. "In the end, it's the betrayals we didn't see coming that hurt us the most. The organization is our brotherhood, our family, the only kin we have. Coming after our housekeeper was stabbing us in the back."

To emphasize my words, I let my blade sink through the back of his left shoulder, straight through his heart before the blade's tip pierced through his chest. He gasped, the sound fading into air as his hands came up to hold his chest, before the life left his body, forcing him to slump forward limply. I placed a foot on his back and pulled, tearing my blade from his flesh and wiping it against his clothing.

"Two more," Wick pointed out, before tossing a lit firecracker in the air, letting the pop and the scream the female couldn't hide guide us. He pointed the light in the direction, searching around until he spotted them. "Fucking glorious. Two for one. Looks like these are ours, little vixen. Hope you're ready."

He didn't wait for her to answer. He stalked forward, a man in his element as he hunted the prey. He toyed with them, flickering the light on and off as he picked up his pace, anticipation for his kill finally getting the best of him. His hand at his side flexed, his fingers opening and closing as he strode forward, catching up to them swifter than the others. He pulled out the bow again, notching the arrows to aim, striking both of them in the back of the thigh, making their legs buckle and crumble beneath them.

They hit the ground hard, but before they could really register the fall, Wick was on them, his large body looming over them, illuminated by a flash of lightning. "They should have protected you, you know."

He spoke to the girl, not even knowing her name. Her lip quivered and tears ran down her face. "I know."

"The thing is, doll, we never would have come after you, never would have looked your direction. You weren't even a blip on our radar, and that would have been ideal for you, the best fucking case scenario. But they had to come after us, our girl. You understand the predicament that puts us in, right?"

She didn't answer, only choked on the sob that bubbled up in her throat, and Wick turned his anger on the guy. His hand darted out, wrapping around his neck as he forced him to stand. "You're the team leader, am I right?"

His face reddened under Wick's grip and his head nodded, but no words came out. "Choking on your own words, are we now? Can't even utter a simple yes when you were so fucking bold behind the steering wheel. Anything to say before you die?"

"Please no. Don't." The girl begged, and Mac gave her a sad smile.

"They would have done the same," Mac offered.

"These pussies?" Austin questioned. "Mac, don't make a saint out of a sinner. If they would have done the same, they would have tried harder to protect her now."

He had a point.

"Take off your panties, doll," Wick ordered, and hysterical sounds broke into the night as she hyperventilated with fear. "We aren't going to fuck you. Calm the hell down."

We were going to kill her, though, but I kept that thought to myself.

She shimmed her panties down her hips and let them fall to the ground, where she kicked them off. Wick bent down and picked them up. Without hesitating, he squeezed the leader's cheeks, forcing his mouth open, and pushed the panties inside. He pushed deep, shoving them down so far that his whole finger disappeared inside the man's mouth. The man's eyes grew wild as he fought to work against the material blocking his airway, trying to free it from choking him.

Wick walked behind him, holding him up with an arm around his chest as he forced him to look at his girl. With Wick's lips to his cheek, he spoke. "Now, while you slowly die, suffocating on something I know you fucking love, you can watch her die. Mac."

Mac's hands shook as she stepped forward. "I'm sorry."

She offered an apology, and for a moment, she hesitated, and I thought she wouldn't follow through. She couldn't. I wouldn't fault her for it. We were killers. She was too fucking pure for us. But then she raised a knife into the air, holding it behind her head for a moment before swiftly bringing it forward, straight into the girl's heart. It was quick. Still, I knew it would weigh heavy on Mac. Mac released the handle, not bothering to remove the knife as the girl went limp, crumbling to the ground.

Wick laughed. "Did you enjoy that?"

A muffled protest was all he managed before Wick brought his hand up, sticking two fingers into his mouth to push at any of the material that might have worked its way free. He crooked his fingers upward, and the man's body convulsed. "Did you know a few strokes here activate the gag reflex?"

Another stroke from Wick, and he pitched forward. "Only, with the panties that were just against your bitch's cunt blocking your throat, you can't fucking vomit, can you? I would hate to die choking on my own fucking vomit. Wouldn't you?"

He frantically cried out, struggling as he grew weaker, and Wick used that opportunity to shove his fingers into his mouth, right to the hilt of his hand, forcing one last gag before vomit slowly streamed out, obstructed mostly by the blockage, leaving him choking until he was lifeless.

Wick let his body fall, cleaning his hands against the girl's dress before he took out his phone and snapped a few photos. He sent them in and within seconds, a call rang out.

Eleven fifty-nine, and the last housekeeper was dead.

CHAPTER FIFTY-THREE

MAC

"What about this one?" I held up a sleek black dress accented by gemstones.

"That one's nice," Asa confirmed before he reached behind me, pulling a dress off the rack. "But this one is better."

"That one will have my ass pouring out of it," I huffed.

"All the better," Wick added as he tossed the dress over his arm, despite my objection.

His arm was full of dresses, all of which they picked out and none of which were my choices, but I'd let them have this. It was their ceremony, after all, their praise for keeping me alive and my acceptance fully into the organization.

It had been two weeks since the night in the field,

and I still got a little nauseous thinking about it. Another minute. Another fucking minute, and it would have been our heads on the chopping block, our bodies being buried, our greedy ambitions plastered for all the organization to see. But we made it, and Wick was smart about it. Taking a photo and sending it only ensured we didn't alter the time of death and secured our lives.

"You know, I could shop by myself," I reminded them.

"But why would you when you've got three hot men trailing behind you, making all the females jealous?" Austin's satisfied grin beamed at me.

"That's flattering yourself, isn't it? No one is jealous," I said.

"Really?" Asa quirked a brow. "Because I just got my ass pinched while we were walking through a crowd, and I'm not sure if it was the female or male who did it."

"You aren't put out either way." I bumped shoulders with him. "But really, I can shop by myself. Shopping with the three of you is overwhelming."

"How so?" Wick barked out, and if I needed a physical example, it would be him.

"Well, for one, you stalk behind me with a scowl, and it makes me feel stressed."

"I'm not responsible for how you feel." He shrugged and fuck, I wanted to punch those luscious lips and devour them at the same time.

"I didn't say you were. However, I can't control

how I feel either, and when you're trailing behind me, with your brows furrowed, and a sigh slipping from your lips every two minutes... I get antsy."

"I am how I am." He used the arm full of clothing to gesture forward, urging me to not stop in the middle of the aisle.

"You mean an asshole," I clarified as I passed.

"An asshole whose face you'll be riding tonight while you scream my name and beg for me."

A gasp to the side alerted me to an old lady nearly hidden behind a rack with her small stature and crooked back. "I'm sorry. He was joking."

Wick turned to the lady. "I absolutely would never joke about such things, ma'am."

"Good heavens." She clutched her pearls, actually clutched them. Then she leaned over and whispered, "That one's a keeper. My Gary used to love to feast, and it's the ones with passion like that that keep the marriage going."

This time it was me who was clutching my pearls. Well, if I had pearls to clutch. But then she winked at me before sashaying, cane and all, past Wick to continue on her way.

"Did you hear that? I'm perfect marriage material." He beamed.

"What about the other two?" I used my chin to gesture to Austin and Asa, who were standing close together, heads bowed as they both looked at something on Asa's phone.

"Come on Mac, we both know they can't eat you

like I can. I make you see stars." So fucking cocky, all the damn time, and it was true. He made me see stars to where my vision was sparking with them.

"That's okay, but you can't fuck like they can."

He blinked a few times. "Excuse me?"

"I said what I said."

"Do you know how many lashings you're going to get on that sweet little ass when we get home?" he threatened, and maybe I was a sucker for punishment because, damn it, I was looking forward to it.

"I've got homework to do."

"Classes can wait." He stepped closer, speaking lower into my ear. "I can't, Mac. Say the word and I'll take you into the dressing room and plow you so fucking hard the wall I'm fucking you against will bend."

How could something so dirty sound so fucking sweet? "With Ethel listening? I could never."

"Good ol' Ethel and her pearls would cheer me on, though let's be honest, I need little cheerleading. I know what I'm doing."

So fucking cocky.

So fucking mine.

I reached over, grabbing the stack of clothing from his hand. "I think I got it from here, big boy. Have you seen the price tags? I can't afford to soil these clothes."

"But I can," he purred.

I patted his chest before pushing him back. "You stay. Austin, you come."

Austin was at my side in seconds, and I stifled a laugh at Wick's face. "Oh, so he can go, but I can't?"

"He respects boundaries. You do not," I pointed out.

He thought about it for a moment before shrugging. "Fair enough."

I took Austin's hand, dragging him through the door of the empty dressing room. I picked the biggest room in the back, the last one with the most space for me to make piles, and began trying the clothing on. Austin was a saint where I knew Wick would not have been. He buttoned, zipped, adjusted. Anything I asked, and I never questioned that he would behave himself. Besides a few kisses here and there out in public, and some lingering heated looks, he was a boy scout.

Where Wick was bad decisions and filthy words, and Asa was flirty praises and sneaky touches, Austin was always sweet, always kind, always like a best friend, just like he had been before this whole thing started, before I joined their organization.

"That's the one." Austin's eyes were on fire as he gazed upon my dress, but he didn't reach a single finger forward to touch it.

"This one?" I smoothed it down my hips. "Do you think red is my color?"

"Baby, any color is your color, but that dress is perfection." For the first time since entering the dressing room, he stepped forward and captured my lips for a quick kiss. "Go show your boys. I bet they will be practically on their knees for that dress."

That was a little dramatic. I'd never seen Wick on his knees for anyone. Asa though, I thought his knees were his favorite place to be, preferably with Austin or me standing before him naked.

I followed his orders, pushing open the door and walking through the hall of the dressing rooms until I exited the door. Beside it, my men slouched, chatting, but when they saw me, they straightened up and their mouths fell open. The silence was heavy as I fidgeted with the hem of the dress. "Do you like it?"

"I'd like to fuck you in it," Wick proclaimed.

"He means you look so damn hot we're instantly hard," Asa corrected.

"I'm not sure if that's the look I'm going for," I specified.

"Oh, it's the look you're going for," Wick confirmed. "We're buying it."

"You haven't even seen the other dresses yet," I argued with him.

"It doesn't matter. We're getting it." He was adamant about the fact. "Try on whatever else you want, but that one is coming home with us for sure."

Austin stepped up behind me, his arm wrapping around my waist as he pulled me back to his chest. He leaned in, kissing my neck before nibbling his way to my ear and whispering, "Told you. It's perfect."

With a sigh, I pulled away. "Fine."

Austin followed me back into the dressing room

as I stomped my way back to my pile of clothing. He didn't dare say a word as I picked up more clothes to try on. But the more clothing I tried, the moodier I became, because as much as I hated to admit it, that dress was it. Nothing compared, nothing hugged my hips as well, or displayed the curves of my body.

I rolled my eyes at the smirk he wore. He found it amusing, and I absolutely did not. "Something funny?"

"Mac, we've been friends for a long ass time," Austin stated.

"I know."

"And in that long ass time, I've rarely seen you in a dress," he pointed out.

"Because you three ruined my good dress the night you drugged me and tied me up."

"We rewarded you with an orgasm," Austin reminded me, as if that made up for it all.

"Oh yes. I forgot. How did it slip my mind? Oh, wait..." I paused for the dramatic effect. "It was lost between the fits of hysteria and the pondering of my death."

"Focus," he demanded. "I've known you a long ass time, and I've rarely seen you in a dress. But that dress, I could see you walk around all damn day, and I'd never grow soft."

"Eww."

"You could do absolutely anything in it. Dishes. Mopping. Filing your feet for all I care... and that dress would still tempt me. The fabric against your hips. The teasing slit up the thigh. The hint of cleavage that promises a taste of heaven. But it's not just the dress, Mac. It's you."

"I feel like that's both a compliment and an insult. I don't need to file my feet. They are as soft as a newborn's bottom." I smiled before reaching up and pinching his cheek.

"Missing the point," he ground out as he pulled away from my grippy fingers.

"No, I got the point. I just like torturing you a little." I smiled, then reached up with my other hand and patted his cheek. "Thanks for improving my mood."

"Sure," he said dryly. "Anytime." He picked up the dress and a few other articles of clothing. "Get dressed. We'll meet you outside. I think I heard rumors that if you were a good little girl, you'd get a pretzel."

"How could a gal resist?"

"You can't." He opened the door. "You love free food."

Four hours later I was fed, fucked, and financed, all of a girl's favorite F words. As promised, the boys paid for my dresses; they fed me food, and when we got back to our place, Wick fucked me within an inch of my life before demanding my pretty little ass put on some clothes because we were getting ice cream.

I showered, put my hair in some pigtail buns,

tossed on a pair of yoga pants and Asa's hoodie and was ready in fifteen minutes. Wick took a leisurely thirty minutes, allowing me time to get some school work done. When he entered my room, he was looking fly as hell and delicious enough to eat. I stumbled off my bed and up to him, gifting him a kiss before I said, "I thought we were just getting ice cream."

"We are." His eyes roamed over me, and even covered fully, I swore his gaze heated.

"Why are you looking so bougie?"

He laughed. "Bougie? Really?"

I pulled on his shirt, and he leaned down for another kiss. "You know what I mean. Like, you put in effort."

"I've got a meeting after."

"A meeting?" I knew what that meant. An assignment was coming his way, or would it be our way, since we were a team now?

"Yep. Not sure if this is a solo or team project, but I'll let you know soon enough." He reached a hand out. "Ready?"

I took it willingly, my fingers curling into his as he pulled me down the stairs, and it was hard sometimes to think there was a time I hated this guy. A time when we fought, and he won every single round. A moment when I almost let my doubt consume me and my naivety ruin whatever it is we had by outing the Saints.

I should delete that paper.

I would.

Tonight.

Because even if I wanted to now, which I didn't, I couldn't betray them like that. Fame wasn't worth the risk of losing them. Chasing my dream wasn't worth losing their trust.

"Whatever you're thinking, you must be in deep," Wick commented as he parked the truck on the curb next to the ice cream joint.

"Thinking about your butt in those jeans," I lied.

He got out and stood by his open car door, then twisted to look at his own ass. "This old thing? You like what you see?"

I rolled my eyes. "You know I do."

"Be a good girl, and I might let you bite it later."

"Wow. The offer is nearly irresistible." I scrunched up my face. "But I think I'm going to have to pass."

"I'm sure some ice cream will change your mind." He slammed his door and jogged around the front of the truck, opening my door before I did. "A little rocky road, some fudge sauce..." He wiggled his brows. "I know how you like fudge sauce."

I blinked a few times, wishing I didn't hear what he said. "Yeah.... about that. I feel like that's more of Asa's and Austin's favorite topping. I'm more of a marshmallow fluff type girl."

"Yeah?" He gifted me with a rare view of his pearly whites as he smiled.

"Yeah." His hand found my waist as he pulled me

in to capture my lips. "That's exactly what I like to hear. Come on, little starfish, let's get some ice cream, and if you're lucky, and I sure as fuck hope we both are, we'll have time to create some marshmallow fluff before I leave."

Why are boys so gross and obsessed with sex?

"Starfish? That's new."

He linked our fingers and pulled me toward the ice cream parlor. "Yes, well, after I fuck you, you always sprawl out, taking up as much space as possible, looking like a damn starfish. It seems fitting."

"Fair enough." He pulled open the door, and I walked inside, throwing a glance over my shoulder. "But maybe if you didn't fuck me boneless, I'd be more conscious of space."

"Sweetheart, if we don't fuck you boneless, we're not doing it right." And that was an indisputable fact. "Now behave. There are children around."

"Yes, sir." I saluted him as his eyes warmed. "I'll behave."

Then I skipped forward, ignoring his growl as I ordered my ice cream.

CHAPTER FIFTY-FOUR

AUSTIN

"Are you nervous?" Asa asked as we lounged in the living room, eating popcorn and shoveling M&M's into our mouths.

"About?" I was flipping through the channels, searching for something to watch. It was all the same old shit.

"Mac becoming official?"

I looked toward him, his long hair pulled back, but a few strands were wild and loose. I loved pulling his hair. "As far as I'm concerned, she already is one of us. Hell, she's been a part of me since the first moment I laid eyes on her in class all those semesters ago."

"I guess so."

I watched him as he tossed a handful of popcorn

in his mouth, his throat working, Adam's apple bobbing. "Are you?"

"Am I what?"

"Scared."

"Come on, I can kill people with a flick of my wrist. I know of at least twenty ways to hide a body that no one will find."

"Only twenty?" I teased.

"Well, that's my fast list." He laughed.

"And that has nothing to do with fear." I kicked his foot with the tip of my own.

His head lolled to the side, his gaze penetrating through me, before he finally cracked. "Maybe I am scared, just a little. We've lived with Mac a couple months now, and I don't know, I guess it all seems too perfect. Like the ball will drop any moment, and she'll be gone."

"Perfect?" I snorted. "The first few weeks I thought her and Wick would murder each other. I wouldn't count that as perfect."

"You know what I mean. We survived the sweep. No one killed her. Our status among our team and within the organization elevated. Hell, that stunt we pulled in the middle of the field... it will go down as a legend. And sometimes, when something seems too good to be true, it is."

"Not with Mac. She's an open book." Every expression, thought, opinion, were right there with her. She was practically incapable of holding back.

"You're right." He sighed as he leaned forward,

then used his arms to push himself up. He stretched, a thin sliver of skin above his waistband on display, taunting me.

"I'm always right."

"You fucking wish." He cracked his knuckles. "I'm going to nap."

"Lazy ass." Though I would admit, a nap sounded divine. "I think I'm going to mail in this essay then maybe crash too."

"Lazy ass," he repeated my sentiment. "I'll keep a spot open."

"Who said I'm napping next to you?" I asked his back as he walked away from me.

He glanced over his shoulder. "You will."

"Cocky bastard," I mumbled under my breath, and he didn't bother trying to deny it. He knew it was true. It was that trait that made him infinitely more attractive, too.

I followed behind him as we moved up the stairs, but when he turned, I went a different direction, instead going into Mac's room to borrow her computer. It was on her bed instead of her desk. She was probably working on something before Wick took her to get ice cream.

I picked up the laptop and put it on her desk, before pulling out the chair and taking a seat. When I opened it, the screen came instantly to life, waiting for her password. It was her birthday, probably the worst password a person could have, yet she trusted us with it, so I guess it didn't matter. I made a mental note to remind her, yet again, to change it. If her laptop got into the hands of someone else, trying to seek revenge for something we'd done, having a simple password like her fucking birthday would only make it easier for people to get a glimpse into our lives.

Of course, who was I to lecture her? I used her birthday for my own fucking password and now someone was probably out there enjoying my porn subscription. I cringed, so fucking thankful I put nothing of importance on that fucking machine. I could have been so fucking dumb and careless.

With a final pound of the enter key, the screen opened up to her screen, and I briefly let my eyes roam over a report she was writing on the importance of global warming and the need for renewable resources over one-use items. I hummed out loud, not even realizing that Mac had felt so passionately about recycling and Mother Earth. I guess you learn something new about a person each day if you're around them long enough.

I wondered what else I'd learn about our girl.

I clicked out, minimizing the screen in search of the web browser. I had the mouse hovering over the web icon, ready to click it, when a folder in the upper right corner of the screen caught my eye.

SAINTS.

The capitalized word boldly called my name as I brought the mouse to the icon and clicked. In seconds, the folder opened up, a display of documents that made my stomach sink. I swallowed hard, not wanting to believe what I was seeing, but fucking terrified that if it was true, I'd disregard it and risk us all.

ASA DOMINGUEZ

CHADWICK MOORE

AUSTIN BRUIN

All documents with our names, and if I opened each one, I knew about what I'd find inside. Information, too much fucking information about us, more than enough to ruin us.

Betrayal stabbed me deep in the gut. Hurt gnawed at my heart.

I forced myself to move the mouse, to hover over the document, then click as I opened it.

The Unraveling of the Saints of Sin
   A journalism exposition
   by Makenna Wright

I didn't want to read further, but try as I might, I couldn't tear my eyes away as I read all our secrets, all the sins we committed legally that were brushed under the rug under the guise of an organization that claimed to do good.

We *were* good. Had she not realized that by now? Didn't she know us at all?

And the worst part? The part that made the acid

in my stomach burble and burn and forced me to fight back heaves, was that the piece in front of me, the piece of work that exposed every single thing we held dear to us, that was our literal life or death, was fucking good. Mac was fucking *good*.

She was good at pretending.

Good at betraying.

And good at writing pieces that could ruin us.

I sat frozen in front of the screen for longer than I'd like, longer than I'd ever admit, until the rustle of movement at the front door tore my gaze away from the screen toward the open bedroom door as I waited for Mac to come up. I didn't know what I was going to say, or how the fuck I'd address it. My hands were shaking, my heart beating so fucking hard I heard my pulse whooshing through my eardrums.

Each step they took up the stairs seemed to slow time.

I stood, waiting and wondering what the hell was about to happen, what the hell I would say. Did I betray her, or let her betray us? I adored her, possibly even loved her. Hell, I wasn't sure yet. I'd never been in love. Never uttered the words to anyone and truly meant it. But my team? They had been with me for years, had my back like no other. I may not have uttered the word love, but I knew, deep down, that I thought it.

This betrayal was going to break us. Hell, I was already broken, and I hadn't even spoken to her.

At the top of the landing, their steps grew louder,

each one thumping as they walked closer to the room. "It has to be quick. I can't be late."

Wick's voice was heavy with lust as he directed her toward the room, and when they entered, they both froze, their eyes on me, and I was sure that all they had to do was look in my eyes and see the hurt, the betrayal, the harm the broken promises had caused.

"Mac," I ground out, then let the word hang in the air because I didn't know what to say, didn't know how to open my mouth and accuse someone I trusted so wholeheartedly of betrayal.

But it turned out I didn't have to. She saw the look, made the connection to the open screen in front of me, and stepped forward. "Aussie, it's not what it looks like."

Her hands were held in front of her. Her attempt to lessen the situation went unnoticed as Wick stepped forward. "What isn't? What are you talking about?" When neither of us answered, he looked between us, seeing the war we fought silently between each other. "Mac? Austin?"

When we didn't answer, Wicked stepped forward, getting in my space, and he looked at the paper in front of him. "Wick. You've got to listen to me real quick."

She was begging him when Asa stepped in. Wick turned. "Did you write this? About us?"

"I—"

"Did you write this!?" he roared, and for a moment, I thought he would charge at her.

Asa stepped in front of her, a protection against Wick's temper. "Calm down, we'll figure this out."

"Did. You. Fucking. Write. This?" Wick punctuated every word, anger dripping from him.

"Yes," she gasped. "I wrote it, but—"

"Get out!" he shouted. "Get the fuck out of our house."

"Wick," Asa cut in. "Just—"

"Right fucking now! Leave. Don't you ever fucking look back, either." He took her wallet off the desk where she left it and threw it at her. Then grabbed the cellphone she left behind and tossed that too.

She missed, not catching it as it bounced to the ground. "Wait. Just listen..."

She was begging him, pleading, and he refused. "I've seen all I needed."

"Austin." Her pleading eyes met mine. "Austin, it isn't what it looks like."

"So you weren't writing a paper to out the organization?" I asked because even though I read it, I wanted to believe that wasn't what I saw. I wished my eyes were lying. Wished I hadn't read the words that would damn her. But I had. I couldn't deny that, and they crushed me.

"I was," she admitted. "But—"

I turned my back and closed the screen down. I didn't want to hear more, not now at least. Not when my feelings were too raw. Asa turned to Mac. "Listen, I don't know what happened."

"She fucking betrayed us, is what fucking happened," Wick bellowed. "This is your one fucking chance to leave, Mac, because if I ever see you again, if I ever look into the fucking whites of your eyes, it will be when I kill you."

I turned just in time to see Asa push her shoulders out the door as she begged for Wick to listen. All pleas hit a wall, none making it through to Wick because, in his mind, she betrayed us. She was now our enemy. And maybe she was, but there was still a part of me that wanted to protect her.

"Mac," Asa instructed. "Let him cool down a little, then come back. We can talk about it then. He won't listen the way he is, you know that."

"I was going to delete it," she promised Asa.

"Too fucking late," Wick growled as Asa and Mac disappeared.

"She could die out there," I stated when they left the room.

"She'll die in here," he snarled before he picked up the lamp, the nearest thing to him, and sailed it across the room, shattering it against the wall. "She's dead, either fucking way."

CHAPTER FIFTY-FIVE

WICK

Once I started, I couldn't stop. Maybe it was something in my DNA, some remnant from my psychopathic father, or a thread left by my mother. My mother before my father broke her, not the shell of the woman after. But as soon as the lamp released from my grip, it opened a whole wave of anger, rage, pain, and everything near me became rubble at my hands.

I threw anything I could grab. Tore nearly everything in the closet. Ignored Austin as he slipped out of the room, that fucking traitorous article still on the fucking laptop he held tightly tucked under his arm. I didn't care about that, didn't care that the Saints could have been outed at any fucking time. I only cared about my trust that had been irrevocably broken.

I trusted her. My trust was a fucking gift, and with how rarely I gave it out, it only hurt more now that she broke it. It was my fault. I let my guard down. I trusted my team, believed them when they claimed that this was it, she was it for us. I trusted my heart when I watched her plans in that field fall into place, felt it beat only for her as she took a life. I should have trusted my heart less and my brain more. It had never led me wrong.

I reached out, my fingers grabbing the last thing untouched, the floral canvas I painted just for her, and I paused. My fingers glided over the raised layers of thick paint, tracing the lines that took too fucking long to create. She fucking loved this. Sometimes I'd walk into the room and she would be staring at the fucking canvas. Other times, her fingers would trail over the paint. She fucking loved this, and I made it. Me. And never in my life had I made a single person happy until then, for her.

The canvas fell from my fingers and onto the torn bedding. I couldn't do it. As much as I hated her in this moment, as much as I wanted to ruin everything she ever loved, I couldn't fucking do it because it was me, the only part of me, that truly made someone happy, and maybe it was selfish, but I couldn't let go of that.

"Done throwing a tantrum yet?" Asa walked in, his hands in his pockets as he surveyed the mess.

I looked around, wishing there was something else I could tear to pieces. "It appears so."

"Good. I canceled your meeting." He picked up a torn-up pillow and raised a brow. I didn't give him the satisfaction of reminding me of just how immature my fit was. It was becoming more apparent by the second. It didn't change the way I felt, though. "Now that the tantrum is over, you can't just kick her out."

"I just fucking did."

"Where is she going to go?" He leaned against the door frame.

"Dorm," I answered instantly. She had a place before us, she could go back there.

"They kicked her out after not being there for weeks," Asa pointed out.

"A friend's house."

His eyes narrowed. "When have you known Mac to have any friends but us?"

He had a point, even if I hated it. "She's not our problem."

"Maybe not yours, but I hate that she's out there with no place to go."

"Good thing she now knows self-defense, thanks to us." Fuck. Maybe I was a little quick to get her out. But she betrayed us. She got what she deserved.

"Your plan is to what, then? Pretend she never existed? Erase her from our memories? Not give her a chance to speak up as to why?"

"It's clear why." I kicked a broken piece of furniture. Why else would someone write a whole essay on an organization unless they wanted to out them? There could be no other purpose, no other intent, than that.

"It's clear to you. But what if she never went through with it, I mean, if we hadn't caught her?"

"Why not delete it?" That was the whole point. If she hadn't had the intent, she would have deleted it. Or hell, never wrote it at all.

"Maybe we should talk to her," Asa tried again.

"Fuck off. I'll slit that bitch's throat if I ever see her again." Even uttering the words made my saliva sour and my stomach tighten.

I didn't know if I'd ever be able to kill her, and I'd never faced this predicament before. Never thought there would be a person who I couldn't watch the light leave their eyes and not feel satisfied. But I didn't want the light to leave her unless it was leaving me too because it was that light, that *fight*, that had made a part of me I thought was dead breathe life again.

"So that's it then? You decide for the entire team, like always." Asa continued to lean against the door frame, his hands in his fucking pockets, looking casual when I knew he was anything but. Wasn't he as angry as I was? Didn't he hate the situation as much as me?

"I'm the team leader," I reminded him.

"You seem to forget the *team* part." He pushed away from the wall and turned, giving me his back. Before he disappeared, he looked over his shoulder, his eyes burning with the anger he held tightly restrained. "You know, we took an oath to protect each other. As far as I'm concerned, Mac is part of our team. She had a paper that went nowhere. The people in this house were the only eyes to see it. What harm did it cause? What crime of betrayal did she commit? You and Austin may feel betrayed, and you're allowed. But you didn't hear her out, don't know her reasoning, and you turned your back on her, like you didn't take an oath to always protect her at all. You don't deserve her."

His back disappeared into the darkness of the hallway, and I couldn't tear my eyes away from the spot. He was right; I knew that. I knew that at the first sign of trouble, the first sign of something hard, I turned away, leaving her alone. I was scared. I *am* scared. Scared that, for once in my life, I felt something and now, I self-sabotaged and fucked it up, but I acted on impulse, and I couldn't stop once I started.

I pushed her away and didn't listen because I was terrified to feel for once in my damned life. And now, I couldn't even fucking admit it out loud. He was right, and I knew it. No matter what Mac could have done or would have done, she was better than I'd ever be. Everything about her was superior, and I needed a reason to squelch that.

I didn't deserve her.

None of us did.

And because I was a selfish, controlling bastard, I lost her for us all.

CHAPTER FIFTY-SIX

MAC

"We'll work it out."

Asa's words as I left the building echoed through me, but it didn't matter. Wick made his thoughts clear, and I was under no delusions that he'd change his mind. He never did.

I wrapped my arms around myself, trying to stay warm even though the temperature outside had dropped significantly when the sky darkened. I should have been smart, should have grabbed a fucking sweater, but all I wanted to do was get out, get away from Wick's anger because I'd never seen him that way. Never seen so much rage consume him, and it scared me. It reminded me just what he was capable of. Of everything I had forgotten because I let myself pretend that the man he showed me was the true man underneath.

But he was a killer. A murderer. An assassin.

It was so easy to forget when he was the same man mere hours ago, licking a chocolate ice cream cone and giving me eyes that made my insides molten and my heart flutter.

He had warned me before and I didn't listen. I wish the past me was wiser, that past me didn't form attachments.

My feet were heavy as I walked, not wanting to carry me away from the boys, but knowing I had no other choice. I had no place to go, and that was my fault. I was stupid and put my trust in them, stupid to think that I could write a paper and still be able to go back to the life I lived before, even though my job no longer existed, and my dorm room was now occupied. I had no friends to count on now. Not when my only friends were three men, my boys, who lived in a house off campus and treated me like I hung the moon.

I found a bench under a tree in the park that bordered the campus. It was secluded, which was both a comfort and discomfort. I needed the alone time, needed the moments away from people, but every rustle of the leaves in the dark had my ears perking up and my body tensing. All the pep talks I gave myself weren't helping. I knew how to kill a man, had done it twice now, yet somehow, I feared the unknown more when I no longer had any of the guys by my side to guide me.

I curled up, tucking my knees under my chin as I leaned against the wooden bench, trying to stop the shivers that racked my body from the chill in the air. If I made it through the night, I knew I could survive from there. I just needed daylight to hit, needed administration to open, and then maybe I could beg for my job back, beg for a dorm. Maybe I could sublet, take a spot someone wasn't using at the moment.

Weirder things have happened, right?

I made it to midnight. Hours had passed, and Wick didn't come. None of them did. I felt the hole in my heart like a dagger tearing it to pieces. I didn't just lose one of them; I lost them all. And for what? To become a journalist like my mother, who died doing that exact thing. It would be a fitting death for me, if that's how I went, at the hands of my men, for my betrayal.

My phone buzzed, and I picked it up, nearly dropping it with my ice-cold hands. My battery was low. I was trying to reserve it, but the view of Austin's name flashing on the screen had me unlocking it in seconds.

The text was simple, but I figured he was still mad.

Meet me at the church. Stop overthinking shit. It's cold outside.

My heart was beating out of my chest, the pulsing

making me shake. The church? Why not home? But then again, if Austin was meeting me without Wick's knowledge, I guess the church where meetings were held would be common meeting grounds.

Unless he was luring me in to kill me.

But this was Austin. He wasn't that type of guy. Sure, he'd killed; we all had. But Austin had a tender soul.

The church was a few blocks from campus, and at this time of night, the roads were abandoned. I held my body tight as I walked, keeping alert and watching every dark alley, listening to every sound. Only a few cars passed because any sane person would be home, in bed, warm, at this moment.

When the massive tree in front of the church came into view, I sighed my relief. There was something about having the end in sight, maybe feeling the warmth of shelter, that eased my worry, if only for a few minutes. As I approached, a light inside illuminated the window, aiding in the comfort. I took the steps slowly, still unsure if I should be here at all.

The handle was cool against my fingers, the metal nearly frozen from the elements as I cranked it down, releasing the lock. The door pulled easy enough with not nearly as much resistance as a door this size should have. When I entered, the room was cast in shadows, the hall poorly lit by candles that lined the stone floor and rested against the plaster wall on five-foot iron candle holders.

"Hello?" The whispered words echoed through

the hall, bouncing off the walls of the building. "Anyone here? Austin?"

My feet thumped against the stone as I walked, my body automatically heading toward the room with the faint glow pouring out the door. When I reached the end of the hall, I turned, walking through the door, into the emptiness of the chapel.

"Austin?" I tried again, walking through the rows of pews, my feet carrying me to the altar. "Where are you?"

When I reached the altar, the door behind me was slammed shut by unseen forces, and I whirled around, my nerves screaming in warning.

I was met with silence, the room vacant as I searched. "This isn't funny."

"Who said it was?" The voice, not one of my guys, boomed from above, and I looked up toward the balcony, but it was black with shadows.

There were no candles up there, no lights to guide me, and when I traveled my palms against the wall by the door, I couldn't find a single switch. My fingers touched the rail of the stairs leading upward, and gripped it, moving upward as I took each step slowly.

This was how nightmares were made, created, orchestrated, and I knew I shouldn't walk toward danger, but my feet carried me, anyway. "Who are you?" My voice radiated, the pitch loud.

"A friend." He paused, then laughed. "Or an enemy."

"How very fucking cryptic of you!" My foot

touched the floor of the balcony and I waited, tilting my ear as I strained to hear, listening for any sign of his location.

"Mackenna." He drew out my name. "You made it too fucking easy for me."

Left. He was left.

I turned in his direction. "I don't know what you mean."

"Don't you?"

"I said I didn't." I stopped, my body wedged in the aisle between chairs.

"I know you. Have you forgotten?"

Who the fuck was he? "Who are you?"

"A friend." Somehow, I doubted it. Still, I racked my brain for every single person I'd ever known, trying to pair the voice with a face. "You came quickly after my call."

His voice echoed from the right, and I changed my direction. "You didn't call me."

"Didn't I?" A manic laugh broke from him, the sound sending a chill through me, causing my skin to break out in goosebumps. "A single text message was all it took for you to come running. How fucking pathetic."

"But that was Austin..." My breathing picked up, fear clawing at me. "What have you done with him?"

"Nothing. Yet." Footsteps that carried away from me had me turning. If I went the opposite direction, we could meet halfway.

"It was your text message?" I gasped, my hand going to my chest.

"It was too easy to get his computer, to access the cameras, to text you like I was him. He never thought about that, only the ramifications for the Saints. I watched you while you slept, you know. Watched you fuck. It was all too easy, too fucking easy, to gain the tools I needed to keep an eye on you. It's only fair after all."

He was closer now. My heart was erratic, panic settling deep in my core. "What's only fair?"

"That I take what they care about before I end their lives." It was stated like a fact, and I'm sure he believed it. But he didn't know my men. He didn't know the lengths they would go through to live.

"They aren't my men anymore." I stepped forward, tracking him in the direction I last heard him speak.

The silence stretched for a long time, and I had no clue where he was as I stood in the dark. Without warning, an arm snaked from behind me, cutting off my airway as he leaned closer. "That's where you're wrong. Just watch, with a single text, how quick they run to you."

Then, he was dragging my body backward as I scraped and clawed at the forearm wrapped around my neck, hoping more than anything that he was right.

CHAPTER FIFTY-SEVEN

ASA

"You're mad," Austin pointed out. "At me. For exposing her."

"Is that a statement or a question?" I threw myself down on my bed. I hadn't expected Austin to be there waiting for me when I finally came back home. After my talk with Wick, I went searching for her, pissed off that my phone was dead, and I couldn't just text. The instant I came home, I put it back on the charger.

"Maybe a little of both." He leaned back in my computer chair, the squeaking reminding me I should oil it.

"You should have called a team meeting and discussed it," I told him.

"Well, I was in shock."

"She's your fucking best friend!" I barked. "She was for longer than you ever admitted to us, longer than she was a part of us, and you let her leave."

"So did you," he accused.

"I didn't know how unhinged Wick was, and judging by the room, it was good to get her out of the house. But I didn't see you out there helping me look."

"I didn't think he would kick her out," he admitted. "I just... how could she do that to us?"

"What *exactly* did she do?" I let my glare sit heavy against his profile, hoping he felt it burn.

"She wrote a paper on us."

"And then... after that?" I pushed.

"Well, she had done nothing yet, but she could have," he tried to remind me.

"Could have and did are vastly different, but I think you know that. And that report. Was it just up and waiting to be found? Did you check the last edited date?"

"Well, no."

"No?" I laughed. "So you snooped in her stuff, broke her trust, then acted shocked when she did something you deemed to break your trust."

"Well..."

I leaned forward, my elbows on my knees. "She wrote a fucking paper. Big fucking deal. But if she did nothing with it, it was not harmful. She's out there, alone, in the fucking dark."

"We can look for her." Austin stood, taking his wallet off my desk. "We'll find her."

"You think I haven't fucking looked? It's after midnight now. Where the fuck do you think she'd have slept if she had nowhere to go?"

"A shelter?"

I rolled my eyes so fucking hard, like he thought I wouldn't check those. Not that I thought she was there. They were all miles away from here, and she was on foot. "I looked. I checked campus, no sign of her. The dorms are locked, as always. Even if they weren't, she's out of a room there."

"Are you sure she left?"

"I walked her out myself." And I hated every second. I'd spent the last few hours wishing I hadn't let myself do it, wishing I had stood my ground and kept her by my side. "I hate to fucking say it."

"Then don't."

"We can't find her in the dark. We could take turns searching all night, but without daylight, it could be impossible. We could check her classes tomorrow and hope she shows up there."

"Do you think she would? All her books are here." He pointed to a pile of books she had brought into my room to study next to me just last night.

Mac hated to be unprepared. She liked to be on time with everything ready, even if her backpack was always a disaster and full of garbage. "I don't think she would skip class unless she had no other choice. She can't afford it, especially if she thinks it's all coming out of her pocket or scholarships. We took away her only source of income when we insisted she quit the student store. We promised we'd take care of her, then we left her with nothing."

"I shouldn't have jumped to conclusions," he groaned before he rubbed his face with his palms.

"You think?"

"I could do without the sarcasm." He huffed, "I already feel like shit."

"It's earned," I pointed out, not sugar coating it. He fucked around and I guess it was his turn to truly find out.

We sat in silence for a while, and I could feel the weight of it pulling him down. In retrospect, I suspect he would have acted differently, asked questions, given her the benefit of the doubt until she proved otherwise. But it was no use turning back now. She was gone, Wick lost his fucking marbles, Austin was throwing himself a pity party, and that left me to truly wonder where she would have gone.

I thought I'd find her when I let her go. Thought I'd let her walk a few blocks, cool off for a moment, work through some things, then I'd pick her up. I hadn't prepared for her to completely disappear, and fuck, that was on me. She was safe out there from the Saints; the sweep was over. But... that didn't make it any easier out there in this world for a female.

With a groan, I pushed myself upward to a sitting position before I forced myself to stand, crossing the space to where Austin sat. My fingers reached his jaw, tightening against the skin as I held his gaze. "She'll be fine."

"She'll be fine," he repeated.

Then I leaned forward, kissing him, pouring every ounce of despair I felt into that single action until my chest was heaving and my dick was a solid rock. Only then did I pull away, watching him mirror the look of hunger in my eyes as we used each other for comfort. "Go get some sleep. We'll look for her tomorrow and figure this out. All relationships have problems, right? Lovers' quarrels?"

"Yeah." He didn't seem convinced. "Lovers' quarrels." He stood, our chests nearly bumping with the proximity, his eyes still smoldering with want and need, but there was also something deeper. A thread of despair, an inkling of regret. "See you in the morning."

I was alone in my room, alone with my thoughts, alone with the agitation that shifted just below the surface of my skin, screaming at me. I needed to find Mac. I should have just sucked it up and borrowed Austin's phone, but I wasn't sure she would answer a text from him. I flopped back down on my bed, my head hitting the pillow, my eyes instantly closing in some mock imitation of sleep. My phone buzzed, and without opening my eyes, I reached over, picking it up. It vibrated again, and I opened my eyes, seeing Mac's name on the screen.

I sat up, fumbling not to drop the phone as I opened the text from Mac.

Mac: *I'm at the Saint's church.*

Mac: *Can you come get me? I'm scared.*

I didn't know what the fuck would possess Mac to go to the stupid church at this time of night, but maybe she was seeking sanctuary. Didn't she know that sanctuary in churches only counted if the church was in operation, not used for some secret government organization whose main purpose was to kill?

Me: *I'm on my way.*

She didn't respond after that, but I guess it wasn't warranted. I debated going to Austin and Wick, but if she had wanted them, she would have texted them. Instead, I grabbed the keys to our rarely used car and drove the few blocks to the menacing church with the massive trees around it casting eerie shadows over the building. I parked on the street, keeping the car in view just under a streetlight in hopes it wouldn't get tagged or damaged in my absence. This part of the neighborhood could get wild.

Hitting the lock on the key fob, I walked toward the church. It was dark, but faintly lit from the inside. I never drove by here this late, but I couldn't say I'd ever seen a light on when I had driven in the neighborhood. Usually, if the Saints weren't using this building, it was deserted. The light must have been Mac.

The door was slightly ajar when I walked up the stone steps. I pushed it open, the squeaking announcing my arrival before my voice ever could. "Hello? Mac, where are you?"

My steps were heavy, the only sound in the church. My flesh pebbled; my stomach knotted. Warning bells were going off, and I knew I should stop, but I couldn't bring myself to halt. As I walked, I took my phone out, sending Wick my location before trying to text Mac. Down the hall and into the chapel, I heard the ding of her incoming text, and I followed the sound.

"Mac." I called her name, and this time, I swore I heard fabric scraping against brick, but that would be insane, right? Mac wouldn't leave her phone in a room she wasn't in. It was damn near her security blanket to have it nearby, even if she had no friends to text. I swallowed the lump in my throat and pushed open the heavy carved wooden doors, stepping into the chapel room.

It was dark, only a few candles lit at the altar, and because of that, it took me longer than it should have to register what I was seeing. But when my brain caught up with the sight before me, I rushed forward, nearly tripping on my own feet as I hurried toward Mac. She was tied and strung up, her hands behind her back, a rope wrapped around her neck, daring her to move. A gag was stuffed into her mouth, and her mascara was streaming down her cheeks from the tears that had fallen. Deep down, I knew I should check the perimeter, I should clear the area and make sure we were safe, but my mind could only focus on her.

Her eyes met mine, begging, warning, telling me

something I couldn't quite decipher as I rushed forward. She moaned behind the gag, screaming something, and I was almost there, almost to her, ready to take the gag out of her mouth when an exploding pain radiated from the back of my skull. I stumbled forward, barely catching myself before another blow to the back of my skull made my vision grow dark, and right before I blacked out, the only thing my mind registered was the muffled sobs of my girl, before the blackness finally claimed me and I passed out.

CHAPTER FIFTY-EIGHT

AUSTIN

I startled awake, my heart beating, my palms sweating.

It had been years since I woke from a dream like that one, but it still tugged at me, making me nauseous with fear, a feeling I had thought I was immune to, a feeling I hoped to have forgotten. Yet it clawed at me, reminding me I too am human, and I've got weaknesses.

And that weakness was Mac.

I knew it was just a dream, but I couldn't get the images of Mac's glassy, lifeless eyes staring back at me out of my head. It was my guilt talking because I knew I was responsible for Wick kicking her out, but I had panicked. I felt betrayed. But Asa was right. She hadn't done harm with the paper, and though there could be the word 'yet' attached to that, I doubted she would betray us like that.

I knew Mac.

I'd known her longer than the others, and I'd never seen her do something so dishonest. She was my family, and at the first possibility of things going wrong, I got scared, and I initiated her being pushed away from us. She wasn't too good to be true. Our unconditional love was.

Love?

The word sent a fresh wave of nausea through me, which had nothing to do with fear and everything to do with how hopelessly doomed I was.

On my nightstand, my phone buzzed with a text from a familiar number, and I grabbed my phone, noting it was just after three in the morning, before I swiped open the screen to read the text.

Unknown: *Hey, it's Mac. Can you meet at the church? My phone is broken, and I'm scared.*

I stumbled out of the bed, nearly falling when the sheets wrapped around my ankles.

My cell buzzed in my grip again, and I looked down.

Unknown: *Leave Wick and Asa, we need to talk.*

Anytime your girl uses that phrase, it can't be good. I shot back a quick reply, letting her know I was on my way and to stay there. I didn't want her roaming the streets this time of the night. We should have put our foot down and never let her out of the house, especially when it was so close to night.

I stumbled as I put on a pair of jeans and tossed on a plain white shirt. Downstairs, I searched around for the keys, not finding the car's, and I sure as hell wouldn't touch Wick's truck tonight. Asa must have them in his room, and I didn't want to wake him. Mac contacted me and me alone for a reason, and I didn't want to betray her fragile trust when she so clearly just needed someone to listen.

Maybe I could get through to Wick after I talked to Mac, have him at least listen to her reasoning without slitting her throat.

The walk to the church was chilly. I didn't run, but I made sure my pace was one of urgency. I didn't have time to fuck around, and I didn't want her to be sitting there alone, scared.

It wasn't until I was nearly in front of the church that I felt the first jolt of unease. The car sitting there, illuminated by the streetlights, looked like the one that we shared. I ignored the nagging unease and pushed through it, not bothering to stop and examine the car as I walked up the steps to the church.

It was dark as I pushed open the door. The hall looked eerie as the faint light of candles in the distance cast the barest of glows. Mac didn't tell me where she was in church, not like the property was massive, but there were a good number of rooms. I followed the light, ignoring the goosebumps that suddenly rose on my arms as I got closer.

"Makenna, this is mighty dramatic, even for you," I called right before swallowing hard.

My foot hit something on the ground as I dragged my feet forward and I stopped, using my palm to feel around until the cool metal of a keyring glided under my finger. I picked it up, wishing I had light to see, but knowing that the weight of the keys in my hand was familiar. Familiar because they were ours.

I should turn around.

Leave.

But the thought of abandoning Mac had my feet moving forward.

We were trained to think rationally in danger, but the thought of Mac being harmed urged me forward, disregarding all I knew. I care of nothing, but her. Always her. She was worth more than my own life and I'd do anything for her, to protect her.

The last door was closed, but light streamed from the cracks. I followed that sliver of light, searching for my girl, my best friend, the only person I'd probably ever loved. The handle stuck when I pressed it down and I had to throw my weight down onto it to get the lock to dislodge, allowing me to push it open.

The light went out.

The second the door opened, the light flickered and poof, black.

I didn't allow myself time to acknowledge the warning signs. I just stepped into the darkness. From the other side of the room, sounds echoed, but even if I squinted, I couldn't make out any shapes.

"Mac? Is that you?"

The sound, the struggle, the... plea? It increased

as I stepped forward, using my hands to feel around, searching my way through the room to the sound. My fingers brushed against wood, and I knew without seeing that I was touching the pews, the same ones we sat in as we held meetings, deciding we were to play gods and take fate into our own hands.

With the pews against my fingers, I knew it was a straight line to the altar, and even without sight, I somehow knew that was where I'd find her.

"Mac? Are you hurt?" I pressed on.

A muffled sob broke from somewhere ahead, but no words aided to comfort me. I fought the urge to run forward, knowing that if I tripped in the dark, I'd do neither of us any good. I made it to the steps of the altar, my foot hitting hard, bringing me to my knees to kneel. A sound had my hand reaching forward, touching warm flesh, and before I could process what I was gripping, lights flickered before the room was illuminated.

My eyes burned.

The brightness was too much after fumbling in the dark, and I shielded my face, getting a glimpse of Mac and Asa tied up before me, like an offering at the altar.

And right before the weight of the chandelier came crashing down, crushing my body, before I had a chance to fully register the sight of my family before me, my mind grasped a single detail of the last hour.

The number that had texted me, it was my own.

Pain radiated, spreading through every nerve as the weight crumbled upon me, and right before I lost consciousness, I looked toward Asa and Mac, allowing them to be the last thing I saw before blackness consumed my vision.

CHAPTER FIFTY-NINE

MAC

"How long do you think it will take him to get here, Makenna?" Mason smirked as he paced.

He was unhinged, certifiably crazy. That was a fact I'd learned over the last few hours as I filtered in and out of consciousness, as I struggled against my bindings, as I begged and pleaded from behind a gag, hoping that he would just take me and spare the lives of the men I'd become so fond of.

My vision blurred as I tried to turn my head, pulling the rope around my throat a little too much for comfort. Asa was next to me, and if I stretched my wrist just enough, I could almost brush against his skin. But Austin? He laid in a crumbled pile on the floor, tied up like a hog and completely unconscious, blood smearing the surrounding ground.

I nearly choked myself out, fighting against the pull of the rope as I watched, in what seemed like slow motion, as Mason cut the rope, crashing the light fixture onto Austin. It was big, welded iron held together by rivets and candle wax that had melted in place so long ago that it was nearly a glue. The weight of it had to be twice the weight of Austin and the sound... the way the iron collided with his body... would forever be embedded in my mind as a haunted memory. That was if I lived, of course, but the chance of that wasn't likely.

Everything depended on Wick now, and Wick would never come for me. Not like Austin and Asa had.

"Well?" Mason prompted when I didn't answer him.

"He's not coming." My words slurred and muffled around the gag, but Mason understood completely.

"That's where you're wrong, Mac. I've watched you, seen every move you make through your camera feeds on Austin's computer. Watched the way he looked at you, the way he fucked you. Hell, he made no secret of that at the party, now did he? You remember the party, right? The one he threw mere hours after slaughtering my entire team."

"They tried to kill us," I tried to argue, but the words were barely audible.

"I think he will come. A little lovers' spat would never stop a man like Wick." He tapped his knife on his chin as if he was thinking about some crazy, deranged thought. "Which of your team should I kill first?"

What? No. There was no way I'd pick one over the other. That was insanity. I cared for them all equally, even Wick, even when I'd hated him, and I'd gladly take the blade for him, gladly feel the pain, before I picked him to die. I shook my head, denying that their deaths were even a possibility to me.

"This one then?" He strolled forward, stopping in front of Austin. He reached forward, his fingers gripping Austin's light strands, now stained with the dark shade of spilled blood. Austin's head pulled back, his eyes still closed. A faint moan and the rise of his chest were the only signs that he was still living.

Asa and I both pulled at the ropes that dug into our skin, praying that one of them would break. Together, we both struggled, the rope gagging me as I leaned forward, my wrists burning from the pull, my arms aching from holding the same position for hours.

"No?" Mason dropped Austin, letting him sink to the floor on his knees before his body collapsed sideways. "This one then?"

He stepped toward where Asa hung close to me, twirling his knife in his hand while I adamantly denied my desire to have him harmed or killed. His knife stopped mid-flip, the handle fitted perfectly between his fingers before he ran the blade over Asa's torso.

"Do you know what type of damage could be done if someone was stabbed in the wrong place?"

Tears fell from my eyes, streaming down my cheeks and neck, pooling in the tattered cotton of my shirt. The muffled croak that left me was broken with despair. "No."

"Well..." He ran the blade teasingly over Asa's skin, and Asa's body held tight as he refused to look at me, his eyes trained on the cathedral ceiling as his breathing came out in heavy pants. "One wrong move, one stab wound, could end a life if it's just right."

His fingers reached up, probing Asa's skin, and I tried not to look, tried to keep the rope around my neck slack, but my head turned and stretched toward him, anyway.

"The secret to successfully causing damage is to get them between the ribs." Mason's eyes found mine, and so quick I couldn't track, the knife jutted forward, sinking into Asa's skin to the hilt. Asa's body fell forward, and his jaw tightened, but he refused to make a sound. "There it is, perfect. Was that deadly, do you think?" When I didn't answer, he shrugged. "Guess we will wait and see."

He dropped the bloody knife, and it bounced once, echoing off the high ceiling. Then, he stomped back to Austin, taking his arms and pulling him forward, dragging him over the stone before pulling him halfway up the steps and dropping him. He stepped back, his hands on his hips as he surveyed us. "Perfect."

A phone appeared in his hand before the flash nearly blinded us. He concentrated on the cell for a moment, typing out something before it disappeared in his pocket again. "Perfect. Now we wait."

CHAPTER SIXTY

WICK

A vibration tore me from my fitful sleep. My eyes remained closed as I fought to fall back into slumber. My brain muddled through thoughts, only picking up single words that each urged me to open my eyes, and still I resisted, my body too tired to listen.

Another vibration had me jumping, my body shooting up as thoughts of the night flooded me.

I reached onto the nightstand, my hand feeling around until my fingers brushed my phone. I grabbed hold, pulling the phone off the charger and bringing it to my blurry eyes. It was an unknown number, with a picture attachment. I opened it up, staring at the screen as my vision came into focus and my heart pounded.

Unknown: *Come join them. Maybe if you get here in*

time, you can watch me repay the favor your team bestowed upon mine before their death. If you're late, you can help bury the bodies.

My hands shook as I looked at the picture. Each of my family was bloodied and bruised. Mac and Asa strung up at the altar, Austin unconscious on the floor. Mac's eyes, the fear and panic that the photo captured, made me nauseous. I caused this. I didn't protect her like I promised I would. Didn't eliminate the threat that I knew deep down lurked in the background of our lives.

This had to be the last team member of Team Martinez. Why else would they taunt me about coming to them? Threaten me with the rape and torture of my team? Although I seemed to be too late for the torture part, I'd fucking die before I let any of them get raped. Not while I was alive.

I nearly fell off the bed, my sheets wrapped around my feet as I struggled to get free. I fell asleep fully clothed, and thank fuck for that because I didn't have the time to get dressed, not when my team, my family, were in danger of dying. I shoved my feet into my boots and strapped on whatever weapons I could find. He could come after me, he could kill me, but I'd be damned if I didn't make him suffer first.

I took the stairs two at the time, grabbing the keys to the truck off the small table by the door before pulling open the door and rushing outside. The truck was in the garage, and I pushed a button to open the door, and ducked under the aluminum panel as it rose, not willing to wait to get into the truck.

I was in the truck, keys in the ignition, before I could think about what to do next. The engine roared to life, and I sat for a moment, taking deep breaths, preparing myself for what could be the final moments of my last day on earth. I failed. I knew that. I made promises, and I never kept them. I let my stubbornness and life trauma consume me, and it led to this.

I picked up my phone, hitting forward on the photo before I typed in a name, then typed out my message.

I made a promise to keep her safe. I've failed her. I've failed you. Don't let my failures lead to her unmarked grave. She likes roses.

I hit send, not sure why I added that last part, but if we died, I didn't want her to go into the afterlife without the simple beauties she loved. She deserved more; she always had. My Vixen. My true North Star. I strayed away.

Another moment to collect myself and calm the nerves that I thought were long since numbed, then I reversed out of the garage, down our driveway, and out onto the street. The drive took me two minutes, tops. I barely had the engine off before I was throwing open the door and rushing out. I jogged up the stone walkway, up the steps, and didn't bother waiting before I pushed open the church's door.

"Where the fuck are you?" I screamed, my voice amplified by the plastered ceilings.

I knew the fucker wouldn't answer me. He wanted me to search him out, to find him. It was a game, and I'd fucking play it. I didn't hide the sound of my footsteps as I stormed through the building. When I reached the end of the hall, I threw open the heavy wood door and nearly stumbled back.

I knew the photo that was sent was real. But somehow seeing them like that, seeing the brokenness and damage that had been caused because I failed to fully trust my team, still caught me off guard. Austin was still unconscious, his body laying at an awkward angle on the stairs. Asa hung there, his pale chest rising and falling, as his blood dripped on the floor. And Mac... fuck. What had I done to her?

Her arms were tied up, blood soaked into the rope, no doubt from her struggling and her neck... fuck. A rope held her neck tight, the purple and blue bruising under the restraint noticeable from here. He would die, even if it took me out. There was no way I'd let him get away with harming my family.

Mac whimpered, the sound bringing my eyes back to hers. She looked up, then back at me, then up again.

I nodded once, understanding.

I hung right, taking the stairs two at the time. When I reached the top, I removed a gun from my waistband. I palmed the heavy metal in my hand as I traveled slowly through the rows of seating, searching for the fucker who did this to my family. I needed a face, a name, a body to blame before I burned this whole place down with my fury.

"Where the fuck are you?" I boomed. "Show yourself, unless you're the fucking pussy I think you are."

I was taunting him, hoping to make him furious enough to come at me. I'd be ready.

My ears strained, listening, observing, but no sound alerted me of a location. I stepped carefully, keeping my body in the center row, giving me the opportunity to peer over the balcony and use my height to check the other rows of seating.

It wasn't until section three when I saw the barest of movements in the front row. I hurled myself over the chairs, jumping to the space between the chairs and balcony, but there was nothing there. A growl left me as I bent over, searching under the seats. I gave up, chalking up what I saw to an illusion created by my mind in anticipation of what was to come.

I stood up, letting my gaze find Mac's again as I peered down at her. I'd end this for her. I had no other choice.

I turned away, no longer able to look into the eyes of the person I let down so thoroughly. A step later, I was forced to my knees, the pressure of a boot in the small of my back making my knees buckle. I didn't hesitate when I twisted, firing my gun blindly, hoping to hit him, but he was gone, moved out from behind me and toward my side, the bullet missing him completely.

A blade embedded into my shoulder blade, tearing a grunt from my throat before unseen hands wrapped around my neck. "You were supposed to be the strongest. But look how easy you fell."

It was my fault. I got distracted by the sight of Mac and let my guard down. "You want to kill me? Do it."

"That would be too fucking easy, and now it's just the four of us. I've got all the time in the world." His putrid breath skimmed against my cheek, and I clenched my teeth before I threw my elbow back, connecting with whatever part of his body I could while slamming my head sideways into his.

He stumbled, taking me with him, knocking my gun out of my hand. I turned my body, facing him as I raised my arm, pulling it back before slamming my elbow into his nose. Blood instantly sprayed over me, but it didn't stop him from using his palm, pushing it against the blade that was protruding from my shoulder. A howl left me, the pain searing through my torso as I struggled against the pressure of his palm. I kicked up, my knee meeting his groin, disabling him enough to push him off me.

I stumbled to my knees, forcing myself onto my feet before he rose. I looked around, searching for the gun, but I spotted it seconds too late as he picked it up from under a seat, twirling it around his finger before tucking it into his pants at the small of his back.

"Thanks for the present," he gloated, and for the

first time, in the dim light, I could almost make him out. "What else do you have on you?"

"Fuck off," I spat as I widened my stance, making my body larger as I looked for opportunities to move. There were none. I was trapped between him, the seating, and the balcony, with at least a fifteen-foot fall. "You think you've won just because you've got my weapon?"

"No." He laughed. "I think I won because I have your weapon, your team, and your girl. I wondered how long it would take you to come to us. Turns out, it was quicker than I guessed."

"What else would I do this early in the morning?" I pointed out, trying to act calm when inside, I was a mess. My muscles were coiled so tight that a single movement could force them to snap.

He took a step toward me and I reached down, shimmying a knife from my boot, and held it up in warning. He laughed. "You think I'm afraid of a knife?"

"You've seen what I can do," I reminded him.

His chin jutted toward the balcony. "You've seen what I can do, too."

Fucker. "They're just scratches."

"You wish. Tell me, how long do you think he'll last before he bleeds out?" I didn't look over the ledge, knowing that if I took my eyes off the man in front of me, he'd use it to his advantage.

"He'll be fine."

"So fucking confident of that. It's like you forget I

single handedly managed to take down three of your team, all while you slept."

"If you took them down, I guarantee it wasn't a fair fight." Another step closer had my fingers holding the blade so tight that I knew my knuckles were white.

"How I took them doesn't really matter." He shrugged and, for a second, his face came into focus, his nearness enough for his identity to click.

"Mason, isn't it?" A little closer and I could swing this blade at him. "It matters how you did it. Catching them unaware after luring them here, it's a coward's move, don't you think? Why not face them head on?"

He didn't answer the question, instead opting to talk about how genius he thought he was. "It was easy, you know. All I had to do was take Austin's computer. Sneaked away while you two fucked and the whole damn party watched. Nice job, by the way, though I bet I'll make her scream louder than you ever could." I ground my teeth as he continued. "Once in, I had access to your cameras, learned your schedule, and knew exactly when to hit. Bonus was his phone number was still linked, allowing me to see all the messages you shared."

"You watched us?" The thought of it made my skin crawl. I felt sick at the thought of him leering at Mac in moments that were private and for us alone.

"Daily. Fucking in the kitchen together: poetic, might I add. I've watched it on replay."

I might actually vomit. I'd never felt more violated. My mind flashed to every time, every position, every moment of bliss that we had shared. He was going to die, even if I died. Without warning, I charged forward, my knife catching his arm before he pushed back, charging into me, toppling me onto the ground. I kicked him off, raising back to my feet as he staggered to his, holding his bloodied arm.

"Lucky move," he praised.

"Not lucky enough. I only got your arm," I taunted.

He rushed forward, his head bowed, and with nowhere for me to move, he plowed into my stomach, pushing me against the balcony. My back bent over the edge, and I teetered between the safety of the balcony and the possibility of death. His hand came up, wrapping around my throat as he bent over me, holding me in the precarious position. His face leveled with mine, his eyes bulging, and his neck strained with the weight and strength he used to dominate me.

If he wanted to kill me, fine. I had nothing more to lose than what he had already taken. But I would not go down without a fight. I refused. Pushing against his hold on me, I connected my head with his forehead. He howled in pain. His face was already fucked, and I hit him where he already hurt, but I'd take any pain I could cause him at this point.

With a curse, his hand loosened, while his other went to his forehead. A bump had already formed, the skin split from the impact. He touched the bump as I kicked at his knee, causing his body to crumble, his fingers scratching my neck on his way down. With his hold off of me, I grabbed his hair, using my knee in one swift motion to his jaw, causing a crack to echo in the building, mixed with his cry of pain.

His eyes flashed with anger, and he tried to say something, but with his jaw stuck at an odd angle, nothing came out. I smirked as I reached up, removing the blade from my shoulder. "Team Moore has always been the strongest."

That was a fact.

"We may leave here broken, but I knew we would leave here," I promised. "We done here?"

He struggled to his feet, his eyes never leaving mine. A low growl left him as he watched me. I should end him now, I knew. But something inside of me wanted to see him struggle first. I wanted to watch as he fought to speak. I wanted to see just how much the blood pouring from his nose and head would stain his shirt. I wanted to view his suffering with my own eyes before I dared do the final plunge of my blade, and maybe that was the error of my ways because while my mind filtered through all the ways I could torture him, and my nerves danced with glee at the prospect, he charged.

His body slammed into mine, his arms wrapped around my torso as my back hit the low wall of the balcony. It didn't stop me, only slowed the descent as I hurled over the edge, taking Mason with me. I hardly had time to process the fall, only the sound of Asa and Mac's horror as the air rushed by me. I twisted, turning us so that he would take the brunt of the fall and hopefully die in the process.

I wasn't so lucky.

The impact of the ground meeting our bodies was jarring. The pain of my arm crushed underneath my body, combined with the air that was forcefully pushed from my lungs, incapacitated me. I gasped, trying to breathe, but for a moment, I think my body forgot how.

The moan from under my body had me rolling. I hadn't successfully turned, so his body only partially protected me from the fall, but it had to be enough. I hurt everywhere, my body in so much pain that even rolling to lie on the ground made me breathe hard. I tried to move my arm, the pain all consuming.

"Fuck," I muttered, and even that hurt.

Mason rolled to his stomach, and that he could even move after a fall like that was impressive. Dragging his leg to the side of him, he propped himself up, before he looked toward me, his eyes burning with so much hate that I felt it in my veins, spurring me on as I gained energy I thought I had lost. I sat up, my eyes wild as I fumbled around with my one good arm, searching for my knife.

The search lost me too much time, and the seconds it took me to look gave Mason the advantage. He threw his body over mine, forcing my head to hit the stone floor so hard that I instantly grew dizzy. My vision blurred, but I refused to let the blackness take me. I jolted my hips up, causing him to lose his balance.

I turned, practically crawling, as my eyes spotted a bloodied knife a few feet away. But he was faster. My fingers gripped around the cool hilt of the knife as the butt of his gun, my gun, plowed into the back of my skull. I flung my head backwards, knocking the gun out of his hands. It skidded out of reach as my vision blacked out for a moment, but I pushed back. Using the blade in my hand, I arched my arm as I rolled over, slamming it into his stomach.

He grabbed the knife, blood spurting around the handle, and looked at it. If he removed it, he could bleed out. If he didn't, he had a chance at living.

"You stabbed me," he mumbled under his breath, his words slightly slurred through his damaged jaw. "I've been stabbed."

I reached forward, trying to fight against his weight on top of me to grab the handle and pull it out, but even in his current state, he was quicker. He grabbed my head, slamming it into the stone. His fury was unmatched by the little strength I had left as he repeated the action, pinning me in place with his weight and using his dwindling strength to cause me harm.

"I can't wait to fuck her," he whispered as I tried to fumble for my boot, trying to grab the one remaining blade I had there.

"You can't handle her," I grunted.

"Good thing I've got all those training videos, then. Thanks for that. She'll be a good lay. Especially when she fights it."

"Leave her the fuck alone," I ordered, knowing damn well that another hit to my head would render me unconscious.

My fingers met the blade, and I worked to grip it and pull it out. "I don't think I will."

Fuck.

I had gotten her into this mess. Her pain, her injuries, it was all my fault.

My knife was in my hand and I leaned forward, ready to plunge it into his back, when he brought the weight of his elbow down onto my broken arm. My vision swam and my stomach rolled. The sound that left my throat was primal. In my weakened state, with the distraction of pain, he turned around, forcing my fingers open to drop the knife.

When it clinked to the ground, he picked it up. "Thought you could sneak this in?"

I didn't bother replying. It was clear what my intent was.

"I told you I'd kill you, Wick. It's all I've thought about for weeks." He threaded his hand into my hair again, pulling my face up to meet his. "Anything you want to tell her before you go?"

I couldn't speak even if I wanted to. Instead, my eyes found hers, begging her to forgive me. Begging her to understand that I knew I fucked up, but I would always come for her.

"Nothing? Nothing at all?"

"Stop." Her gag muffled her voice, but it didn't hide the tears she shed for me, for Asa, for Austin. "Please don't."

I swallowed, my throat dry as I tried to speak. "Always." I licked my lip, my scalp burning from the hold he had on my hair and my body heavy with the weight I couldn't seem to move away from. "North."

I hoped that was enough. I hoped she understood. That even in the worst of times, she was my North Star, my home, the one thing, the only outcome, I picked in this life.

Before I could say more, my head slammed down again, hitting the floor in rapid succession, making me lose count as my consciousness faded.

Mac screamed, her voice nearly hoarse as she begged me. "Eyes on me, Wick. Don't look at him. Only me."

She was sobbing, words falling from her mouth, but my mind was too muddled to understand. All I could focus on was her beautiful face I never deserved and the tears that trailed down her cheeks. I wondered if she'd forget the way I tasted when our lips touched? Would she still run her fingers over the rose painting and think of me? Would she live that long?

He released my hair, his arms arched over his head with my knife in his hand, the last of his strength fueled by pure adrenaline as he danced the line of life and death.

"She'll scream my name louder than she ever screamed yours," he taunted as his arms rushed toward me, blade poised over my heart. But I couldn't look away from her, I didn't want to. Even with my vision spotting, my mind hazy, and the cusp of death creeping near. I never took my eyes off her.

And for a moment, her eyes veered away from my gaze, and with the last breath I could manage, I whispered, "Eyes on... me."

As if it made a difference that I died not watching her beautifully marred face. It was my last wish, my only request in this life to carry me into the next.

A sound loud enough to make me flinch echoed in the room, but I couldn't compute it. Above me, Mason's body jerked. The blade fell from his hands before he swayed, finally resting as he fell completely backwards, his torso hitting the ground, his legs still tangled with my body.

Thump.

Thump.

Thump.

Heavy footfalls came closer as my vision tunneled. And right before it fully crept in, seconds before I succumbed to the darkness that had been dragging me under, a pair of boots stopped in front of me. The man bent down; his eyes leveled with mine before he spoke.

"She always was more than one person could handle."

CHAPTER SIXTY-ONE

MAC

"Turns out the son of the serial killer was shit at doing his job." I jumped at the sound of the voice, my fingers flexing into Asa's shirt before I pushed myself up to sit, searching around me for the speaker. "Calm down little sister, it's me."

My eyes followed the voice, landing on the chair, where my brother lounged, his legs spread, his arms casually slung over his thighs as he leaned forward. As if Asa could sense my turmoil, even in sleep, he squeezed my side from where his arm was wrapped around me.

"You..." My voice broke, unable to complete my thoughts.

"I left. I know that. But it's complicated, Mac."

He looked up, and the familiar eyes that I finally could place burned into me.

"You could have said something," I accused.

"I never planned on it. Family is a weakness in this field, you know that."

That stung. The thought that my brother, my only family, had no intention of coming back to me. "I see."

"It was to protect you. You see how this life is," he explained.

"You could have denied me this life."

"I could have. But the truth was, when I saw you up there, when I saw your name on their forms, I didn't want to. Admittedly, I might have pushed harder, nudged them toward you. I wanted to be closer. I wanted you nearby. I just thought those fuckers would have done a better job at it."

The urge to protect them surfaced fast. "They protected me through the whole sweep. This was more than that. This was personal."

My brother, Jonas – or as my boys knew him, Jones – smirked. "I guess they did okay. They aren't enough, though."

"Fuck off," Wick muttered from where he laid on a bed on the other side of the room. I was thankful that they were all here together. I imagine that was some sort of government pull. The machines attached to them all beeped in unison. The sound should have been annoying, but it only calmed me.

Wick had a concussion, a broken arm, a stab

wound, and a few busted ribs. Nothing that would keep him down long, at least that was what he claimed.

Austin was equally broken, with a head wound that would have him on watch at least for the next twenty-four hours, even though he was finally shaking out of the unconscious haze and was fully responsive.

But Asa... I squeezed him, not caring about the yelp from the pain it caused. I almost lost him. Twice. If my brother hadn't showed up, if he hadn't gotten to the hospital in time, if they didn't have a surgeon ready and waiting... he'd never have survived. He'd lost too much blood. The damage from the blade was fixable, but barely. He flatlined, and for a moment I thought I'd lost him for good. My stomach tightened and coiled at the thought, tears running down my cheeks before I could stop them.

My brother leaned back. "I see the leader of Team Moore is in good spirits."

Wick didn't bother to open his eyes when he responded. "Mac, you could have warned us your brother was a douche."

"Still your superior," Jonas reminded him.

"Not in my hospital room." Wick tried to move, but ended up groaning from the little, jarring movement. "You could have warned us that your sister would be a pain in our ass, Jones."

"And play all my cards in the first round? What type of agent would that make me?"

"A considerate one," Wick grumbled.

"I'm not a pain in the ass." And I swear all four men in the room snorted. "What? I'm not."

My brother ignored my protests as he scrubbed a hand over his face. "I think we can agree that you will not be outing the organization."

"No," I agreed, then I sighed. "I-I just–"

"Wanted to be like mom. I know. But Mac, she wasn't who you thought she was. Neither of them were."

"She wasn't a journalist?" My voice broke as I spoke. My entire world as I knew it, my entire life shattered, my dreams ruined, my heart snapped.

"I mean, she was. But that was a cover. Every fucking thing we do has a cover. Do you think I would have just been recruited as a regular ol' student at Sablewood University? We got in because we were dependents. It's in our blood."

"I mean, I was just..." I grappled, but that wasn't fully true, was it? If my brother held a position in the organization, then I clearly wasn't just recruited. "I wasn't, was I?"

"They picked you, if that's what you're curious about." He leaned forward again. "But we might have planted the seeds, urged them in your direction."

I didn't know what to say. "I was a pawn this whole time?"

"It's not personal. All housekeepers start out that way." He looked around, his eyes on the bodies of my men in hospital beds. He lowered his voice. "They didn't know, of course. This right here, this was all them. They care about you, Mac. Don't let our family history or the fact that we manipulated both you and them to cloud the situation. They. Picked. You."

They picked me.

Even when I thought of betraying them, they picked me.

"Was—"

"Yes," he replied.

"You don't even know what I was about to say." I scowled.

"Yes, Dad was a Saint, and Mom was a house-keeper. Retired mostly. Lost two members of their team and went into retirement. The traveling journal-ism, that was a cover for the selective jobs they took. Their deaths weren't accidents." He stood, looking over the room before bending down and whispering in my ear. "Leaving you was for the best. I hope you know. But I sure as fuck am glad to have you back in my life. Tell Moore to come visit me when he's mended. I'm moving up, and I've had my eye on him to take my position."

I had so many more questions, so many things I wanted to say, but I was growing tired, and maybe, for now, it was best I didn't know.

I watched his back as he walked toward the door, and I was furious with myself for not seeing it sooner. I should have recognized the man under the mask, should have figured out the whole time that my brother would never abandon me unless he had a reason to do so. But time had passed, and he had changed. Both of us had. He had grown taller than I remembered, broader, and muscle now replaced the childhood chub that he had seemed to carry into his teenage years.

When he reached the door, he turned around. "Oh, and Mac?"

"Yeah?"

"I knew you'd survive this bunch. They are about as pigheaded as you are."

Then he was gone, and the room was silent again except for the rhythmic sounds of machines reminding me how lucky we each were to be alive. I lifted the blanket up to my cheek, wrapping my arm around Asa's torso again, careful of his stitches. And when I rested my head on his shoulder, letting sleep pull me under, I could have sworn through his sedated thoughts, he mumbled.

We choose you.

CHAPTER SIXTY-TWO

AUSTIN

"Are we going to talk about it?" I stared at Mac's naked silhouette as she showered, not giving her privacy.

"No need." She lifted her arms up, running her hands through her hair, and my cock went instantly hard.

It had been almost two weeks since the incident and fuck if it wasn't the longest time of my life. She wasn't mad at me, at least that's what she said. But it was what she *didn't* say that had me twisted up in turmoil.

"I think we should," I pushed.

"I think we shouldn't." She pulled aside the glass door so that her face peeked out of it, as if I couldn't see through the glass. "I'm hours away from initiation, and if I think about anything else right now, I might barf."

"Why? You're a shoo-in."

"Have you forgotten the many murders I've seen take place at that very altar?" She raised a brow, and I realized just then that maybe that was the problem. She continued, "What if they decide to butcher me?"

I stepped forward, my eyes burning into her. "First, your brother is our section leader. You won't be butchered. Second, you're afraid, aren't you? About reliving that day."

"Aren't you?" Her voice was weak, tortured.

"No." I shook my head. "But to be fair, I was unconscious for most of it."

Her eyes fell to my head, which was still healing with stitches and fading bruises. Her voice was small, distant, when she said, "I thought you were dead at first."

"Babe." My voice softened, and even though she was soaking wet, and I was fully clothed, I didn't hesitate to reach into the shower and pull her closer to me. "I'm fine. You're fine. We are all fine."

"I know." She buried her face in my shoulder. "I know."

We stood like that for a while. Neither one of us wanted to break this moment. She needed reassurance, and I needed her touch, any way I could get it. It was something I'd missed the last few weeks. I thought she was mad still, angry that my snooping caused this mess, but maybe that wasn't it at all.

Maybe it was the fear, the terrifying realization that we all were human, and humans die.

"Just so we're clear..." I tangled my fingers in her wet hair. "You're not mad about me reading the essay, are you?"

Her head shook from side to side. "No."

I blew out a breath. "What can I do to make you feel better?"

"Let me skip the ceremony." She answered fast, as if she'd been thinking about it the whole time.

"Not going to happen." I chuckled at how quick her shoulders sagged. "But... what *will* happen is we'll go, we'll get it done, and we will be there every step of the way, holding your hand and showing you we'll never leave your side again."

Her wet fingers clutched my shirt tightly. "What if you make more enemies?"

"No one lives their lives without enemies, Mac."

"But- Like..." She swallowed. "What if- I can't- I-"

I dropped to my knees in front of her, distracting her with a kiss to her thigh, letting my lips skim the tattoo she got to match ours. The one with the Saints emblem. I mumbled against her skin, "If we have any enemies, we'll worry about it then. Now I'm only worried about making you cum and getting you to that ceremony."

Her hands fell to my hair; her fingers threaded into the strands and pulled. "Can we skip the ceremony and just cum all night?"

I bit the tender skin on her thigh. "Nope."

"Fuck." She hissed out, but my tongue lashed out, sliding between her slit, tasting her cunt, and any other objections faded into a moan.

She tasted so fucking good. My cock was already steel. I could stay like this all night, on my knees, water cascading over us, soaking through my clothes, if the world allowed us. But I knew time was limited and anything more than a couple of minutes would only enable her procrastination. I let my tongue slide through the junction of her thighs, pulling her moisture into my mouth before I flicked her clit.

"Oh god, do that," she ordered, and because she demanded, I disobeyed. Instead, I concentrated on spearing her with my tongue, pushing her thighs wider to allow me access to push my tongue in and out of her body. She writhed against me, begging and pleading for more, and I refused to give her what she wanted, taking my pleasure from the sounds that spilled from her lips.

"Touch yourself," she begged. "I want to watch you."

The desperation in her voice, the want and need behind the command, had me freeing my cock as I knelt in front of her. With one hand, I stroked the length, running up and down the hard span before squeezing the head. The other hand reached up, sinking two fingers into her body as I finally gave her what she so desperately wanted and sucked on her clit.

She went frantic, sobbing for me to make her cum while her legs shook, her whole body weakening, being held up by my shoulders and mouth alone. Her fingers tugged hard, guiding my head and mouth to the exact spot she wanted me as I devoured her pussy, consuming the most delicious part of her with a frenzy I'd been holding back on since we came home from the hospital, too afraid that she was too fragile to handle it.

I knew my mistake now because nothing about Mac was ever fragile. She was fierce, loyal, and even when we broke her heart, she so quickly forgave us.

"You're so fucking beautiful," I praised her against her flesh, letting my words vibrate through her, loving the moan that escaped. "We don't deserve you."

That was the truth. We didn't deserve a girl like her, but I'd fucking try every day to meet the standard she deserved. I swirled my tongue on her clit as my palm worked my cock faster and my fingers pumped into her harder, curving just enough to brush against her sensitive bundle of nerves that drove her wild.

"God. Austin. I can't–" Her chest was heaving; those beautiful breasts rose and fell above me. "Make me cum."

I'd never deny her, not again. I bit down on her clit, sucking hard, while pressing my fingers forward, and she exploded, her cunt squeezing my fingers like they were my cock, pulling them deeper into her body as she broke into pieces, sobbing my name and pulling my hair, grinding into my face.

Another three strokes, and I was coming, warm ropes spurting from my cock and landing against her bare skin as she cried my name.

I'd heard nothing so sweet.

I worked her body until she slumped limply against me, then I stood, turned off the water, scooped her up, cradled her naked wet body against my still fully clothed one, and carried her into the room, where I proceeded to dry her off, lotion her, and worship every inch of her body until she resigned to the fact that she was ours and she'd never have to question it again.

Never again.

CHAPTER SIXTY-THREE

MAC

The red dress fit me like a glove, and my men couldn't keep their eyes off the sway of my hips. Even with the two orgasms Austin gifted me earlier, my body was wound tight, terrified of entering the church again. I forgave them; they forgave me, and in the scheme of everything that had happened, the situation was just so utterly unimportant to dwell over. I would not betray them. I couldn't. But I broke Wick's trust, and he broke mine, and that was something we were trying to work through.

From the moment I stepped foot on the stone tile floor, I felt nauseated. I wanted to think we were safe, and I knew we were, but still my mind wanted to replay every moment of those early morning hours.

I felt the pain, the sorrow, the resignation that I was going to watch someone I loved die.

Loved.

That word was so fucking heavy. It'd weighed me down for weeks with its truth.

I loved these men. All three of them. And if given the opportunity, I would have died for them, if it meant they lived. That they, too, were clearly willing to die for me made me question if they felt the same.

"I've got you." Wick squeezed my palm in his. "Always."

I had heard that before, until he didn't, but I wouldn't let my doubts cloud the fragile truths we had formed. I wouldn't ruin us because of a small misunderstanding that escalated to an extent that neither of us could have expected. But I couldn't just accept that all was well either, not when inside, I was more scared than I'd ever been.

To my other side, Asa had his arm around my waist. "It will be over before you know it."

I looked over at him, his face pale. He should have been home, recovering, not here at a swear in ceremony. I should be comforting *him*, not the other way around. I leaned toward Wick, standing on my toes even in heels so that I could whisper in his ear. "We need to get him sitting."

He glanced over my shoulder, eyeing our team-mate. "The front pew should be open for us."

My heart raced faster the deeper into the church we walked. We already did our offering, reciting the verses I long since memorized, and now we only waited for the ceremony to begin. People filled the pews behind us, the room slowly filling. It wasn't until the gong rang out, announcing the meeting would soon start, that people's chatter slowed and the room grew silent.

Another gong, and the heavy doors, the same doors I once struggled with all my weight to open, slammed shut. Panic clawed at my thoughts, its nails sharp as it fought its way out, threatening to spill from me. But beside me, my men sat, looking calm and collected, as if their lives had never been in danger in this very room. With a deep breath, I collected myself, forcing my nerves to calm, so that I reflected the same demeanor as the rest of my team.

"It will be okay," Austin promised, and fuck, I hated that he always was the one who comforted me when I was afraid.

"It's almost over," Asa assured me, always the one to follow up on Austin's comfort. "You'll be home to your carnival fish in no time."

"Promise?" I bit my lip, letting my teeth gnaw on the sensitive flesh.

"I'll fuck you so hard you'll forget this night," Wick chimed in, a small smirk forming under his mask. There was my guy. I'd expect nothing less than a thorough fucking from him in times like this, times of need.

My brother stalked up the steps, sparing us a glance and shooting Wick a glare, letting him know he heard what he said to me, and he didn't appreciate it. It spurred Wick on and he leaned forward, his lips close to my ear as he promised, "Lick you from front to back, while Asa and Austin watch."

My face heated, my body burned, and I tried to look ahead, to keep my focus on Jonas as he took to the podium, but Wick's breath still fanned against the shell of my ear, reminding me he always fulfilled the promises he made.

I tried to keep my focus on my brother as his hands encompassed both sides of the podium. His eyes met the crowd as he cleared his throat. I reminded myself that the past did not control me and that my fear was unwarranted as images flooded my senses, reminded me of what it was like to be strung up from the ceiling right where Jonas stood, with Asa bleeding out next to me. With Austin unconscious. And Wick, god... With Wick seconds from death as his eyes only watched me.

I was helpless.

Useless.

And yet, they still stood by my side, even though I couldn't protect them like they trained me to do. I couldn't even protect myself.

"I don't know if I can do this," I whispered as my brother spoke to the crowd of people, talking about tradition and unity, acting like I could make a difference being here.

"You're doing fine," Wick assured me. "Perfect, actually."

"I didn't save you," I whispered.

"I didn't save you either," he reminded me, and that may be true, but it was different. He fought hard. I could hardly fight.

"You tried," I pointed out.

"And you think that I'm supposed to believe that you hopped up and helped him tie you up there? No. I've seen the bruises, the scars. I know you fought just as hard as I did. Just because no one was there to see the struggle didn't mean that struggle didn't exist."

"Then why are all of you acting like we didn't almost die in this building?"

"Practice," Wick reassured me.

"We've got a lot of traumas packed away," Asa joked before my brother shot him a look, silencing him.

If it was anyone else speaking but my team, I knew my brother would call them up and decapitate them while he spoke, but we were Team Moore. And by proxy of me, his family.

Family.

I still hadn't come to terms with it. This whole time, my parents were living a double life, agents of the Saints, working for the government tactical team of assassins, and I had no clue. Not the same parents who stayed up all night decorating for a birthday party for their child, or dressed as the clown when the clown didn't show. They couldn't have been the same, even as I knew they were.

Was that what my life would be like one day? With these men?

I looked straight ahead as I watched my brother talk, but still I spoke to my guys next to me. "Do you want kids?"

Wick coughed, naturally catching the attention of those around him. He held up a hand, while holding his chest, letting them know he was okay, while Austin and Asa's bodies stiffened next to me. It was finally Austin who asked through lips that hardly moved. "Are you–"

"God no." I shook my head, and I swore they all relaxed. "It's just... my dad was like you. He killed people, but also read me bedtime stories, and I can't compute that both existed together."

"I see," Wick finally managed. "I think I can speak for all of us when I say–"

"If you'd please come up to the podium." My brother's eyes were on us, clearly knowing we weren't listening. Fuck, we missed what he had been talking about, not that it mattered. Not listening soothed the anxiety of being here, even if it was marginally. But if we were anyone else, we'd be dead. I'd seen firsthand what happened to a member of the organization if they stepped out of line.

We rose, along with one other team and their housekeeper. Following their lead, we fell to our knees on the steps below Jonas, waiting for further instructions. He paced in front of the row of members, his face behind the mask serious, even though I could spot his eyes twinkling slightly.

"Today we welcome two new members into our organization. Housekeepers, as you know, are the heart of the team, if a team opts to take one on. They fought hard for their members, gave it their all to keep them alive to see this day. Now they drink to the unity they have formed, to a bond greater than that they are born into, because it's forged in blood, our blood."

He took two goblets off the podium and made a display of pouring wine into the cups. When he was satisfied with the amount poured, he handed a goblet to each of the team leaders.

We'd been in this position before, when I vowed to be a part of them, vowed to give my life to the cause, and drank their blood. Before, I was afraid to bring that glass to my lips, afraid to drink the combined life force of us all mixed together. But now I couldn't wait. My mouth watered at the possibility, the feeling of closeness with them anticipated by the second.

I wanted this.

I wanted their blood coursing through me.

I needed that tether to tie us together after the turmoil and triumphs that had consumed us these past weeks.

Wick placed the goblet on the step in front of him, producing the bone knife from his boot. Without taking his eye off Jonas, he brought the sharp blade up to his palm, slicing through it. With blood dripping down his arm, he handed the blade to Austin, who repeated the action. When Asa received the blade, he turned to me and grabbed my palm. After placing a kiss on my forehead, he ran his blade through the tender skin, slicing it open. Blood instantly welled, but we didn't acknowledge it. Instead, he faced forward, sliced his own palm, and placed the knife on the floor in front of him.

"Fill this cup with life. Create a bond that is unbreakable. Forge a path that you will walk together," my brother ordered us.

Wick picked up the goblet of wine, tipping his hand over it and draining the blood that pooled in his palm into the wine. He passed it down the line, each of my men emptying a palm full of blood into the liquid, until it was my turn. I tipped my palm, watching as each drop plopped into the wine, making the tiniest of splashes.

"It is a great honor to join the Saints." My brother spoke when the goblets contained all they needed to. "With this drink, you become one of us. Specialized Agents in Intelligence and National Tactics, a Saint. An honor that encompasses your lifetime, from this moment until the day you take your last breath. Housekeepers, do you accept?"

"I do." I spoke the words without hesitation, and they were mirrored a few meters away by the only other surviving girl of the housekeeping sweep.

"You may drink to an unbreakable, impenetrable

bond." Jonas nodded toward us, giving us the okay to move forward.

I brought the rim of the metal cup to my lips, the cool sensation a stark contrast to the warm wine and hot blood that sloshed over, dancing over my tongue, igniting my senses into an inferno of lust and need. I gulped down mouthfuls, pulling the addicting liquid into my mouth and nearly rolling my eyes back with pleasure.

"Enough," Jonas barked, and I pulled the goblet away from my lips.

Asa reached up, taking it from my hand and placing his lips in the exact spot mine had just left, tipping it back to drink. After a few gulps, he handed it to Austin, who took his sip and handed it to Wick. When it was empty, Wick slammed the goblet down on the stone step.

"Saints," Jonas addressed the crowd in front of him, "I'd like to welcome the newest members of our organization, the heart of their team, our new house-keepers."

A cheer went up, but I couldn't focus on it. My mind was solely on thoughts of my men, my heart beating in time with theirs as their eyes burned into mine. In one quick movement, my men stood. Asa grabbed me. Ignoring his stitches, he tossed me over his shoulder as they stomped out of the room. The action only made the crowd cheer louder.

By the time we made it out of the church, my body was on fire. Each jostle of the steps descending the building made me squirm in desire. There was no tenderness when Asa laid me down in the truck's backseat, only rough mouths and hard kisses, promising me that when we got home, behind closed doors where no eyes could see, I'd be punished for drinking that wine so greedily.

And when we finally made it home, they fulfilled that promise, punishing me to the brink of insanity, not relenting until my body was boneless, my mind blank, and I was buzzing with the feeling their mouths left behind.

If this was what it was like, what they promised from the beginning, long before I was sworn in as officially theirs, then I'd say yes all over again, agree to all the dangers, and let lust rule my decisions. Because by now, I was certain if there was a heaven, we'd not be going to it. But a slow trip to hell with these men at my side would be worth every torturous moment.

Always.

EPILOGUE

WICK

"You're late." Jones peered over a piece of paper, glaring at me.

I wanted to tell him that it was because I was balls deep in his sister, but somehow, I didn't think that would earn me any favors. Nor would I mention that right at this moment, she was on her knees, tied and gagged, waiting for my return. I cleared my throat. "I was preoccupied."

"If you make any notions that have to do with my sister, I'll cut your balls off. Just so we're clear. My sister is a virgin, and that will always be how I see her."

I pursed my lips, not able to meet his eyes. His sister is most definitely not a virgin. Anywhere. But he was my superior, and I wasn't about to break his delusional bubble.

"Keep making that face and I'll gut you where you sit." Jones leaned forward. "We aren't here to talk about your team."

"I didn't bring it up," I pointed out.

He glowered at me, unamused. "I'm questioning my decision."

"Regarding?"

"Starting next year, I'm going to progress further into the organization. My team and I will no longer control this sanction, as we will move to a district level."

"Does Mac know?" I questioned, knowing that she would be gutted if he left, especially after she just got him back.

"It will be of no concern. I'm not planning to cut ties now that she is one of us, just so you know."

"I appreciate that." I nodded.

"We've been watching you," he remarked. I could literally laugh at how hilarious that was. They watched everyone. There were no secrets from the organization. I opted to stay quiet instead. "Except for that minor incident that almost got my sister killed and your team wiped out, we've observed that you possess the skills and drive that are needed to lead. I respect that even in that circumstance, you had the forethought to reach out and make us aware of the situation, instead of rushing in. That's another asset we admire."

"I–"

He cut me off, not letting me speak. "The sheer number of teams that were eliminated in the sweep were staggering. Ninety percent of those numbers were deaths at your team's hand. You recognized threats before they came. You stayed alert, trusted no one, and utilized the skills you learned throughout your time in the program to keep your team safe."

"We–"

"The boldness that was implemented," he broke in, refusing to let me speak, "during the last night of the sweep was unheard of. In the organization's history, no team dared to push such limits. Not only did you push the limits of time and risk death, but you did it smartly, providing time stamped images to eliminate the possibility of rebuke."

I couldn't take credit for that. Before he could say more, I blurted out, "That was Mac. I mean, it was all of us, but it was Mac's plan."

"Even more reason to consider your team."

"I don't understand, sir."

Jones leaned forward, his elbows on the desk as he eyed me long enough to make my palms sweat. "My team is being relocated."

"As you mentioned," I reminded him.

"We are looking for a team to be our replacement. We think that team is Team Moore."

My mouth opened and closed like a fish gasping for air. I had to swallow a few times before I could work out words. "With all due respect, sir. We don't qualify."

"An expert now, are you?" he taunted.

I wasn't an expert, but I read the contract. The contract we signed that allowed us to have Mac in our lives. "As stated in the contract, by taking on a house-keeper, the ability to move forward and be promoted will be void. We picked Mac, and we'd pick her again."

He sighed. "I wish we had made the choice to have a housekeeper instead of success, but we can't turn back time."

"She is worth every sacrifice."

His hand slammed down, making me jump before he smirked. "That's what I want to hear when it comes to my sister."

That absolutely wasn't necessary, but to say so could still get me slaughtered. It was the way of a trained assassin, I guess. "Agreed."

"Housekeepers are forbidden for teams moving forward for promotions," he confirmed.

"As I thought."

"Unless..." He let the words hang in the air so long I couldn't stand it.

"Unless?"

He was so fucking smug I wished to lean over his desk and punch him in his masked face. What the hell was the point of the mask, anyway? At this point, we were literally family. Finally, he broke, a smile lifting one side of his lips. "Unless an exception was written and signed by a minimum of five superiors."

For a moment, I couldn't quite compute what he was saying. My thoughts were moving slowly, struggling through my molasses filled brain. If what he was saying was true, then...

"Sir?" I questioned, clearly needing him to dumb it down for me.

"I'm leaving at the beginning of next year, and I've vouched for Team Moore to take our place. The signatures have been obtained. Your spot is secure. All I need is an agreement."

I- Fuck. This was a dream. A dream I never thought possible because we'd picked Mac over this route, but now that both were obtainable, I didn't know what to say. It was a joke that I'd one day have Jones's job, but never my true reality. I wanted to agree, wanted to take anything they offered me. But I couldn't just jump without thinking.

"What does this mean for Mac?"

My question softened his gaze. "Less blood, less danger."

"Less, but not a complete elimination," I pointed out.

"Not in this line of work." Lord, don't I know it? Always in constant danger.

"Is she free to get a job anywhere, or will they assign her a position in the organization like the rest of the team?"

"You would be the only one required to work in

the agency. Your other teammates could be assigned outside jobs that still coordinate with our plans and operations. Mac has greater options, as standards are lightly enforced for the females. However, she too would be offered an inside job. In addition, your team would still be called on for highly classified jobs."

"It's safe then, for her, I mean."

"Safer than your current position." His fingers flexed. "Listen, I was considering you for this promotion prior to you taking my sister on. Bringing in a housekeeper ruined that until I found a loophole. I respect you. You're close to the greatest this organization has ever seen. When I saw Mac's name on your paperwork, I nearly choked. I couldn't believe we'd done it. Well, that I did. I worked so fucking hard to get her attention from any of your trio, but you were stubborn, kept to those vows you took. It was a miracle that I ever got her paired with Austin repeatedly for labs. She belongs with you and by proxy as a Saint. I can't give her up again. So, if you reject this, if you willingly put my sister in more danger, make her life harder than it has to be, fuck with the plans I put into action, you'll die. I'll even make it look like an accident."

"So I don't really have a choice."

"No." He blinked slowly.

I stood up, holding my hand out to Jones, the guy who might as well be my fucking brother-in-law. "I'll take it."

He pushed his chair up and stood, grasping my hand. "Good choice."

"Nice talk," I mocked as I pulled my hand from his before turning toward the closed door.

My fingers had just wrapped around the cool metal of the handle when Jones's voice stopped me. "Oh, and Moore?" I didn't answer, only paused, waiting for him to speak. "Welcome to the Saints. When you're in it, you're in it for life."

As if I didn't fucking know it.

I took my time walking up the steps to our place. When I opened the door, I let it slam behind me before tossing my keys into the bowl filled with our pocket clutter. I paused for a moment, loosening my tie, listening.

Not a sound.

My tongue darted out, licking my lips. My cock was already hard, knowing what I'd find.

I let my boots hit heavy on the steps of the stairs, not bothering to skip the steps that I knew squeaked. I wanted them to know I was coming, wanted the anticipation of what was to come to make them shake.

At the landing, I paused, gathering myself before I pushed forward, turning toward my room, where I knew I'd find my team. I didn't knock, only turned the handle, pushing it open. The vision in front of me was the most glorious of sights.

Some might call it sick, but I call it team building.

I dropped my tie into my laundry pile before daring to look. "Has our team behaved?"

I directed my question at Asa, who lounged in my office chair, a magazine casually in his hand. His foot was kicked up on my desk, and I didn't know how he did it. With Mac and Austin bound up like an offering, I would have caved an hour ago.

"A little fussing here and there." Asa paused. "Nothing my cock didn't stop."

I swallowed hard at the images that flashed in my mind. I'd have to rewatch that later on the camera feed, savor the time I missed. "Not quite the saint I was willing to give you credit for."

Asa let his feet fall to the floor. "We are all just men in the end." Mac snorted and Asa added, "And woman."

I stepped forward, running my fingers through her loosely tied hair, toying with the strands. Her head tilted, nuzzling into my palm. "Such a good girl."

The simple words caused her eyes to heat. Our girl melted at praises, soaked her panties for them. My finger skimmed down her neck, teasing the tiny little strap of her silk slip. These fucking slips drove me wild, absolutely mad with want, and she knew it. "Did you put this on to punish me?"

She shook her head, the ball gag not allowing a single word to slip from her pretty little lips. "I think you're lying."

"She is," Asa confirmed, not afraid to throw her to

the wolves. She would have been eaten by the wild
either way. "Picked it out just for you right before I
tied her pretty little wrists."

"And she's done well?" I questioned, knowing that
she had been afraid to surrender. Afraid to trust me
to tie her up, to silence her. She was haunted. The
memories of that night hunted her thoughts, stealing
moments from us, and I wouldn't allow it any longer.
I couldn't let her see a rope and think blood and
death followed when lust and love could equally wait
on the other end.

"So fucking well," he confirmed as he stood,
strolling toward us before he smoothed her hair from
her eyes. "Didn't even object about the gag."

"Look how pretty your mouth stretches around it.
Is your jaw tired, little vixen?" She tried to talk, but
only sounds spilled from her throat, as drool dripped
down her chin. "Fucking gorgeous. And him?"

"Only behaved once my cock was in his mouth."
Asa sighed, and I swore, even with the round black
ball in his mouth, Austin smirked.

"Figures." I rolled my eyes and stepped to the
side, letting my fingers thread in the strands of
Austin's hair before I jerked his head back, forcing his
eyes on me. "You had orders and you disobeyed."

He shrugged his shoulders, amusement in his
eyes. I guess next time I shouldn't make the punishment so damn tempting. I slowly removed my belt as
I circled around them, making the leisurely stroll all
part of the game as they anticipated what I'd do next.

I circled them twice, before I snapped my belt, circling it around Austin's neck and pulling his body back into my thighs. His face reddened as he strained against the pressure, but his eyes boldly looked into mine as I peered down.

"So fucking defiant. Always." I let the belt slacken, granting him air as I stroked the red lines on his neck. "Did you like when Asa shut you up with his cock?"

He nodded, no fucking hesitation. In fact, the thought made his cock jump, straining and twitching, already weeping with precum. I tilted my head to the side, eying him thoughtfully. "I've never been sucked off by a man before."

Austin's eyes rolled in ecstasy, the thought clearly something he wouldn't object to. I tightened the belt, tilting his head so his focus was back on me. "Today won't be the day for that."

His shoulders dropped in disappointment, and I loosened my belt again, using my boot to kick the small of his back, pushing him over onto his stomach. I offered Asa my belt, before I dropped to my knees behind Mac, wrapping my arm around her, and pulling her against my body.

"Austin wasn't behaving," I reminded her, as Asa stepped forward, snapping the belt against Austin's bare ass, leaving a red welt in its wake.

In my arms, Mac's body stiffened, a cry halted by the gag. With her hands pinned between us, she couldn't reach for him, couldn't stop the belt from laying a second row upon his creamy skin. "Shhh, he likes it, baby. Don't you, Aussie? Tell her."

Asa reached forward, unlatching the gag and tearing it from Austin's lips. His heavy pants filled the space, and when he didn't speak, Asa cracked the belt against his skin again. He hissed; a curse fell from his lips before he finally confirmed, "So fucking good."

Her body relaxed slightly as she watched the push and pull of her men, the enjoyment they both got out of the moment. I reached down, teasing my palm over the silk that covered her body, roaming my hands over her stomach before bunching the material in my hand. "If I touch your pussy, am I going to find it soaked?"

Her throat worked around a swallow, but she didn't answer me. She didn't need to; I knew the truth. Still, my fingers danced along her skin before I dipped between her legs, finding her cunt dripping. "You dirty girl. You really do like this. I wonder what your brother would say if he knew his innocent little sister gushed at the sight of her teammate getting whipped."

She turned her head toward me and glared. I grinned. Who fucking cared if talk of her brother made her uncomfortable? It amused the fuck out of me. Especially since he was too damn squeamish to acknowledge that his sister gets her brains fucked out daily.

I didn't bother to remove the ties on her wrists, or the gag, when I freed my cock and stuffed her cunt full of it. Her body instantly pulsed round my dick, and I fought not to moan because she felt that damn good. I leaned over, grabbing Austin's hair and dragging him over toward us. I pushed his face between her thighs, and without instruction, he knew what to do. His tongue darted out, teasing her clit, running along my cock, teasing both of us.

"Fuck." My fingers gripped Mac tighter, probably leaving a bruise on her pristine flesh, but I couldn't release her if I tried. The feeling, the stimulation, both incredible. "Fuck him."

A slow grin toyed with Asa's lips as he took in my command. He didn't take his eyes off us as he reached an arm out, finding the bottle of lube on my nightstand. He dripped the liquid down Austin's ass, before his hand disappeared. I was familiar now with the sounds they made, familiar with what was required to be in their special type of relationship, and I knew by the hitch in Austin's breath and the clench of his hands that were still tied behind his back, that Asa was prepping him.

"It's his favorite part," Asa informed me when he caught me watching.

"Yeah?" My chest was rising and falling rapidly, the urge to move faster fighting with the urge to draw it out.

"He likes the moments that border on pleasure and pain." His fingers gripped into Austin's skin, and his hips jutted forward, not giving any warning before he impaled himself inside of Austin. Austin's whimper ended on a moan, only confirming his truth. "It's why he liked when I used the belt."

I let my fingers roam under the silk, pinching Mac's nipples lightly as she rode my cock, no longer needing me to do a damn thing, her body eager to cum on its own. "Do you like a little pain too, vixen?"

I asked, but I didn't wait for an answer. I pinched her nipple again, this time harder, and her body gripped my cock as she pitched forward, a muffled cry escaping. I did it again, this time twisting, and that, combined with the angle of my cock and Austin's tongue, caused our girl to explode, her body milking mine as tears fell from her cheeks.

With her chest heaving, her body limp against mine, I jutted my hips up, brushing her hair down as I whispered against her cheek, "That's our good girl, one more baby. One more and I'll release you."

She shook her head, trying to argue, but it was no use. I wouldn't change my mind. I pushed Austin away, leaving Asa to finish what they started as I reached down, finding the swollen nub, dancing my fingers over it.

She cried out, her body shaking from the single touch as I circled it gently. "Look at you, sweetheart. You're dripping all over my thighs, making a mess of my slacks."

"I told you she'd like it," Asa grunted as he pulled Austin's head back, slamming his hips hard into Austin's body. Austin's eyes were closed, sweat dripped down his temples, and if the world ended in this moment, I was glad it would implode with the bliss in this room.

"Do you like it, baby?" I asked before I reached up, removing the gag. Spit trailed out of her mouth as she panted, her chest so fucking beautiful when it was flushed.

"God, yes," she finally managed.

I tilted her body, angling her toward a mirror against my wall. "Watch us. Watch me make you cum. See how fucking beautiful you are when my cock makes you scream out. Eyes on me."

I didn't look away as I fucked her for us to see. Didn't tear my gaze from her as Asa and Austin found their release. Didn't stop until she begged me and pleaded, her orgasm spurring mine, her eyes locked with my own as her head tilted back against my shoulder, her mouth open in a silent scream.

And when her body was limp, our combined cum dripping down our legs, I laid a kiss on her forehead and closed my eyes for a moment, savoring the fact that she was here. Our housekeeper. So fucking alive when it could have gone so wrong. I swallowed hard, fighting against the emotions, as I hoarsely whispered, "That's our girl."

Thank you for reading!
Like what you read? I would love if you left a review!
Feel like hanging out with me?

Check out my Facebook reader's group, Delilah's
Darlings.
Want the latest updates?
Visit me on Facebook at https://www.facebook.com/
delilahmohan/
Sign up for my Newsletter here!

Other works by Delilah Mohan

PARANORMAL ROMANCE/ REVERSE HAREM
Claiming Claire (A reverse harem shifter novella)
Saving a Succubus
Training A Succubus
Liberty (Keeping Liberty Series)
Justice (Keeping Liberty Series)
Truth (Keeping Liberty Series)
Retribution (Keeping Liberty Series)
Resisted (Wolves of Full Moon Bay book 1)
Refused (Wolves of Full Moon Bay book 2)
Redeemed (Wolves of full moon bay 3)
UMBRA (With the Shadows 1)
BLAZE (With the Shadows 2)
SONDER (With the Shadows 3) Winter '23
Heidi and the Haunters

<u>CONTEMPORARY ROMANCE</u>
Obscured Love (Obscured Love Series, book 1)
Eluding Fate
Ricochet (Obscured Love Series, book 2)
Five Seconds to Love (Obscured Love Series, book 3)

Resisting Royal (The Repayment Series, book 1)
Owning Emma (The Repayment Series, book 2)
Salvaged Girl

<u>Website:</u>
<u>Delilahmohan.com</u>

Made in the USA
Monee, IL
18 April 2024

56860680R00371